FOREIGN TO ME

JOURNEY OF A DARK SHAMAN TRILOGY

BOOK 1

DALE ALLEN-ROWSE

WOLF VISION PUBLISHING, LLC
MOUNTAIN CENTER, CA

Wolf Vision Publishing, LLC
P.O. Box 157
Mountain Center, California

www.DaleAllenRowse.com

ISBN (book): 979-8-9865306-6-6
ISBN (ebook): 979-8-9865306-7-3

where personal wisdom follows transformation. It is a cinematic joy reading Allen-Rowse's first novels, and I am all the better for it!

I just finished reading Dale Allen-Rowse's recent publication of *Foreign To Me* and found it to be a shining success! This first book of a three part series brings to life Jack Daw, a physically flawed yet handsome, brave, and resolute protagonist who's life choices embody the themes of Robert Frost's herald poem, The Road Not Taken. This story details the evolution and journey of a queer man who consciously decides to leave behind a stable, unfulfilling life of "okayness," in exchange for authentic spiritual, psychological, and sexual freedom. To walk away from life, to take to the highway and the Canadian wilderness, to strike out upon a road less traveled, and to tear down the oppressive walls of malignant, Judeo-Christian ideology, in exchange for Shamanic practices— that is the raw gutsiness of Allen-Rowse's Jack Daw. On so many levels I am inspired by this book, for it demonstrates how challenging and pushing against the status quo, societal norms, and traditional spiritual practice can bring a man to stand strong in his own personal truth — the truth that queerness is rightness, and taking to one's own road will make "all the difference." This book is for anyone who believes in living an authentic life.

"Dale Allen-Rowse's first novel takes the reader to a place that is reminiscent of earlier gay novels such as *The Fancy Dancer* or *The Catch Trap*. The characters are familiar, rough around the edges, even tattered at times. Allen-Rowse takes the reader into the mind of Jack Daw in a way that is immediate, raw, and not always comfortable. Being inside

Jack's head feels like riding in a pickup truck on a dirt road. It's not always easy to shift gears.

The imagery, the sounds, the smells, all the senses are engaged, but moreover, the reader is enveloped in constant, turbulent waves of emotional energies. It's often a bumpy ride for Jack and the other characters. Allen-Rowse gives the reader enough to make them real, but not enough to know everything. There is a compelling uncertainty in the story.

This is definitely not a finite story; it is only the beginning to what this reader suspects is a much larger, deeper, more painful tale. The bumpy road promises curves as well."

~JEFFERY DOWNS, MA

AUSTIN, TEXAS WRITING CENTER DIRECTOR

AT ST. EDWARD'S UNIVERSITY

"This book begins in devastation and burns in a slow reveal to a new pain. Traveling through man's vices and our relationship with others, the path lands us squarely in ourselves. Anyone carrying a wound through life will benefit from this journey up the mountain with Jack as he faces one of humanity's most significant challenges. Dale Allen-Rowse artfully adds fun and playfulness with notes of hope and curiosity into a human tragedy cocktail. Pass this book on to a friend – Jack's journey has pearls of wisdom that the world needs to hear.

I look forward to more from this first-time author."

~MIDGE MEADE, PORTLAND OREGON

GRATITUDE

I would like to thank my husband, John Allen-Rowse, my sister Laura Rowse, Annette Sanders, Jennifer Anderson, Professor Derek Currin and Micah Schwader.

To the amazing tribe who helped usher this work into existence, thank-you.

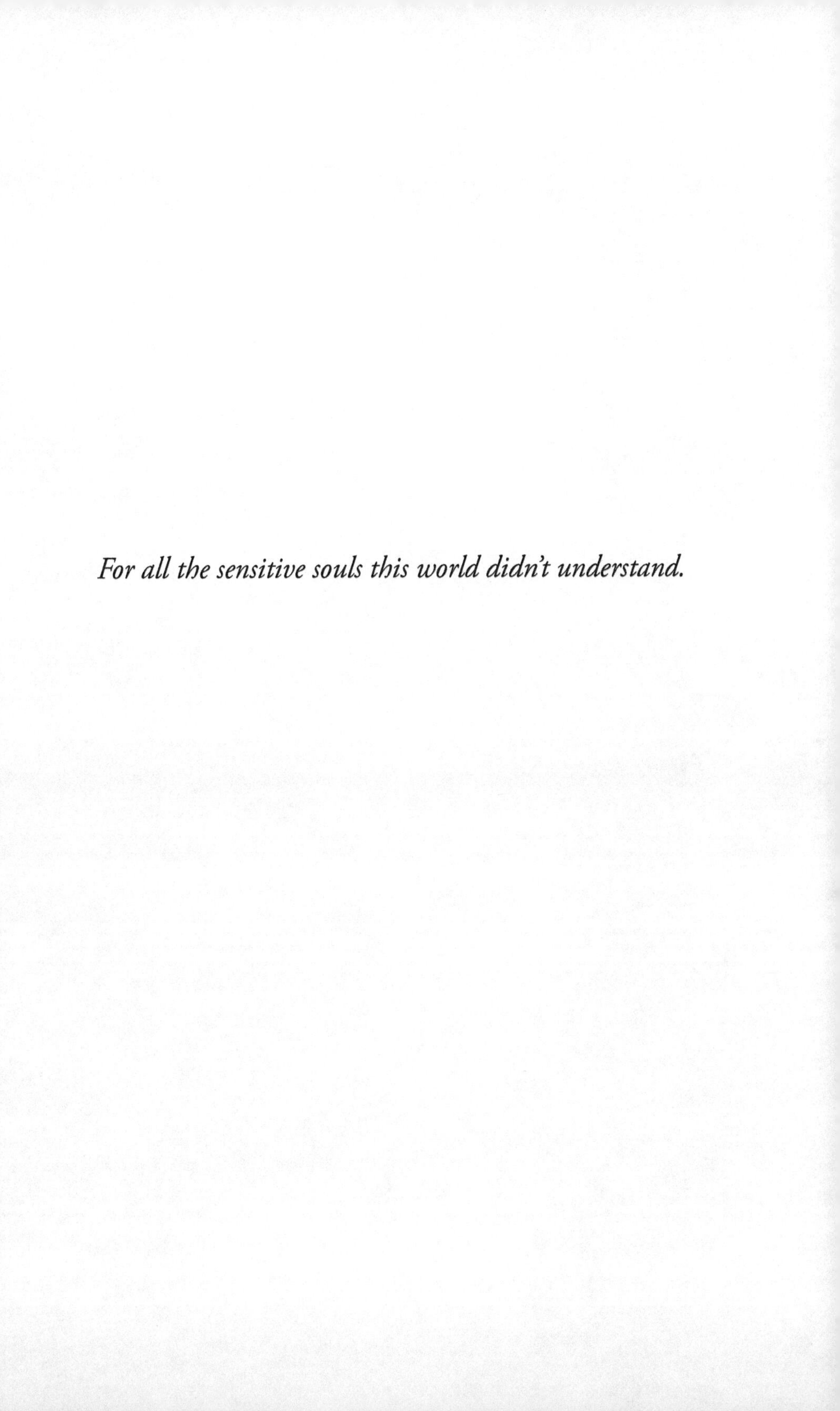
For all the sensitive souls this world didn't understand.

*"Life is a school where you remember what
your soul already knows."*

~ ANONYMOUS

TABLE OF CONTENTS

PROLOGUE

Standing in the employee parking lot of Plexus Foods, Jack exhaled into the dark Canadian heavens. "I don't get it." He just had the worst day, and he simply didn't see the point of the exercise anymore. He focused on the North Star, his star. "How I wonder what you are—because how can you expect me to do this world right when I arrive to it so…?" Before he finished his thought, his boss's word "ineffective" rang in his working ear. "How?" Jack shook his head for answers. "How does any of this make sense? I thought…."

He grabbed a joint from his bag and lit it while still mad-wondering at the Gods. "I thought you were supposed to be, you know, conspiring for my success or some bullshit." Jack paused and closed his eyes again, dragging hard then exhaling smoke. "Em told me that. She knows about these things even if she…." Jack didn't want to think about it further, so he stopped and refocused on the night's horizon. "I thought in this place we were supposed to learn how to be kind and walk each other home, because that's what I learned in your god damned church!" He shouted heavenward. "Well fuck your god!"

Jack recoiled at the thought of a singular Christian God, especially an idle God. The one who stood by and watched; the one who did nothing. The one who had never intervened for him.

In that moment, Jack felt his ten thousand emotional scars all sear at once within his queer self. Just thinking about it made him feel unsafe. He exhaled. "So tell me…." Jack sent heavenward, continuing his assault on the one who bore silent witness when he was thrown to the floor, his pants removed— and he could never forget the mind-bending pain that ensued. To this day, if he gave much thought to it, he could still feel the power-seeking gaze of his step father's eyes tracking his every move, he could feel his hands forcefully gripping his waste, and he could hear the loosening of that belt buckle. With his face painfully crushed into the floor, the smell of the musky orange carpet permanently merged with his psyche, because it was there where he first learned how to protect himself and run for his life.

"How can you in your fucking infinite wisdom send us here to this bullshit world and have *that* be the assignment?! Tell me. Tell me what I need to do to make this all better—because honestly, I don't get it." Jack grabbed his face, feeling its unnatural arc and deformity. He wasn't sure he still saw the point of it anymore.

He hopped in the truck and flicked the remaining joint out of the window as he started his old hunk of a beast – an '81 Chevy that he bought from the estate of a neighbor who had passed away four months ago. Putting the truck in drive, he held the clutch as he gunned the engine to announce to the world he still had some control over his movements despite his frustration with a life with so little direction or meaning.

As the car took off, he glanced in the rear-view mirror checking first for traffic and secondly to see if by some chance, or by some miracle the distorted and scarred right side of his face had been transformed — he longed for the ruggedly handsome face that could have been, but the singular bold hazel eye starring back, gave no such report. He beat the steering wheel with his hands, and under his breath exclaimed, "Damnit. God, dammit!" He searched the rearview mirror again to see his busted-in side that endlessly looked back at him with disappointment.

He didn't like to do that. He didn't like to hold his gaze in a mirror, but today… *Well fuck it,* he thought as he left the parking area of the salmon-packing plant that voided his soul and routinely left him feeling empty. He touched the ever-present frostbite on his ears from life in a freezer, packing dead fish. What purpose did this all serve? Laying out the evening's catch onto frozen metal sheets to be packed into crates for shipping and then revisiting those same fish in the morning was a task any trained monkey could carry out. And yet, that, up to this point, was his entire purpose in life. That was it.

Jack pointed his vehicle toward highway 97 and started to speed, his mind revived with the slight pump of adrenaline and the freedom of not living under the thumb of his boss, Mr. Wren. *What a disgusting human.* He was the kind of guy who enjoys being a manager, not to build an effective team or set records for productivity, safety, or efficiency. No, Mr. Wren was the kind of guy who got a sick and obvious pleasure out of making other people feel smaller than him.

As Jack approached the main on-ramp to the 97, he slowed, then pulled over as he felt hot, embarrassing tears . *Why?* he thought. *Why any of this? Why am I doing <u>this</u>.*

With the last thought formed in his mind as a statement, not a question, Jack made a decision. Today was the tipping point and he wasn't going to participate in the garbage life he had created anymore. He was done, and he was finally ready to tell Em his truth.

THE VISIT

As Jack rounded the last bend of the road to his trailer, his shoulders dropped. Not in a manner of relaxation or exhaled beingness but more in resignation. He had created the mess that awaited him behind his front door. The stuff. The brown shitty carpet that he never bothered to rip out and the girl that held him in place. For better, not so much. For worse, also the same. Their relationship wasn't painful, and it wasn't great. It was okay. It met a bar of okay-ness that Jack expected from life.

As Jack shut off the engine, Banjo, his pit mix mutt, did his best to showcase enthusiasm at Jack's arrival despite his ten-plus years. He was a good dog. *Funny,* Jack thought to himself. *I'd never know if Banjo had a shitty day. Hell, every time I pull in, he acts like I'm his long-lost brother returning from war.*

He threw open the front door of the mobile home with much more force than was necessary, but it felt right given the day he'd had. Jack cursed as the door snapped right back at him. Because, why not? Why should his front door be any different than the rest of this world?

Em wasn't home yet. *She probably took a double shift at the hardware store where she worked,* Jack thought to himself. He looked around the house and then into the backyard. "Backyard" was a very generous term for the bare dirt patch out the backdoor that was barely defined by a broken-down wire fence that no one cared about. Jack often thought about tearing it down and maybe planting some sod where the dry dirt-patch constantly threw dust around. But why? Would it make any difference to their lives? Grass wasn't what Em was clamoring for.

Jack walked out the back door, beer in hand, and resigned himself to the top of the picnic table that he had made a few years back. He was proud of his woodwork. It was one of the many things he prided himself on despite his obvious shortcomings. At least he had that. At least he could, on good days, still make something out of nothing. The question was, why didn't he spend more days like that? The word "ineffective" echoed in his ears from earlier.

Jack's mind swirled. What next? What now? *Am I done for real this time?* He thought to himself, *Is this it? Is this as good as life gets?* More to the point, *Is this as good as life gets for me?*

As he sat there, finally in the presence of silence, he let his guard down to be present with Banjo. *What a dog*, he thought to himself. *This mutt is as weathered and raggedy as they come. But maybe that's why we get each other.* Jack guzzled the beer and then took a hard drag off his mokee pipe in a slow, deliberate manner. The mix of tobacco and weed eased into his lungs. He closed his eyes as he fell into himself.

Jack's thoughts began to churn as if carried on the energy of the swirling wisps of smoke. *Why does the world not want this silence, this air of non-judgment, because if it can exist here over this ramshackle of bullshit, why can't it be better everywhere? Anywhere? Why is this state of quiet so anathema to people? Why the insanity of human commotion and endless stream of noise? Why do we not value peace? Why do we not value silence?* His soul ached. A slight breeze picked up a fistful of dirt from the dry patch and sent it downwind. Jack watched it float off with inexplicable envy.

As always, he waited for the combination of beer and smoke to relieve the edge of the day. A day he hated, which was like most days. However, unlike most days, Jack suddenly had the slightest twinge of desire to know what it might feel like to be happy. Maybe even content.

He looked down at Banjo and was glad to think he always lived in that cheerful place.

Just as he felt his spirit lift from Banjo just being Banjo, he heard tires churning on gravel on the unpaved driveway. He assumed it was Em returning from wherever she had been. He noted his newly perturbed state in response to this intrusion as he walked around the trailer, rather than coming through the house, avoiding having to deal with possibly fanning yet another flame of dispute, over the dirty condition of the house.

Coming around to the front yard, Jack was surprised that it wasn't Em's car pulling into the driveway. "Who the...?" he said under his breath just as a man he didn't recognize stepped out of the old Dodge.

"Hey, Jack, it's Den," the stranger said.

Jack tried to shield his good eye from the blinding headlights while also trying to see who "Den" was. *Den,* his mind searched. *Den. Den...*

"I'm sorry, who?" Jack said. He was still trying to see the man's face in the flood of the headlights. Jack walked to the side of the car to get out of the beam of the lights, which were now starting to give him a slight headache. A common occurrence, given his degenerative neurological brain "situation."

"It's Den, you fucknut. Dennis from Kelsey. Your old neighbor from, I don't know... maybe your old life and high school? Or are you too good to remember us now that you have *all this*?" Den pointed with his chin in the direction of Jack's trailer and Chevy Blazer.

Jack had to stifle a chuckle, thinking, *This guy. This guy who comes out of nowhere from my past thinks what I have is valuable enough to be a big shot. Ha! That's both completely laughable and completely pathetic.*

"Oh, hey Den. Is it Den now? Sorry, I didn't realize you were going by that."

"Yeah, my lady said it might open new doors for me. Make me seem more, you know, employable." He betrayed his emotions behind this with an exhaled sigh, showing he clearly didn't believe his girl's promise of more. They both knew there wasn't more. Not here. Not in the middle of nowhere British Columbia, where dead animal carcasses were more prevalent than opportunity.

"Oh, cool," Jack said, feigning interest. "Why the sudden visit? Can I help you with something?"

"Maybe," Dennis said, not looking directly at Jack, which, for some reason, made Jack instantly nervous, even though he couldn't pinpoint why.

To get Dennis to spit it out, Jack replied, "Okay. With what exactly?"

"I'm in trouble, Jack," Dennis finally mustered.

"Oh, jeez, Dennis. Why? Why me? C'mon, I haven't seen you since we graduated high school, and you just show up with a carload of problems hoping I'm going to help you? Is that your plan?" Jack said, his voice leaning into his frustration, most of which had nothing to do with Dennis. He had been on edge all day with his relationship being on the line, and tonight was "the big talk," and then there's this new problem standing on his front lawn.

"This is not a great time for me," Jack threw at Dennis like a dagger.

"I know," Dennis replied.

"You know? The fuck you do, Dennis. What do you know of my life?"

"Okay. Okay… God. Settle down. Maybe I don't know about your life now, but I know where you come from. We used to be buddies. Or at least I thought so."

Jack leaned back on one heel, adjusting his stance and hopefully his attitude as well while saying again tersely, "What do you want?"

"Can we go inside and talk?"

Jack's eyes flashed to his front door as he felt a tinge of shame about letting his old friend see the conditions in which he lived. That thought was immediately followed by the memory of "Den" being impressed by "all this."

"We can go around back and sit on the picnic table." Jack said over his shoulder, resigning himself to this imposition. "This way. Want a beer?"

Den agreed with a nod, and in a few minutes, they were sitting in the yard, each unsure of what to say next.

"So, what's going on?" Jack started.

Long pause. Chug from a cold bottle. Exhale.

"Do you remember Larry?" Dennis started.

"Catfish Larry?" Jack inquired, chuckling.

"That's the one."

There was a long pause as Jack's mind recounted how "Catfish Larry" was the craziest son of a bitch he ever met, always the life of the party but also a complete failure when it came to understanding the value of emotions in others. The name "Catfish" didn't come from his love of Cajun foods but rather how he'd lure underage girls into compromising situations online. Shared photos. Trust in little secrets. Topless photos. Nudes. All of which he could use to gain the upper hand should things not go the way he wanted. It was so crazy to Jack how this relatively good-looking guy would rather play this foul game rather than just be honest about who he was. He wasn't a bad guy other than this behavior, so why even go there? It made no sense.

"So, what about him?" Jack began, "Didn't he go to jail?"

"Yeah," said Dennis. Silence. Another swig. "And I got his girl pregnant. He gets out next week."

"And you, in your infinite wisdom, figured I'd be the one to help you out of this mess? Why?" Jack could feel his frustration over this massive imposition return.

"I had to get out of Kelsey, and, Dude, you're the only one I know who's not there anymore. I had nowhere else to go." Silence. "I don't know what to do," he said quietly.

"Jesus, Dennis. This isn't fair. I have a life." Jack felt the lie of that last sentence as it left his lips. "How in the hell did you even find me?"

Dennis looked at the ground. "I swung by your parents' place. Said it would be great to reconnect since I was heading out this way anyhow. They gave me your address. Truthfully, I was a little surprised they had it… after… you know… given how you left-n-all."

"So, you lied," Jack said pointedly. "That's always been the best way to get something out of them."

"Well, not exactly. I was heading this way once I got your address," said Dennis, still looking at his feet.

"So, what's the plan, Hotshot? What did you think was going to happen once you got here?"

"Well, I thought I might stay a few nights just to clear my head, then maybe head down to Comox or Campbell River to look for work. Maybe just start over."

"How? With what?! I'm assuming if you're here that you have nothing," said Jack, not even trying to be polite anymore. A very small and unfamiliar part of Jack's soul was enjoying that someone else was worse off than him at this moment.

"That's not true. I have money," Dennis said all too sheepishly to be an actual fact.

Jack looked into Dennis's face, feeling just as weary as his old friend looked.

"Then why are you here?" Jack said flatly. "Why not just tootle on to butt-fuck BC to begin this imagined new start?"

"Because my money hasn't come in yet, and I need a few days to lay low until I can get it."

At that moment, the recognizable rattle and tenor of Em's old Mercedes came to a halt out front.

Jack looked at Dennis. "Fuck," he said with fists clinched. "She's not going to be happy about this."

Dennis held his measure, saying softly, "I get it. And I'm so sorry, but please. I just need a few days, and then I'll be gone."

"You know you've always been a huge pain in my ass. That said, I've always been grateful for how you stuck by me and remained my friend even after the accident. You and Mel were the only ones who did. You're cashing in those karma chips now, aren't you?" Jack was tired of this conversation and just wanted it to end. He wished all the conversations he would have that night were already over.

"Please. You were my only option left," Dennis managed as they started walking out to the front of the property.

THE VISITOR

As the two men were coming around the trailer, Jack watched Em kill the engine and lights of the vehicle, then step out into the night air. Her annoyance at seeing the two men approach was palpable to Jack even before she said a word.

"Hello," she managed in a near-friendly tone as she waved her hand toward them. "I didn't realize we were going to have a visitor?"

With that being posed as a question, Dennis's breath caught before saying, "I'm Den."

Jack shot him the "Are you fucking serious?" look that also conveyed "You are pathetic."

"Um. I'm Dennis," he continued. "Nice to meet you. And... uh, don't be mad at Jack. He didn't know I was coming. I just kinda showed up. So, I hope that's okay."

Em replied coolly, "I guess that remains to be seen." She walked toward the trailer's door and barely broke stride as she entered the home.

Tired and resigned at this point, Jack nodded to Dennis to follow him in.

Jack entered the trailer using a more appropriate level of force not to have the door ricochet back into him again. Em put away her coat in the front closet by the front door as Dennis followed Jack into the adjoining fake wood-paneled living room.

"Babe," said Jack. "Dennis is an old friend, and he just needs a few days to get on his feet."

"And this is my problem, how exactly?" Em muttered, not bothering to look in their direction. It was clear that any modicum of politeness she'd decided to portray initially had since left the building.

As Jack finished ushering Dennis into the living room and pointed for him to sit on the sofa, he said, "Babe. Can we at least talk about this?"

"Fine," Em said. "In private," making her intention for the next impending conversation known.

Clearly embarrassed for having just sat down and now getting back up, Dennis excused himself and stepped outside to have a smoke.

As the tattered door closed, Em looked at Jack. "What the hell is this? No notice, no phone call, no heads up. You're always doing this. Choosing the needs of others over us."

Jack walked over to Em and held her in both hands by the shoulders so he could look more squarely into her eyes. "Babe. I know this isn't a great time with us working so much, but it's also a good time if you look at it that way. Since we're now both employed, we aren't home all that much, and it'll just be a few days. If it's too much of an imposition, maybe he can just stay in his car and come in for meals and a shower and stuff?"

"Two days," Em finally acquiesced.

"Okay. Two days," Jack repeated.

There was a long silence before Em finally got to the heart of her underlying mood. "So…? What about the conversation we were supposed to have this evening? Since we're now 'entertaining guests….'" She didn't continue, and while her air quotes came off as childish, they did not disguise her upset.

"Emily." Jack did his best to reassure her by using her full name. "You know I'm just not ready." This answered the silent hanging question that had nagged Jack all day. How does he tell her he's not ready (or willing) to have kids? He just didn't see his future like that. The cat was now, out of the bag.

"You're a fucking joke," she said with absolutely no emotion.

Silence.

She continued. "Here I am wasting my life waiting on a guy who will not commit."

Jack interrupted her abruptly. "It's just that…."

She, in turn, interrupted loudly, "YOU'RE GOING TO BE A GOD-DAMNED CRIPPLE IN FIVE YEARS!" She screamed. "And I was willing to take that on IF you could commit to me! I want kids, Jack! I want to have a family. And a life! Why won't you give that to me!?"

He finally said it. "I'm just not that guy." Instantaneously, Jack questioned whether he knew what kind of guy he was.

"NO," she snapped back. "You're just not that guy for me."

Silence.

She continued. "And maybe I'm not that girl for you."

Jack's walls immediately went up, cutting him off from his words.

Silence.

"SO!" She screamed. Her temper was finally on max.

Silence.

She reached for the closet. "For two years now, I've bailed you out." She grabbed her suitcase. "For two years now, I've hoped that you would…." She stopped herself. "I gave you money for that fucking piece of shit car. I took care of you when you were sick or having a bad day physically. You can't function on your own anymore, Jack. You really fucking need to come to terms with that. You…." she paused, then resumed. "I've been on the phone a lot today with my sister in Victoria. They have work there for me if I want it. She'll even let me stay with her and her family for a bit until I can find my own place."

She ripped their cork-framed dream and vision board from the wall, broke it in half, and then threw it to the floor. Watching the thing hit the ground, the push pins scattered while Jack, for the first time, saw that it held all of Em's dreams, and very few of his. She continued to pack while Jack held silent vigil in the corner of the room. As Jack closed off, one of the photos of a Disney Cruise for kids landed near his feet. In the confines of the room, Jack could feel the void between them expanding, but he knew that both of them had a clear understanding that this was where they'd eventually end up. Jack just couldn't give her what she wanted. A cost too great because then there was nothing for her in exchange for her becoming his full-time caregiver. They both understood this.

"It sounds like you have it worked out then…" Jack's voice trailed off like an unfinished thought.

"I'm not stupid, Jack. I prepare. I'm the one who has their shit together, and well… I deserve better."

As her words rang in his working ear, he didn't disagree. She did deserve better than a 'ineffective' mess.

Em had clearly thought through this plan of action as she worked through a prepared mental list for this eventuality. Jack was shocked at how efficient she gathered her things and headed for the door. He couldn't help but wonder what his escape plan was. Shouldn't he have one too? Or was this perpetual state of okay-ness enough for him? That thought made an indescribable sadness rise within him. He hoped Em would interpret his tears as sadness over her imminent departure.

Jack watched Em leave and walk into the living room. He chased after her.

"I feel sorry for you," Em said as she reached the front door. "And it's sad that you just can't let yourself be open, or honest, or loved." She fidgeted for a second looking for her keys, giving Jack a second to catch up, so they were face to face on the home turf side of the door.

Jack looked into her eyes as she let fly the final words that would haunt Jack's mind forever. "You're not good-looking enough, to also be an asshole."

Jack felt this as it was intended. She had nicked the jugular on purpose. She knew how sensitive he was about his bashed-in face, deaf ear and fake eye. The truth landed like a boulder on his heart, which fell into his stomach. For a second, he thought he would puke.

Emily stormed out the front door and past Dennis, who was leaning on his car smoking. He immediately sat up straight as if he was a fifth-grade student and the teacher had just walked in the room. Em started her car and in seconds was gone.

"Hey, Jack…" Dennis called softly in Jack's direction.

Jack, still standing in the door, looked down, and with what he had left, he replied, "I told you today was not a good day." Jack then closed the door and went inside.

NIGHT FROM DAY

Jack sat on the old green plaid sofa with Banjo at his side, head on his lap. His soft, doggy eyes stared up at him, letting Jack know he was still his buddy. Jack clenched his everything—steal innards, aching heart.

All of this was no surprise to Jack. They had planned that this evening would be "the talk." They had both prepared for the impending potential outcomes. But still, it's always painful, particularly when one party hurts the other by not being what the other person needs. Emily's gut punch hit more squarely because she knew Jack's buttons, soft spots, insecurities, and personal truths. Armed with that knowledge, the sword she summoned cut and cut deep.

Dennis opened the front door to look around to where Jack was sitting with his back to the door.

"Jack…," Dennis whispered.

Silence.

"Jack…."

Jack strained to be decent. "I need a minute."

"Yeah… I get that, so I'm just going to hang out in my car for a bit. I have…." Dennis didn't finish the sentence.

In the silence, Jack picked up the conversation thread with, "When I head to bed, feel free to make yourself comfortable, but I need to be alone for now."

"Understood," Dennis said, closing the door. "I'll be here if you want to talk or something."

Jack exhaled once the door closed.

You're not good-looking enough, to also be an asshole played back in his mind. She was right about that. His hand reached up to touch where his rebuilt temporal bone was, his finger reading the Frankenstein bent-brail of him—it's the sort of thing left behind from skull fractures that break wide open and have to be rebuilt by man; they never quite look as like nature intended. Jack would often hold his right hand over the scars, fake eye, and deaf ear. He closed his eyes and for a brief second, relived that day – the day that changed his face – and his life, forever. Jack recalled the moment clearly…

At the age of twelve, Jack looked up to his big brother Ben. They were ride-or-die buds. He was as sure of that as anything else in his world, so when he was struggling with questions about personal stuff, he figured he'd ask his big brother.

Jack had noticed that Ben had stepped into a role of Jack's protector after losing their real dad and being raised by a stepfather hell-bent on making his boys pillars of the church. Jack had spent his life trying not to upset his parents' apple cart. More than once, one of the brothers had said the wrong word, given the wrong glance at the wrong time, or giggled during their stepfather's sermon, setting off a cascade of consequences falling somewhere between biblical and downright evil. Jack had always felt that Ben would care for him, as an older brother was expected to do.

"Ben…" Jack started as they finished cleaning the stalls and brushing the horses.

"Yeah. What's up?"

Jack shored up his nerves. "What's it called when maybe someone feels different inside?"

Ben immediately stopped what he was doing. "Different, how exactly?"

"Different in how someone feels about who we're supposed to be."

Jack could tell he had Ben's full attention from the look of surprise on his brother's face.

"Jesus, kid. You're twelve." Although Ben looked uncomfortable with the conversation, he continued. "Well… there are some feelings that are bad and some that are good. The trick is to figure out which is which and then do that. What exactly are you getting at?"

"It's just that I was at Mellie's house on the reservation, and there was a drag queen on TV." Ben's face pinched as Jack continued. "And we got to talking about how maybe there are different ways of being, you know, a man."

Ben's face turned to disgust. "What are you trying to tell me?" he responded with obvious distaste for the conversation. Jack knew Ben wanted something better for both of them than their step-dad provided, but he seemed very uncomfortable with Jack's questions.

Jack was rounding the back of their young mare Tawny when Ben straight out asked him, "You're not a sissy faggot, are you?! You know kids like that get hung on fence posts like scarecrows."

Although Tawny blocked his view of Ben, Jack could sense the tension his brother was feeling.

"That's not what I'm saying, Ben." Suddenly, for the first time in his life, Jack felt unsafe in Ben's presence. He was taken aback and confused about why THIS conversation would be the thing to take down all they had built up as buddies. Jack didn't understand why he suddenly felt like he was kneeling before his stepfather rather than tending to the horses with Ben.

"Then out with it. What are you telling me? Be specific. I don't have time for games Jack. I'm busy." Ben turned his back toward his brother, and while Ben was still in the stall with him, Jack had never felt this alone *or abandoned. Again, he didn't understand the genesis of all this tension and weirdness.*

"Mellie was telling me about how her tribe views these things. That some things are not one or the other. Sometimes they're both. Or neither. Do you think that's true, Ben?" Jack could feel himself getting smaller as he walked to the back of the stable to address Tawny's backside and flank.

"Listen, bud. It's like I started to say. There are good feelings, and there are bad feelings. We can't always be the best judge of which is which. That's why we have the word of God to lean into. It's how you know what is right and what is wrong. No offense, but Mellie's tribe ain't exactly in touch with the good and evil our bible teaches."

"But what if what's right for me...." Jack tried sheepishly. A tear volunteered itself to the surface of Jack's cheek.

"Listen, Jack," Ben interrupted, clearly ready to end the conversation. "Dad isn't around as much, and he asked me to be the man of the house, and as such, it is my job to rip the wheat from the chaff. You got me, KID?!" Ben screamed this last "kid" with frustration and fear as he slapped Tawny's flank for emphasis. The horse startled just as Jack rounded the horse's backside, causing her to kick.

The last thing Jack heard was the horse's scream and the internal crack of his skull being popped open. As the horse's hoof made contact with Jack's temple, he lost his innocence and any closeness he would ever have with Ben. Meanwhile, his right eye jangled out of his skull, and with it still intact, he viewed the ground getting closer until everything was suddenly dark.

BROMIDE

Jack sat numbly for a while. Not because of Em leaving but because that was his survival mechanism. When he was in that place, nothing could touch him because there was nothing. No world, no emotion, no stress, no heart, no people, no spirit. Just nothing. And to Jack, that was the best he could do in the moment.

With Banjo asleep, his head in Jack's lap, he charted his next course of action. He was also very aware of the lateness of the day and that he had to return to work within hours. Jack finally got up and went to the bathroom, where he opened the rusted medicine cabinet that complained every time it was opened.. He rifled through his prescription bottles. *Fuck. Fuck, fuck, fuck… Did Em take my meds? Well… not all my meds but the ones I need for sleep? Good God*, he thought. He just wanted this day to end but had no clue how he would sleep now? His chemical dream parachutes were gone, leaving him gut-punched that he'd be forced to be earthbound for this night.

Reaching for the last orange plastic tube, he read the label. "Sedo-neural - Contains Bromide. Do not mix with alcohol."

"Oh, thank god," Jack said out loud, and he pressed his forehead into the cold glass of the mirror. He popped open the white cap and washed two pills down with his beer, feeling relief in seconds despite there being no possible way the drugs could affect him that quickly. But they would, and that was good enough for right now.

Jack walked into his bedroom. It seemed eerily still and vacant. He sat on the edge of his bed and took a few deep inhales from a roach he had snuffed out in the ashtray on the nightstand. He started to feel calm… Well, maybe not calm exactly. Numb was a better word but really, what's the difference? Jack turned out the last of the lights and rolled onto his side naked under the sheets as he heard the front door open. *Fucking Dennis*, Jack thought. *God damn piece of shit Dennis has to show up now.* His thoughts slowed with each passing second. He knew his cares would eventually give way to induced sleep.

The last thing Jack wanted to hear was Dennis's voice, and yet there it was, very quietly from behind the open bedroom door. "Jack? The dog is on the sofa and won't get down."

Jack didn't respond. The last thing he remembered was Dennis getting in bed with him like they used to when they were kids. If he allowed himself to care, it was probably okay by him. Maybe he didn't want to be completely alone tonight despite what his energy was giving off.

Dennis carefully pulled up next to Jack and whispered, "I'm sorry." Then, like when they were little, he spooned Jack for a minute before rolling over and going to sleep.

OPTIONS

Waking the next morning, Jack rolled out of bed to the familiar smell of brewing coffee and something cooking in the kitchen. It took him a minute to manage underwear and put together the shards of memories from last night.

"Hey!" Jack said, coming into the kitchen. "You didn't have to…" he finished that sentence with a gesture meant to convey the word cook.

"I just feel really bad about showing up unannounced, so it's the least I can do," Dennis said as he handed Jack a cup of coffee. "Sit."

Jack was happy to comply. He was trying to unfuck his mind from yesterday's events and wipe clean his brain to face another day of packing dead fish in a freezer. The pay was the only reason he stayed in this dead-end job. The job itself was horrid. His boss was even worse. Even still, the events of the previous night made it seem like it had been weeks since Mr. Wren called Jack "ineffective." Ineffective. The word stung in Jack's mind again.

"So, we didn't really have a chance to…." Jack thoughts were cut short by Dennis interjecting.

"I know I have a lot to explain, but I need you to know that my finances are legit. It's not a drug deal or anything, but I sold one of my canoes to this guy who said he'd pay me when his next commission check came in. It's supposed to be here by Friday."

Jack was taken aback by this news. "Hold up. Canoe? Commission? What the fuck are you even talking about? We haven't seen each other since high school, so you're going to have to fill in some of the pieces here. You make canoes?"

"Well, kinda. I guess," Dennis added. "I don't so much make them as I fix them up and paint them, so they look cool. I've been trying to sell them online, and well, this is gonna be my first sale."

"Oh, jeez, Dennis. So, is this a real thing or what? Just level with me."

Dennis's pride continued, "Nah. He took down my banking info and is going to wire me the cash."

Jack internally face-palmed so hard he had to put his head back and just breathe for a second. "You did fucking what now?"

Dennis's face dropped. "Well, yeah. You know, with computers and such… That's how they do it now. They just wire or something. I mean it's 2008… you do banking online and stuff now, right?"

"Dennis," Jack added in a serious manner that changed the entire tone of the conversation. "I appreciate you saying this, but I don't think your sale or grift or whatever this is, is going to happen. How well do you know this guy? How do you know he's not just ripping you off or stealing your bank info to bury you financially or steal from you?" The "bury you financially" bit was a reach, but Jack thought it might make him seem smart. He felt pretty confident about his affairs ever since Dennis's "all this" comment. *All this, like it's a fucking Beverly Hills estate.*

Dennis paused, then started in with, "I don't need you to trust me on this. Why don't we wait until Friday and just see what happens? If the money doesn't come through, I just head back to my parent's place. If it does, then we can talk options."

Jack burst into laughter. "Options! Oh my god! Options! Ha ha…. Oh my god. Wow… that's amazing. Phew," Jack said, wiping the tears from his eyes with the back of his forearm, trying not to spill his coffee. "Options." He managed one last time through a fading guffaw. "Oh my god. That's brilliant. Thank you." Jack sat back up in his chair. "Oof… God, that felt good to laugh." Jack had a brief recognition that he was being a complete dick to his friend – something he would not normally do – but this guy showed up in the middle of Jack's shitstorm, and therefore he was going to get the worst of Jack whether he liked it or not. Jack didn't have anybody in his life to blow smoke up his ass and lead him to believe it was all going to be okay. So why should he do anything of the sort for Dennis?

As Jack collected himself from his outburst, he realized that Dennis was just staring back blankly. "That wasn't a joke," Dennis said picking up on the fact that Jack was being an uncharacteristic asshole.

Seeing that Dennis was hurt, Jack changed his tone. "Awww… c'mon." He stood up and put his hand on Dennis's shoulder. "Okay. We can wait until Friday to see if your money comes through. You can have the run of the place while I'm at work. Just please take care of Banjo and don't smoke all my weed. Em took most of my meds, and I'm not due for a refill for two more weeks."

"Aye, aye, Captain," Dennis joked. Jack still had an uncanny ability to bring the mood back to laughter and light when he wanted to.

Jack showered and got ready for work, leaving his meds regimen for last. He hoped Dennis wouldn't see this part. Noting his physical condition wasn't great from the stress of the prior evening, he stuffed his pockets with those pills he thought he might need midday. Then he kissed Banjo as he left the trailer and closed the door behind him without officially saying goodbye to Dennis. In truth, he was just happy to be back outside and alone. He could breathe there. He was safer there.

As Jack pulled into the parking lot at the food processing plant, he mentally braced himself for what usually came next.

Closing the Blazer door, he turned to see Annie also doing the same.

"Yo!" Jack shouted. "How's my favorite lunch lady?" He laughed. Annie was an old-timer who was a taciturn and prickly gossip. Jack would respond to her moods with charm and warmth, challenging himself to blow away the dark cloud that followed her wherever she went. He loved the days when he ran into her before anyone else at this hell hole. Maybe he could make one person's life better, even if he couldn't do the same for himself.

In spite of herself, Annie laughed in return. She waved in his general direction and kept walking.

Jack punched the clock with his paper card noting 8:05 AM. His mood fell as he realized his tardiness. "God damn it," he said under his breath as he scanned the hall side to side. Fortunately, Mr. Wallace Wren, the flagship of terrible bosses, was nowhere to be seen.

Jack never could figure out why Mr. Wren stayed when he clearly hated it here, hated him, hated everything. That thought had barely crossed his mind when a voice inside him said, *And what about you? What is this judgment you're going to levy against another while also doing the same? Is this how we're going to play this? Is this who you are?*

Jack shrugged off his mental chatter and headed to his locker, grabbing his gear to be in place and working by 8:15, where he'd be until 5:00, save for a few small breaks, each of which would be devoid of pleasure or relaxation if Mr. Wren were in the vicinity. Just a glance from the small-minded man left employees with the feeling they were doing something wrong, even if they were on a legally-mandated break.

Wednesday was Wednesday. Nothing new. Nothing special. It's hard to get fired up about mid-week fish processing.

Five o'clock eventually rolled around, and, as always, Jack stank. He grabbed his things and jumped in his truck as the sun was setting. The stench of dead fish was overwhelming in an enclosed space. He rolled down the truck window and stuck a flame in his mokee pipe. He didn't know why he preferred this combo of weed and tobacco, but he did, and as he was gaining in years, he was allowing himself more and more to have what he wanted. He no longer felt the need to over-explain or clarify with anyone who he was and what he liked. Telling Em that he wasn't ready to have kids was probably the strongest example of Jack's newfound self-focus. He hadn't enjoyed hurting her but smiled at the thought that he held true to himself.

Once home, Jack opened the front door with a twinge of anxiousness in his stomach. No Dennis. His absence did not calm Jack's uneasiness at all. Far from it.

Jack walked into the bedroom. No Dennis. Then into the backyard. Still no Dennis.

Well, what on God's earth? Jack thought to himself as he noticed that Banjo was also missing. Now he started to panic a bit. *Where are they?*

Regardless, Jack was beat and wanted just to enjoy a beer uninterrupted, an activity very much stolen from him during yesterday's fucked up mess. Jack noted he hadn't thought much about Em until now. Her words, "You're not good-looking enough, to also be an asshole," were just about all he could hear when she did enter his mind. Every time, Jack's fingers would involuntarily trace the bumps, scars and unnatural flesh that made up his face.

"Aaaa!" An exclamation of self-hatred escaped his lips as he could feel himself once again going down the rabbit hole of *why am I so fucked up?*

Often, when Jack was alone, he picked apart the broken parts of himself. The super messed up childhood, his physically abusive stepdad, and his mentally abusive mother, who would say things to him that no child should ever hear from a parent. His physical issues. His health issues. His undefinable sexuality and his desires to bed practically anyone, man or woman. His walled-off emotions and matching heart. His brokenness on every level. Nothing was whole. Nothing was good. His past was shit. His future… well. He didn't go there because it's not an option when you're staring down the barrel of a future in a wheelchair. Exploring that reality was way too terrifying… *Even for a badass like me.* This last thought made him laugh out loud.

Badass? Where? How? Jack thought to himself. Who was he kidding? He couldn't even make it through the week without both chemical and metal crutches. He eyed his braces across the room that he'd need when the meds stopped being enough. Most days were still pretty good, but when they're not… well. It could be bad.

Jack went over to the medicine cabinet and grabbed his concoction of assorted pills as a precaution. When taken proactively, it significantly increased his ability to function normally.

Fucking Em. Ugh. Why? The answer came to him the moment he thought it. She wanted him to hurt too. That was the worst way she could do it. Check and mate.

By 6:00, Jack was in a decent mood, watching TV and enjoying his second beer when Banjo popped through the door, followed quickly by Dennis's dumb face and matching gait.

Dennis and he had been pretty close in high school, and he sometimes wondered what had happened to him. Dennis and Mel were the only friends who always stood by him… even after the accident when they tried to help Jack relearn life and the basics such as tying a shoe, reading with one eye, and hearing with one ear. Jack remembered how anxious it all made him. It wasn't the accident per se; it was the reentry into life that seemed insurmountable. He was entirely different. The world was not.

At the front door, Dennis turned to Jack, holding up four fish on a wire. "Dinner is served!" He laughed.

Jack was secretly glad for the company, and if you pressed him on it, he would tell you that he was also secretly happy to reconnect with Dennis. It was good to see him. It was good not to be alone right now.

"Now, this is the life!" Jack grinned. "I wondered where you fuckheads went."

"Gah," Dennis muttered as he made his way to the kitchen, trying his best not to drip dead fish juice on the floor. "They were swimming pretty good today. You got something to go with this?"

Not even looking up from the TV, Jack muttered, "Um… iceberg lettuce? Maybe tomatoes?"

Dennis rummaged through the fridge. Closing the fridge door, he shouted over to Jack. "You know how they do those cheap yet somehow fancy iceberg lettuce wedges in steakhouses and stuff?"

"No," Jack responded.

"Well, never mind. I got it covered. It'll be awesome." The smirk on Dennis's face was unmissable. Jack could tell he enjoyed having this task and, in a way, purpose.

With that, Jack felt *the* twinge. *Fuck.* He hated that twinge. It always started the same when an episode was coming on. Jack internally started to panic because his medications were depleted, and he felt utterly unarmed and unprepared to deal with the impending eventuality.

Fuck, he again thought to himself, but as always, he pulled himself together and steadied his tone to address the room. "I'm just going to pop into the bathroom." He said over his shoulder as he headed for the hall.

Once in front of the broken medicine cabinet, Jack paused. It was as if, in that moment, the dam broke. He stared at his deranged face where his crushed eye socket met his rebuilt cheekbone. The tiny crack in the glass, mirroring back his life and how it had split him in two—on one side of him everything was as it should not be, and on the other, was a jawline that could trample hearts. Then, as always, his hand made its way to his face to cover it up so he could remember what he looked like when he was whole.

Tears streamed down his face as the buried memory resurfaced the way it always did…

"JACK!!!!" In a high-piercing tone.

"JACK!!!" It was his mother's voice.

"JACK!!!" Screams of terror mixed with sobs.

"JACK!!!" He was semi-conscious and floating in a hospital bed.

JACK!!!!" Medicated and falling into himself.

"JACK!!!!" The only functioning part of him was one ear, which replayed his mother's wail every time he stepped away from holding back the memory. Then it was silent again. Dark again. Nothing again.

Jack pushed away the memory as he reached into the medicine cabinet, taking a complete inventory of what Em had left him. *Seroquel, check. Thank God. Lamotrigine, check. Thank God. Prednisone, check. Fingolimod, check.* Everything else? All the meds to help weather an actual attack? Well. That was all gone.

Fuck, Jack thought. With the impending attack crawling up his arm, he knew that if he was thrown into a full dystonic attack tonight, there was little he could do to make it less scary for himself or Dennis. He knew what was coming, and he knew he had already taken his safety precaution drugs, so now all he could do was wait, see what happens next, and hope that Dennis was up for one hell of an education on a topic that, in Jack's experience, even most doctors knew nothing about.

FLOORED

Jack came out of the bathroom and quickly headed for Dennis in the kitchen. "We have to talk…"

Dennis's look of joy while cooking dropped from his face. "Sure. What's up? Was it something I did?"

"No," Jack said under his breath. "It's just that. Well… I… Something is about to happen that I need to prep you for."

Dennis put down the lettuce he cut, his face becoming stone-cold serious. "What's going on?"

"I have a pretty serious neurological movement disorder, and I'm about to have an episode. I can feel it coming on now." Jack said this as he looked out the window, past Dennis, with a blank gaze that disallowed him from focusing on anything in particular.

Dennis moved toward him. "Is that what Em was going on about? I overheard her say you are going to be crippled in five years. I was hoping she was exaggerating. You know, just being mean in a heated moment."

"She wasn't exaggerating, and I need you to know what happens next because Em stole my meds that I need to weather this when I'm in a… um…situation. It's been a long time since I've had to face this without medical support, and I don't know how it's going to go." Jack paused. Dennis waited. "Well, to tell the truth, I never know how it's going to go."

God damn it, Em! Jack thought to himself. He drew in a deep breath. *Now what?*

Dennis arranged himself to get under Jack's gaze so that he could see his eyes. "Dude, you look fine to me. I think you'll be okay."

Jack could feel time running out. He could feel the twinge taking possession of his right ring finger, the place where it always begins to make itself known. "Fuck Dennis. C'mon. We're running out of time. Just listen to me. It's a neurological disorder, and I can feel my brain starting to collapse. Of course, you can't see it, fucknut, but you'll see how it's taking me over."

Jack grabbed Dennis by the hand and led him into the bedroom, where he stripped the bed and grabbed a wadded-up sheet from the closet. Dennis awkwardly stepped in to help as he could.

Twinge. Ring finger. Twinge. Right forearm just under the elbow. Twinge. Right bicep. Twinge. Right shoulder. Jack could feel it start to take him over as it always does. Soon, Dennis would be more aware of what was happening to Jack's body than he was. But for now, Jack was the only one in tune with this mystery.

"Listen, Dennis, Em was right. I can't be on my own."

By this point, Dennis's face was filled with concern. "I mean… What's going to happen, Jack? How can I help?" His voice was getting slightly more desperate as he could see Jack's right hand starting to curl into itself like a kid's would when he's imitating a T-rex with short hard, contracted curled-up hands. Jack began using only his left hand.

"So, here's what happens next," Jack said as he felt the devil within him claim the right side of his neck, forcing him to bend to its will and pulling his right ear toward his shoulder. "Just keep me from hitting anything or injuring myself. First, I'll probably be in contorted positions as my body constricts." Jack was speaking quickly now. "If it's really bad, my arms, chest, and back can stiffen to the point where I can't breathe or get air. If I pass out, this is good. Just let me recover. My brain resets with sleep or unconsciousness."

Jack finished adding the rubber sheet to the bed, then, starting to limp, he made his way over to his tobacco box, where he began packing weed into the bowl of a pipe. Looking back over his shoulder, Jack felt the right side of his face drop. Dennis's eyes went wide, but he seemed to steady himself.

For his part, Jack was not the least bit shaken that half his face no longer worked. "I might shake or move weirdly like I'm having convulsions. This is the part where I can injure myself. Just keep me from banging my head or something."

Jack paused. Just stopped. The room fell eerily quiet. Dennis moved toward Jack as Jack's headspace resigned, like someone giving up. Jack lifted his head. His face was now that of someone with Bell's Palsy; his physically damaged side now completely offline as it drooped untethered, making his fake eye resemble that of an evil doll like you see in scary movies.

Jack felt like a monster. He could see he was scaring his friend. "If it gets worse from there, I'll just go limp. For me, this is the scariest part because it's when my mind disconnects from everything. I have no thoughts or access to my body. I have access to nothing. Sometimes I don't even know who I am or what my name is." Jack could now feel the juxtaposition of a tear rolling down his cheek while the thing inside him slithered and snaked across his chest and down his other arm. "If I get into this state…." Jack paused, looking down to his crotch. "If I make a mess, I'm sorry. Just leave me, and I'll take care of it when I'm awake."

"So how can I help? What can I do? I don't want just to watch, Jack. What can I do?"

Jack didn't want him there at all, but his embarrassment over letting someone see him like this had to take second place to needing help and needing that help now. Jack understood this.

"Just don't let me hit anything…" he trailed off. Then this was the tough ask. "It sometimes would help when Em would be near me so I could hear her breathing." Jack's internal demon was now in full possession of his torso, which yanked him violently into contortion. The internal hellion lurking in corners that curled all the way up into this brain, carelessly flicking neurological switches on and off as it went. It was now affecting Jack's speech and ability to form words. "Touc and quie scheech" Jack shook his head, trying to knock the English language back into him. "…helps me have soko kee pall…." Jack, frustrated, shook his head again. "FUCK. Gives me an feedo kee. Fuck! to know SEESHO. FUCK. Where da. keeto I AMmmm."

Jack felt Dennis reach to balance him as Jack's spine twisted into a question mark. "You need me to breathe. Right?" Dennis's repeated, his panicked voice rising. "It helps know where you are. Is that what you meant? JACK. JACK!"

Jack dropped onto the mattress as his legs started to buckle. His arms and chest were now so contracted that it affected his ability to breathe freely. He was beginning to wheeze. Finally, with the tinniest corner of his lips that he still had control of, he managed. "Cho-cho." Damn it. "Poko." *Fuck*.

"Pot." Jack had to stop and try the next word thoughtfully. "Can." Breathe. "Keeto," Jack wanted to cry. "Sometimes." Breathe. Pause. "Help…" Jack knew he had just seconds before he dipped below the surface of this world. "I feeko. che-chen deedo. CAN… cheee… HEAR YOU."

With that, he was gone.

Silence.

In the deafening void that followed, Jack slipped below the surface of his mind. His internal monstrosity was now entirely in charge of what happened next.

UNMOORED

Like being thrown out of an airplane, it began.

Jack's non-verbal mind braced as he plummeted. The rush of wind, violent and abrasive against his skin, only it wasn't air he was falling through; it was energy. He hit the hard surface of it with a crush so violent he gasped. "AAAAAAAAG!" his mind screamed as his physical body reacted by asphyxiating his rib cage and lungs. That, in turn, produced a gagging hiss as the last of his breath was forced out of him. The world became darker than the blackness of the ocean's depths as Jack was forced to twist into hideous gothic positions. Mouth open in a permanent silent scream. Eyes bulging dead and unfixed.

Jack fought, but had no other option than to endure the trampling of him, by him. The crush of his muscles attacking making breathing impossible; his master only allowing Jack tiny sips of air as he felt himself continuing to fall.

Just put me down! Jack begged for unconsciousness. He begged it to stop. Jack knew the gentle cast of sleep would be his only way out, but today his mind wasn't done with him. Not yet. Not this time because fear and stress feed it, and on this day, Jack's internal hellcat was stronger than strong. It thanked Jack for the new dark energy it needed as it wound up for another destructive blow.

Jack's spine undulated. His good eye, unfocused and dead, was a match set for the glass one that had long failed to blink, see or move.

CRASH! Jack broke through the surface of the icy dark water.

CRASH! He dropped out of the bottom of the sea, flailing.

CRASH! He hit the solid form of water again, desperate to get air but instead choking on freezing, salty seawater as the torrent of icy wind blasted his skin.

CRASH! He slammed onto the ocean floor then was pummeled by more massive roiling waves of energy. He was drowning.

CRASH! He dropped through the bottom of it again as it ravaged him endlessly, utterly impartial to Jack's withering condition.

Through layer after layer of water, air, earth, he fell. The slamming and jerking making his mind rattle and mush; it was a dark place, a place where no thoughts could form.

Jack wailed involuntarily. "NO!!!!!..." Then just a quiet whimper, "Please..." as the next massive contraction of his abs fully sat him upright then slammed him back down onto the mattress again, bashing the back of his head violently into the bed.

Wave after wave mashed and pulverized Jack. Only Jack knew that it wasn't earth or water or air that he fell through. In this state, it was solely his insides that so violently squashed and crushed him. As his body betrayed him, he knew not to fight. The most effective action was to let go and ride the wave of energy forcibly expressing itself through him.

The dark matter reached into the icy water and grabbed Jack, pulling him violently up into the air. Jack detached. Became nothing. Resigned. It then threw him through more layers of earth. BANG! Then falling. BANG! He hit the ocean. BANG! The velocity increased as the beast was simply toying with him. BANG! CRASH! Freefall. Jack's guts threw him as he twisted and flailed through no space and nothing real or tangible. Falling. Nauseous. Twisting. Falling. *Please, God,* Jack thought. *Please.*

And then he felt how close he now was to the great void of nothingness, the final phase of this sick game over which he had no control.

Falling.

Falling…

Please, Jack thought once more.

The anticipated release finally arrived and Jack was instantly transported to the space where nothing exists. Jack tried not to scream at the elimination of anything and everything and the overwhelming terror of absolute silence. Here, the terror is the nothingness, like being pushed out of a spaceship and floating through deep space. No up. No down. Nothing to grab hold of to stop the spin of you… but you're not even sure that you're spinning because all thought is gone. You don't know. You can't think. Once Jack crossed that threshold, he lost all access to his body and mind. Everything was as blank as death. Or maybe death was much more lively and peaceful. Sometimes Jack wished the beast would throw him there instead of here.

In this new place, the place of white nothingness, Jack's brain entirely disconnected from everything. He couldn't think. He couldn't move. He had no control over his body, and this is where he lost his bowels. Jack had no angst about such a thing in this place, for he could not even perceive it… but he could hear. Barely… but there it was.

"Jack?" he perceived off in the distance. And while Jack was incapable of processing a thought around this, at least it was something in the vastness of this obliterated world. Jack started to breathe again. Slowly and very shallow, but it was something.

This was the final stage; it always was — and with his brain completely flatlining, Jack's body went limp. He could not recount where he was or who he is. Jack dropped into this with only a vague awareness of how scary it is to be this detached from thought. No brain. No body. Just nothing, which Jack tried to fold himself into. Wrap himself in the nothingness to join the still. Sometimes Jack could even find peace here, his body alien to him, a stranger on the other side of the room.

THURSDAY

When Jack awoke the following day, Dennis was still asleep next to him. He opened his eyes and assessed what he had control over. Head, check. Neck, check. Arms, check. Legs, check. He continued to lay there next to Dennis and thought about how he dreaded the next few impending conversations. Those talks were never awesome.

Finally, Dennis's eyes opened, and he rolled onto his side to face Jack. Then, very quietly and with concern, Dennis asked, "Are you ok? How do you feel this morning?"

"I'm not exactly sure yet, but I think I'm ok," Jack said as his discomfort over this conversation grew. He didn't want pity. He didn't want to have these conversations. He didn't want to talk about it. He didn't want to see the fear in his friend's eyes and voice. Jack knew he scared people because what he had was, in fact, scary. Something right out of a Stephen King novel… only his situation was real.

Dennis, somehow recognizing Jack's tamped soul, tried to lighten the mood with, "I'm pretty sure in olden times you would have been burned at the stake for witchcraft." This made Jack laugh.

"Yeah…" Jack said as he rolled over onto his back, taking off the covers to let his skin breathe.

Dennis sat up and swung his legs over the side of the bed. "How about some breakfast? Are you still going to work?"

There was dread in Jack's voice as he said, "Yes."

Fifteen minutes later, Jack had showered, and they were eating breakfast in silence.

"Thanks," Jack finally managed.

"Oh, it was nothing. I barely noticed that anything happened," Dennis said, looking out the window to avoid Jack's gaze.

"Dennis…" Jack began.

"Yeah," replied Dennis.

"All I ask is that you don't do that." Jack adjusted himself in his seat. "Don't minimize the experience to protect my feelings. It's not helpful."

Dennis looked confused. "I'm sorry. I guess I'm not…."

Jack cut his comment short. "I know you're trying to protect my feelings, but I know when it's bad because I can see it in your face… so if you tell me it's one thing, which I know isn't true, but you tell me it is, then I feel crazy. Like I have to question what happened when I'm not in a position to assess these things. So let's just please live in the same reality. Just be honest with me. That's helpful. That helps me gain clarity around a situation like last night."

Dennis thought about it for a minute. "That makes sense. Sure."

Standing, Jack grabbed his coffee cup and headed to the bedroom. "I gotta get to work. I assume you'll be here when I get back?"

Dennis was stroking Banjo's head. "I guess so. If that's cool?"

"Sure," Jack said, then paused to turn back around. "Thanks again for helping me out last night. I'm sure that wasn't easy for you."

Dennis replied with a wave of his hand and said, "I'll see you tonight."

Jack felt slightly better emotionally with those few initial conversations behind them but was still assessing his physical condition as he hopped in his truck and started the engine.

What Jack hated most about having a big episode like that was the brain-drag hangover that he'd often experience into the next day. It's like having a foggy brain after waking up from a long hard nap. He wasn't running on all cylinders mentally, and Jack was still trying to resuscitate certain parts of his body that weren't wholly accessible to him. His right arm was always the most significant issue. It's not like it was numb or tingly but rather just significantly powered down, operating on half battery. As a result, his brain refused to communicate with that limb fully.

At work, he parked the car and hurried into the line to enter the building. Annie was a few spots behind him, but Jack didn't wave or smile this time. His sullen mood was still very blue.

Clock punch… *And look at that!* Jack thought as he read his timecard. *7:47 AM. I'm even early today.* Trying to reassure himself, Jack thought, *Sure, I might go fully poltergeist in the evenings, but no one knows. No one can tell. My scars are on the inside, and there's nothing easier to hide than that. A wave and a smile. Just that simple.*

Jack had been a serious athlete in his younger years, but he was also somewhat prone to injury. He had had more concussions and head trauma than most and stress fractures in his legs was not uncommon. Especially his shins. But his learning how to perform injured and rally for the team served him very well. It taught him how to compensate for the parts that weren't working by using the things that were. He could still sling dead fish all day even if one arm was operating at 50% or less. But, again, no one could tell. No one had to know.

As the day wore on Jack did his best to evade his boss until around 3:00PM when he heard, "Jack," Mr. Wren burped. "What's going on there? You seem to be even slower than you normally are. Is this what I'm paying you for?"

Jack stared at him as he thought to himself, *Ummm… you're just an employee here like the rest of us. YOU don't pay me for anything. Plexus foods does, and while you might be a higher-ranking asshole in this food chain, you're still just a cog in someone ELSE'S very lucrative wheel. So please. Spare me the power trip.* But instead, Jack adjusted his face to look pleasant and came back with, "Ah. Yeah, I kinda hurt my hand in that damn freezer door. You need to get that fixed." Jack was a master at this. Placing the blame of his shortcomings on the plant and dropping the subtle hints that maybe Jack should file a lawsuit for poor working conditions.

Mr. Wren stood there with his doughy-sallow face and sunken dark-little-eyes. No response. It's as if he was going on a power trip by just hovering, making it clear that he could do whatever he wanted, and today was the day he'd observe and take mental notes.

Jack turned back to the crates and iron plates. *God damn*, Jack thought. *Ugh… just go. Don't watch me. Not today.*

Jack did his best not to show his lame arm, slightly curved spine, and other hangover issues from yesterday's massive attack. He was determined not to let Mr. Wren see any weakness, so when it looked like he was holding one of the freezer trays with two hands, he was only using one while the other was a prop. Jack smiled over his shoulder and just kept on walking.

But Mr. Wren had a different idea. He moved in closer to Jack, making the younger man instantly uncomfortable. So close that Jack could smell his breath … a wretched mixture of stale Coca-Cola, chronic mouth-breathing, and menthol cigarettes.

"I'm watching you, Daw. Don't ever think you're getting away with any nonsense. You know how I feel about hiring your type, but, in this case, I was given no options. If … or should I say when …. you fuck up, on the other hand, I will have all the options, and you will have none." Mr. Wren said the last part too gleefully for Jack's taste. His boss walked away, not even trying to conceal his delight as Jack breathed fully for the first time since the encounter started. He could now return to hauling the fish and freezer trays with one arm.

To Mr. Wren, this was probably just a run-of-the-mill interaction with a hated employee. But, for Jack, it was the very last straw. He decided then and there to do something entirely out of character. Now all he had to do was carry out his plan. The one that would ensure him both cash, and freedom.

After Jack's shift he sped home, and as he was coming through the front door, Jack greeted Banjo. He then veered into the kitchen to grab a beer.

"Honey, I'm home," Jack joked over his shoulder in the direction of the rest of the house.

Dennis came out of the bathroom. "Oh. I didn't realize it was this late. And for what it's worth, you'd make a terrible wife. With that fucking face, you're far too ugly, and from what I've heard, you're terrible in bed."

Jack laughed despite himself. "Probably true," Jack said… "Except for that last part. I'm a fucking stallion." This comment sent both men into laughter given Jack's well-known, yet not-talked-about history as a hustler, womanizer, manizer and everything in-between-izer.

When silence returned to the living room, Dennis headed past Jack, informing him, "I bought a few things for dinner, plus we still have some trout from last night. You didn't seem much in the mood to eat." Dennis winked at Jack, in an obvious attempt to normalize their conversation around an otherwise potentially sticky topic. Jack appreciated that.

An hour or so later, Jack had smoked some pot and was opening his second beer when Dennis commented that dinner was ready.

"How'd you learn to cook?" Jack asked as he sat down.

Dennis, delivering the plates to the table, said, "You know… my old lady would work late some nights, and I had to step up. She is really particular. Always made me watch these YouTube things and try and do some fancy shit."

"That's how you know about the iceberg lettuce thing," Jack said, waving his fork toward the fridge as if the lettuce was still in there. "I was pretty sure you weren't touring the countryside visiting fancy steakhouses."

"Huh, yeah, I guess." Dennis was lost in thought and gave up only a pathetic chuckle.

"Listen," Jack said, looking Dennis squarely in the eyes. "I know you want to do right by Wendy, but you gotta realize the tourists just don't come to Kelsey anymore. If that's the lot you're after, you need to get to someplace more interesting. Someplace people want to visit. Honestly, I think you're onto something, but you need to either increase your online presence and sell like on eBay or something, or you need to get a small set up or shop or something."

"So, move?" Dennis asked quizzically like it was a brand-new thought. It was always amusing to Jack to watch a small-town mind consider leaving the nest for the first time. It was as if you were asking them to crawl out of reality and into television, where all sorts of wondrous and hideous things might happen. Enticing, sure, but terrifying at the same time.

"Well, clearly Kelsey ain't doing you so well, Dennis," Jack said with more tone than was intended. "You're running around with someone else's lady, so you don't feel right there, plus you live with your parents. Maybe you just need a fresh start?"

Ignoring the conversation, Dennis looked at his friend squarely in the eyes. "Can I ask you about last night?"

"Sure," Jack said as he prepared himself for the usual questions. "And no, it doesn't hurt if that's what you're going to ask me. I mean, I get sore from the cramping, but…."

Dennis cut him off. "I mean, you look good. You look fit. You don't look sick."

Jack had to clarify this point for the one-millionth time in his adult life. "Because I'm not sick." They both paused. Jack could see the confusion growing on Dennis' face.

Jack clarified, "People tend to put everyone with a situation in one bucket called 'sick people.' To me, someone who is sick is ill or doesn't feel well. That's not me. Do I look sick?"

Dennis managed, "Well, no, but last night…," he trailed off.

"Dennis." Jack leaned in closer to convey a sense of closeness between friends. "I know that was probably super scary for you, and I'm sorry we didn't have a chance to talk about it more at length before everything went to shit, but you have to trust me. I am okay."

I don't think you are, Jack. What I saw wasn't anywhere close to okay."

"I know. And I know it's hard to wrap your mind around it but look at me now." Jack stood. "Everything is good. I can do push-ups." Jack dropped and gave him ten to prove the point. "I can run around the block." Jack ran in place. "I can probably even kick your ass in arm wrestling."

Dennis swung his arm up onto the table with a chuckle. "Okay. Loser does the dishes."

"Ha!" Jack said in delight as he grabbed his friend's hand and sat down. He was mostly sure his limbs were done betraying him.

The match lasted four seconds before Dennis's strength failed. He made loser groans as he made his way to the sink to start cleaning up. Jack found this all highly entertaining, especially given the state of his arm earlier in the day.

"How'd you get so fucking strong? And how is it someone your age is in such good shape?" Dennis inquired after a long silence.

"For serious?" Jack looked up while still rolling a joint.

"Yeah. You know… I mean, I don't know anyone our age who looks like they're in your type of condition."

"Want to know my secret?" Jack laughed.

"Absolutely!" Dennis said, stopping what he was doing to train his full attention on Jack.

"It's my brain disorder. You know how working out and contracting your muscles gets you into better shape…." Jack said without posing it as a question. "Well, it's the same for me, only I don't have a choice as to when and how I'll 'work out.'" He emphasized the words "work out" with air quotes.

"You're kidding me?" Dennis said, slightly annoyed. "One of the side effects of your fucked up brain is a killer bod? That's seriously crazy."

Jack laughed with embarrassment. "Silver linings, I guess." He just wanted to think and talk about other things. Things with less sting.

Dennis finished the dishes, and they headed out back to smoke that joint.

FRIDAY

Waking up Friday morning, Jack felt pretty good. His neurological storm had now fully passed, and he was firing on all cylinders. As Jack got out of bed, Dennis stirred. Walking past him on his way to the door, Jack pushed Dennis just hard enough to knock him off the bed, his body hitting the floor with a thud.

"Haha," Jack said as he left the room.

"Asshole!" he heard as he stepped into the bathroom. A slight grin crossed his face as he gazed sleepily into the mirror. "You're not good-looking enough, to also be an asshole," rang in his ears, balanced on the precipice of both the mirrors and Dennis' joking truth.

"Never mind," Jack said to his reflection, and he opened the cabinet to start his medicinally propped-up day. Blue small. Check. One yellow. Two white for now. One big blue and two orange for mid-day.

When Jack was done showering, he was delighted to smell the scent of coffee brewing as it floated on air yet again throughout his home. Jack quickly got dressed then joined Dennis in the kitchen.

"I have about twenty minutes before I gotta head out," Jack said as he sat. Dennis handed him his coffee. "You know, I could get used to this."

Dennis looked confused. "Didn't you and Em work like this? Did she cook or make coffee or even breakfast?" Dennis still seemed to be harboring anger toward Em for taking Jack's meds. His tone did not conceal this.

Jack, on the other hand, seemed over it. "Meh. Kinda. Not like regularly or anything. She liked to sleep in when possible. I'm more of a get up early and tackle the day kinda guy."

"Can I ask you a few more things about your brain situation?" Dennis followed up.

Jack, lost in thought, came back with, "No… there's no cure. Yes, I've seen every fucking neurologist this side of Alberta. Yes, they can only manage symptoms. No, there's not much research into my condition because it's not fatal, just extremely invasive and debilitating. Did I miss anything?" Jack had about 30 seconds left of leveled patience. He just didn't want to talk about it. He never did. Too unpleasant to think about.

"I was just going to ask if you're okay. Like for real. How are you going to manage on your own?"

The last of Jack's face fell as he looked into his coffee cup. "I don't know, Dennis. Honestly, I don't know…." His voice disappeared but then resumed with, "It's mostly controllable with meds and lifestyle changes like reducing stress and not pushing myself too hard. Stress and fatigue are the key triggers."

"And you're going to live in North America AND avoid these things? You're what? Going to find some Zen bunker, hunker down, and avoid stress? Kinda not how it works out there, Jack. How do you feel comfortable driving or working with something like that just beneath the surface?"

"Dude, I'm fine."

"C'mon… You're not fine."

"Look, it only happens late in the day when my brain gets tired or stressed. It's manageable otherwise, okay? You just caught me on a bad day. Big stressful life events are challenging. Em leaving, while not a complete surprise given our history, was one of those events." As

Jack said Em's name, he allowed himself the first pang of loss, which was more than enough, and he knew he didn't need to deal with that again. Enough feeling or thinking about her. Moving on.

Jack deflected with, "I gotta run. Just going to finish this," he said, pointing to his breakfast sandwich that Dennis had made. "It's perfect for people on the go!" Jack said in a humorous voice like he was in a cheesy commercial that celebrated healthy breakfast treats for fast-paced American lives. "Hey, it's all good," he said over his shoulder to at least give a sliver of an answer to Dennis's question.

Jack was out the door and starting his truck in another ten minutes. *Another day, another dollar.* That thought was quickly followed with, *Well, actually, it's more like another day, another $135 net.* He had done the math more times than he cared to admit, and he knew that if he was going to make a new path forward, he couldn't afford to lie to himself anymore.

Arriving at Plexus Foods, Jack's beast of a vehicle hummed to silence as he put the truck in park. Jack felt for his meds in his pocket, triple checking that their support was all in for this day.

When Jack got to the time clock, Mr. Wren was standing in front of it, arms folded, lips tight in judgment.

"Well, Mr. Daw. So glad you could join us on this fine day."

"Um? Thanks?" Jack said as he grabbed his timecard and approached from the side to paper prove his timely arrival. 8:00 on the nose. *Phew,* thought Jack as he moved away from Mr. Wren as quickly as possible to throw on his work-issued coveralls, coat, and toque that kept his head warm. Unfortunately, the woolen cap never covered his ears adequately, and he secretly wondered if the company made them that way on purpose to keep people just cold enough not to fall asleep.

Jack arrived at his station in the fish-laden air, grabbed his gloves, and reached for his first fish in the freezer. The dead salmon reminded him of his hardened limbs when in the midst of an attack. Hardened carcass. Unnatural flesh. He hoped death precluded the fish from the mental anguish that came to him during an episode.

Jack's task was to carefully lift the fish from the frozen tray to avoid breaking a fin or other parts. The goal was for the fish to arrive perfectly intact to far-flung stores, markets, and restaurants. Mr. Wren was very clear about this. Damaged catch was less valuable and a direct reflection on Plexus Foods' reputation.

All morning, Jack pried the fish from the frozen plates on which they were lying dead. Jack liked to think of this as a Zen exercise. To him, it was the attention to small details like one does with the perfect origami fold or the ideal turning of wood. He didn't know why he prided himself on this task, but he often said to himself, *Fish on, fish off*, a comedic take on the Karate Kids "Wax on, wax off." The task was menial, but Jack always did his best to be precise. This, in turn, gave his job meaning and gave him a reason for the toiling hours. In a way, it was like a silent walking meditation – an internal journey for one.

At 11:30, Jack took a break for lunch. As he walked out of the freezer section where he was housed for most of the day, Jack focused only on removing his freezer gloves. When he looked up, however, he noticed Mr. Wren looking down on him from the area's upper level. Jack gazed up and managed a very fake smile that was so unnatural it confused his boss as to its purpose.

"Mr. Daw…" Mr. Wren let the words hang in the air as Jack moved around quickly, acting much busier than he was.

Jack halfheartedly waved, trying his best to scoot out and dismiss himself from this place and the present moment.

"Mr. Daw!" Mr. Wren snapped, starting down the metal stairs to meet Jack eye to eye in the cement arena.

Jesus, mother of Saint Francis, Jack thought to himself, shedding the remainder of his clunky yellow waterproof gear.

Jack turned with a, "Oh hey, Mr. Wren." The lie of his cheerfulness peeled at his insides and mocked his current duplicitous gesture. "Glad you could make it by today. Boy, I can't believe how busy we are given that this time of year is often...."

Mr. Wren, clearly not there for chit-chat, interrupted. "Mr. Daw. It seems HR might have a few questions for you regarding your..." he paused to train his gaze directly into Jack's fake eye while also indicating with his nose in the direction of the issue. "Sorry, do you prefer disfigurement or...." Mr. Wren trailed off again, pausing as if to punctuate this next moment with some sort of sick weighted point. "Defect?"

The word washed over Jack as his boss's digs always did. Jack thought to himself, *You power-tripping fuck*, as he smiled and said, "Ah. Not a problem. Happy to see them after lunch." Jack tried to skirt around his boss's hefty frame.

"Not so fast, young man." Mr. Wren stopped him with an open hand to Jack's chest. Jack recoiled at the touch, his midday hunger suddenly replaced with a feeling much closer to vitriol. Jack just wanted out from under this... well... whatever this was. Mr. Wren continued with an oily smile, conveying concern without directing it toward Jack.

"Also, did you ever take that two-week mandatory training to work in this department? Seems, according to your file, that somehow that was missed." Mr. Wren took a slight step toward Jack, his unmistakable breath invading Jack's personal space even more than his physical body. Jack swallowed hard but held his ground. Next, Mr. Wren walked his massive frame in a tight circle around Jack. "It would seem to me...." Mr. Wren paused while eyeing Jack up and down as he always did to prove he was the boss. "Seems to me that someone with your limitations shouldn't miss that. In fact, I think it's most important that you, of all people, fully understand how to be a proper employee here. With your disabilities you...." Mr. Wren made a gesture like he was knocking on his skull like one would a door, "...might need to drill the basics into that little brain of yours."

Jack was resigned to enduring the moment but also gave it as little mind as he could, his eyes darting around the room, trying to find something appropriate to look at but finding nothing. "Ah… well," Jack started, "when I was hired, they, excuse me, you were very short-staffed in this department, so I kinda just learned on the job." At that moment, his department mate Phil was heading for lunch. "Phil!" Jack said way too loudly to redirect the focus now being unloaded on him.

Phil turned around at the sound of his name "Wha…." He didn't finish the word. "Oh, hi, Mr. Wren. Didn't see you there."

Jack internally laughed at, "Didn't see you there" because Mr. Wren's massive girth was very difficult to overlook.

Mr. Wren, unimpressed at the exchange, flapped his hands toward himself, suggesting that Phil should step towards them, which he did. "Phil. You do well here. Always have, and I appreciate that, but I fear there might have been a valuable step skipped when we brought on little Jack here… and well, given his condition," Mr. Wren motioned with a pen toward Jack's damaged face. "We need to make sure protocol is followed properly to avoid any problems. Insurance issues and all. I'm sure you understand." The man's fat face wrinkled in meaningless fabricated thought, more to prove a point than to show thinking, care, or concern.

Ugh. Mother fucker, Jack thought to himself, continuing to mentally distance himself from the moment while also pulling his neck to one side the way one does when physically escaping an unpleasant smell. "Not a problem, sir," Jack started. "How can we take care of it?"

It was Phil's turn to intercept the conversation. "Mr. Wren. Jack's doing a good job… he's working hard and well… yeah, he can only see with one eye and hear what's around him with one ear, but he is getting the job done."

Mr. Wren turned his mass slowly to Phil, eyes sending the message that he wasn't impressed. "The man is a liability, and we cannot have this. Otherwise, it can be a real problem for Plexus, and none of us wants that. Do we?" Mr. Wren was slowly articulating each word either to emphasize his power or feign that Jack was incapable of following along at average conversational speeds. Either way, it grated on the nerves of both workers.

Phil continued, "I mean, obviously not, and if you'd like, we can catch him up." Phil seemed very clear on what this exchange between Jack and his boss was meant to convey, and he was doing his best to back Jack up.

Mr. Wren changed the subject as he gestured to the staging and washing sinks, "It's more about the food cross-contamination courses that he missed. We are bound by Provincial law to train all employees on this. Gotta protect the public, you know." Then, turning back to face Jack, Mr. Wren placed a hand on his shoulder, which once again Jack internally reeled from, doing his best not to breathe in the air that escaped his employer.

"The course isn't up for negotiation, Mr. Daw. You'll head to HR now to sign out the VHS video courses, which you'll complete this weekend. Then, on Monday at 5:00, I personally will make sure you fully understand the material." Mr. Wren creepily smiled as if to falsely reassure Jack that it was in his best interest to let Mr. Wren "help."

The man's sweaty hand, still on Jack's shoulder, tightened as he pulled up next to Jack's face. "Just here to help, kid… By the looks of you, we think this would be best. You know… to avoid any 'accidents.' People who are prone to such things aren't good for the company."

"Understood and not a problem," Jack said as his boss finally stepped out of his personal space. Jack exhaled as Mr. Wren made his way back up the metal stairs.

"Now, Mr. Daw! We can't have you…." his sentence wandered off into silence, "I'm sure you understand."

Jack understood alright. Somewhere deep inside himself, he understood that this was not the life he was intended to lead. Then, from a place he couldn't quite grasp but thought might be a remnant of his recent neurological storm, Jack heard the words, *You should thank that man for this moment.*

Fuck that, Jack fired back … wishing his dystonic hangover would just subside already.

After grabbing his gear, Jack headed to the HR office. After a knock on the door, Jack heard "Come in," and he stepped in to see Mrs. Whitely in her usual plain clothing. Jack always liked Mrs. Whitely. She had helped get him on board, and she was helpful enough with ancillary paperwork that Jack struggled with. "You wanted to see me?"

Mrs. Whiteley sat behind her desk, put her glasses on, and inspected Jack's employee folder that was already front and center on her desk. "It appears we have missed a few of your onboarding courses. The province requires them. You know… just a food processing thing to make sure everyone understands food hazards and best practices."

"Ah, yes. Safety First!" Jack said, his internal voice mocking him while the external one conveyed compliance.

Mrs. Whitely failed to be charmed and looked over the top rim of her glasses while handing Jack a stack of video tapes. "Watch these, then complete the online test." She reached into her desk, flipped through neatly organized files, and pulled out a sheet of paper. "Here's everything you need to know. Just follow the directions."

"Got it." Jack paused, unsure what to do next.

Mrs. Whiteley then snuck in, "We'll also need to review some of your medical history, Jack. Please verify that this is your primary doctor's information with a signature. Mr. Wren is just concerned about any potential insurance liability. Our policy doesn't cover impaired workers."

This took Jack by complete surprise as he thought, Impaired? *Da Fuck she talking about? Impaired. Gah. I hate this place.* Jack signed on the line after visually verifying Dr. Bentine's information.

"That's it, Mr. Daw." She turned away to reach for the filing cabinets behind her, showing she was done with Jack, who was doing his best to leave her office ASAP. Just as he was about to escape, she said over her shoulder, "Oh, and Mr. Daw…" there was a pause punctuated with slight concern. "I suggest you do your best on this. I know Mr. Wren isn't thrilled how you were brought on without his consent, so…."

"Not to worry. I'm all over it," Jack interrupted with a wink as he walked out the door

Finally, sitting down for lunch, Jack noted he only had twenty minutes before returning to his station. He ate quickly but was interrupted by Annie standing over him.

"May I ask you a question?" she said, acting as if she was trying to cozy up to a longtime friend.

"Sure," Jack said between bites, mouth still half full. He moved his chair a bit to make room for Annie, who seemed determined that this conversation needed to happen.

Annie cozied in closer, her older life-wrung chest almost touching Jack. "Word has it you have some kind of mental problem. I just want to make sure you're okay. Was it because…." She gestured toward Jack's misshapen temple. "You know… an accident or something?"

Jack stuffed the last of his food into his mouth and took a long sip of his iced tea. He wasn't sure why Annie's interrogation didn't bother him more. He knew this was the gossip machine's mayor simply paying him a visit for her next ovum of scandal.

"Not really," he said, finally answering her question. "I mean, sure. A lot of my brains fell out from my accident, but the doctors managed to stuff them all back in there. I'm good."

"Huh," Annie replied gruffly. "People said maybe you were goofy or something, but I didn't believe it. To me, you seem like a guy who's maybe different in other ways. Wasn't sure…" She trailed off. "Anyways, good luck to ya. Hope Wren doesn't give you too much trouble."

Different in other ways? Jack thought to himself as he watched the middle-aged lunch lady shuffle away. Maybe she was off her rocker. That said, Jack was feeling undeniably stuck and friendless at the moment. He hated having this type of attention focused on him.

On the way back to the "fish house," as the employees called it, Jack felt his phone vibrate.

"Dude!" Dennis sounded unusually energetic. "Dude. I got the money! The guy from Colorado actually sent it to me."

"Dennis, that's amazing. So happy for you… but listen, now isn't a great time. I'm just about to start my afternoon shift."

"Okay, okay…. Maybe you can help me plan my next move when you get home. I'm still kinda thinking Comox because it's still afford-able, but maybe Nanaimo. We can talk later."

Jack was surprised that Dennis announcing his departure deflated his already tired mood, but he knew he could file that away just as he did with Em's departure. Mail that never gets opened. Addressed to no one. Never to be sent, or read.

As the large clock on the wall above the cement floors struck 5:00, Jack was washing off the stink of day. He was in a relatively good mood and couldn't wait to get home to talk to Dennis about his financial score. With a final brush of the soap wand, Jack felt the presence of someone behind him. He turned. Again, it was Mr. Wren. *What is this guy's obsession with me?* Jack thought as he hurried.

"So, I'll see you Monday, Mr. Daw. We can review your under-standing of Plexus policies and procedures then," Mr. Wren said while closing in on Jack's personal space. Jack, this time not holding his ground, took a few steps back until his lower-back was against the rim of the wash sinks. Jack looked around nervously, but it was after 5:00, and everyone was gone. He was alone with the fat man.

"You know, Mr. Daw… we could save some time next week by just reviewing a few of the basics of Plexus policies now. How's that sound?"

Jack was feeling cornered and very exposed. He wanted out of there. He wanted to get home to Dennis so they could celebrate.

"Turn around, Mr. Daw. Let me see if you understand the basics of scrubbing in for this position. You do know how to do this properly, don't you? It'll be reviewed with me now or on Monday. He gently put his hands on Jack's shoulders to turn him to face the wall so Jack could get his hands back into the sink.

Jack could feel the fear rising in him as Mr. Wren's stomach brushed his waist. He felt like prey. He wanted to cry because this place… this place, where he gets turned like this, is all too familiar.

Next, Jack's brains blasted backward into his past without his consent…

SCHISM

"Now, son," he recalled his stepfather telling him as he towered over teenaged Jack. "Come sit," his stepdad indicated to the space on the pew next to him. "This won't hurt a bit, I promise. It'll be good for our community to see the power of the Lord firsthand before them, so thank you for agreeing to be a pillar of our community. You're very brave."

Jack's instinctive need to do right by his stepfather was in a vexed battle with his internal voice writhing in fear. Jack hadn't agreed to anything, and he didn't know why he was feeling weird and flustered. Jack didn't know what was coming next, but he knew it was about him and not about him. Jack was perceptive like that even at that young age.

"We need you to come to the front of the congregation and sit…" he said as he pointed to a small plain wood chair already placed center stage. Jack's initial thinking was that perhaps they wanted to ask him questions about his faith or something? Why was that chair already set out in the middle of the stage like that? Why did that chair induce fear in Jack's stomach? Why did it feel so wrong?

"No problem," Jack squeezed out, his desire to impress his stepfather with his strength and character currently outweighing his newfound nervousness over something he couldn't put his finger on. Lately, his stepfather had been talking a lot about strength and character in his sermons, something Jack knew he had in spades.

The service began, and like a fairy dust spell, a hush settled over the congregants.

Jack's stepdad began the service at the podium like he did every Sunday. "Today is a special day."

The crowd responded in unison, "Amen."

Reverend Daw continued. "Today is a day where we see the mysterious ways of our heavenly father in action. Today we thank God for his many gifts and the bounty of his love." The reverend then made a few community announcements as Jack's mind drifted, only to return to his stepfather saying, "Let's begin with 'Christ the Lord Is Risen Today,' number 57 in your hymnals."

Again, Jack's mind was wholly distracted over what might happen next as he fumbled endlessly to find page 57. Jack began to sing with the others while pretending to be engaged in the present moment.

"Christ the Lord is risen today; Christians, haste your vows to pay; Offer ye your praises meet...." People in their pews began singing in whatever key they wanted or knew. "At the Paschal Victim's feet. For the sheep the Lamb hath bled...."

Up front, the old pianist was plunking away, leading the clunky crowd in a kilter-key song. "Unto Thee, O Lord, do I lift up my soul." The crowd continued as Jack honed in on the strangeness of lyrics. "For the sheep, the lamb has bled? Oh my God, I trust in Thee, Let me not be ashamed, Let not mine enemies triumph over me."

The discord finally halted, much to everyone's relief as Reverend Daw once again found his place at the podium. He cleared his throat.

"As many of you are aware, we have had some challenges in our family. Much like all of you." Part of his charm was gesturing to everyone in attendance. "So, Marilyn and I thought we might demonstrate the power that our Lord has here today. It is within all of us to help right the wrongs of those we love and right the wrongs cast upon us."

"Amen," rumbled through the crowd in low tones. A few hands were raised heavenward.

"Now, before we get to the sermon, Deacons Ward and Borey and myself wanted to show you what it means to love our family and yes…," pause, "…show love and affection to our young men." The crowd grumbled in agreement. "We all have to make these choices in our lives to be one with our creator."

Jack's stepfather, to punctuate the moment, then slapped the podium as he rejoiced, "Do not grieve! For the joy of the Lord is your strength!" Recognizing this truth in them, the crowd waved low as their murmur of hallelujah started to find its voice.

Amens now met Reverend Daw, "So do not fear! For I am with you!" Waving hands now met a slight sway in several of those bearing witness. "Do not be dismayed. For I AM YOUR GOD." The chorus of elation started to take form as Pastor Daw felt the congregation's building voices wash over him, the lights bright on his face, the feeling within him of God's righteousness finding root.

"I will strengthen you and help you!" More hallelujahs rang out. "I will uphold you with my righteous hand!" He waved to the sky. "The Lord is my strength, and he promises VICTORY over my enemies!" Once again, Jack's stepfather hit the podium with a CRACK that resonated throughout the sacred hall. He paused. A quiet began to settle over the crowd.

"Jack," his stepfather said warmly in his direction. "Won't you join us on this fruitful day? The Lord is my shepherd, and so with open arms, we welcome one of our flock."

Jack stood up and walked in silence. He walked the way a boy would who was both terrified and wanted to make his stepdad proud. The internal battle was visible on his young form.

Jack wasn't sure why he felt like crying in this moment, but he knew he was strong. He knew that about himself if he didn't know or believe anything else. Jack stepped up the few stairs onto the church stage and turned to face everyone where he was surprised at how blinding the lights were. Realizing this, he relaxed a bit. He couldn't see them. It's just bright air he was looking at now. "Just bright air," Jack told himself.

To Jack, this was less scary. Standing in the blinding glow, he looked to the podium where his stepfather now stood next to the plain wooden chair. So nondescript this wooden chair, but a chair that, nonetheless, Jack would never forget.

"Jack, please sit," his stepfather said, opening a hand in the direction of the oddly placed chair. Reverend Daw continued with, "How do we love one another? How do we heal those we see hurting?"

Jack, sitting in the notably hard and uncomfortable chair, was now thinking perhaps he might have a chance to share somehow? He wasn't sure because the more his stepfather went on and on about healing and helping and loving and overcoming, Jack wasn't sure where this was all headed. Was it about his busted face or something else? He didn't know.

"We love them. That's how we help them. We return them to the fold… and we are here to do that today. Deacons Ward and Borey, please join me. Others, as you feel the spirit move you, please feel free to join us in whatever manner you feel moved to."

The three men were now around Jack with his stepfather behind him and the two others flanking him.

"Deuteronomy 23:1." The Reverend paused looking heavenward. "No one who is emasculated 'or damaged'," Jack's stepfather paraphrased to seal the double meaning, "shall enter the assembly of the Lord." The crowd now sat silently blinking as Jack felt tears well in his eyes, but had no idea why. He didn't understand the extreme fear he was experiencing at that moment.

"My son Jack is such a blessing to Marilyn and me, and we seek the Lord's truth in our parenting.…" Long pause. "Not our word… but God's word." Once again, the low grumbles of amen began softly. Their echoes from the ceilings planted seeds of the pastor's righteousness as it went on air.

Mr. Daw then placed his big, firm hands onto Jack's shoulders, pinning him in place. "1 Peter 1:14. As obedient Children, do not be conformed to the former lusts and damage which were yours in ignorance." The floorboards in the room started to rumble; Jack even saw its form taking shape. "But like the Holy One who called you! Be Holy Yourselves!" Jack's stepfather began speaking loudly into Jack's good ear. "We all have sinned. We all are sinners…." The congregants now beamed their faith off their faces while being moved to the spirit of the Lord.

"As a man of faith, I know that I must protect my children… And sometimes that means saving them from both others and… themselves," the crowd's agreement manifested through wild waving. "My son here." He looked at Jack proudly. "He deserves to be the man he was meant to be…." Reverend Daw walked around the chair to face his son as Jack started to panic and squirm visually. Jack could feel his heart begin to beat wildly. Still, he didn't know why.

"Jack," his stepfather said the boy's name plainly while standing before him, backlit in a cast of blinding bright light. A face full of pity and shame washed over the Reverend as he continued, "I begin the laying of hands to heal you, Jack. You deserve to be made whole." The Deacons then joined in the ritual by adding their hands to the surface of Jack's newly forming impenetrable shell.

"Dear Lord, we call upon you today to heal my dear son Jack from ALL which bedevils him. We are ALL sinners, and we ALL deserve to be made whole." The crowd's volume grew as it stirred itself with shouts and hallelujahs.

"We call upon you to oversee my boy. Please, Jesus, make him whole. We call upon you to deliver your divine justice NOW! Bring it to us. Bring your mercy to my broken son for his wounds glare, and we ask that you use your might to restore him to that which he once was." Others from the congregation were now marching to the stage to help heal Jack, their crush gaining on Jack's fourteen year old frame. Their rising heat sickened and terrorized small Jack.

"I can't breathe," Jack finally said, his face turned upward, hoping for light or air. "I can't breathe!" Jack's voice strained to find air, but the continued squash of fat bodies pushed the air out of his lungs, making his cry for help futile. The roar of the crowd, now in full fever pitch, chanted, "Do not grieve, for the joy of the Lord is your strength." Jack fought to find a sliver of hot air. "So do not fear, for I am with you; do not be dismayed, for I am your God!"

Jack was now desperate. "I CAN'T BREATHE. I CAN'T BRE-ATHE! PLEASE! SOMEONE!"

The crowd continued joyously, "I will strengthen you and help you; I will uphold you with my righteous right hand."

Jack fell internally and externally in this moment, a first for his psyche. His body could not compete, his young mind desperate for escape. The crowd continued wildly, "The Lord is my strength and my song; he has given me victory!"

Jack lifelessly bobbed as he swayed with their sweaty hot mash moving to and fro. Jack was soon unconscious. His departure. His escape. His last thought before everything went dark was, "This isn't real," then the world was gone, and so was he. He was safe.

With the crowd finding a less frantic tone, people began returning to their seats, broad, wide backsides reclaiming familiar territory. Slowly, the crowd dispersed. Slowly, they removed themselves from the rejoicing dog pile under which Jack had been enfolded in hot sweat, hot tears, and hot unbreathable air rank with putrid body odor.

At last, Jack became visible to those around him. He was a slump. He was the lifeless body of a dead child just pulled from a hot car.

Jack started to revive with gasps of air. His stepfather looked at Jack, barely breathing, and the shock of this sight registered on his face, both because of the physical condition of his child but moreover because Jack indeed had not been made whole. Jack was still broken.

With Jack's consciousness returning came the awareness of the Deacons still on each side of him. These puppeteers propped him up to give the audience someone to stare at. Jack's stepfather walked to the podium where he kept a spare towel, which was often needed when the exuberance of the Lord's message left his brow drenched with sweat.

"Here," his stepfather said to Jack's face as he threw a towel into his lap. "Go clean yourself up." Deacon Ward then hoisted the boy onto his shoulders the way Jesus would carry a lamb. The crowd cheered their blessings, for, on this day, the Lord's work was done.

Mr. Ward sat Jack on the floor of the stage wing, his back slapped wetly against the wall as he stared with hate at his stepfather still on stage. Jack tried to rouse himself. He knew the ordeal was over. He knew they were done with him. He knew they had done what they came to do on this day.

"I will go clean myself up.." Jack seethed. "but not this second." His mind was still mush. Regardless, he was doing his best to sort out what had happened because this wasn't just life to Jack; this was love.

Jack's mood began to clear, and his first thought was that he knew it wouldn't work. Jack knew his fucking face wouldn't heal. Jack knew he wasn't a good enough Christian to receive God's mercy. Not now. Not after all this. Because if such a thing as mercy existed, it would have shown itself before now. But it didn't, and Jack knew he only had himself to blame for his shortcomings.

As Jack got older, he would look back on this moment and think, "That's how they groom boys to be raped." His indoctrination was complete, and next time he'd be more prepared and seasoned. Next time he'd know better how to survive this.

With a jolt, Jack came back to the present moment. His hips were still being pressed firmly and repeatedly into the metal wash sink at the back of the fish house while Mr. Wren continued to explore Jack's broad backside with his thick gut.

Without thinking, Jack darted the way a cornered animal would. He ran as he swam through the murkiness and swirls forming in his mind. Jack took flight and sped down the hall then ran like hell out the employee exit.

"Mr. Daw!" He could hear in the trailing off distance, but Jack didn't stop. He ran. He got as far away as possible not to gain air until he found his truck in the parking lot. Swinging his car door open, he threw himself in and sat for a moment, eyes wide, adrenaline pumping in his ears. Jack put the car in drive and sped off never wanting to return, despite knowing he had to. In a life like his, there was no other choice.

CAKE

As Jack pulled into his driveway, he was happy to watch Banjo make his daily trek to greet his dad. The days were already getting noticeably longer and dusk was still settling over the single-wide trailer that he called home. With the sight of the dog, a smile returned to Jack's soul.

"Who's a good boy?" Jack asked while encouraging the dog into a higher level of excitement.

"WHOO-HOO!" Jack heard as Dennis came crashing out of the front door and landed in front of him. "Dude… I can't believe it! It actually worked! I sold one of my canoes!"

"I'm so happy for you, Dennis!" Jack did his best to be upbeat, but he was still shaken from the disturbing entanglement with his boss. "Did you cook?"

"Not yet," Dennis said while bounding back into the trailer. "BUT…. I have a surprise. A little something to toast to new beginnings."

Jack was just glad to be home. He pitched his old boots off and unloaded onto the sofa. He was beat. "Dennis, while you're in the kitchen, can you grab me a beer?" Within seconds, Dennis had one rocketing toward Jack's forehead. Catch. Twist off. Glug. Ahhh.

As he sunk into the couch, Jack was happy for Dennis but needed a minute to change his mood and get out of work mode. *I better take my meds*, Jack thought, rising despite not wanting to. He headed down the hall and into the bathroom, where he popped a few pills to protect Dennis and himself from another terrible night.

"I'm gonna go lay down for a minute," Jack said, closing his bedroom door as he saw Dennis's dejected face as he continued to futz around the kitchen. "It's been a day. Just need twenty minutes." The hope was for Jack to reset his brain in case he was already heading down the path of another neurological storm. He didn't want to have to deal with that today.

The unmistakable smell of bacon-wrapped steaks soon drew Jack out of the bedroom. Minutes later, they were enjoying Dennis's celebration dinner.

"How is it?" Dennis asked expectantly.

"Oh wow," Jack said mid-bite. "You are going to make some lady very, very happy. This is amazing."

"Thanks." Dennis beamed. "I think I'm getting the hang of this. I thought it might even be fun to take some classes or something. You know, once I get settled with Wendy."

The reemergence of Wendy's name brought up questions for Jack. "So… you and Wendy, huh? That's still part of the plan moving forward even with your concerns about Larry?"

Looking slightly bewildered, Dennis nodded his head while finishing a mouthful of potatoes. "Yeah. Like I said before, I think I love her, and well… she's pregnant, and we're going to have a kid… and well… I'm pretty excited about that. Besides, I don't think 'ol Catfish Larry is violent or anything. Who knows!? Maybe he found himself a new 'girlfriend' in prison." They both laughed despite the slight stink of homophobia that his joke was laced with. Of course, this wasn't lost on Jack… but it was still funny given Larry's notorious womanizing.

"So, what's the plan, Dennis?" Jack leaned in to get closer to Dennis. "Because if you don't have one, I think I might." A sly but wide shit-eating grin appeared on Jack's face. Dennis hung onto Jack's every word. Jack knew that Dennis just didn't know how to do this next part of life on his own. Dennis leaned in to listen closely.

"I need outta this crap job of mine," Jack began. "I need a new start; you need a new start, and that two grand you just landed is the ticket for us both."

Dennis's hands clenched as if he would be hit with something he didn't want to hear. "So…" Dennis gestured a "well, fucking out with it already" in the air.

Dennis's new-found physical animation amused Jack, so he led with a slight chuckle, then, "So…! Here's what I'm thinking. How would you like to buy this place and move Wendy up here to start your new life? You'd be out of Larry's view, no danger of accidentally running into him at the grocery store or something here in Port Hardy. You could have a fresh start, and I can even put in a good word for you with a few guys I know who are hiring."

Dennis's eyes blanked and widened. "The fuck…?" He drifted off as he sat back in his seat. "Jack! I mean. How would… It's not like…." Dennis seemed incapable of finishing a sentence in this state, so Jack relieved him of his stammer.

"Listen, I was able to score this place for next to nothing, and while it's probably worth fifteen grand, I'd be willing to take a small upfront payment then just send me, say, $500 a month until the amount is paid off? Would you be open to an arrangement like that?"

"But, Jack," said Dennis, deflating into thought. "I mean. It's just that…" pause. "I mean, you'd be willing to do that for Wendy and me? I mean, you'd help my family get a house and a job!? For real, dude? I mean…" Dennis just could not stop sputtering in disbelief.

"Dennis, listen. You need a setup like this now that you will be a family man. You need a house and a job. We can set that up here. Hell… I'll even spend the next two weeks helping you fix the place up. Which brings me to my next part of how this is all going to work." Jack paused more for the theatrics of it than to recoup his thoughts. "I need to get out. I want to do a little driving to clear my head and just reconnect with nature, myself, my thoughts… it's just that, well… Em leaving and all, it just feels like a sign that I need to get out of here. Start over, just like you."

"But, Jack," Dennis tried but was silenced by an open palm slowly moving toward Dennis's face.

"Shhhh…" The gesture and the word were meant to be slightly comical and relay that there need not be hesitation or questions.

"But where will you go? How will you manage, especially given your…" Dennis paused, unsure of how to name what he was thinking. "…problems. Do you think you can manage okay? I mean, I certainly don't want you here stinking up my new grand palace, but…." Dennis started to deliver laughter along with his next words. "…seriously?"

"Dennis. I'm fine. I can manage. It'll be another ten days before I can get my prescriptions refilled then I'm free to head out. The wild west awaits me!" Jack joked.

"But what about? How will you, you know, make money and where will you live, and how will you get new meds or see your doctors or all that?" Dennis looked a combination of confused, excited, and concerned.

"I will be fine. As for money… well… I have a plan. Besides, if you give me a down payment on this place, maybe a thousand bucks, and then you send me $500 a month, I should be fine."

"Jack. You honestly expect to get by on five hundred a month?"

"Not exactly, but as I said, I have a plan. First, I just need to know if you're buying this place. It's the last thing holding me here, and Dennis," Jack's tone was now serious. "I need to get out of here."

"Well… yes. I mean, I still can't believe you'd help me get a house like this. I mean… I never owned a house or something like that before, but it would be amazing for Wendy. She's going to be pretty excited, especially if you can help me get into a job or something?"

Jack now pulled his chair around to be next to Dennis. "We can work out the details, and I see it as you helping me out. I might need to come back on occasion for a doctor's appointment or something, and having a place to crash on the odd occasion would be the best way you can help me out. Well… that and the monthly payments." Jack laughed.

"You really see it that way? Like, me buying your house is your best option right now?"

Jack put his arm around Dennis. "I need your help, and this is the best way you can help me."

A huge smile breached Dennis's stupid face as he radiated joy and delighted in prospects yet to be realized. Jack could see that Dennis had hope again.

"Let's do it," Dennis said, putting forward a closed fist in anticipation of Jack doing likewise.

Jack did the same, and a deal was struck not by handshake but by fist bump. That's the bro-code these two had. It was a bittersweet moment as they both seemed to realize the two weeks before their new beginnings was the time they had to share before everything would change.

And so it was.

CLEAN BREAK

After a weekend of helping Dennis fix up the trailer for Wendy's arrival, on Monday morning Jack arrived at work knowing what had to be done and that it had to be done quickly. There was no backup plan, so his only option was to see this through.

Jack started his shift eyeing the broken door of the freezer that he had often complained about to Mr. Wren. It was five minutes to 8:00, and Jack knew he had a tiny window of opportunity. Precise timing was going to be very important to pull this off.

Jack knew painful and embarrassing conversations with Mr. Wren awaited. He knew H.R. awaited, and after verifying his doctor's contact information on Friday, he knew concerned talks about his condition awaited as well, a situation he had found himself in much too often for his liking. The only time he could do this was now – before any of these bricks fell, before he was told he was an insurance risk and before he was tested on policies and procedures he had not brushed up on over the weekend.

"The time is now," Jack said under his breath as he walked over to the heavy aluminum-clad freezer and eyed the heavy metal device that would finally move his life forward. Jack steadied himself, renewing his commitment to his plan.

The top hinge was already nearly dislocated from its location, and the bottom one showed its age flaked in decay and rust. Jack took a breath then calculated the exact trajectory of a falling heavy slab from its location to the floor. He was set.

To freedom, he internally toasted, then jammed a long-handled metal paddle used to unstick frozen fish carcasses into the space between the door and its jamb. Jack carefully scanned for witnesses. Finding none, he kicked the wedge with his full strength to liberate the swinging metal mass.

The door complained but didn't come free the first time. Jack kicked the paddle even harder. Finally, with the sound like a tire iron hitting a fire hydrant, the door cast off. Jack had half a second to react. As the monster panel fell, Jack threw himself to the floor, making sure his right arm would land where the metal plate would fall, but he also wanted to ensure his hand wasn't crushed. A broken forearm would mend cleanly. A fractured hand would not. Jack braced himself for the looming pain.

In an instant, slam, crack. Jack could feel the silence wash over the factory floor as the searing pain rushed at him, unyielding in its scope and ferocity. Jack screamed in pain and triumph, knowing the worst was over, and he achieved his goal.

The blinding pain of his broken forearm was so intense he couldn't breathe and most certainly couldn't move. The post-crash silence was quickly broken by clamor, chaos, and out of view voices. Phil was the first on the scene.

"Jack!" Phil's eyes widened. "Oh my god, Jack. Hold on, buddy."

Within moments, other workers started to arrive as Jack continued to wail. It was mostly real, but a dash for show. Jack had a very high pain tolerance. He often mused how he could will himself into doing the unimaginable if the goal was shiny enough. Hell, he had run an entire season of track on a stress fracture that didn't have time to heal and that he was determined wasn't going to hold him back. In this moment, one of the hardest things he had to do was contain his glee. Pain be damned, he'd just earned a ticket out of this hell-hole.

A few men gathered to lift the metal behemoth from Jack's pinned right arm. When medical assistance arrived, it was clear his arm was broken. One could quickly tell this by the unnatural arc, not to mention the massive swelling now taking over. Jack writhed in pain but made sure not to move his arm. He had done enough damage to himself already.

"Are you right-handed?" the first paramedic asked, trying to slip a brace under Jack's fracture.

Jack thought this an odd first question but answered nonetheless. "Yes." Jack had no further resources to ask why despite wondering. The medic continued to work to get the arm bandaged and compressed while strapping him to a stretcher. Other medics now milled about, and Jack could hear questions from the onlookers, speculation as to what happened, and the like.

Mrs. Whitely from H.R. arrived, and Jack tried to manage an apology. She said, "Think nothing of it," and she'd see him soon. Jack was strapped into an ambulance and was quickly whisked away. That's the moment when he allowed a slight smile to meet his face. He had done it. He had dodged being fired or being put into some lesser category than every other employee. He now had full benefits of workers' compensation and time off to heal, which would be enough to implement his next move.

As they unloaded Jack from the back of the vehicle, the medic looked at him and, in a reassuring tone, said, "It's going to be alright."

You got that right, sister, Jack thought to himself.

It had been several years since Jack had to break the law to escape an oppressor. He was far too familiar with the sweet, sweet taste of freedom to feel even the slightest pang of guilt for what he'd done then or now. In fact, despite the intense physical pain in his arm, that familiar sweetness swiftly began bleeding onto his lips.

He was free.

BANDITS

Dennis practically ran into Jack's hospital room, greatly alarming the nurse. He hurriedly made his way to Jack's bedside. "Damn, dude. Are you okay? What happened? I came as fast as I could."

Jack looked up at him with a slight smile that Dennis wasn't expecting and said, "I'll explain the details later… but for right now? Yeah… Imma going to enjoy this stuff to they pain killer concoction gave." Jack was clearly on some heavy medication and speaking slightly drunk. A look of amusement and relief crossed Dennis's face.

Dennis stayed with Jack for the rest of the day until Jack's arm was in a cast, and he was sent home with some killer narcotics. *This ain't so bad*, Jack thought to himself as his brain steeped itself in chemicals. He sat both wearily calmed and cheerily intoxicated in his IV drip mood. Dennis then drove Jack home and got him comfortable on the sofa, mokee pipe in hand. Dennis sat on a small corner of the couch near Jack and put his hand on Jack's chest. "Damn, dude. Seriously, are you okay?"

"I am," Jack responded as the slight grin kept showing itself. "And I want to tell you exactly what happened, and why."

Dennis was visibly taken aback. After a slight pause, Dennis prompted with, "So…?"

"So, you're my brother, right?" Jack was still slurring his words but somehow managed to form irresistible puppy dog eyes. "And brothers,"

Jack paused for drunken dramatic effect, "brothers keep each other's secrets."

"Yeah, dude, of course. C'mon… I already know that after you ran away, that you were a escort," the two men laughed. "So… I think we're good on that front. You can tell me anything, Jack. C'mon… What's up?"

Jack's eyes landed on a tree outside. "So… I kinda did this to myself. I orchestrated this. I pulled the broken door off its hinges and threw my arm under it."

Dennis looked more confused than ever. "Okay… But? I mean … Well, why?"

Jack took Dennis's hand that was still on his chest and put his hand on top of it. Jack needed a second to close his eyes, breathe in his newfound freedom, and feel the closeness between them. It was a brief moment, but one Jack needed. It was one memory he could always recall as safe.

"I had no other options. I need to escape, and well… this path forward will afford me the most options and resources." Jack paused and looked into his friend's blue eyes again. "Now I can be on medical leave and get paid. I can prepare for my trip and have money to plan for what's next."

Jack's gaze dropped from Dennis's eyes and, as he looked out the window, he thought out loud, "It'll buy me time. I need to get my meds next week, and I can't go anywhere until I get those refilled…." Jack's voice trailed off then reemerged with "… and I just couldn't be at that place anymore. I think they were going to fire or demote me or something. I'm not sure. Now at least I have cash for a while, and I can have time off to help you with this 'Casa de Dennis.'" They both quietly laughed.

"Help me with Casa De Dennis, eh?" Dennis's eyes were smiling. "How you going to do that with a clipped wing, my friend?"

"Dennis… You've seen how my brain situation most often affects my right arm. Hell… it's often useless anyhow, so not a huge loss here. I know how to get by using only my less dominant hand."

"You are one twisted mother-fucker, Jack. You know that? Now shut up and rest. Dinner will be ready in a bit."

Over the next ten days, Jack and Dennis were together almost 24 hours a day. They had learned to enjoy each other's company again, and they remembered why they worked so well as friends back when they were boys.

The mobile home started to look nice. A freshness now replaced the stink of old. Wendy had made her way up to see them the day after Jack broke his arm. She couldn't believe the news that she and Dennis now had a home. She cried and pulled Dennis close. As a couple, the gratitude they felt for Jack's gift was immeasurable, and the financial arrangement, while made with a fist bump, was a commitment that neither party would break. Besides, Jack knew he still held the title, and if his friend did mess up, well, it would be within his right to repossess the home and sell it to someone else. He was generous, but not stupid. "Trust but verify," he had once heard somewhere.

The day before Jack could refill his prescriptions, he was asked to come in to see Mr. Wren and Mrs. Whiteley. He agreed and arranged for Dennis to drive him to the meeting.

Arriving back at the Plexus Foods building, Jack internally shuddered. *Ugh,* Jack thought. He had not missed this place. Not one bit. He made his way up to the third floor where the offices were located and ambled over to the "Human Resources" door.

"Ah," Mrs. Whiteley said as Jack's face peered from behind the door. "Come. Sit. Mr. Wren will be here shortly. Can I get you anything?"

Jack sat and said he was fine. He then flipped through his phone, trying to avoid further chit-chat that could lead to awkward topics of conversation such as how their medical background check went; however, Jack was a bit curious if any of his outlying conditions would prove problematic.

Mr. Wren arrived and pleasantries were exchanged. Jack was asked again to sit, an action not shared with Mr. Wren, who stood at the side of Mrs. Whiteley's desk. Jack couldn't tell which was less desirable, to have this monster sit next to him or loom over him. Both were terrible.

"Well, Mr. Daw," his boss muttered while eyeing him up and down. "You're fortunate you weren't more seriously injured." Already Jack detected a tone in Mr. Wren's speech indicating he thought Jack was up to something.

"Thanks," Jack said to the floor, not making eye contact with either one of them.

"We just wanted to check in and see how you're doing and then review company policy as to how to proceed forward. But it is good to see you," Mrs. Whitely continued. "I was worried… you know. But, I mean, we all know you have a lot of other things that you're dealing with."

Jack was surprised how this latest turn of events made Mrs. Whiteley more compassionate toward him. That was never her strong suit in his experience. He also wondered how far she'd been digging into the "other things" he was dealing with.

Just wanting this whole thing to be over, Jack asked, "So now what? What are the medical leave procedures and stuff?"

"Standard policy is based on a doctor's recommendation. We've reached out to Dr. Bentine to begin with. We had requested a consult with him already and will have to add this to the list of items to discuss. We just need to ensure that you're 100%." The "in the head" part was not spoken but implied. They had to understand better if Jack was a risk they could bring back into the building.

"I have some reservations, Mr. Daw," Mr. Wren began in his usual manner. God, Jack hated how that man said his name – "Mr. Daw." The pronunciation of his single-syllable name was unnecessarily drawn out and intonated with some suggestion of wrong-doing. Just hearing his name from that man's lips made Jack associate it with terribleness, creepiness, and yuck.

Just then, Mrs. Whiteley was asked by her secretary to join her for a few minutes on a suddenly pressing matter. She politely excused herself. Now it was just Mr. Daw and Mr. Wren, once again alone. Jack, however, knew better than to arrive at this meeting unarmed. Mr. Wren continued. "Like I said, Mr. Daw, I have some reservations."

"Oh?" Jack said flatly with no emotion in the direction he was already staring. "About what exactly?"

Mr. Wren repositioned himself to a more menacing stance over Jack. A power play that no longer bothered Jack because Mr. Wren was no longer his boss in his mind.

Mr. Wren looked down upon him, coughing out, "Well, you see, I had the maintenance crew take a look at what exactly happened there with your accident."

Jack cut Mr. Wren off instantly: "How many times did I tell you to fix that fucking door?" Jack now stood, making Mr. Wren look small, despite his rotund shape. The older man took a cautious step backward.

"How many people have witnessed me complaining about that broken-down shit hole ice palace? The conditions have never been great, and if you like, I can walk you down right now and point out about a hundred other things in the fish house that are completely worn out and about to break. When was the last time things in this building were inspected for safety? Did you document my concerns, Mr. Wren? How about the concerns expressed by Phil and the others? Because you know that part of your job as our manager is to record safety concerns, investigate them, and, if necessary, see that repairs are made. Did you do that, Mr. Wren? I'd sure like to see your safety records, if so. Don't think for one second that I didn't keep a journal of all the times I complained to you about the condition of that door." That last part was a lie, but Jack could see he had his former boss over the ropes, and he was ready to make the knock-out blow however necessary.

Mr. Wren's power stance continued to weaken, and his typically smug facial expression was replaced with one of abject fear and surprise over the complete shift in the power dynamic.

After a minute or so of silence, Jack followed up with, "Huh? Answer the questions, you bastard. Because my blood is on your hands, and I'm really curious as to how you're going to make it right."

Jack took a step toward his boss, saying in a very steely, serious tone, "Since you seem at a loss for words, I'll tell you exactly how this is going to go, you fat fuck." Jack now drew a long metal device from his pocket and pointed it toward Mr. Wren's plump neck, a move that alarmed the boss man who was used to only a one-sided power play.

Jack continued, "I know who you are, and I know what you are, so I'm going to make you a deal that's a win for us both." Jack looked behind him quickly to make sure Mrs. Whiteley hadn't returned. "You're going to keep me on workers' compensation for as long as the Province will allow. You're not going to check-in or need notes from my primary care physician. If you do, I will get the other guys I've been speaking with about your predatory ways, and we will come forward and bury you, get you fired, and generally run your ass out of town." The device in Jack's hand got closer to his boss's throat, a move that was meant to send a clear threat. Jack was a nice guy but also calculating and clear on how to take care of himself. He'd done and seen far worse than this, and he didn't have a choice in this instance. Life had made him scrappy as hell.

Mr. Wren stammered and choked out, "Now settle down. I'm sure it's all okay. We'll see that you get taken care of." Jack was pleased that his bluff had found purchase. Indeed, there were others, so now Jack knew he had real leverage.

Jack continued, "I won't ever get you fired or come back here again so long as you do this. See to it that my medical leave is paid out as long as possible." Jack turned to walk out of the office. "I'm not joking, Mr. Wren. If you come for me, I will come forward and bury you. The line of employees willing to help me in that regard is very long, I assure you." Jack's intended message had been delivered. He had no reason to stay.

Walking past Mrs. Whiteley at her secretary's workstation, he turned his head with a, "It's all worked out, Mrs. Whiteley. Mr. Wren said I'm free to go and that if there is any paperwork or anything, he'll take care of it. So email me anything you need signatures on."

With a slight bounce of "I am awesome," Jack pocketed his stylus and left Plexus Foods for the last time.

GIT

The remaining days that Dennis and Jack shared before Jack's departure would always be remembered by both men with fondness. Dennis had seemed to discover how cooking and caring for Jack gave him a greater sense of purpose.

On the last Thursday of April, Jack finally had his consultation with his doctors to get his prescription refilled for another six months. *Phew!* Jack thought. *It's time to go.* Where exactly was yet to be seen, but Jack knew where he wanted his pilgrimage to begin. He had been making plans behind the scenes and found it hard to contain his excitement.

Dennis commented often about him being so proud of their work on his new home. They had painted the place in light neutral tones meant to be calming to the new baby and mom. The carpets and drapes had been replaced, and Jack and Dennis had purchased some furniture, including items for the baby's room, at a thrift store. Artificial grass covered that old patch of dirt in the backyard with several clunky, plastic children's toys on top.

The morning after Jack's doctor appointments, he was packed and ready to head out. Dennis fixed them breakfast, and they sat in relative silence as they shared their last breakfast.

"Looks like you're all set," said Dennis trying to cut the quietness of the moment. "You sure you'll be okay?"

"Yeah, man." Jack sat in stillness, acknowledging that he didn't know if that was true. "Like I said last night, I'm going to hit the open road and visit a few people I've been meaning to catch up with. From there, I'll see where my soul wants to land."

"And just so I know you'll be alright, what exactly are you going to do if you have another really bad night? I won't be there... to...." Dennis trailed off.

Jack got up from the table and motioned over to Dennis to follow him, which he did. Opening the back of Jack's Blazer, Dennis was surprised to see how the thing was now tricked out. There was a nice flat bed, some crates of cooking supplies and a camp stove, a few fishing poles, and hunting knives. Jack had made this into a kind of lux situation. Dennis's face showed he was impressed.

"And check this out," Jack said as he hopped up inside and pulled a few cushions out from under the slightly raised bed to place around the perimeter of the bed. Again, Dennis looked impressed. This newly added bank of cushions around the bed circumference could only be for one purpose.

"Ah, perfect!" Dennis laughed. "Your own padded cell."

"Ha," Jack yelled. "Yeah, kinda. I just figured I should have a place to weather any bad situations. This will ensure I won't hurt myself. And!" Jack said as he pulled out a plastic bag from the pharmacy. "Look." Both men peered into the bag, and Dennis almost lost his shit when he saw the package of adult men's diapers.

"Oh, my God. Dude. That is both completely hilarious and...." Dennis wasn't quite sure how to finish that sentence.

"Gross?" Jack asked.

"Smart," Dennis reassured. "I'm glad you're prepared, but you have to call me if there are any issues. You know I can help even if I'm just on speaker. You can still hear me, and that might make a difference one day. Just promise me."

Jack put the diapers away and turned back to Dennis. He put one arm up on Dennis's shoulder, so they were side by side in a dude hug. "I promise. And thanks for everything. While yeah, your showing up here was a total surprise, I'm glad it worked out that way. I'll maybe even miss you."

Both men's eyes were wet with a pang of sadness, but Jack knew this was for the best. He knew Dennis knew that too. They went back into the house where Jack finished the last breakfast bites, grabbed his remaining items, and then called for Banjo to load up in the truck. It was go time.

LOCATION

Leaving Port Hardy, Jack said a "thank you" from his internal to the external, to the space he called home for the better part of a decade. Jack drove south on Route 19, making his way through Campbell River, Comox, and finally arrived in Nanaimo to cross over onto the mainland.

While waiting for the ferry to arrive, Jack was lost in thought and mindlessly itching under his cast with his tablet stylus when he felt it. Twinge. It was his right ring finger complaining once again. *Fuck,* Jack thought to himself as he immediately raced for his meds in his backpack. *Fuck, fuck, fuck. Not now!* Jack was scrambling and spilling the contents of his bag, a move that disrupted Banjo's nap. Without moving, Banjo cocked one eye as if to say, "Really, dude?" The dog was not impressed, but neither was he, as he noted this was the first time he'd ever had an episode *this* early in the day.

At least today, Jack was pharmaceutically armed and prepared, not like last time when he was stressed and defenseless from Em emptying his chemical resources. Jack found what he needed and downed them with a half-empty bottle of water. He hoped that he'd have some time to get himself together to assess what type of an attack this was going to be. Would this be just losing access to a few body parts, or would it be yet another grand mal of neurological storms? Only time would tell.

Twenty minutes later, the queue of cars was inching toward the gaping mouth of the ferry boat, and so far, Jack was mainly okay. *Not too bad,* he thought to himself. His right arm was offline, and his face was starting to droop, but other than that, he was doing better than expected. He counted his blessings.

With the cars finally parked in rows, Jack's physical departure from Vancouver Island was beginning. The mental departure had happened some time ago. Jack's heart leaped as the ship started to move in a way that indicated all systems were go.

The ferry trip wasn't going to be long, and Jack could have stayed in his vehicle, but he felt the need to go up top and watch the island disappear and slip away into his past. He wanted to witness and feel the freedom he had been dreaming of. His trek was finally beginning, and not being in this moment was not an option.

Jack secured Banjo in the truck as he fished out his walking cane to make his way up the steep metal stairs to the upper viewing deck. This was not an easy task given that he was in the middle of an attack, and while it didn't seem to be a padded cell, shit your pants type of event, it was bedeviling him, nonetheless. Finally, with a bit of a heave and solid push from his working, non-cast-bound arm, he freed himself into the blast of fresh sea air.

Jack was surprised at how few people there were atop the vessel. In his experience, this farewell to the island was always well attended, but not today. Secretly, Jack was glad for this moment of grace, given his current struggles just to remain upright. He turned around a few times, pivoting on the one foot that still worked, taking in the full spectacle of the view. Then he made his way to the guardrail of the ship's aft so he could stop and properly "Bon Voyage" his old life as it slipped into the distance.

Of course, it wasn't just Port Hardy, his trailer, and his job that Jack was leaving on the island. Jack was leaving a lot of torment behind as well. The type of pain that lived deep within his soul and had long threatened to make him a permanent prisoner of its grasp. And while this agony was undoubtedly capable of following him across a body of water again, Jack was hopeful he could begin to shake loose from its constant stronghold somewhere along this new path.

Jack tried to shake these thoughts. Once he got settled against one of the guardrails, he noticed a distracted young woman in her thirties fishing for a notepad in her bag. When she saw Jack, she suddenly stopped what she was doing. From 20 feet away, her eyes focused on Jack's left side in profile.

Against the backdrop of boat rails and sea, she, for reasons unbeknownst to him, felt drawn to look hard at him, as if she recognized him from some other time and place. Uncomfortable with her gaze, Jack turned to face the other direction.

Despite his obvious attempt to avoid interaction, the woman approached him.

"Hi," she said, reaching out her hand. "I'm Sarafina."

Jack felt slightly annoyed at the intrusion into the last moment that he had to say goodbye to his place of youth. But, in truth, it wasn't just this woman injecting herself into Jack's moment that was a problem for him, but also that she pulled up next to him on his right side. For Jack, it would have been easier to tolerate if she was on his "good" side where he could see and hear her more clearly and not have to consider her thoughts about his damaged skull.

Jack physically struggled for several seconds. He couldn't figure out how to manage a handshake since his right arm was dead, and he needed his left to prop himself up. This dance was all too familiar to him. The moments where someone is handing him oranges to hold, yet his hands aren't working right, or when someone asks him to follow, and he can't get up from a chair.

This was always a bit alarming to people around him. Especially people who had watched his seemingly impenetrable frame walk into a room and take a seat. And then suddenly he couldn't move? Couldn't stand? Couldn't take a plate when offered? It made no sense to the onlooker, for they couldn't see Jack's brain. They didn't know it was now a switchboard of busted, shorting-out wires and blown fuses. Arm, yes. Leg, no. Eye, yes. Back, no… This was the internal language of dystonic Jack. Sometimes things worked, other times not. And never with rhyme, reason, or fair warning.

"I'm sorry," Jack started. "I'm having a bit of a situation here. It comes and goes… anyhow, I'm Jack. It's nice to meet you." He hoped she couldn't perceive that he was offering niceties through clenched teeth, but there were two solid reasons why small talk was not attractive to him right now.

After Serafina awkwardly withdrew her hand, Jack decided to settle into the moment. It was always a source of embarrassment for him, but this woman didn't seem thrown, so Jack let it go. He exhaled and looked at Sarafina's warm smiling face. She was the embodiment of a field daisy, and Jack couldn't help but note her general air of sun and earth. Her long strawberry curls were doing an easy frolic on the sea-scented air while seagulls yammered their usual yells.

Slight discomfort returned, however, as Sarafina continued to stare at Jack's face. To Jack, this level of rudeness often felt confrontational, and his default response was to retreat. But today, given his physical issues, there was no abandoning this moment or place. He had to stand before her.

To break Sarafina's very direct gaze, Jack spoke up, "So… is there something I can help you with? I assume you didn't just come over for a closer look at *this*." Jack indicated his broken parts.

"Oh!" she said as her moment of concentration broke. "Oh… I'm sorry. I didn't mean to stare. I was just so fascinated by…" Her response was a trait from strangers Jack had become adept at handling, because heck, no one knew how to finish that sentence. Not even him.

Jack focused his gaze far off into the distance, putting up an emotional wall in Sarafina's direction. He wasn't feeling safe, a feeling that was always amplified when he was physically struggling. His best defense was to block her and move his attention in a new direction.

Jack noticed a look of horror cross her face before she reached into her bag and pulled out a pad of paper and a pen.

"I'm so sorry if I…" her voice stopped. "I find you very interesting, which probably sounds completely nuts, but I study people's energy, auras, physical and character traits, and chi. I'm working on my graduate thesis in anthropology for U VIC."

Jack just wanted to be left alone and continued to stare off into the distance while he listened. His only return was a flat "Okay," though he suspected this journey would force him to be more open to new situations, and bleh, people. Nonetheless, now was most definitely not the time for his first lesson.

Despite being inundated with boat, seagull, and onlooker noises, the air between them suddenly felt dead. Jack did nothing to relieve the stranger of her foot that she seemed to have stuck into her mouth.

"Would you be open to letting me ask you a few questions for my research paper?"

"Listen, lady, uh, Sarafina… I'm not doing so great over here. I can barely stand up, and if you don't mind, I'd just like to be left alone." Jack felt an internal sense of relief in setting a firm boundary with this woman.

Sarafina's energy deflated a bit. She reached into her bag again and produced a thin leather strap with a rough forged tag that said, "Be Here." She showed it to Jack, saying, "Here. Excuse my intrusion. It's just that I am curious about your story, and… well, I can see that perhaps now is not the best time."

Jack was thinking, *Ugh. God. Now what?* as she continued.

"May I?" she asked, indicating that she wanted to put the necklace on him. Jack had no way of moving off the rail or doing anything else, so he acquiesced in the hopes that if she did this, she'd leave. He didn't love people using him as freak-show entertainment. This always put him in a bad, closed-off mood.

Sarafina put the thin leather strap over his head, bringing her in closer to him. She didn't retreat much when done, a move Jack thought was very bold and highly invasive. "There," Sarafina said. "I make these for friends. If you ever want to talk or anything … Well, here's my card." She retrieved one from her bag and put it in his jacket pocket. "It would be nice to get to know you better, Jack." She turned and walked out of view as Jack finally exhaled his turmoiled state into the salty air.

Jack steadied himself solidly against the moving ship, reached into his jacket pocket, grabbed the woman's card, and threw it into the ocean. "Just don't," he said in an imperceptible whisper. His comment was far more directed at humanity in general than toward Sarafina. "Just fucking don't," he repeated.

Jack was still struggling to prop himself up with his cane but managed his way down to the parked cars, where he prayed his right foot would come back to his control before he had to drive off. He entered the vehicle and leaned his seat back as Banjo tried to brighten his day with welcome licks and that ever-wagging back-half. Jack was feeling shaken and walled-off. Mostly, per his plan, he just wanted to disappear into the endless woods where voices were not heard and judgment didn't exist.

FLIGHT

Jack roused from an unintended nap when the ferry jolted to announce its mooring to the mainland. Cars in rows started their engines as Jack gratefully realized that his right side was back with him. *Oh, thank God,* he thought to himself. The nap did the trick and reset his brain. He was feeling a lot better overall. Methodically, the cars ambled their wheels onto Canadian soil and began their trek toward a freeway.

"USA," proclaimed a signpost with an arrow to the right. "Ugh," Jack exhaled aloud. He had no interest in that country's brash ignorance and punitive ways. What kind of country lets sick people go broke and then manipulates citizens into cheering their suppression? Jack always thought America's priorities were that of a petulant, unevolved child. Their wars and guns, their obesity, their disdain for culture, and their criminally piss-poor education system. Not to mention their over-crowded prisons, institutionalized racism, and purported "separation of church and state" even though the country was controlled by the "religious right" and white supremacists; both groups joined as political bedfellows in their mutual disdain for his kind.

When the 99 North sign came into view, Jack could feel the flutter of excitement in his soul. He reached over and gave Banjo a scratch to edify the mutt and exalt the truck cab in general. "Woohoo!" Jack thought as he turned left toward Whistler and Pemberton. This was really happening.

The journey along the Sea to Sky Highway was always one of Jack's favorite experiences. The road seemed to take flight as the vehicle rose above the ocean below. The views were breathtaking yet deadly because the road was terrifyingly winding and narrow. Many travelers had lost their lives trying to navigate both the road and the view. Siren songs seemed to be heard here.

By mid-afternoon, Jack was beat, mainly from the emotional turmoil of the day. He happily pulled over at his favorite coffee shop in Britannia Beach. A cup-o-Joe might be the answer to Jack's slowing mood.

On the way back to the truck, Jack looked down to see a round sliver of a clamshell. It was about the same size and scale as his fake eye. *What's the difference?* he thought, and then wondered if anyone had ever replaced their missing eye with a gift from nature.

People were always amazed when Jack could pop his fake eye out on command. More so, they seemed fascinated that fake eyes weren't round like marbles. The entire socket isn't empty, so it's more like a big white contact lens that lays dead in his hand as it stares back at him. Given the way he'd lost his eye, he was lucky his stepdad was willing to pay for the replacement. Of course, it probably served the family's vanity more than it served Jack. With the number of stares and whispers he encountered on any given day, he might as well have gone back to wearing an eye patch as he often did in his twenties.

Jack finally kicked the shell aside and got on with the day. Banjo pooped on cue, and they were back on the road. They were a good team, Banjo and Jack. They understood each other. They were all they needed. They were content.

Several more hours of driving graced Jack with Banjo's repeat performance of "farts of death in an enclosed space." Eventually, Jack saw the sign for Alta Lake, which was his planned destination for the night. "Ah," said Jack as he pulled off the highway. "We made it." This was the first victory in a methodical escape from his past.

Jack loved this new way of living because of how easy and compact it was. There was no need to pitch a tent, just grab the kitchen supplies and make ready the meals and campfire. But tonight was a celebration. Jack felt that his first night of freedom should be celebrated with good food, good beer, and who knows, maybe even good company if the stars were aligned. Jack's new sense of freedom brought his swagger back, and he was feeling his power restored.

After relaxing a bit and getting Banjo fed, Jack figured it was time to head out and see what was around. The sun would be setting soon, so it was best he got his bearings now. As Jack walked up to see his reflection in the driver's side window, he ran his right hand through his hair with an attempt at a sexy, "How you doin'?" But of course, he clubbed the side of his forehead with his cast and instead came off like a muddled wannabe. Jack spit out a quick laugh.

"God," he said to himself. "I can't even get the basics of human flirtation right anymore. I'm just not the same as I was before my brain issues started five years ago." Jack paused. "Human flirtation? Who speaks like that? Ugh…" Jack felt like he was always doing his best, but in the past several years, he never quite hit the desired mark while he physically struggled.

Those who encountered Jack would disagree. Fake eye and bashed head aside, the guy was undeniably sexy. But it wasn't just his steely jaw or chiseled abs that got them. Those things were detractors for some of the people who pined for Jack. Notwithstanding his good looks, the guttural attraction both men and women felt for Jack came from somewhere deeper. He simply seemed to know something they didn't. Something important. Something life-altering.

Frustratingly, for those who dared to try to cozy up and bring him closer, Jack never shared that part of himself. It was as if he didn't even know it existed. The closer anyone came to Jack's core, the faster his sex language would take over. Intimate bonds that could have been spiritual were quickly shepherded toward the physical. Sex, for Jack, was the easy part. And right now, easy sounded really damn intriguing.

Reaching the south side of Whistler where the people who work at the resort lived, he found his usual haunt but was surprised it had been renamed "Astral Bar." *Weird,* thought Jack. "Hope it's as good as it was before it changed ownership."

Jack parked the car and went in, where he was greeted by dim lighting, AC/DC's "Touch Too Much," pool tables, bank seating, and multicolored Christmas lights dropping from the ceiling. The vibe reminded Jack of late-night carnival rides and tricky games where one might win a cheap stuffed animal. He sat at the bar along with a few other journeymen. Jack previewed the menu, and the indecision of what to order was registering on his face as the bartender approached him.

"My name's Kent. Welcome to my bar. Any decisions? Any questions about the menu?"

Jack looked up and muttered, "I'm not sure exactly."

"Another few minutes then," Kent said, and he hurried off.

Jack had just reestablished his nose in the menu when he heard the woman two barstools down offer, "I strongly suggest the Astral tequila flight." In her late twenties, she was a young woman accompanied by a handsome, mixed-race guy who didn't seem to notice or care about the exchange.

"Excuse me?" Jack said, feeling instantly flustered, the way one does when caught dining alone.

The young woman raised a shot glass from a wooden tray that held three others, two of which were already empty. "The Astral Tequila Flight. The new owners are trying to be fancy or some shit, so they do these, I don't know what you call it, sampler trays."

Then, as deadpan as any human could muster, she cheered the air with a raise of her arm. "To fancy!" She raised her arm slightly more, then downed the amber shot. "Besides…" she paused, the burn of the alcohol taking her aside for a second, "It's a lot cheaper when you buy four shots this way than any other." She then turned back to her date. Jack couldn't hear what they were discussing but was intrigued by her spirit.

Kent returned without any words as Jack looked up and indicated toward the young woman with the tattoos and two very tight braids falling out from under her baseball cap. "I'll have that tequila thing she's having and your classic cheeseburger." Kent nodded and walked off.

Looking around the bar and taking in the bizarre decor, Jack was surprised when he felt something on his left side. It was the chatty, dark-haired, tough girl dropping her last full shot glass next to Jack. Without looking in Jack's direction, she sat down and said, "I'm Sam." Then as her date sat next to her, she continued with, "This is Jordan."

"I'm Jack." There was no effort to shake hands by either party. Instead, to retain their pretense of cool, they all stared straight ahead. Still, they occasionally nodded in the direction of the other two, a move that hoped to send a message of apathy and ennui but served to casually check one another out.

Sam spoke to the air directly in front of her. "You work around here or something? Never seen you around. Not that we've been around much either lately." Jack could sense the story she was trying to pique his attention with, but he didn't pursue it.

"I'm just passing through." Jack offered no follow-up information. He was always walled off and hated chit-chat with strangers, but he at least had Sam on his good side. Maybe she wouldn't notice his misshapen skull in the dark bar.

"Oh," Sam followed up. "From where… or should I ask, to where?"

"Well, originally from Kelsey Bay, but I've been living in Port Hardy the past few years."

"An island boy," Sam teased. "Where you headed to, champ?" The "champ" was punctuated with one of her fists landing on his shoulder.

Champ? Jack thought. *Champ, as in Champion?* Her use of the word slightly threw Jack, but she was a tad drunk, so Jack gave it a pass.

"Up north, via YoHo. It's a bit of a trek, but it's kinda what I need right now. To just get away."

"Get away, eh?" Sam leaned in. "Get away from…?"

AC/DC continued in the background – this time "Thunderstruck" – while neither party spoke. Jack wasn't sure how to formulate the next words.

"I guess my past. You know, just time for a clean break." As the words came out of his mouth, he realized that his casted arm made him seem like he was running from real trouble.

"Ah…" Sam said as she sprawled across the front of the bar the way relaxed drunk people who have abandoned their sense of personal space do. "A clean break." She then reached over and lightly knocked on Jack's cast as if to see if anyone was home. "Time to start over. I've been there a few times."

Jack's food arrived, and he ate hurriedly and without apology. He was starving. Once done, he sat up and refocused on his glass of water and tequila shots. Sam raised her last shot glass and yelled a tad too loud for Jack's taste. "To new beginnings and clean breaks." Jack wasn't sure this made sense, but his mood and environment weren't going to allow him to judge anyone. Not tonight. There was too much to celebrate. His first night on the open road.

Just let go, the voice inside his head rang. Little did he know, that voice was about to become a notable companion.

Having finished her tequila, Sam stood and had Jordan follow her over to the pool tables. Jack remained sitting as he watched the young couple begin their racking of balls. Jack was intrigued by these two, and they seemed friendly enough.

So, what else am I going to do with myself tonight? he thought. *Cuddle gassy Banjo in my truck?* The old dog slept through most of everything and, in the large scheme of things, was often not great company in this capacity. Besides, opportunity seemed to be afoot.

Jack waved at Kent, the bartender. "Make these last three shots into boilermakers." He had three pints of frothy cold beer a minute later with the tequila shots perched by a hanger on the sides. Jack grabbed them, dropped his debit card on the table, and then walked over to Sam and Jordan.

"This round's on me," Jack said, hailing the air between them, which was quickly met with cheers and woots.

"On you, eh?" Sam said in her flirty way, walking up to face Jack head-on. A slight register of surprise came across her face. He got it. This was the first time she saw Jack straight on. Before this, she had only seen his "good" side. Jack knew that moment of registration. He knew it couldn't be helped, but the next words out of her mouth caught Jack off guard. "You're very handsome, Jack."

Without thinking, he openly laughed in her face. "Oh really?" Jack stammered. He wasn't sure why he gave this reaction, but there they stood. More than anything, Jack couldn't tell Sam's intention. Was she ribbing him? Was she making fun of his fucked-up face, or was there something else at play? And, slightly more importantly, as far as Jack was concerned, was whether the beautifully-skinned Jordan was also interested in this game.

"Yes…," Sam said, slowly looking into Jack's eyes. "Really."

This was not a situation Jack was familiar with for some time now. Someone was cozying up to him with bold flirtation and calling him handsome. He was thrown and even more thrown over the fact that he was thrown. He used to be able to handle this. He used to have swagger and know how to handle himself, but the depression over his deteriorating physical condition had since robbed him of even the memory of what that felt like.

"Uh…" Jack backed up a bit. "Uh, well… I don't think so but, thank you."

"Why do you not think so, Jack?" Sam said, leaning in closer. Jack could smell the liquor on her. "Is it because of this?" She used her index finger to make a circle on his right temple. This was a move that made Jack super uncomfortable. He froze as Sam repeated, "You need to stop. You're very handsome. Scars and all. In fact, I'd say it's the scars that make people interesting. Shows they have lived. That they've been through shit. If that isn't their story, I can't relate." She booped his nose.

Jack paused and, not knowing what else to say, followed up with, "That's true but c'mon… I'm not exactly handsome." The words now ringing in his ears were, "You're not good-looking enough, to also be an asshole." He was ashamed to not just take the fucking compliment.

"Is that the story you tell people like me…?" The long staggering pause was followed by, "Or is that the story you tell yourself?" Sam's eyebrow cocked as her eyes danced with delight. "Enough," Sam said as she pushed away from Jack and headed back over to Jordan, who was easily a foot taller than her.

Wow, Jack thought to himself, catching the first full-bodied glance of Jordan. *That is one sturdy dude. Maybe he's a hockey player or something.* Jack wasn't sure.

At that moment, Jack's inward conversation was broken by Jordan talking at him. "You wanna play?" Although he said this while holding a billiards stick, Jack got the feeling that billiards was not the game that he meant. Jack swallowed hard and made his way over to Jordan. "Sure," Jack said. "I got game."

The threesome quickly downed the first round of boilermakers as Sam took the lead in eight-ball. *God, she's good,* Jack thought. *Even drunk, this girl can hold her own.* He was impressed.

Into the next round of drinks, the flirtation increased with Sam hanging on and hugging Jack like they were longtime friends and Jordan coming up behind Jack and hugging him, making Jack feel small. Not just in stature. Jordan was a big dude who could tear Jack apart if he wanted to. Jack wanted him to.

Sam was waiting against the pinball machine in the corner while Jack took his turn. She called Jordan over, and they started kissing while she still had her eyes on Jack. They seemed to be either lost in the moment or moving from pool to a different game. This was a move that wasn't lost on Jack. He stood there like a statue until Sam broke from Jordan, grabbed Jack by the hand, and pulled him over to the game area they had turned into their lounge. Sam pushed Jack's butt against the front of the pinball machine, kissed him full-mouthed once, then slammed him back onto the glass.

Jesus, lady, Jack thought to himself. He felt the power of her thrust even in his inebriated state. But Sam wasn't done. She reached down, grabbed Jack by the shirt, yanked him clean up, kissed him deeply again, then turned him around so now she was the one with her butt against the buttons and levers. Sam kept holding his shirt aggressively as Jordan came up behind Jack. He was kissing Jack's neck softly. It was becoming clear that Jack had a choice to make, but not an unfamiliar choice. Jack pushed back against Jordan with just the slightest arch in his back that sent the message, "Let's go, cowboy."

It wasn't Jack's first time at this rodeo. Far from it. After running away from home, he had survived a portion of his young life as an escort in Vancouver's west end. Not something he talked about, not that he had any shame around it. Nonetheless, people tended to put the entire concept of sex workers into a thought prison where it didn't belong. Jack was lucky that way. He had no gender boxes or thought prisons of this type. They served nothing and added no value to one's life. Jack simply saw nothing worthwhile in adopting these imaginary constructs – concepts alien to him but inextricably and wholly part of the North American psyche. Jack saw this as wrongheaded, pointless, stupid, and infantile. Porn stars and prostitutes came from all walks of life, and for many, it wasn't demoralizing or drug-related. For some, it could be beautiful, but for Jack, that was never the case. He had dark demons to exorcise, and being a hustler was simply the playground that he chose as its venue.

The memories of how it all began came flooding back...

FISTICUFFS

Jack was seventeen when he placed his first ad as a sex worker. He was nervous, but also knew that he was far more qualified than most to do this. He quickly learned who to trust, what attracted the wrong type of people, and how to get himself out of trouble if needed. But more than all that, Jack learned how to be a "special service." His body worked fully back then, so it was just the facial scarring that he had to work around. And work it he did, because, in time, Jack would realize that in this circle of flesh lust, him looking like he could take a hit, was a significant perk. Jack's ad was simple, and the words in innocent type beneath the photo of his ripped abs read: "Anything you need me to be," then his phone number and his fake name, Colton.

Jack had just one rule when meeting anyone from his ads for the first time. Before anything began, the client had to hit him and hit him hard because Jack had learned that cops aren't allowed to do this. Talk about separating the wheat from the chaff. Besides, Jack liked the tone it struck with paid dates.

Most of his encounters were almost identical to a call he received from Guillaume DuBois, a French Canadian banker who had very specific tastes. Jack would always confirm over the phone that the photo was him but that his face was kind of banged up and had scars. To this news, Guillaume responded in a French accent, "Even better."

Jack showed up at Mr. Dubois's West-End condo and was ushered in. Guillaume greeted him, asked if he wanted water or anything, then took him into his bedroom. Jack explained his one rule before they began, and Guillaume came alive with this news. SMACK! Guillaume's backhand landed across Jack's face so hard it threw him into a wall. Guillaume grabbed Jack and started wrestling with him, pulling at his clothes and demonstrating that he was in charge. The next thing Jack knew, he was naked and being handcuffed with his hands behind his back. Guillaume then walked him to the shower and scrubbed him down hard, telling him how important it was to be clean. Jack was silent. "Right faggot?" Guillaume screamed like a drill sergeant into Jack's deaf ear. Jack was silently still. "I fucking said, right FAGGOT?!" The elder man screamed as he pulled Jack's head back violently by his hair that he heard his neck crack. Jack again was silent and still; because he knew what came next... this time, another violent backhand that kicked him off his feet, threw him into the tiled wall where he then slammed onto the wet shower floor. With his hands still cuffed behind him, Jack got to his knees and looked up at his savior; he was more animal now than man, and it was from this basement of his emotional hell that Jack would let loose.

"HIT ME!!!" SMACK!

Jack no longer recognized his own enraged voice. "HIT ME!!!" SMACK! "AGAIN!!!" Jack screamed with all his might. "HIT ME!!! AGAIN!!!"

Jack tasted his own blood pooling in his mouth, dying his teeth crimson. Slowly he surrendered to the shower floor, feeling the warm water rain down on his skin, That's the stuff, *he'd think to himself,* That's it right there.... *He red-smiled with his eyes closed.*

While Jack remained on the tile floor listening to the gentle shower fall onto his naked skin, a sense of warm inner peace washed over him because, for Jack, this was always the moment when he felt the most alive.

SMOKE

"You want to get outta here?" Sam asked Jack bringing him back to the present moment. He found it notable that she had asked this question without looking to Jordan for input. It was clear that conversation had already taken place — now they just needed an answer.

"Uhhh… sure?" Jack said, trying hard to be cool. It registered almost immediately that he was failing because, at that moment, Jack couldn't remember what normal arms do in relaxed conversation. This nervous fidgeting amused the other two. They grinned, and each grabbed one of Jack's hands to haul his ass to the bar.

After Kent rang them up, they were quickly out into the parking lot breathing cold air, which didn't faze them, given their intoxicated state. "This way," Sam laughed as she started running stupidly toward the road. "It's just fourteen houses this way," she yelled exuberantly. The two men held hands and ran after her.

Banging loudly and drunkenly through the front door, Sam had Jack's shirt at the pits again and was heaving him around. It was becoming apparent to Jack that this was the little lady's thing. He didn't hate it.

Next, Sam and Jordan were getting naked and making out when Jack grabbed a plastic water bottle from the kitchen and ran into the bathroom. He used this trick as an escort while on the run from client to client. Unfortunately, he didn't always have time for a proper shower to get himself "ready," so this quick life hack would, as Jack liked to think of it, would "evacuate the dance floor."

In less than a minute, Jack was rejoining the action. Given his past, Jack knew the difference between making love and fucking, and today, the three of them came to fuck the house down.

Sam once again grabbed Jack by his short and threw him on the bed. A move that lit up Jack's eyes. *Oh yeah?* Jack thought. *Bring it. Gimme all you got, Sam.* With that, a stinging hot slap met Jack's face, and in delight, he thought to himself, *This is going to be fun.*

Ninety minutes later, they unmeshed from one other. A bed of sweat, grease, God knows what bodily fluids and a whole lot of panting and trying to catch their breath. There's always that one laugh that someone chimes in with. This time it was Sam with a light bird's laughter. She rolled over next to Jack so that she was just inches away from his head. "You're something else. You know that, Jack?"

Jack laughed to himself and, without formally agreeing, sat up against the headboard where for the first time, he took in the clap-board cheap apartment and its attempt at 'shabby-chic'. Jordan, on Jack's left was next to chuckle, followed quickly by Sam who reached for a joint.

She lit it, then exhaling smoke, Sam said, "Jack. What sign are you?"

"Taurus." Jack puffed then passed the joint to Jordan. "But I don't, you know, really follow that stuff."

Now it was Jordan's turn to try and speak while exhaling. "I didn't much either before meeting Sam." Pause. Hold. Blow. "She's kinda amazing at this stuff. Trust me." Jordan coughed while trying to clearly say, "I don't fully get it, but you know, life is hard, and any edge up you can get, I say take it."

"Let me see your hand," Sam said to Jack as she leaped from the bed naked. She returned with a flashlight, a book, a pen, and a writing tablet. Sitting back down on the bed, she grabbed Jack's hand to shine a light on his palm.

Okay, Jack thought to himself, *I'm going to need to get out of here soon. Just came to fuck, not for a personality test.*

Sam went quiet, then grabbed Jack's hand with both of hers. "What?" Jack inquired. He was unclear as to what exactly was going on.

"It's just that…" Sam trailed off, then resumed, "It's just that I think you…. Look here." She was pointing to the meaty area at the base of the palm below Jack's pinky finger. "Look. See?" She pointed more fervently. "What do you see?" She quickly consulted her book again.

"Um, I don't know," Jack said, feeling dumb.

"Look!" Sam said. "Look closely. What's that shape called?" Now drawing with her finger along the lines of Jack's palm.

"A figure eight?" Jack guessed.

"No, dummy, look!" Jack watched as Sam grabbed her pen and wrote on his hand. It was a Yin/Yang interlocking symbol. "I've never actually seen one of these before! This is amazing, Jack." Sam threw these words wildly at him while quickly thumbing through the book in her lap again. "Look," she said, holding out the book for the guys to see. "It says: *A very rare occurrence is when the mark of the yin yang appears on the hypothenar. When the yin and yang are balanced here, the soul of its owner is integrated and balanced. In the personal unconscious, the undifferentiated (or unassimilated) opposites of the personality are projected: a man's anima, or hidden feminine aspect, will be represented in the unconscious by feminine anima images and vice versa. A woman's animus, or hidden masculine aspect, will be represented in the unconscious by masculine images.*"

There was a long silence.

"So… what does that mean exactly?" Jack asked, confused.

"Jack, listen," Sam said. "We are seen as our truths are to us…" Pause. "…and I think there's a truth here that you need to be aware of. This symbol…" She pointed again to his palm. "…is fucking rare, and it only finds its way to those who are achieving balance in their lifetime. You have that in you, Jack."

Jack laughed quietly and uncomfortably; it was time for him to leave. He looked up, thinking, *Much too much, didn't come for this, gotta go, bye.*

But Sam continued, not letting go of Jack's hand. "Tell me who you are, Jack."

The mustard and turquoise room fell silent as Jack's safety walls slammed into their "Go Fuck Yourself" positions. *Why?* Jack thought. *Ugh, this is getting weird…*

"Jack!" Sam demanded his attention back. "You are harmony and balance in genders. You are someone who walks the in-between like some of us say we do, but you do so effortlessly and without thinking because that is who you are."

Jack started collecting his things. This was too much for him. This was too intimate.

"Jack!" Sam yelled after him. "You can't ignore this stuff!"

A naked Jack then spun around with crazy flashing in his eyes and yelled with a ferocity that Sam wasn't expecting. "I FUCKING KNOW, SAM!!" Jack screamed. "I KNOW WHAT I AM, AND I DON'T FUCKING WANT IT!" Jack immediately felt embarrassed for the outburst, but it was something he had needed to let out for a very long time, and he wasn't particularly thrilled to have done so in front of two strangers he just fucked.

"I know," Jack said quietly, head hung. He sat on the edge of the bed and started crying. Jordan grabbed him in his big arms, pulled him onto the bed, and held him while Sam wiped away his tears. "I know," he kept saying through tears. "I know."

MIST

It was almost 4:00 AM when Jack left Sam's house. He had just stepped into the night air to walk back to his truck when he recalled that Banjo was no doubt sleeping soundly without him. Jack was about four doors down from Sam's place and was lost in thought when he was slapped back into the present with the never-welcome twinge of his right ring finger. It was back.

Oh shit, Jack thought as he picked up the pace. *Damn, damn, fuck, damn,* he continued cursing while making a break for his vehicle. *God damn it!* Jack thought as he began to hobble and run. He hated this part of his life, and every time Jack forgot, or rather just lived an everyday life without the constant internal medical checks, he would be viciously reminded of what was in charge of his body. He hated that the moment he abandoned his darkened problems and just lived carefree, the monster within him would rise. Jack was never allowed hubris around this. Not at all. Not for one Goddamned day. Jack willed himself to go faster.

Twinge went his right forearm. *Fuck,* Jack thought in response. *I gotta make it.* But, unfortunately, Jack's truck was not yet in view.

God... I'm such an idiot. Not even 24 hours into this trip and, ugh, mess. Why Jack? Why can't you fucking remember that you don't get to live with abandon. You just don't. Not anymore. Jack fell back on the memory of how this all began. A memory that broke his heart every time he recalled it…

"Hey, Jack," Ricky called from the kitchen of his newly purchased trailer home. "You got a beer?"

"Yeah," Jack yelled back as he continued packing weed into his pipe to ease the edge of the workday. This should be nice, Jack thought, heading down the hall of the shitty brown trailer toward Ricky's voice.

They each grabbed a beer and headed out into the backyard, where a frenzied Banjo was waging war against an upturned tree root. Seeing this, Jack encouraged his dog with, "Kill it, boy! Kill it!"

The guys laughed as they sat on the top of the picnic table, which was always customary — a better view from there.

"Nice evening," Jack continued as the rays of last light animated themselves across his face. "It's nice having you here… and I know it's not much, but I have big plans of fixing it up. I'm just happy to have finally found a place that I can afford," Jack said while clinking his bottle against Ricky's stationary beer.

"Great to see you too. Or should I say, formally meet you," Ricky replied. They had been chatting online for a while but had never met in person until today.

"Toi aussi," Jack joked, watching the sun slip away.

They sat in quiet discomfort the way people do when they're newly in each other's presence, and potentials and possibilities for the evening are running through their minds. It was at that moment that Jack felt something weird. The muscle that controlled his index finger contracted involuntarily, lifting his finger from the bottle. Jack was familiar with muscle cramps and the like, so he shook out his hand, and it dissipated.

After they had finished their beers, Jack had a surprise for Ricky. "C'mon, you hungry?"

Jack's guest replied with a nonverbal dude shrug meant to convey "yes." Jack grabbed Ricky by the hand, pitched the bottles into the recycle bin, and pulled them both into the seats of his Geo Storm hatchback, which already housed a cooler picnic. It was a gesture Jack hoped would convey his feelings toward his date. Jack wanted to make things pleasant for Ricky.

"Where are we going? Dinner or something?" Ricky said as Jack nodded back. "You're not going to drag me out into the woods and kill me or something?" Ricky was boy-grinning in a full, stupid dick-bending hot sexy smile; a trait that Jack found completely irresistible and, oof, hot.

Jack, still looking forward, eyes on the road, said flatly, "Maybe. But probably some parts of you more than others." They both laughed. Twenty minutes later, they pulled off the freeway onto a dirt road, no doubt making the previous joke slightly less funny to Ricky. But then, just a few hundred feet up the road, the most incredible view opened up before them.

"Wow ..." Ricky said, mouth open.

"You like it?" Jack beamed excitedly. "I packed us some food and stuff. Thought maybe we could open the hatch and sit in there and have dinner."

The guys enjoyed themselves, and Ricky was taken with Jack's intense effort to create a very nice and thoughtful date. Then it happened again. Jack's index finger involuntarily peeled itself from the glass he was holding. Jack, now slightly more perplexed, shook it out again. He wondered if he had somehow messed it up at the lumberyard earlier that day. The guys resumed their meal, which was heavily peppered with flirt.

Arriving back at Jack's home, he turned to Ricky seated beside him. "You want to come in and watch a movie or something?" The "or something" was pregnant with possibility that jump-started Jack's imagination.

"Sure." Ricky nodded as he exited the vehicle. "WooHoo!" thought Jack, racing for the door and fumbling with his keys.

Once inside, Jack fished out two more Coronas and got them settled on the couch. Grabbing for the remote, Jack noticed he couldn't turn the

TV on. He couldn't work the remote. His index finger wasn't responding, and for the life of him, he couldn't tap the power button. It wasn't that he couldn't do it but rather that his brain had lost the channel. Jack focused hard, but nothing happened. "What the...?" he thought out loud, which caught the attention of Ricky seated next to him.

"What's up?" Ricky said, then swallowed more beer.

"Meah..." a sound meant to convey slight displeasure. "I'm not exactly sure. This finger is giving me some kind of trouble. Maybe I strained it or something." Jack thought nothing more of it and turned his attention back to his date.

Over the next eighteen months, Jack would watch the trend of this anomaly find new homes at different intersections of his body. First was the index finger, next the same finger on the other hand. Then the thumb, then his neck, and other fingers. It inextricably continued to work its way through Jack's body to find new homes to dwell, control, terrorize, and delete from Jack's system.

One night, Jack was lying down watching TV when his hands went dead, and the muscles that controlled his forearms contracted involuntarily to bring them up like two hooded cobras, one on either side of him. Jack watched in absolute amazement. His hands just hung there in the air, and there wasn't a thing Jack could do about it. He was stuck, and he didn't know what to do. Jack was legitimately panicked.

The next day, he phoned Dr. Bentine to make an appointment. It was an appointment that opened a new path toward a potentially crippling life where no one had answers, and each person he spoke to had conflicting information, all of which made the path of uncertainty morph into a soul-sucking blackhole. Not much hope there. Down went Jack. His mood, ability to care, and hope for a better tomorrow were all being leached out of him one appointment at a time.

Jack recalled the worst moment of it. Each month, he would report to his doctors the muscular abnormalities that found new ground within him. A cold report of the seeds that were being planted, which new locations were inhabited, and what were its latest terrifying expressions. Its key signature, unexplainable loss of control, rendering some parts in hyper contraction while others disconnected entirely from the motherboard of his mind. There was no rhyme or reason as to how it was devouring Jack's body, but it was, and it was not a thing that could be understood, not by him, and not by doctors.

But all that was one thing doctors could evaluate. However, the next phase of it no one could have foreseen. Jack then had to report that during episodes, it was not only taking his body, but it was now also masticating his mind.

Jack's last conversation about it with God was only a few months into his reports to doctors. That was years ago now, but Jack could still remember it. "God, listen… I know I…." Pause. "…well, we both know we haven't always gotten along, but I'm calling in a favor if you can still hear me." Jack started to cry and shake uncontrollably, leaving him unable to remain seated in an upright position. The rest was only said internally while his face fell toward the earth and pressed itself hard into his brown bedroom carpet. "Please. Please, God… if you're out there. Please. I am begging you, please don't take my feet. That's all I ask. Please don't take my feet. Please just let me have them… I can't… I don't…. PLEASE! Please just leave me them. Please just leave my feet. I don't want to be in a fucking wheelchair or something. Please. Please. Please. That's all I ask. Please don't take my feet. Please."

Jack's prayers, as always, fell on non-existent ears, so that was the last of them. The scourge did find its way into his ankles and then his toes. It decided its final home would be a clubbed habit of deformity at the end of Jack's legs while mental neurological storms raged.

Running from Sam's house in the cold night air, Jack shook off the old memories and continued to make his way quickly to the Blazer, which was now finally within his view.

Twinge. His right arm was rapidly dying.

Twinge. He could feel his left arm begin to do its curl of death too.

Twinge. *FUCK!!!* thought Jack, now in a sprint against the impending. He knew from experience that he would not be able to start his car if both arms were offline. He sprinted.

Twinge. It was slithering toward all four extremities. Jack was panicked, but reaching the vehicle, he unlocked the door quickly, started the engine, and frantically sped off for the campground.

SILENCE

Jack woke the next morning unsure of how he was.

He didn't seem to be in any pain, and the truck didn't stink. Jack did the math and put together his "dance floor" situation last night and added one more silver lining to that hot stroke of luck.

More fully rousing himself to see what would move, it appeared that last night wasn't too bad, neurologically speaking. *Dodged another fat bullet there,* Jack thought as he began putting things back in order.

Upfront, Banjo sat looking at him with blinks and wags of happiness. Jack's heart melted like it always did when met in this way. "Okay, boy. Let's have a walk and some breakfast." Jack's tone quickly faded from perky to *fuck, I'm getting old,* as the drumbeat of his hangover pounded him from the inside.

Jumping out of the back of the truck, Banjo took Jack for a walk, as was customary. As they made their way around the campground, Banjo pointed out all of the interesting things. He even stopped to smell a rosebush, which reminded Jack that he needed to emulate Banjo more in his everyday life, even if the dog was stopping to smell another dog's pee instead of the roses. Jack now had a new cheer for his dog's efforts: "Champ." Jack smiled.

Back at the campsite, Jack pulled together a quick bite for them both. He felt pretty good despite the slight hangover, lack of sleep, and a mild dystonic storm. He knew a hike or a jog would clear the befuddled webs of yesterday's tequila, so he suited up. Jack always loved working out because it was a time to reconnect to himself. To feel himself work. To feel himself breathe and push and struggle and win. To feel like a whole person. Sure, with age, he wasn't what he used to be, but he had to fight if he wanted to unearth himself from where he had been. He was laced up, so off he went.

Jack attuned to his breathing as his feet began padding their way around the small lake. 1, 2, 1, 2. The pace set, all systems firing, focus forward, heightened alert, go. Someone once asked Jack what his favorite thing was to listen to while he jogged. He didn't answer out loud, but, in his mind, he said, "The Universe." Today was no exception, even though it had been a while since they had spoken. The mountains of British Columbia opened that morning to the sky. "Ah!" Jack's spirit said, cracking wide open as he rounded the curve to the lake. This is where his soul lived. This is where he could hear himself think. That was always part of Jack's issue, a noisy, unrelenting brain.

Jack continued to run, with heartbeats and drumbeats singing energy into his ears. Faster. Jack was pushing himself. Faster. Get to the ...

There was always a point in Jack's workouts where he'd hit "smooth air." He discovered it when pushing himself to inhuman extremes in athletic competition. No pain. No earth. Just flight. It was the place of superhuman strength; it was "the zone," the hyper-focus of the present moment when everything else slipped away and disappeared from the noise. That was smooth air.

There was also the rare feeling of being fully present like one must be to navigate the world at this speed. Here, there are no split-second decisions at full throttle that can falter. Not a one. The mind has to achieve a state of total comprehension of everything surrounding it. The brain knows there is no room for mistakes at this speed. Amazingly, the mind will bend time to achieve the necessary level of attuned perfection to escape injury or death.

Rounding the final mile, Jack's spiritual high beams amped up. It was the call and echo of all that is, a connection to Mother Earth and all her children. It was clarity. It was mindfulness, and he harnessed the power of it all as he pushed and pushed and pushed his legs until they physically could not go faster. Jack breathed this in deeply. The legs responded. For today, that was enough to fill journals of gratitude.

Nature was Jack's church. He felt here what folks who went to "regular church" referred to as God. He felt at once impossibly large and infinitesimally small. He felt a kinship with everything around him – trees, water, mountains, grasses. He felt and respected their age and he listened to their wisdom. In turn, they allowed him to drop his shame and sorrows and become one with them. And, perhaps most importantly, they forgave him when modern life forced him back to a bleaker existence.

Jack returned to the campground and found Banjo asleep in his usual position on the truck's passenger side. He stopped for a minute and took Banjo's face into his hands.

"You know what, boy? I'm glad we're on this adventure together. There isn't a soul on earth that I'd rather be doing this with. Banjo agreed with a yawn that landed his head on Jack's chest for a closer cuddle. Jack noted that he was happy for the first time in a long time. Legitimately happy. The kind of happiness that stems from the inside finding its way out rather than what he had been doing ever since his diagnosis. He'd been forcing "happy" on himself in a way that never quite worked. Jack noted that happiness doesn't come from the external; it comes from his connection to spirit, his surroundings, and the hug he shared with Banjo. Jack stroked Banjo's head and said a prayer of gratitude. He had once heard that if the only prayer you could manage was "thank you," then that would be more than enough. That's what he could do today, so that's what he did. *It's a start*, he thought.

"Next stop, Shuswap Lake," Jack announced to his pup. Banjo's ears perked up for the simple fact of meeting his friend's excitement.

Their destination was a beautiful place with a name that felt awkward to verbalize. Jack laughed, remembering his encounter with his neighbor at the grocery store a while back. Jack was going on and on about where the best place to relax is when that name popped into the conversation…

"You know, Shuswap. Shuswap Lake? It's up near Salmon Arm."
"Ain't never heard of it," His neighbor Al said while feigning thinking. "Shoe-What-Now?" That's the part that always made Jack snicker. Every time. "Shoe-What-Now"? Hilarious.
"Shoe-swap… but pronounced like Shoe-schwap." It's the Schwap bit that lets the locals know you're one of them.

Jack and Banjo were several hours into their day's drive when it was time to stop for lunch. Jack decided on a roadside diner in Ashcroft. It was a small town but had great food options because it was at the intersection of the two main freeways, the "99" and the "One." They were both happy to get out and stretch, use the washroom, and grab a bite.

Forty-five minutes later, they were back on the open road and feeling refreshed. After a hearty burger, Jack's hangover had finally diminished. "Worth it," Jack thought to himself, reliving the beauty he had shared with Sam and Jordan. He was grateful for the experience, but Sam's words, "Tell me who you are," were a pesky gnat that he wasn't able to swat away. Jack didn't know why.

Around 3:30 in the afternoon, the Chevy pulled off the main road and headed toward the lake. Jack was ready for a nap, and Banjo, well, Banjo had done little else. At his age, he'd earned this as his signature move.

Jack paid the fare for the campsite and found the perfect spot furthest away from the road that backed up against the endless park forest. *Perfect,* Jack thought to himself, feeling pleased with his new surroundings. They parked, pulled out the cooking items from the back, and cleared enough space on the bed for a nap. It wasn't long before they were both asleep in a puppy-pile cuddle.

NIGGLED

The dynamic duo was up from their afternoon nap when someone pulled into the neighboring campsite. Jack looked up from his chores and pretended to be cheerful with a wave, but inside he was thinking, *Bleh. People. Why?* He hoped his fake cheerfulness read correctly to his unwanted neighbors. They seemed okay enough, Jack guessed. A nice nuclear family with all the originality of florals for spring, as the movie line goes. Jack ignored them.

Jack was well into cooking his foil-wrapped hobo-pack when the empty campsite to his other side received guests as well. *Mother Fucker of Saint Hades fucktardia,* Jack thought to himself. *These people have the entire campground to choose from!* He guessed it was like locker locations at the gym. It didn't matter which one you chose; the neighboring one is *always* in use when you need to access your stuff – and usually by some old fucker intent on air drying his balls. It was the law of inconvenience when surrounded by others.

Jack's new neighbors were an older couple in a newer VW bus thing. Jack didn't know they had updated such a vehicle. He guessed it ran on corn husks and banana peels or some shit. Jack retreated behind his truck, where he could hang out with as little notice or intrusion as possible. After the epic events of last night, he just wanted to be quiet. It was a great night to see the stars and be alone.

Sitting back into his lounge chair with Banjo at his side, Jack balanced his dinner plate on his knee. He could have seated himself at the picnic table, but this hideaway spot where no one could see him felt right for the moment. Just then, Banjo started to bark.

"Excuse me," a voice came from the direction of the wholesome family.

Aargh, Jack thought to himself. *I came all this way to get away from people, not this.*

"Banjo!" Jack yelled, getting the dog back in order.

"Hi there. How are ya?" the stranger's voice chimed.

Jack managed a meager "Yep. Hey there. How can I help you?" His tone was not exactly brimming with curiosity, friendliness, or joy.

"Yeah, hi. We're the Olson's. Up from Idaho. Anywho, I just wanted to say, smells great, whatever you're cooking."

Bleh, Jack told himself. *Did Papa Olson seriously just come over to tell me my cooking smelled good? I mean, what now?*

"Yeah, thanks," Jack finally said in the man's direction. Jack offered no lingering open questions, statements, or follow-ups.

"If you need anything, we're right here. Just saw that you're flying solo tonight, and well, we thought we'd make this part of the campground a little more family-friendly."

"Cool," Jack replied while noticing the fish decal on the back of their Subaru family Jesus wagon. The crucifix always made Jack's skin crawl because of his history and the brutal way it inflicted maximum human pain. But they probably didn't see it for what it was on its face. Instead, they most likely lived an "alternative" reality where death = life, and praying to a torture device hung on the wall wasn't darkness but a path to salvation.

Jack remembered back. "For we are ALL sinners," his stepfather would bellow at the pulpit. Then again, for emphasis, Reverend Daw would repeat it in a hushed tone. "We are all sinners." This felt heavy to young Jack. The entrenched messaging was dark and abusive and delivered like the burden of the cross.

Sinners. Sin. Jack was confused by the concept, and most often in his life, this was a concept used as a cudgel of rank human oppression and judgment. There was no joy there. There is no lightness there. There was no love there. There was no empathy there. Not amid those pews. *Fuck em',* Jack thought as he continued to physically and energetically remove himself from his neighbor's awareness.

Most of the early evening was uneventful, which Jack was more than grateful for. It started to get dark when Banjo wandered into the neighboring camp with the VW.

"Oh, hello there," Jack heard from the neighboring site.

"*Oh jeez. Banjo!*" Jack thought, making his way to the woman's voice.

Jack stepped out of the brush into the cleared site. Sure enough, Banjo was insisting the neighbor love on him. "Oh, gosh, I'm so sorry for his intrusion. I'll tie him up."

"And hello to you too," the woman said to address Jack's presence. "Who's your love-bug friend here?" She continued giving the dog a good tummy scratch now. Banjo assisted by putting himself in a dead bug pose to "help" her get into the good spots.

Jack laughed awkwardly, trying to keep the mood light and hide his internal embarrassment. "This is Banjo," Jack said, now reaching for his collar to clip him to his leash. "He's my co-pilot… and mostly a good buddy. Tonight, however, he seems to have forgotten his manners."

"Well, welcome, and it's nice to meet you, Banjo!" she said, giving the dog one final enthusiastic rub. "I'm Theta."

"Uh… hi. I'm Jack." He wasn't sure what to do next and felt awkward. "We should…"

Theta cut him off as the man she traveled with exited the VW. "This is Jonathan." Jack noticed how fit they both were for their ages.

"Well, hi there, young man." The long-haired gentleman said with an outstretched hand. "Doing some sightseeing? Where from?"

As they shook hands, Jack was still feeling exposed, and he was doing his best to sidestep the chit-chat. "Yeah… just come up from Port Hardy. I'm headed over to the Banff area to catch up with a friend." Jack, lost in thought, let slip, "Might head north after that. I'm thinking Dawson City."

"Oh, nice! Sounds like quite the adventure for you two," Theta chimed in while Jonathan put a hand on Jack's shoulder, leaving him feeling a bit tense.

Why is this man touching me? Jack wondered but then relaxed into it, sensing the man's calm presence. The dim light was beginning to cast long stretching shadows.

"Are you traveling alone, or do you have a partner?" is a question that Jack always struggled with, especially when said in circles that were trying to suss out his sexual orientation. To Jack, he didn't have a "sexual orientation" per se. He didn't identify in any box that had been explained (and defined) for him. Nothing fit other than the basic concept that who he is, is balance. He considered himself both and yet neither. When people asked him how he identified, he responded, "I identify as Jack." He thought that should be enough.

"On this adventure, my partner in crime is this one," Jack said, loving on Banjo's ears with hearty scratches.

"Would you care to join us?" Jonathan said, pointing to the campfire.

Not knowing what to say and feeling a little caught off guard, Jack politely excused himself. "Maybe later. I have a book that I'm really into. If I finish it in time, I might stop by." This invented book was a total lie.

"Well, good enough then…." Jonathan said. "You're always welcome."

Banjo and Jack walked through the brush via the fastest way from their site to his. He had some whittling he wanted to work on, so he opened the back of the Chevy, turned on the camp lantern, and grabbed his favorite tools and a gnarled piece of wood. From the moment he found the stick, Jack thought the spirit of its form was simply waiting to be uncovered, if he listened close enough. As was his custom, Jack would "live" with the wood in its original state to hear what it wanted to be before he started in on it. Jack was always fascinated by what wood would say to him, how it spoke, and showed him where to place his carving tools. This relationship between him and his work went beyond that of man and stick but instead lived in a place just beyond the physical – the realms where we go to dream and wonder. Jack held the stick in his hand as he laid back on the bed, just eyeing it, turning it, listening to it. "What do you want to be?" he silently asked. "Show me."

The next thing Jack knew, he was being awoken by what sounded like loud crashes and music coming from the direction of the neighboring site. *What the?* Jack thought to himself, still just figuring out that he had fallen asleep. Banjo stirred but went right back to sleep as Jack jumped out of the back of the vehicle only to be met with flashing lights and more trumpeting music. Jack headed in the direction of the sounds and quickly realized that the Olson's were showing a Goddamn movie on a Goddamn bedsheet that they had strung between two Goddamn trees. *Are you fucking serious?* thought Jack as his newly awoken walk was replaced by a white-knuckled "fact-finding" mission.

Jack walked right past Mr. Olson, who was cooking on the outdoor grill of their RV.

"Ahoy, neighbor!" Jack heard from behind him, which instantly caused him to question Mr. Olson's ability to grasp critical parts of the English language. *Ahoy? Seriously? Ahoy? Gah.* Jack turned around.

"Oh, hi, Mr. Olson. I see you're playing a movie."

"Yep. Yep. The kids here wanted to see Titanic again so well… we invited the whole campground to enjoy a family-friendly evening on us."

Jack was curious how this man could think that his "generous" offer, extended to the entire campground, was beneficial to anyone considering it was only being used by his immediate family. At least the "Ahoy" made sense now. "Ah," said Jack, folding his arms.

"Yeah, we tried to invite you, but you were taking a nap. Care to join us? It'll be good family fun." Jack was highly perturbed by the man's continual use of the term "family-friendly." That phrase usually translated directly to "no degenerates like him, no faggots like him, no queers like him, no freaks like him, no non-gender conforming people like him, no sex workers like him, no hippy types/free spirits like him, and no people of any other faith other than Christians… like him. On and on, the list of ways that Jack was unacceptable unfurled in his mind. He wasn't safe here.

"I see… but the thing is, it's a little loud for your neighbors, and the flashing lights might be a bit much for…". Jack was cut off.

"Oh, stop – no need to be a pansy like that. C'mon, let me grab you a beer. The men of the place can hang out, and… any chance you're a Steelers fan?"

O-M-Jesus in Bethlehem, thought Jack. *He's not going to make this easy.* "Yep, I'm good. I just thought I'd come by and see what the racket was all about."

Mr. Olson swung an arm around Jack's neck and started a joking chokehold on him while walking toward the cooler next to the smoking BBQ. "C'mon, this'll be fun."

In the one second that Jack allowed this behavior to be thrust upon him, he asked himself why guys like this can't hear him. They think what they have is so amazing that they want to "share" it with the world whether the world wants it or not. They can never keep their dick of "this is what's best for you" in their god damn pecker shorts. Jack thought it might be time to go full Bobbit and bob it.

Jack pushed the man off him, saying, "Listen, buddy. Your campsite is pretty loud, and the flashing lights are pretty distracting. It's kinda not cool to push your agenda on everyone else." Jack walked away. "Just keep it down if you can… I don't want to be bothered by this anymore."

Returning to Banjo, Jack sat on the tailgate. "So now what, boy? Maybe a walk?" The utterance of the word "walk" was always met with enthusiasm and butt shaking. Banjo jumped out into the night air and headed down the drive. Jack locked up, ran after him, and clipped his leash on.

Their walk was a success, and with a newfound branch in Banjo's mouth, they circled the last bend and headed back toward their camp. They were about back to the Blazer when they passed Theta and Jonathan's fire. At this point, it was burning bright and making the surrounding trees dance in dappled night light. Banjo gave a good yank and proudly showed Theta his latest capture.

"Oh! Oh, my goodness," Theta said in surprise, almost spilling her drink.

Jack rushed to retrieve his petulant pup. "I am so sorry… here, let me."

"Oh, he's fine. It was Jack, right?" Jack nodded in agreement while still trying to snag Banjo's slithering leash.

"Banjo!" Jack said, trying to get the damn dog to stop moving.

"No, really, Jack. I love seeing this guy." Theta gave the dog a good scratch. "Reminds me of ours who passed a few years ago. I miss her," she said with a look of warm memories on her face. "Would you like to sit? We'd love the company if you feel like joining us."

Jack thought about it. Pros: Something to do. Cons: It's something to do that involves people. *Bleh,* Jack thought while weighing his options against his undefinable mood. "I guess," he finally said as he sat next to her, folding his arms. Just as the two were about to say something, another loud smashing sound was accompanied by flashes of light on the newly erected drive-in movie two spots up.

"It's even more distracting from my site," Jack said deadpan, meaning to be slightly funny. Theta mused and took a sip of wine.

"People," Theta said with a slight shrug. "What are you going to do? Here," she said, handing Jack the full glass of wine that sat next to her. "It's Jonathan's, but he hasn't taken a sip, and he might be out for the night. The man just cannot stay awake past a certain hour. Besides, he's been working a lot, and it makes me happy to let him rest and catch up. A good dose of R&R. That's why we're here." A long pause between the two as the fire crackled and glowed. Theta then raised her glass toward the noisy neighbors. "Although with this shit, whatcha going to do?"

Jack laughed. He was not expecting this elegant, long-necked woman to cuss openly. He instantly liked her ability to be real with him. Jack appreciated this. She had a regal Mother Earth quality to her. Jack did not doubt that Lululemon was a large part of her wardrobe.

The conversation to this point was fairly one-sided as Jack sat with his arms crossed with a wine glass in hand. Jack felt her eyes on him, so he took a chance and looked in her direction. "You okay, Jack?" Theta said in a motherly tone. "Where are you coming in from?"

Jack shrugged more, not because he was cold but just to shore himself up. "Like I said… I'm just passing through to YoHo, then headed up to Dawson. I just wanna get away. I need some me-time."

"That's a very nice thing to do for yourself. How we take care of ourselves is the hallmark of how we take care of others. I see it as being generous and balanced in these areas. I'm lucky I have reached a place in my life where I see the importance of these things."

There was another long silence.

Theta reached over and touched Jack's shoulder. "Everything okay? You seem awfully quiet."

"I dunno know. I'm just kinda that way, I guess."

Theta rearranged her seat to face more in Jack's direction. "And why do you think that is my friend?"

"You know…" Silence. "It's like those neighbors. I just don't understand things or people, I guess… and like even the people in my life, well…." Another long silence. "I guess that's just the way it is. It's never made sense to me."

The fire crackled and sparked its joy as Theta's forehead pondered what Jack had said. She then offered a laugh under her breath that conveyed that she understood. "Life is just that, I think. A series of confusing signals. It took me a long time to let that be okay." She lifted her head from its place down in thought to greet Jack's face with fireside warmth.

That evening, there was often silence between Jack and Theta as they reflected on life and bemused the absurdity of it all. Theta seemed to have a connection, a rooting that grounded her. Jack liked this quality in her. She gave an aura of ease, for she could, at her deepest core, allow there to be what was. Nothing more. Jack thought that it was a unique superpower. He always thought that everyone had one unique quality or gift that they brought to earth to demonstrate and model for those willing to be open to it. He certainly knew his out-of-the-box persona was potentially one such example.

The evening was wearing long, and Jack wanted to head to bed, but the crazy noises, screams, and flash-bangs coming from his neighbor kept checking him in place. "So, in this type of a situation…." Jack nosed in the direction of the lights and movie screen noise. "I mean, this doesn't bother you?"

Theta grinned and sat back further in her chair, her long, elegant grey hair surrounding her face while the glow of embers embraced her. "Jack…" she said, eyes bright and caring. "That's life, Jack. All of it." Theta stood, which threw Jack. "Come with me." He wasn't expecting there to be a tour or a late-night walkabout. "Come," she said over her shoulder as her wrap lifted with life from the night's cool breeze. Jack and Banjo stood and followed her onto the campground road.

"Come," she said, extending a hand in Jack's direction.

This left him super confused as to how to respond. *I mean…* Jack thought. *Uh… panic… hand… what to do… no thanks… I'm good… leave me alone… what are you doing…? This just got weird.* Jack slowed, visibly not knowing how to respond to the outstretched hand, a move that seemed not to be lost on Theta, who then took the initiative to step toward him and fished a reluctant hand from his side.

"Let's take a look at something." Jack was dying inside. *Much too much.* He was not feeling safe. *You need to back the hell up, lady.*

"This way." She grabbed Jack's hand and led him in the opposite direction of his walk with Banjo earlier that day. Jack acquiesced.

Theta held his hand and walked them down to the lakefront, where Jack could hear the call of loons. This unique bird call was his favorite sound in the world, and it instantly lifted his sense of vitality and wellbeing. Jack exhaled, now realizing he hadn't been breathing deeply. A gush of his air met the night with a heavy sigh.

"There we go," Theta said to Jack in a manner that was much too personal and close for Jack's taste. Jack's nerves were rattled from the intrusion, and he found himself a bit relieved when the walking tour stopped. His relief was short-lived.

"Take off your shoes." Theta said.

"I'm sorry… what?" But Jack's words were met with the void of her as Theta was already halfway to the water.

"Jack…" her soft song rang across the lake. "Come. Ong Namo Guru Dev Namo."

Mother of Saint Francis in weirdness, fuck-fuckia. Jack had a habit of making up new swear sentences that amused him. It was a perk he had assigned to moments of unpleasantness. It was like a little gift he could give himself when things weren't great.

Banjo was crazy for this adventure, and he strained the leash in Theta's direction. *Bleh… Why?* Jack thought. He never understood why life always presented all of this interpersonal and talking stuff when he preferred to be alone. That's what felt right to Jack. Taking off his shoes and heading in the direction of the shore, Jack walked into the space next to the tall, elegant woman and froze. That's what Jack could manage. Theta did the rest.

"Here. Come," she said, pulling Jack to the earth. "Sit." She planked her shoes on the grit of the beach and sat on them. Jack did the same while Banjo took a few steps into the shallows and stood, slow wagging his tail and breathing the night air. The tranquility of the space was undeniable. "Sit, sit, sit," she continued, demonstrating how Jack was to arrange himself just like her. "Ong Namo Guru Dev Namo. Close both your eyes…"

Jack's energy flashed as he beat back the moment with an anxious, "I only have one eye."

"If you say so, Jack." Theta's voice softened her eyes in meditation. "Ong Namo Guru Dev Namo. I bow to creative wisdom. I bow to the divine teacher within."

God. Now what? Jack thought, still very uncomfortable with what was happening. He watched her face as she dropped into stillness. Jack internally rumbled and protested. Not only did he not want to meditate with this woman, but he also wanted to get up and jog back to the campsite. He eventually decided that would be even more awkward. Besides, Banjo was enjoying himself, and Jack wanted to watch his buddy smile for a bit.

"Come," Theta said, not opening her eyes. The command confused Jack since they were already next to one another.

Come where exactly? Jack thought.

"Come." She was perfectly still, so Jack played along, closing his eyes. Sensing this, Theta gave them a few minutes to feel the space, allowing Jack to settle slightly, not a familiar space for Jack. Usually, there were too many jagged bits. Too many parts of himself that weren't acceptable.

A few minutes later, Theta asked, "What is real for you here, Jack?"

"I'm sorry…?" Jack paused and tried to reframe the question internally. "Well, I guess it's a nice night and all, but maybe that's not what you mean. Should I get…?"

He was interrupted quietly yet directly. "Jack…" Silence.

"Oh, you mean like here today stuff. I mean, there was this moment this morning when I was jogging around…." He was doing his best not to show his nerves.

He was cut off again with her quiet, "Jack…."

"I'm sorry now. What was the question exactly? What is real for me here? I guess…."

One more time, Theta called him out without opening her eyes. "Jack…."

Jack was more confused now than when they began. He sat in silence, feeling hurt, terribly awkward, and well aware that whatever words he offered to the moment were going to be seen as "wrong" by the tall crazy lady. *People,* Jack thought. *Why? I am terrible at this 'getting away from it all thing.'*

The moment was still. The loons echoed on the lake as the gloaming folded into the last light. Jack sat wondering if he shouldn't have just minded his own business. "It's just that…."

Theta opened her eyes to focus them on Jack. She reached over and put one finger on his lips to silently hush him. Jack's eyes went wide in surprise for a second, but then he settled back into the moment as she put another finger on the center of his forehead just above the brows.

Tapping Jack's lips with her finger, she said, "I bow to the creative wisdom. I bow to the divine teacher within. This moves back." Then tapping his forehead with the other finger continued, "This moves forward."

"Oh," said Jack. "It's like that class I took with… Oh, that's right! I remember it now. Yeah, they had that saying there too. What was it? The Adi Mehandi or Ali Babbah… or something?"

Theta exhaled and turned back to face the lake. "Jack. Be still. Be here."

The "be here" felt familiar to him for some reason. Suddenly, he remembered the woman on the Ferry. Jack thought back to their odd encounter and her gesture of an unexpected gift. He felt for the leather strap still tied around his neck. "*Be here*," it said to him. Jack's response was, "*Okay, got it.*" Jack pretended to sit with a still mind, practicing how to "be here." Again, he failed miserably.

The noise of Jack's mind raced from what he had done this morning to memories of Dennis to Banjo, and what the heck was he doing now? Where was he? Jack scanned the surroundings, only to find his buddy a few feet away napping. *Okay, good,* Jack thought. *Now, what is this exactly? I mean, this lady seems legit, but… I mean….*

In the end, Jack felt he should have just stuck to himself.

Sensing her neighbor's noise, Theta said quietly, "Ong Namo Guru Dev Namo. This goes back. This comes forward." However, she said it without touching his lips or forehead this time. There was a long silence. "Repeat it, Jack."

Fine, He thought. "Ong Namo Guru Dev Namo. I bow to creative wisdom. I bow to the divine teacher within."

"Good. Now… Be here, with me."

This is nice-ish, thought Jack. He breathed deeply and remembered the encounter with his neighbor Al and their conversation about Shuswap. *Shoe-what-now?* Jack internally chuckled every time the memory struck him. *Shoe-what-now?*

"Ong Namo Guru Dev Namo. I bow to the creative wisdom. I bow to the divine teacher within. This goes back. This comes forward."

Yeah, yeah, lady… I just want to enjoy the moment. It's so crazy how some people just feel like they can always interrupt, Jack thought to himself.

"This goes back. This comes forward." Theta breathed again into the night air.

The routine was getting old to Jack, and he was feeling the day being leached out of him now that it was dark, and he was starting to feel a bit tired.

"This goes back. This comes forward."

Jack gave up just enough to focus on her words. *What exactly?* he thought. *This being my mouth goes back. Back where exactly? Like into my neck?* He wasn't sure but tried to focus on a general idea of his mouth going backward.

"Your voice is what to abandon first."

Ooh… my voice, Jack thought. *Not my mouth or lips. Yeah, sorry, that was a bit confusing but okay, let's roll with that.*

Jack tried sitting without his voice. While he easily managed to sit without speaking, the chatter of his mind wouldn't allow him to achieve anything that approximated stillness. This wasn't lost on Theta.

"Jack," she said, turning to face him again. "Can you quiet the noise inside you?"

Ha! Jack thought. *The noise inside me. That's a weird thing to say. Noise? Noise. I mean, like what noise exactly? I'm sitting here perfectly….*

Theta shifted to be in front of him and placed her fingers back on his head and lips. She didn't say anything; she simply breathed, which seemed to be a deliberate instruction. "Quiet. Be still, Jack. Let it happen. You're okay."

Jack's eyes opened, and he moved away from her in a bit of a panic, but she didn't give any effort to stand or move from her place. "Yeah, well, it's getting kinda late, so maybe we should just head back or something," Jack said standing, awkwardly dusting himself off.

"Just do me one favor before we go," she said, smiling.

Oh, my hell. What is it with these people? For the briefest moment, Jack wondered if there was much difference between this lady and Papa Olson back at the campsite. They both had a clear agenda, and they both thought nothing of forcing it onto a stranger. But, somehow, Jack realized, Theta's message and methods were slightly less offensive. It probably was because their thoughts weren't based in a community that demands forgiveness as a path to salvation, because for one to demand forgiveness, means they also demand sin, or something to forgive—and Jack refused to see his creation as needing such density of thought.

Ugh. Fine, Jack thought as he sat back down.

"Look at your boy." Theta prompted. Jack did. "How is he? What's he doing?"

"Umm… you know… he just hangs out, sleeps quite a bit. Of course, he's ten now… so.…"

Theta raised her hand to silence Jack. "Look closely, Jack. Look at your boy. How is he being?"

Now totally out of his comfort zone and tired of being silenced, Jack sat confused. Finally, he exhaled and looked at Banjo.

"There!" Theta said. "You were silent for a second. Did you feel that? Can you do it for a second more?"

Okay, time to go, Jack thought. "Yep. Totally awesome. Thanks, but I think it's time to head back." He stood, put his shoes on, and brushed himself off.

Theta stood as well, grabbed her shoes without putting them on, and continued down the path. "This way," she said. Jack followed, like the lost tend to do.

Theta was soon in front of the Olson's campground. The lights of the movie flashed in the night while blockbuster bangs rang through the crisp night.

"Come. Sit."

"I was just going to.…" Jack offered, trying to get out of the moment and just return to peace and solace. But unfortunately, he also realized that solace would be a bit of a challenge while the movie clamored on. But, again, he had nowhere to go or anything better to do.

"Just for fun, let's try this one more time," she said, patting the ground next to her. Jack sat. "Put your son Banjo in front of you, close your eyes, and detach. See if you can get less noisy even in this location. Be Banjo. Adopt his calm manner."

Having gone through this exercise with her once before, Jack had a reasonably good understanding of what this was. He sat, closed his eyes and focused on Banjo and not the surrounding movie-noise chaos. "Do it with me." Theta scooted in front of him, grabbed Jack's hands in one hand, and placed her fingers from the other on his lips and forehead. For Jack, this was an intrusion, and he couldn't help but feel angsty and uncomfortable. He shook off her hands in protest.

"So, Theta… I'm not exactly sure what you're hoping to accomplish with this little make-a-wish, hug-a-tree experiment, but it's kinda making me uncomfortable."

Theta paused for a minute before choosing her next words. "You are uncomfortable, Jack. It reads all over you but especially in your mind, which seems very cluttered and noisy. Does that feel like a fair assessment?" Jack wasn't moving. "Understand, I'm not judging you but rather sharing my experience of you back to you, and my assessment in the short time I've known you is that you're uncomfortable for no reason or any reason. You seem to wish for alone time but somehow even that is elusive to you."

Feeling like he had just been caught in a lie, Jack agreed by nodding his head but then followed up with, "Sorry, it's not that… I guess I do not fully understand what we're doing here."

Theta looked into Jack's eyes. "You'll never gain peace out here," she indicated to the movie screen, "when there's no peace in here." She tapped his forehead with her finger.

"Yeah, sure… it's just that, you know, with my past and stuff, family stuff and you know…." Jack stopped talking mid-sentence.

"Jack, I see who you are to this world." Pause. "A place that is very difficult to navigate when you're a sensitive boy." Jack started to cry quietly, which caught him totally off guard. "Never listen to those who make you doubt who you are, especially those who offer judgment and dense, dark energy. It's up to you to save yourself from that." She paused again. "If you so choose. C'mon. Just one more time. Repeat. Adi Mantra."

Theta put herself next to Jack, who felt like a total dope. Finally, Jack resigned himself and closed his eyes while his ear filled up with the clang and clatter of the film.

"Adi Mantra," Jack repeated.

"I bow to the creative wisdom. I bow to the divine teacher within," Theta lead.

He repeated, "I bow to the creative wisdom. I bow to the divine teacher within."

"Ong Namo Guru Dev Namo."

"Ong Namo Guru Dev Namo," he said with eyes closed, cleansing his mind with a newfound tone.

"There. Focus on Banjo. Be still with a quiet mind like him."

Jack exhaled and did his best to further clear his mind, where in the darkness of his mind, a pink vastness revealed itself for a very brief second. It sounded like the ocean and was very calming to Jack. He opened his eyes, and saw Theta who was joyful and quiet. He could tell in her glee that he had done it if only for the briefest of seconds.

"You, my friend, are going to be a monk in the world. I believe you have that in you. Well, actually, I believe we all do, but there's depth in you, Jack. All that pain and noise…? It's just the rubber band on a slingshot. I promise you that the height one can hit in life is tied to how far down one has been pulled and stretched down. Once you find this, you'll discover the purpose of your past. But it'll be up to you, Jack."

They stood and shook off the dirt and sand. Jack headed for his truck but turned around briefly to say goodbye to Theta. She was gone. Jack was confused when he felt a hand on his shoulder.

"Here, I want this to be your thinking cap." She pulled out from behind her a beat-down old straw cowboy hat. Jack laughed.

"Oh, wow. This is amazing. I love it. It'll be very cool on my drives."

"I'm glad you like it. Wear it when you do your driving or thinking or wherever you connect with something other than yourself."

"I appreciate that, Theta. You're very kind."

She was already halfway back to her VW when she turned and told Jack, "Be good to yourself, Jack. Banjo is your teacher from now on. So be Banjo until you find your way." And then she was gone.

LEDGE

The next morning Jack woke to find Jonathan and Theta had taken off. The Olsons were still present in boisterous clamor, which only made Jack want to get the hell out of there. So after a quick walk with Banjo, a jog, and a shower, Jack drove to a gas station for gasoline and the other fuel, a.k.a. coffee.

Jack was hoping to connect with Mellie in YoHo, but she was on a trip to see her mother and wouldn't be back for another week or two. This left Jack some time to explore the lake and surrounding area. After the last night, however, public campsites were no longer on the must-do list. So Jack drove around the lake to look for a private hang-out spot that might serve as a free campsite for the night. Rounding the tip of the lake, Jack found just the place.

"What do you think, boy?" Jack said to Banjo as they jumped out of the truck, both excited for their new sequestered home. Jack did a final walk around the site to make sure no one could spot them from the road. They were well hidden, and Jack exhaled, knowing they'd have time to enjoy the lake and just be.

Jack found a sandy spot for the campfire and secured the kitchen items under his Blazer so he could hop in the back and put on his swimsuit. It was time for some R&R. He grabbed a wakeboard from his truck and headed out to the shallows. Banjo, as always, walked into the water to his knees and stood there with his tail slowly wagging as

Jack dove in and headed out with his float. Reaching the middle of the lake, he pushed the foam board between his legs and sat up to enjoy the view. Jack paused and breathed out people, stress, judgment, and his past, much of which he was still processing.

You're not good-looking enough, to also be an asshole, Jack remembered.

We're judged by the truths we tell ourselves…

Banjo is your teacher now.

Who are you Jack?

Be here.

It all ran through his noisy mind as he self-soothed and tried to make it make sense. He laid back on his board and took in the warmth of the sun on his face. Peace.

Jack and Banjo spent the better part of the day relaxing, taking naps, and exploring their surroundings.

Finally, at last light, they headed out for their evening stroll then jumped into the back of the vehicle to sleep. Rolling onto his side, Jack put an arm over his pup for warmth and moved into quiet reflection.

"Banjo is your teacher now," the woman had told him. He still wasn't quite sure what that meant. He repeated the thought, searching his mind for meaning. Jack looked at his dog but not just superficially, for he knew that wasn't what Theta meant.

In retrospect, the memories of her intrusiveness and his discomfort were gone. Instead, the chance encounter with the woman had moved him. He remembered feeling warm energy from her like a loving parent who exuded empathy and care. Whenever Jack felt this from others, it was painful because it called out what he hadn't received at home. He had grown accustomed to telling himself that it didn't matter because none of it was real. Jack was good at that. Sometimes his only comfort came from walling himself off from the deadness within him.

Jack held Banjo under one arm while his mind escaped him and returned to one of the flashbacks that would often haunt his soul and curl its way into his consciousness…

"*Now, Jack,*" *his mother's tone was sharp.* "*Whatever made you think that you could take the car? You don't even have your driver's license yet.*"

"*I have my learners permit, and it's not like I don't know what I'm doing. It was just down the road and back. Not a huge deal. Stop freaking out.*" *But his parents were freaking out, more because they had been taken for fools than the actual borrowing of the car.*

"*What does Psalm 34:13 tell us, Jack?*" *his stepfather said, clearly displeased.*

Jack was silent, which was his usual course of action for moments such as this.

"*Keep your tongue from evil and your lips from telling lies.*"

"*Yes, sir.*" *Jack said, not lifting his gaze but thinking,* This fucking guy. This moron quotes about 'telling lies' when I just fully admitted what happened and why. Idiot.

Jack's mother left the room as his stepfather moved toward him. "*I've about had it with you, Jack. Why are you constantly acting out? This is unacceptable behavior for a man of God.*"

Fuck your God, *Jack thought, preparing himself for what usually came next, but then Reverend Daw stopped just short of Jack's face.*

"*This time, there will be real consequences, Jack. You need to learn your place.*" *Jack could feel his stepfather's breath slap at his face. He wasn't scared. He was done with this asshole.* Walls up. Nothing is here. Nothing is real…

It was roughly 7:00 PM when Jack's mother stepped into his room, where he was lying on the floor listening to music. "*Jack, I'm heading out. Your father…*" *Jack chaffed against the word* "*father.*" *The best he could accept is what the Reverend was to him biologically, and that was not a father. In truth, he was Jack's uncle. Nope. The guy in this house was not his father and never would be. His father was kind and warm and often spoke with a twinkle in his eye. Jack admired him and loved to recall the few moments he'd had with him. The things he could remember were few — the relaxing warmth of resting his head against his dad's big hairy chest chief among them. They were good memories of what life was like before his unexpected death on their bathroom floor.*

As Jack listened to his music with the sound of his mother's car trailing off into the distance, his stepdad walked into his room with disdain in his eyes.

Sitting on Jack's bed, he said, "Come sit next to me." This was a sentence the Reverend would say just before the shit hit the proverbial fan. This was always an entrée into a talking to or verbal smack-down. Jack didn't care. He was impervious to it now. "We have a problem, son…"

Gross, *Jack thought.* Son. Not in this lifetime. Fuck off.

"…and I think you need to…" another sentence left to hang in the air unfinished.

When he could get really honest with himself, Jack didn't understand why he was acting out, and it wasn't until much later in life that it finally made sense. He was in his late twenties when he read the saying, "The child who is not embraced by the village will burn it down to feel its warmth." When he read that, his behavior as a young man became understandable.

Reverend Daw grabbed Jack by the hand and led him down the wood-paneled hall as his teenage mind flashed through every scenario of what might happen next. Jack realized they were alone, and he fought as his stepdad practically threw him by the arm into his parent's bedroom. Almost hitting the floor, Jack steadied himself and stood to face "dear 'ol dad."

"I know what you are, Jack." His stepfather was fuming. "You know…"

There was a long pause as the Reverend looked skyward and ran his hand through his hair, exasperated. "One rumor I might be able to over-look, but…." More silence. Jack began to cry silently while his stepfather adopted a back and forth pace. "This boy, Sheldon. Deacon Ward's son." Jack's guts shook. "When I heard about…." His stepfather couldn't say the words. "Jack, come here." He did as the Reverend asked while the big man scooped up Jack's hands in his. "We need to pray."

Pray? *Jack thought,* or prey? *His eyes darted around the room, searching for an escape. He felt trapped and unsafe, but perhaps this is the atrocity he was guilty of for seeking out a corner of honest affection in this world. Something Sheldon offered, but a crime for which Jack would be severely punished. He understood how this worked.*

"*Dear heavenly father…*" his stepfather began quietly. "*Please be with our dear son Jack for he is lost and needs to be returned to the fold. We ask for your merciful blessings, and please help our family be righteous in all our endeavors.*" Jack's hands were starting to tremble as the man began shouting in his face while holding them tighter and tighter. "*2nd Chronicles 7:14 tells us, 'If my people who are called by my name humble themselves and pray and seek my face…'*" Jack's hands were now being crushed in the grasp of his stepdad's fists. The cracking of joints was silenced by a white-knuckled death grip now completely covering his hands. In the same manner as the crucifix, this was devised to deliver maximum pain.

"*Dad?*" Jack whispered.

"*…and turn from their wicked ways, THEN! Then, I will hear from heaven and WILL forgive their sin.*"

"*Dad? You're hurting me.*" Jack managed as tears rolled down his face.

"*Jack! You must know what danger your soul is in and as the man of this….*"

"*DAD!*" Jack yelled. "*You're hurting me!*"

Ignoring his stepson's words and doubling down on his issuance of frustration, the man shouted, "*You are an embarrassment, Jack! An abomination!*"

Jack knew this is who he was to the Reverend by his mere existence.

"*You must repent!*" The good Reverend threw Jack to the ground, knocking the wind out of him. Jack turned to face his red-faced stepfather, but found he was unable to put any weight on his wrists. "*You must prostrate yourself before the Lord!*"

Jack tried to recover and shake out his hands… he wasn't sure if anything was broken; the pain was scorching. "*Dad, please…*" he said, but then *his stepfather's hands wrapped their weight around his neck with shocking strength as the total weight of the man descended upon Jack's teenage frame pressing and squashing his face into their tainted orange carpet.*

"Prostrate yourself before the Lord all mighty, Jack!" Jack was just trying to assess the situation with his mangled hands and throbbing wrists, but so much was swirling and tumbling as his stepfather wrestled him into a prone position before the cross hanging above his parents' bed. Jack fought back, making his stepfather all the more enraged. It was clear that what was "right" or righteous had to be taken into the elder's hands.

"PROSTRATE YOURSELF, JACK! Show me you are willing to repent for your sins! You must."

Jack wouldn't. Not willingly. He wanted nothing to do with this.

The next thing Jack could recall was coming to and being unsure of where he was. The waking up was warm and serene, like waking up from an afternoon nap. He just wanted to go back to sleep, but then the moment of where he was all came rushing back. He had only been choked out and unconscious for a few seconds, but he would always recall the orange glow that moved through his spirit and echoed like the tinkling of bells on a summer breeze. Jack longed to return there… And that was the moment Jack found the other side of his mind. Previously, he didn't know it was there. He didn't know one could slip behind the wall of this world into another. He didn't know this was the escape hatch; until now.

Gaining his senses, Jack realized what was going on as his stepfather was on top of him, using all of his weight to force Jack onto all fours and violently force his face into the carpet. Jack's hands, couldn't hold him up. He couldn't put weight on them, his red wrists were crushed and possibly broken. Jack wasn't sure of the extent of the damage, but that was impossible to assess while his face was being repeatedly slammed into the ground. From this spread position, Jack realized that his stepfather had pulled down his pants and was entering him from behind. Jack screamed from a place of unholy hell and tried desperately to fight, but the emotional betrayal of what he was experiencing robbed him of his strength. It took everything from him. The crushing emotion of the moment left Jack with only one option, which was to heave and sob. He tried to will himself back into oblivion – to seek out the orange light just on the other side. In doing so, Jack became the embodiment of nothing. He went slack, and he left himself back in that room, a room where his body might be, but he was not. Not now. Not during this.

The next thing Jack remembered was being alone in his parent's bedroom. With red tender hands, he quickly gathered his jeans back up around his waist and bolted. He could feel the mixture of blood and the Reverend's semen draining out of him as it seeped into his pant leg.

Jack bolted, only to be stopped by both his parents, who were in a quiet hush in the corner of the living room, essentially blocking his path to the front door. But why was his mother there? They both turned in unison as Jack eyed wildly at alternative escape routes. He was utterly unable to understand why his mother was home. Was her leaving a ruse? How long had she been home? Did she actually go? Did she hear his screaming? Nothing made sense at that moment.

"Jack," his mother started. "We know…"

And that was all Jack was going to accept or allow. He was not going to accept any more Goddamn words from these hateful people. He rushed the door, hunkering down to deliver all the force he could muster. Given his track background and experience in field sports, his power in this arena was significant and he intended to inflict as much pain as he could. His Taurean nature was alight—his life force catching an unknown fire.

His mind ran wild; it was as nature would have prescribed, and in this place he connected to something deeply feral. He was no longer someone's child. No. It was far too late for that. Before his parents, he was a wounded teenage beast that seethed in the living room. Jack ran, then slammed into his parents, knocking his mother over a chair while his stepfather was knocked into the wall behind him. Jack kept running right out the front door.

The last thing he remembered about that God-forsaken house was his mother screaming after him out the front door, "God is going to get you!"

Jack was fine with that. Let their cunt God come after him. He would body slam that mother fucker too. Jack had found his hellfire, and it wasn't going dim any time soon. He ran faster than he knew possible and further than he knew he could go. Jack didn't stop until he reached the city. A journey that took two days on foot.

Years later, when his mind would briefly pause on that moment, he would recall how it was the most confusing thing that had ever happened to him. Why hadn't he fought harder? Why was this betrayal so deep that all he could do was lay there and cry? Why had he essentially allowed this to happen? How could someone think their anger was worthy of inflicting this kind of pain? Why was his body of so little worth or consequence? How could a self-described "man of God" deliver such a punitive measure by force, by rod, and by the staff of man?

DUSTED

After a week of exploring and campfires and hobo packs and sunburns, it was time to move on. Jack knew Mellie would be back from her trip soon, and at this point, Jack thought it might be okay to be in the presence of another human.

Mornings were always a special time for Jack and Banjo. They'd walk together and have chats about how messed up the world was and how glad they were to be off that treadmill. Jack hoped out loud that he would make it to a bank in the next town to make sure the Plexus Workers' Compensation checks were still rolling in. Jack also wanted to head to the grocery store and the Provincial sanctioned liquor store (because Hail Canada! and its lack of freedom to purchase liquor elsewhere). Lastly, they'd make their way to the a weed dealer that he learned about from a local. Jack took the buffet approach to few things in life, but weed was one exception. So that was it. Their next stop was set, and other than that, there was little need for human interaction. For them, it was just easier that way.

They had been on the road about two hours when they pulled into Revelstoke. Like many Canadian towns in this part of the world, it was a place that felt like winter, even in summer. There was a decent grocery store in town and a few restaurants Jack had heard about, so they decided to make a pit stop for supplies and lunch.

"Stay here, buddy. I'll be right back," Jack said, giving Banjo a kiss while popping on his "thinking cap." He then closed the truck and headed into the local hardware store, where he helped a "gimpy dude" through the front door. Jack was immediately disappointed in himself for thinking the word "gimpy."

Whatever, he thought, wishing to dismiss it lightly but knowing what he had just done was call himself gimpy, lame, or fucked-up. It was a match. He looked into the reflection of the glass door and what stared back was gimpy. Gross. Defective. Broken. "It doesn't matter," he told himself as he continued into the store.

After wandering around a bit, Jack finally laid his hands on the rope, rods, reels, and chisel he needed. He was making his way back to the front of the store when he caught a glimpse of something out of the corner of his eye. He turned. It was the disabled guy taking a tumble. *Oh shit*, Jack thought, running in his direction as the man on crutches fell to the floor.

"Are you okay?" was what Jack led with as he quickly searched the man for blood and bruises. "You don't seem to be cut or anything."

The man laid still with his green eyes focused blankly on the ceiling, a move that Jack found quite distressing. "Are you okay?" Jack repeated as the auburn haired man started to chuckle.

"Am I okay?" More chuckling… "Am I okay? Sure fuck. Why not? Yep, mate. Just a few crutches and legs that don't work right but yeah … I'm bloody fantastic."

Jack was silent. "Can I help or…" Jack felt horrible that he had mentally disparaged and looked down on this guy when he was this guy for all intents and purposes.

But for the grace of God go I, Jack thought. *Ugh… I'm such an asshole… Maybe Em was right.*

"Sure, mate," the man said with a slight accent. "I could use a hand up."

Jack pulled the man up, doing his best not to club the guy with his cast as it dawned on him that they were roughly the same age. Jack was maybe his junior by a decade but possibly less. It also wasn't lost on him that he was just served a dose of panic that he's usually on the other side of.

"There you go." Jack lightly dusted the guy off, ensuring he had his crutches back in hand. "My name's Jack."

"I'm Thad," he said, looking distrustingly in Jack's direction. "Anyhow… thanks. Sorry about that. Sometimes… well, it's complicated."

"Is it now?" Jack teased.

"I'm sorry, Jack, was it? I appreciate your help, but yes… it's fucking complicated." Thad turned, brushing Jack's hands off him. "I'm good, thanks."

"Hey, listen," Jack stepped back in front of him. "I was just trying to make light of the situation. No hard feelings, okay?"

"Fine. Whatever. Please just leave me alone."

With that, Jack realized the guy was embarrassed and was walking towards the exit. Jack wondered if he had forgotten something or if it had been their interaction that was making this guy so uncomfortable that he was now leaving. He didn't know, but it all made him feel very sad. Now he was the asshole. He was the lady on the ferry. He was the Olsons. He was the unrelenting jerk when someone just wanted to be left alone. "*Shit,*" Jack thought as he watched Thad hobble out onto the street.

Damn, damn, damn, damn, damn! Jack thought. He tried to tell himself it was okay, but he knew by firsthand experience that what he had just done was far from it. *Hubris,* Jack thought. *That's what always takes me down. I think I'm hot shit, that I'm strong, and I got it all together… That I'm doing okay….* Jack hung his head. *When I know none of that is true.*

In that moment, Jack fully grasped how he was often just a little boy standing in the dark whistling, telling himself that he was okay.

Jack felt horrible as he collected his items, paid, and then left. *Now, where was that lunch place again…?*

PERFECT

Jack pulled the Blazer out on the main downtown road looking for Rusty's Burger, the drive-in that still served the old-school soft serve. *God, that brought back great memories,* Jack thought as he found it, parked, and headed inside.

"Two Jerry Burgers and a medium diet coke… and fries… and gimme a Peanut Chocolate swirl. Um… in a cup, please, not a cone. I need to finish…." Jack just stopped talking like he usually did when he felt uncomfortable.

He paid and found a table near a window where he could sit with his back against the wall and keep an eye on his truck and Banjo. Jack was about halfway through his mess of chow when he looked up and saw a recognizable figure. *Shit… It's the handicapped guy,* Jack thought, rushing his final few bites. *Damn it.*

Thad was ordering a meal for himself while Jack couldn't stop watching it all unfold. *"How's he going to carry that to the table? I mean, yeah, I can… but how's he going to…?"* Jack stopped his thoughts and put his head down to try and finish lunch quickly, then exit. He looked up again, wiping his face when the two men caught sight of one another; their eyes locked. Jack tried to manage a meager tight smile, but it came across as painfully uncomfortable and resigned. Jack noticed Thad gave no expression in return and kept working his way around the seating to find one where he could keep an eye on the lady who had taken his order. Thad looked briefly deflated when Jack caught his gaze and indicated that the seat across from him was free. "Care to join me?" Jack asked.

Thad stood silent for a minute. He was clearly reviewing scenarios.

"Come. Sit." Jack smiled. "It was Thad, right?"

Thad didn't move, not trusting what this exchange was about. Jack stood. "Do me a favor. I hate eating alone." He motioned to the empty seat. Jack did his best to seem trustworthy. Thad finally stepped in his direction.

"How about I buy you lunch?" Jack said, helping the man sit.

"Well, I just paid … so."

"Ah. Yes. Of course," Jack said while simultaneously thinking, *I'm a complete moron.* "Hey, listen … I'm sorry if what …."

Jack was cut off by a still unimpressed and quiet-hearted Thad saying softly into his chest, "Don't worry about it."

"Can I tell you something?" Jack started trying to see under Thad's reddish eyebrows. Pause. "I get that you probably don't trust what people say to you. I get that when someone tries to make light of your physical issues that you assume they're mocking you."

"Why?" Thad asked. "Why do you get that? Because of your fucked up face? You think that's the same, do you? Because it's not."

"*Argghhh…*"' Jack thought. "*Why is this just all coming out wrong?*" But in an instant, his internal voice reminded him of what this moment is like when he's on the receiving side of this conversation. So the answer to his question was immediate as the thought, *This moment is weird because I'm weird in this moment.*

Jack took a deep breath and regained himself. "Nah. Oh sure… it's a shit show up here." Jack poked his right temple. "But that's not what I'm talking about." Jack reached across the table to touch Thad's shoulder. "I get it. Your life is super complicated, and none of this is easy. I get that there are probably days where you're exhausted from your situation even before you get out of bed." Silence. "I'm just trying to let you know that in a way, I relate to what that's like. Can you just let your guard down for a second so we can talk?"

Thad twisted in his seat, took a breath, then set his crutches to the side where they could rest against the wall.

"I wasn't making fun of you. Just, you know, trying to make you feel better, let you know that the situation was okay. To be, I guess, light in the moment… but I also know what it's like for others to wing off the course of your reality and deliver fake observations in an attempt to spare your feelings." Jack retrieved his hand to point at his face. "It's not just this I have to deal with in life. And yeah, you don't get a break from your physical issues, whereas I often do… and I'm so sorry that you have that burden to bear." Silence. "Do you have people at home to help out?"

The long pauses between them were notable yet also not completely uncomfortable as they both often needed time to choose the right words or process what was being said. Thad's food arrived as Jack noted he didn't answer that last question.

"If it's okay, you eat while I talk," a statement that was out of character for the usually reserved and tight-lipped Jack, but this handicapped man was damn handsome. *Maybe something worth pursing…* Jack thought as Thad nodded and unwrapped his burger.

"This isn't something I normally talk about. I just don't usually think about it, but maybe …" Jack changed tact as the voice in his head prompted, *Stop being weird, just be real. Call a thing a thing so you can be in his reality and not a sugary version thereof.*

Jack continued, "Let me cut to the chase… I've been living with a potentially crippling neurological movement disorder that will most likely put me on par with your troubles by the time I'm your age." Thad stopped eating but kept his head down. "It's rare, and there is no cure and very little research on it because it's not fatal. However, that doesn't mean it's not bad or life-altering because it is progressive, and it's already in every Goddamned corner of me. And yeah… I get that I look fine."

"Trust me," Thad interrupted and nosed in the direction of Jack's face. "You don't look fine." This caught Jack off guard, and he sputtered a dumb laugh in spite of himself.

"Touché." Jack smiled hard, knowing he had finally broken through to the man's spirit. *There he is,* Jack thought. *He's still willing to give me a chance. He's just guarded, which I get considering our first interaction.*

Thad smiled, too, as the tension between the two men receded.

"To proactively answer your questions, no, it's not because of my accident. It's a completely separate issue. I've been living with the brain thing for just over five years, whereas my accident happened when I was a kid. And if I'm honest…." Jack was going all in to gain the man's trust. "I don't know how much time I have left before my body stops working altogether. It's…" Jack started into his dessert, pausing briefly to reorganize his thoughts. "If I take how this thing has progressed over the past few years and work that trajectory forward… I estimate I have about five good years left. The doctors, well… fuck them. They don't seem to have any answers."

Thad took another bite of his sandwich while they sat in silence. It seemed fitting to be quiet for a second so that what still hung in the air could be mentally dealt with – an exercise more for Jack than the foreign man.

"I'm sorry, Jack."

"Yeah, me too, but for a long time, I honestly thought I was going to die. The fact that what I have isn't going to kill me is all the gratitude I need for the rest of my life. Sure, my life will look very different than it does now or how I thought it might look in the future, but I'll still be here. I still have a chance at a family, and who knows… maybe kids." Much to Jack's surprise, he involuntarily started crying – a move that gave Thad the opportunity to step in and show compassion back, whereas up to this point, that energy had only flowed in one direction.

"Hey, mate." Thad wadded up his burger wrapper and pushed it aside. "I didn't know." Jack sat back and exhaled, hoping to end his unexpected emotional purge.

"Sorry… It's just more complicated when I look normal, and people just assume that… It's just a lot to deal with." Silence. "Inside." Silence. "So, when I saw your situation, I felt like I could talk to you, but then I know I was way too familiar and casual when you didn't know I am dealing with something similar… well, maybe not totally… I just thought we could maybe relate. You know … to the struggle … and again … I know…." Jack just wanted to shut the hell up, but his brain couldn't seem to find the end of his current rambling, unending sentence.

"Jack. It's okay. And I'm sorry if I misread your attempt at being funny, but you bloody well know that you don't just come upon a stranger who's in a moment of a crisis and start making jokes about what the piss is happening. That's not helpful, Jack."

"I know, I know, and I've said the same thing to those around me … I just never expected I'd be on the other side of it. It's an easier mistake to mess up on that end than I had thought. I'm sorry. I guess I felt like we were on the same level, but of course, you had no way of knowing that."

"Well, mate, I do now." Smiles escaped their walls despite their best efforts.

"So, what's your story? You always been a wreck?" Jack's eyes twinkled from his joke, making Thad laugh.

"Yep, since birth. I got tangled up, and since I was being born at my parent's cottage, there wasn't anyone to figure out what was happening until it was too late."

Jack eyed Thad. "So, is this just normal for you, or does it feel like you've lost a part of you? Maybe a part that you didn't even get to know or experience."

"Dunno. I never framed it that way exactly, but yeah, I guess sometimes I'm somewhat angry for being dealt a shit hand. You?"

Jack collected himself, not exactly sure how to respond to his own damn question focused back on him. "I guess, same. Yeah, I'm sometimes bitter that this has been thrust upon me. I mean, I never asked for this. Some days it just feels like my body is rotting from the inside and all I can do is watch it all evaporate. I don't know if it's different if you've had something from birth or if I might struggle more because I'm losing a life that I once had. I dunno."

The two let a moment go by, then Thad returned his gaze to Jack. "Has there ever been an upside for you in all this?"

The question took Jack aback then he snorted an involuntary laugh. "Upside? Dude…?"

"I'm serious. Have you ever tried to put it in that context, to, you know, reframe it? Maybe give it purpose? Give it meaning or reason for showing up that way."

Now Jack was feeling like the one being assaulted.

"Thad. You cannot be serious."

"Have you ever tried to look at it like that? Maybe what you have to overcome is your superpower?"

Instinctively, Jack knew Thad was trying to help, but this was too much. Much too much. Like, "gotta go" too much. Instead of bolting, Jack tried being frank and direct. "If you're making fun … of …" Jack went silent.

"What we both have is a Ph.D. in shitstorm, but if you work with it from that perspective, mate, you might find a new purpose or calling. I think there might be a job or something out there where your special skills in living like this might be of value to someone. Maybe to someone who needs your insight on such things?"

"And how has this angle worked for you?" Jack said flatly.

"Oh, it bloody well hasn't, but I thought it would be big of me to fucking say so." They both laughed. "Regular people can't get what life is like on this side of okay. It's just not possible for someone to understand unless they've lived it."

"That's true."

"There's a game I play when all else is falling apart. It's called "the perfect game." It sometimes helps me shift my perspective around things." Jack was dubious yet curious. "In any given situation, I ask myself, why is this perfect?"

"Such as?" Jack asked.

"Well … as an example, I guess, let's say you have a noon appointment, and the person you're supposed to meet doesn't show up until 12:30."

"And this is perfect how?"

"Well, that's the whole gist of the exercise. Why is this perfect? Was there a point to it? Was there an opportunity in the thirty minutes you had to wait that if the person had been on time, you would have missed out on? Was there a bonus thirty minutes in your day to gaze at the clouds or witness something that you would have otherwise missed? Or was the late person now able to bring something to you that took them the extra time? Or, at minimum, were you able to model for them an example of who you are? There can be endless possibilities for those thirty minutes that you would have missed out on had the person been on time?"

"And this works for you?"

"Sometimes." Thad took a second to find his next words. "Sometimes it does. At least it helps me find purpose in what might otherwise be seen as negative. So let's think about either one of our struggles. Why is it in your life, and why is it perfect?"

Jack sat blinking as he searched for the answer within him. Then, finally, the nudge came from his inner voice. *Say it. Give it voice.* But for Jack, there was no saying it. There was no formulating benefit to the part of him he hated. "I'm not sure."

"Surely, there's got to be some purpose behind your journey on this path."

While Jack wanted to participate in the conversation, he had nothing. He would not give praise or thanks for that thing while it's eating him alive. "There's no upside here, Thad. There's no fucking way I will show gratitude for this putrid bucket of horse shit that the universe decided to dump in my lap, and now you're asking me to call it a bouquet of roses? No."

"Well, think about it. It took me years to find my answer to that question."

"And…?"

"And it's something we each have to answer for ourselves."

"Can you elaborate?" Jack wasn't feeling the love around this conversation. "Sorry, but I just don't see value in that which is leeching the life out of me."

"But is it?" Thad shot back.

"Is it what?"

"Leeching the life out of you." There was new life in Thad's line of questioning because this exchange was now giving his life's conflicts meaning. "You said it wasn't going to kill you, and yet you have framed it in your mind like your life is over. You even said yourself that at worst, your future will just look different than you thought… and that you're grateful that you'll still be here."

"Bleh…" Jack didn't appreciate being taken on like this. "Yeah… I mean, sure. I said that."

"So, were you lying, or do you believe what you said?"

Jack wanted to retreat, but his curiosity was also piqued. "Yes, I said that, and I guess I mean it."

"So that's purpose."

"Thad. I'm sorry, but I just don't see it that way."

"And that's your choice."

There it was. A thing had been called a thing leaving Jack at the intersection of angst and peace. The truth of it pissed Jack off.

Thad continued. "For me, I try and talk to people who need my insight into my journey with this thing. That gives purpose to why I was given this gift."

"Gift?" Jack snorted. "Gift?! Dude, I'm sorry, but I'm not on board with that concept. So, listen, I gotta scoot. Do you need a ride or something? I'm headed East."

It was apparent Thad was disappointed that their conversation was being cut short. "I'm fine. There's a bus that I take…." However, he didn't say where to as Jack stood to excuse himself from whatever this was.

"Anyhow, nice talking to you." Jack grabbed his keys from the table, thinking, *Fuck this guy. Gift. Yeah… sure. Fucking amazing.*

"Likewise… and Jack, thanks for helping me out back at the hardware store. Perhaps your disorder has taught you empathy for others, even strangers like me who need it. Maybe that's the gift? Your ability to know what it's like for people like us. Like I said, people who live on this side of okay. Your trials have taught you that, helped you feel that, and … just know that your approach might need work." Thad sent raised eyebrows to indicate he was joking. "But you said yourself that you could relate to me, even from the first few seconds of our meeting. That's not nothing, Jack."

"Anyhow, as I said, it was nice to meet you. My dog is in the car and… anyhow, bye. It was good talking to you."

"Same, Jack. I wish you well."

Jack smiled and headed for the door.

BUCKLED

Back behind the steering wheel, Jack headed east. They drove for what seemed like the better part of the afternoon before finding the sign for their destination. Finally, they pulled into Kicking Horse Campground, which was surprisingly vacant considering it was mid-May. Jack paid the reservation fee and drove the perimeter, searching for the right spot. An interior campsite was out of the question for the same reason why Jack always sat with his back to a wall. He eyed one that he thought would be perfect and parked for further inspection.

"C'mon, buddy. This is our new home for a bit. Let's go check it out!" Both their spirits smiled as they bounded down the back slope that separated the campground from the National Park. Within seconds they were at the stream they heard from their truck. Banjo waded in, as he always did, up to his knees to stand there and slow-wag his tail. This was contentment… and it wasn't lost on Jack as he stood still to observe this characteristic of, as Theta called him, his son. Jack thought that was a sweet way of putting it and he smiled as they stopped at the water's edge. The rippling gurgle of white noise and water flowed as Jack sat. He thought he saw something notable, but he wasn't sure, and he found he didn't want to move until this inkling either evaporated or resolved itself. Besides, it was such an incredible day; late afternoon, the sun and water streaming, the just born fresh air, and the smell of woods damp and earthen.

"Whatcha doing, bud?" Jack whispered beneath the lap and purl of the water's volume. The dog stood quiet in slow wag, his smiling energy being exhaled from every corner of him. Slow wag. Slow wag. Jack found it almost meditative, but more than that, Jack was for the first time looking at Banjo and sensing his spirit, his being. It was deeper than just the superficial. Jack felt what Banjo felt. He let that in and then breathed it out. Slow wag.

"WooHoo!" Jack yelled as he stood. They took off down the stream where he took in every second of it, his legs strong as everything, fired on max. It was a vision, a dream, and it was a moment Jack hoped he could recall when the time came, and he could no longer walk. Tears of gratitude streamed from him to join the encircling flow splashing behind his running feet.

They had just reached the point when they thought they should turn back when Jack felt it. Twinge.

"No, no, no, no, no, no…," Jack thought. Ugh, I'm such an idiot. Hubris, Jack. You thought you were okay. You can't ever think that," he told himself, frustrated. They turned and started running back. Twinge. "Aaargh," Jack yelled at the trees hoping beyond hope that he'd have at least ten minutes before things took a turn. Unfortunately, he was too far from the truck to get his meds that he took proactively to guard against attacks. "Damn it!" Jack continued to hate on himself. "Fucking idiot." It had been a while since Jack had to deal with this, and as was par for the course, he would forget he was a God damned cripple, mainly because Jack failed to see himself in that light. The fact that his brain melted, misfired, and cratered into a dark abyss was second to that. It just had to be. Jack ran.

Twinge went his right arm. *NO!* he internally yelled, saving his breath. Jack ran faster as his right arm, cast heavy, dropped like a dead tree, almost pulling Jack off his balance. It was gone. It was offline. It was now inaccessible to him.

"Please, God…" Jack ran. "I can't do this by myself." Jack started to cry, making it more difficult to see where he was going. He stepped on a green rock, faltered, and slammed into the icy water. The shock of it fed the onset of his mental decay. Stress always sped up this process. Jack stood, then his left arm dropped also. Both arms were now completely dead. There was no time to think about it. Jack ran in his wet clothes as Banjo led the way barking; doing what he could to protect his owner.

The more Jack watched his functions dissolve like a sugar cube in a glass of water, the harder he cried out of fear and frustration. He knew this had the potential to be bad. He knew that the worst bouts were when one hadn't occurred in a while. It skulked its way into his spine, and then the usual crush began. Jack didn't know how much air it would leave him to breathe. He didn't know if this time it would leave him stone-cold unconscious as it often could do in minutes. Jack screamed, "Help!" Tears flowed heavily on his face making it impossible to see where he was going, and with dead arms, he had no way to wipe away the tears. The world started getting blurrier and more obscured.

"HELP!" Jack screamed as the beast crushed his spine into an ungodly torque. Jack could only walk now as the freeze of his wet clothes scraped at his nervous system. There was no doubt who would win. Jack started to realize he could die out here if he didn't make it back. His right shoulder was now brought down to touch his right knee. He knew he only had a few steps left before it was all gone, and he'd be free flung into the vast oblivion of silent disquiet. With his last seconds, Jack slumped against the base of a tree as Banjo sat next to him, holding guard. A twinge vibrated in his cerebral cortex as everything slipped into black.

NUMEN

Jack was falling, the air punching at him this way and that. He knew the roll and throng of it because it always started the same, only this time Jack sensed he was falling faster, even gaining speed. The windswept vortex of energy around him made it impossible to think. Jack tumbled through the nothing then walloped the ground's surface with his limp form. On this side of his mind, it was never a recognizable place or planet.

Jack's body convulsed as the air was knocked clean out of him, but he didn't fall through the dirt and sand this time. This time the ground was solid enough to hold Jack still for a moment. He opened his eyes. The hills and landscape in the distance were dead, gray, and blue. A place of misery and muddled confusion but still a place that had form, and he was grateful for a moment to collect himself, sit up, and see where he was. He was amazed that the sense of falling had stopped. It had never happened this way before, and in the barren wasteland, Jack searched for something, anything to gain his bearings. The moment was mixed in its messages, for it felt like mercy to be allowed to tell up from down and left from right, but a mercy nonetheless delivered in the valley of death.

Scratching in the rubble of sand and stone, Jack sat up and found a boulder nearby to put his back on, a first in this place, a rare moment to catch his breath. Jack's eyes scanned the horizon where a blue glow shone just beyond the ridge. It seemed to be getting brighter as it crested into view. Jack sensed the source was coming toward him. He searched for his legs to run, but they were nowhere to be found. They were there attached to him but not of him. There were no other options other than to watch the source approach.

This is it, Jack thought to himself. *This is how I go out. Please let Banjo be okay. Please, someone, find him and give him a good home. I love you, buddy. You are my best friend. Maybe we'll meet again on this side. I'll be here waiting for you.* Jack let his mind trail off to just moments before when they had such joy running downstream together as the late spring rays of dappled light touched their faces and lent them warmth.

The figure approached.

Jack didn't dare move or even breathe. He knew this was the end. No one would find him here. Not in time. The figure was now on the valley floor, a football field's distance away and closing in. Jack wondered if this would hurt, but he was resigned to this undeniable fate. He was ready to go.

When the blue light was just a hundred feet away, Jack could begin to make out its details but could also sense its necrosis. She was made of the stuff that raised the hair on the back of your neck, and she was the silent whisper of death. Jack faced it unafraid because, at this point, the gleaming light was the answer to all the problems of his mind.

The radiant aura stepped into view. She was beautiful, and her glow was soft, silent, warm, and deadly. That was Jack's final clue that this was the end. His mind recounted how hypothermia kills, and how the sense of warmth it provides just before death, is the hallmark of its death-grip. Jack welcomed its flushing glare as its first rays began to lull and engulf him. "It's you," Jack thought. "I have been expecting you for a very long time." He reached toward her for the embrace, thinking, "It's time to go home. People have always been foreign to me."

The figure knelt beside him and did just that; the final embrace— the walking home.

In his last moment, both a tear and a smile presented themselves to bear witness to Jack being embraced, one final time. He let go… *It doesn't matter.* He thought as they slipped off into the vastness of the universe. *Nothing is real…*

The hot sensation of a stinging slap grated abrasions across Jack's blue face as he heard in the far-off distance a man's voice screaming, "I'm pretty sure he's dead. Call 911. Hurry!" The man smacked Jack again, only harder this time, hoping for a sign of life. He then started CPR.

A dizzying light for the briefest second seeped through the murk and gloom. The whiteness of it saddened Jack's soul as he searched for the path back to blue, but in time, it faded back to the black of the in-between. In the distance, the last thing Jack could hear was a woman's screams while the man continued with, "Damn it, Linda. Hurry. He's blue and….

Jack felt the void of eternal darkness envelop him as he exhaled his final breath and said his final farewell.

TABLED

"Beep… click, beep. Breath."

"Beep… click, beep. Breath."

"Beep… click, beep. Breath."

Jack sat at the blue water's edge from the beyond, where he observed the room where his body was, but he was not. From this vantage point, he saw his lifeless body being force-fed air and fluids. Tubes and wires scatter-shocked his form and served what purpose they could, for now. Jack saw Mellie enter the room, where she picked up his hand, carefully avoiding the ports and pipelines of hope. Almost a decade had passed since they had been in each other's presence. He grieved for the time and opportunity lost. This last moment they would have is what life would grant, a moment for the briefest thoughts of gratitude. They were blessed with this time to say goodbye, the time to acknowledge the bond that survivors have when, it seems, they only have each other. Childhood outcasts were like that. They clung to each other for the tiniest allotment of humanity.

Mellie had come to the hospital as soon as she heard. It was nothing short of a miracle that when she called Jack's phone, the nurse caring for him had the forethought to press Jack's thumb on the home button that would unlock it. Jack somehow knew this was true, although the details were fuzzy. He asked the beyond to show him what had brought Mellie to his bedside. The blue waters replied in sepia-toned recollection with images of the nurse and Mellie, as if they were in a split-screen television.

The watery blue vision shifted again, and Jack saw his friend standing over his body, crying, when a tall doctor barged into the room.

"Are you his next of kin?" He asked.

"Yes," she lied to take control. "How is he doing?"

"Mr. Daw here almost froze to death. It seems he fell in a river then couldn't make it back to the road or his campsite. Does he have any preexisting conditions that might help us fill in some unanswered questions? The police would like to speak to witnesses if you were there. I know they already have the Petersons' statements. Maybe you can help?"

Jack wondered who the Petersons were before realizing they must be the couple who found him.

"I wasn't there but came as soon as I heard."

"It'll be touch and go for a bit. We're not certain if there will be lasting injuries or brain damage. He was in almost freezing temperatures overnight. That's more than what most humans can survive."

"Did he have his dog with him? Any idea what happened?"

"The Petersons, I believe, are back at the campground where they found him. Also, here's the business card for the officer who is in charge of the investigation. He'll probably want to speak to you. There are still a lot of unanswered questions. It would be good if you could assist them with this." The doctor turned and left the room.

As the door closed behind the doctor, Mellie searched for something in her purse. Jack couldn't quite make out what it was, but it seemed to be a bracelet. She pulled back the blankets and sheets at Jack's feet and tied it loosely around his ankle. Jack wondered why she would put it on his foot when he realized it was because she was afraid someone would see it on his wrist.

Mellie replaced the covers and tucked Jack in the best she could despite the massive number of wires, tubes, and monitoring machines. "C'mon, Jack. Come back to us," she quietly prayed.

The blue bubbling waters shifted again, and he saw the campground where he left his body. Jack watched as Mellie asked the guard at the park entrance if she knew what had happened to Jack and where the Petersons might be.

"Oh, gosh," the camp ranger said in anxious care. "Yes. Yes, come with me. Nick, I need you to take over for a bit. The guy who died yesterday has family here." A "sure thing" was heard in the background.

A few camping spots away, the ranger hailed in the direction of a couple eating breakfast. "Mr. and Mrs. Peterson, we have one of Jack's relatives here."

Not wanting to take the time to correct the woman, Mellie brushed past her to meet them face to face as they stood up from the picnic table.

"I'm Mellie," she said, reaching out her hand. "Thank you for finding Jack."

"Hi, Mellie, I'm Norm, and this is Linda. We are so sorry for your loss."

"Actually, he is alive. I was with him at the hospital yesterday. He's in critical care, and they've put him into a medically induced coma."

Linda then piped in with, "He's alive? I mean… he wasn't when we…" she dropped her gaze. "His dog is the real hero, though. We have him. He's sleeping in our tent. Do you know the dog's name?"

"Banjo," Mellie managed. "Can you tell me what happened exactly?"

"We were hoping to find some answers as well. We honestly don't know what happened. He was just there…." Norm pointed down the steep hill of the backside of the campsite. "I've never seen… anyhow; it was very shocking. We just hoped we found him in time."

Banjo made his way out of the tent, yawning and stretching as if it were just another day. "Come here, boy," Mellie called him as he ambled over for a scratch and a hug. The dog then started for Jack's Blazer. "I have to get back to the hospital to check on how he did last night. Would it be too much of an imposition to ask you to keep Banjo while I get other things sorted out?"

"Oh, no… not at all. We'll take good care of him, but if you can find out if there's food for him, it'll save us trying to figure that out. The idea of a strange dog in our tent with an upset stomach is something we'd rather avoid."

Mellie smiled in agreement. "Let me see what I can work out." She got back in her car and headed back to the hospital.

Jack wasn't sure he wanted to know more, yet he found himself asking once again for the water's crystal blue clarity.

"Hi, I'm here to see the patient in room 307," Mellie announced at the reception desk. The woman waved Mellie in while answering the phone. Arriving at Jack's room, Mellie almost ran into Nurse Farrow. "Oh! Very sorry. Excuse me. How is he today?"

The nurse collected herself and exited the room without responding to Mellie's question. Jack could see alarm register on Mellie's face. She turned to look at Jack lying lifeless in the sterile hospital bed. Wires and tubes and beeping machines were everywhere. "This isn't what Jack would want," she cried, as the grief on her face blossomed like a dark desert flower. "Damn it, Jack. I always worried about you. Turns out, rightfully so." She picked up his hand as she sat.

"Here are Jack's things," the nurse said, re-entering the room. "You'll need to speak with Doctor Metz. He'll be in shortly." Mellie took the plastic bag and reviewed its items. "Keys!" She turned back to face her friend as a tall doctor approached her.

"Ma'am. Your friend here is essentially brain dead, and we'll need to speak to the next to kin."

Mellie didn't respond. Jack then saw the side of Mellie he had seen all too often in his lifetime. "This information is not correct, sir." Jack could tell she had blocked this news from her world because she couldn't accept it. She would refuse to accept it. Finally, Mellie stood up with the bag of Jack's belongings and left the room. She got in her car and headed to the campground.

"Hi. It's Mellie, correct?" Mr. Peterson asked while exiting his campsite.

"Yes. Hi. Nice to see you again. I have Jack's car keys and was hoping to move his vehicle to the parking lot of my hotel. They said it would be fine if I kept it there for a few days while we get everything sorted out."

Mr. Peterson brought Banjo to her. "How can we help?"

"If you could drive Jack's car and follow me to the hotel, I can take it from there."

Jack watched as they made their way to the parking lot, parked Jack's truck, and checked in with reception to switch to pet-friendly rooms.

"Thank you for everything, Mr. Peterson."

"Please call me Norm." They exchanged a hug before she headed to her room.

After making a makeshift bed for Banjo out of a sofa cushion, Mellie sat on the edge of the bed and watched the gentle dog sleep. Jack watched as Mellie searched his phone, then called his parents.

"Uh… hi. Mrs. Daw? This is Mellie, Jack's friend from school. I'm not sure if you remember me, but we used to live on the reservation next to your house."

There was a long silence. "Yes…?"

"It's Jack. He's in the hospital, and the doctors are searching for his next of kin. He's being kept alive and is on life support. Can you come to see him? He's in the critical care ward at Golden and District Hospital."

Another long silence.

"Mrs. Daw? Are you there?"

"Yes. I'm here."

"Would you be able to make it out here? They need to speak to his next of kin."

"I don't think I can, Mellie." This answer greatly confused Jack and equally enraged Mellie as she staggered her breath in near-shock at the uncaring response from someone's mother.

"Mrs. Daw. I think they need to speak to you about whether to keep Jack on life support. Can you come? Jack needs you here."

"It sounds like in his condition, he doesn't need anything. Jack choosing to be the way he is is what killed his father. You tell him that." She then hung up, leaving Mellie upset. Her hands shook as she hung up the phone.

That was all Jack cared to see. He stood and stepped away from the water's edge. He'd had enough.

"Enough!" He said into the blue haze, hoping never to revisit the place of horrors known as life.

The last thing Jack heard from the whispers back home was Mellie calling her parents. Jack heard her father's voice, and through tears, Mellie did her best to convey what was happening.

"We'll be right there, Mel."

PINION

The following day, Mellie's parents arrived with Reason, a healer and sha-man from home who lived between genders and had access to different information and resources than Mellie or her parents. Jack didn't want to know more, but he couldn't help but sit by the water's edge, peering into the space that held his final form.

Jack witnessed them exchange hugs as Mellie held onto Reason for an extra-long minute. "Come," she said, holding the healer's hand. She led them into the hospital.

"Room 307, please. We're here for…."

The receptionist interrupted her. "Oh, he's not in 307 anymore. Jack has been moved to hospice. They couldn't reach his next of kin, and we need to free up the beds in the critical care ward." Pause. "I'm very sorry, ma'am. He's in 104. Just down the hall."

Jack could tell she was upset as they headed toward the hospice care ward. He knew that she could only hold so much together, which was fine for the moment. She was doing what she could to help, and that had to be enough.

Seeing the room that housed his body, Jack noticed how dim and peaceful it was. There was no movement or sound other than the whir and gush of tubes and machines. There were much fewer machines attached to him here than before, and Jack knew that there was no hope of things getting better if the medical facility was reserving its devices.

No one had tried to make the space anything other than it was: a final stop on the way to the morgue.

The two-spirited Reason stood over Jack's brain-dead body.

"Leave us." His tone was emotionless and direct. Mellie's family didn't question his command and moved to hold vigil in the hall while Jack saw Reason create a space for Jack's impending journey. All in attendance knew their four collective spirits needed time.

Alone in the hospital room with Jack, Reason opened his medicine bag and removed a hand-carved rattle and a drum. Despite being detached from his earthly cord, Jack felt the air change in the hospital room. He heard Reason as he settled to a hum and began his work. Reason chanted low, calling on ears from behind the curtain to listen to his prayers, announcing his arrival to a port in a storm.

"Come," he pulsed into space. The room shifted, energy swirling. Movements from beyond began finding their voice.

Next, Reason addressed the four directions. Facing south, he spoke directly to the winds of that order, saying, "Great serpent… Wrap your coils of light around us, teach us to shed the past the way you shed your skin. To walk softly on the Earth." His tone increased in volume and resonance as he rattled and shook the air around him. "Teach us the beauty of your way." Reason lofted heavenward as he held back the world while the beyond reached to meet his up-stretched hand, the invocation authoritative, bold, and feminine.

The medicine man waited for the spirit to arrive, opening the space and bringing the loving serpent's expanse to this plane. Once he had the winds from the South present, the healer turned with authority to address the Jaguar of the West.

"To the winds of the West, Mother Jaguar, protect our medicine space." The room was a whirl of energy surrounding the two men. Jack could feel its pull on his dead-brain body. It was a vortex that sucked at his tired soul. "Teach us the way of peace, to live impeccably. Show us the way beyond death," his hand held aloft, summoning the beyond.

The space opened the gateway, and Jack saw Mother Jaguar join Reason in the room, holding open her corner of the universe. As the air in the room filled with the swirl of a holy invocation Jack understood that the shaman would need Mother Jaguar's efforts the most, and as he asked for her love and support, Jack saw Reason bow with gratitude.

The winds of the room continued as the power of the rattle and dance became undeniable, making the lights and electronics flicker. Reason turned to address the North. "To the winds of the North Hummingbird. Grandmothers and grandfathers. Ancient ones. Come and warm your hands by our fires. Be with us. Be here. Whisper to us on the wind. We honor you who have come before us and you, dear children, who will come after us. We call on our children's children. COME."

Jack felt a crackle of energy pop and hiss as the Northside opened to mark a new mind, energy, and vibration and he slowed further yet, hearing the great hum now reverberating in the room. It was the sense of all that is, and it was alive, thriving and conscious. Reason turned to the East as Jack's skin tried to square with the cosmic thunder that Reason was manifesting and blasting into the small hospice room. *He's affecting what is… not the other way around.* It was a brand new concept to Jack's dead mind.

"To the winds of the East. Great Eagle and Condor, come to us from the place of the Rising Sun. Keep us under your wing. Show us the mountains we dare to dream of. Teach us to fly wing to wing with the Great Spirit." The universe responded with the clap of reverence as the space of the winged raptors showed themselves with the beating of wings. The air in the room was now a whirlwind of chaos as papers and light loose object began to lift and be thrown. It's life force, it's tempest storm was whole and wise and all encompassing. Reason dropped to touch the floor as the clamor and pandemonium continued its swirling anarchy.

"Mother Earth. We've gathered for the healing of all your children. The Stone People. The Plant people. The four-legged, the two-legged, the creepy crawlers. The finned, the furred, the scaled, and the winged ones." Then Reason slapped the ground with all his might as the massive crack in the floor opened to beam light heavenward beyond the hospital's restrictions. They were now off-grid in another time and another space.

Reason gathered the energy, the masculine, the feminine, the bold, and the empowered. He stood facing the beacon of powerful emission radiating from stones heavenward. "Father Sun, Grandmother Moon, to the Star Nations, Great Spirit, you who are known by a thousand names… And you who are the unnamable." Reason clapped and threw all that he had to give skyward. "Thank you for bringing us together and allowing us to sing the Song of Life. You grant us life, and we thank you."

A light beam from the earth opened as the four directions plus the earth with its stones, plants, animals, and insects arched in reverence up to the skies to welcome the power of the sun, moon, stars, and heavenly spirits. The vastness of all present levied the force of all that is and joined hands to increase their capacity and influence. Reason then addressed the purpose of the moment and knelt on sacred earth to place his loving hands on Jack's lifeless body being held and suspended above the earth. Jack watched close as his corpse was held in the cradle of Grandmother Moon's pull, where the dead were not addressed with words, but energy. All forces turned to lift the trinity of Mother Jaguar, Reason, and Jack from the ground. With her feline steel yellow eyes, The Great One, Mother Jaguar flexed and opened the space beyond death for Reason to enter. Jack watched him arrive.

TUMULT

Becoming aware of a shift in energy, Jack watched as a being filled with light approached him and took his hand. Without words, Jack knew his name to be Reason, a shaman traveling between dimensions.

"It's peaceful here. It is beauty, and it is love. Do you know why that is, Jack?"

The hum of the blue world carried Reason's voice into the distance as Jack let his gaze drift off into the distance. "Not specifically, but I have always felt at home in this place."

"The way of the universe is here." Hearing this, Jack turned back to the shaman who continued his utterance of carefully chosen words. "It is without comment, mind, judgment, or thought. Most do not recognize this place yet you say you know it. This is unusual."

Jack flowed in and out of a radiating blue light as he replied with full understanding, "This place is the model for life. It's like life in the forest; in the trees. There is no lens of the human mind here… Not that the mind is bad but that it is misunderstood and misused."

"Yes, Jack. You see that now?"

The silence echoed his silent yes.

"We are cousins. I know you." The shaman said then pressed his forehead into Jack's as a momentary greeting and blessing. "We know you. All of us know you, but as is everyone willing to know the truth of themselves. It is not truth; it is not perspective. It just is."

The river watered on, gliding down its path.

"Lay here." Reason indicated for Jack to lie in his lap, the shaman's legs crossed in their form. Jack rested his head on Reason's leg, his face turned heavenward. The medicine man put one hand on Jack's heart, the other on his forehead. "Your spirit is strong, Jack. Do you feel it?" Jack closed his eyes in surrender. "But it is also too noisy to cross to where you need to go. You haven't cleaned house, Jack. The spirits ask that you finish your assignment."

With his eyes still closed, Jack realized this resonated as truth. He didn't want it to be true, but he knew it was. Jack didn't like the idea of going back. *I am finally free here.*

"But free of what?" Reason interjected, reminding Jack his thoughts were a thing that flowed freely between them. "Emotions? You can do better. You confuse the brain with the mind. Without clarity around this, you cannot transcend to where you want to go. You cannot go up while holding onto and looking down. Your mind is not here…" Reason touched Jack's forehead. "Your mind is not here." He then flexed his hand on Jack's heart. "Those serve another vital purpose but not the tools for you to use as you have been. You live in a self-afflicted prison, and we understand why but we also need you to understand why not."

Jack did not respond, and the shaman continued.

"You don't belong here, Jack. This place is not what you think. You have reached the in-between, and it is not the freedom you seek. It is not true ascension or that which you yearn for. This is not that space. This is the holding space above the earthly plane, but it is not transcendence. You will never fulfill your assignment in this place."

Jack was in a meditative state. "It's so peaceful here. I won't go back."

"It is peaceful on earth too. May I show you?"

In the purgatory of their position, Jack thought no, but Reason pushed back. "This is not your place, Jack."

"I won't…"

"Quiet, beloved. You do not know what you do not know. This is the value of silence. Let me show you." With that, Reason resumed a chant that summoned all in attendance for this, the reckoning of Jack.

As the blue air spun in a soft circular path, Reason placed the hand on Jack's head onto the back of his neck, just where it met the skull. "Here. This is why you struggle." Great Serpent, come. Show us your might. Show us how we may shed the dead of what was so that we may live in new skin."

The next sensation changed the entire landscape of Jack's understanding. It was as if an extension cord of great influence and power was disconnected, severing Jack from what was, in exchange for what is. It was instantaneous. Reason severed the pull of it, the ken of it, and the wounds of it. There was no other option than to be fully present in this moment because there was no longer a then—only the now. Jack exhaled and breathed in the truth of the Great Serpent. It was freedom previously unknown to him on this earth, most notably in this space by the stream where he came to say goodbye to earthly things.

"Your assignment, my friend, is to sever it. You must if you are ever to be free. Your thought prisons are what keep you stuck. When we hold onto known fears to protect against negative thoughts, we trap that fear inside us. You must be in the universal flow; the exchange that grants fears passage through us, not trapping it or capturing it so that it might be more closely examined and known. Can you feel what that is? Can you allow yourself to flow so that the fears that troubles in you, are allowed to leave you?"

Jack turned inward. There were no memories. There were no wounds or hurts; there were just the blue trees that surrounded them, the fresh air, the spirit of the healer, and him. Nothing more. It was as it is, as it always is, and will always be. It is existence without resistance. It is flow.

"Watch me, Jack. Feel me. Be one with me." Jack closed his eyes and heard the healers message as he melted into the shaman's energy waves. "There is no me here. There is no me against anything or anyone. Simply observe. To go higher, observe that you're observing. To be this free, you do not get to hold onto fears or joys. There is only the flow of non-judgment in this very moment. This is your calling. This is how to evolve to live in the eternal above the in-between."

There was a newfound peace in Jack's body.

"You've been fed darkness, but that does not mean you have to dwell there or pick it up or worse yet, use it as a cudgel against yourself and others."

"So, acceptance is the key," Jack mused opening his eyes.

"No. Accepting something often pangs of something you do not want yet live with begrudgingly. That is not freedom. Detachment is the answer. It's where we are now. It's the cord I terminated to your past. Can you feel it? It's in the detachment of what was, that we find what is. That's where you find peace, Jack. Did you feel it happen like the flick of a switch? It is an instantaneous process, and it removes the lens of your malady."

ZOETIC

The morning after Reason visited him, Jack opened his eyes. He was alone and awoke with the vibration of a deep dream. It was a feeling he had never felt before. There was a buzzing in this body that extended into all things and it lived in him as a sensation that there was no 'over there' or separate from; it was all one. He dialed deeply into its way doing what he could to 'remember' the sensation now newly coursing through him.

Jack looked out the window to see a tree, but for the briefest moment, he wasn't just looking at it with his eyes but more so, he could feel the exchange of energy from him to it and vice versa. He could "feel" the tree and sense its presence and he never wanted the connection to end.

Maybe Thad was right. Perhaps this was a superpower of sorts, but then the sensation began to fade and Jack could sense the flow to all was slipping. He closed his eyes to try and hold onto it, but after a few seconds, it was gone. However, for the rest of Jack's life, he was able to know what that oneness felt like. It was like learning a new skill. Once you have performed it flawlessly, even just once, your body remembers it even when you're old and feeble. It's still there and always will be. That undeniable knowing was now a part of Jack.

After a few minutes, a large, black male nurse entered the room. Jack liked him immediately because it was apparent he was living his purpose. It was simply clear that this guy had a gift that he showed up for each day. It's what he could do to lighten the load of the world for some and provide a shoulder when needed.

To achieve this level of empathy toward fellow humans, one has to have lived through difficulties that many straight white people can never relate to, or even see. Minorities, on the other hand, had no choice. Much of this education was not chosen but rather the lot in life selectively unseen by the silent, myopic majority who think everyone plays on a level playground.

"Oh!" the nurse said as he turned to face Jack. "You're awake?" He then rushed out of the room and returned with a doctor and several other hospital workers. They swarmed to check his vitals and get more information from his newly awakened form which fuzzed his brain and assaulted his mind. He reached for the nurse's hand.

Jack's pleading eyes caught the nurse's attention. Then, in an instant, recognition registered on the large black man's face.

With a nod from the doctor, the nurse addressed the room. "Everyone, please gather what you need, but I need you out. The patient needs to rest." Within a few minutes, they were alone. "I'm Nurse Duarte," the man said, sitting at Jack's bedside facing him. Jack laid silent in his grief. There was so much more he knew now that couldn't be unknown and it terrified him to hold such vast truths of the universe in his mind; this lesson was now a part of him whether he liked it or not.

Jack noted how stimuli were extremely difficult for him in his condition. He just wanted to sleep; not because he was tired, but because he didn't want to be awake.

A tall doctor with a calm and quiet energy entered the room, which Jack found he could tolerate. "Mr. Daw, we weren't expecting you to return to us," he said, news that saddened Jack on a thousand levels. He knew others were hurting, that he had hurt others, that his stupidity almost cost him his life and threw chaos into the lives of all those around him. He hated himself some more while he closed his eyes, closed his heart, and left the present.

"Well, you just rest. We've already called your friend Mellie who's been here at your side every moment she could. You're lucky to have someone like that." Jack nodded in agreement as a slight smile found its way to Jack's face. He was lucky. He knew that, but right now, he couldn't feel that because the residue of the other side and the hum of his experience still entrenched his spirit, and he was trying to will himself back into a different space and vibration. But it was gone, not because it left, but because Jack and his fears did. All of it had evaporated into thin air, leaving him to remember its grounded grace of the free, blue and divine. Jack held onto the contentment while trying to banish that which wasn't. It was an exercise of opposites and extremes, and Jack fell back to sleep in the throws of it.

Several hours later, Jack was roused by, "Jack! Oh my god, Jack. You came back." Mellie began to cry while reaching for Jack's hand.

"I'm here." Jack smiled, his voice barely working. "Is Reason here too?"

"How do you know Reason? You…"

"I met him by the river," Jack said matter-of-factly, not sure why Mellie was confused.

Jack kept his eyes closed as he felt Mellie reaching for something at his feet. Finally, he managed an exhausted, "What?"

"Just checking something, Jack."

Another tired, "What?"

Mellie untied the bracelet, now serving its duty as an anklet. "This." She held up the leather straps woven with duck feathers. Jack opened his eyes briefly and didn't question her more. "My father used these on us as kids to help when we were ill. There's power here."

Jack just wanted to be quiet to search out more of the last fading seconds of his experience. However, the hum in him was now sadly silent. "Very pretty, Mel. Thank you. I've always been fond of feathers."

"Duck feathers. They are very powerful for my family."

"The mighty ducks then." Jack was confused but too tired to care.

"Ducks can navigate water, earth, and sky. For us, their power comes from the beyond, and their healing source is best accessed by someone who lives between worlds and has the balance of both genders. It is for the one who has access to knowledge such as the shaman, Reason… who I see you have somehow met."

Jack wanted her to stop speaking. His mind just wanted to be quiet and search for the hum, the spirit in blue. He listened without comment. This wasn't lost on Mellie, who remained quiet for the rest of the morning while Jack slept.

"Excuse me, ma'am," Dr. Metz said, entering the room. "We're going to need you to wait in the waiting room for a bit while we see what's going on here with Mr. Daw."

"Of course," Mellie replied, gathering her things and quietly leaving them.

Dr. Metz moved to Jack's side to see if he was conscious, causing Jack to open his eyes to see what was happening.

"Good afternoon, Jack. This is quite a surprise to be speaking with you. How do you feel?" Jack didn't answer. All his walls were up. His space had to be protected from the stranger standing over him, and this was by far the most vulnerable Jack had ever felt in his life. His body was not to be shared, prodded, or used on any level with this dealer of poison. Dr. Metz continued. "We're just going to run some tests to see if…."

"The fuck you are. Step back from me, sir." Jack's words were more air and wheeze than sound.

"Now, Jack, we just need to…."

Jack couldn't sit up, making him all the more afraid because he couldn't protect himself from what he felt might happen next. "What is your name? Please step back from me."

The doctor did just that and, in a soothing voice, said, "I'm Dr. Metz, and I've been here with you ever since you were admitted. We're just so happy that...."

"Dr. Metz, I'd like you to leave." There was a long pause as the tall physician took in the situation the best he could. "NOW!" Jack did his best to yell, but because of the condition of his larynx, it came out as a hoarse whisper. The doctor left the room, and Jack began to relax back into himself, but he could feel how shaken he was. A negative hum consumed him internally as its jagged and shaky senses pulsed in Jack's frayed electric nerves.

As he was settling, Mellie reentered the room.

"Hey, Jack…" she started with all the overplayed fake caring she could manage, a move Jack was all too familiar with.

"Mel… just be real with me. What's up?"

Again, she dialed up the saccharine. "We all know you've been through a lot, but it seems like the people who are here to…."

"Mellie! Cut the crap. Be real with me. Say a thing if you came to say a thing." Jack was doing his best to remain calm, but the metronome of beeps around him was gaining in pace and betraying his efforts.

Mellie gave up the language of fake confections. "Jack. You need to let…."

"I won't do it. They can keep me here as needed. I can agree to that and to being monitored, but they are not to inject me with anything. They are not to give me pills, and I will leave if that's not acceptable. I need to know you have my back on this." At that moment, Dr. Metz walked into the room to join Mellie's inquiries.

"I couldn't help overhearing your conversation." The tall man crossed the room to do his best face-of-care at Jack. He then put his hand on Jack's shoulder.

"Sir. You need to back away from me." This time the doctor didn't, a move that heightened Jack's aggressive and angered state.

"Can we at least talk about this? The correct course of treatment? I think perhaps when you better understand…." Jack was now furious and shaking inside because all of this was being forced upon him while he was more tired than he had ever been in his entire fucking life and while he could not move away from the situation. Again trapped, he just wanted to be left alone. Jack never understood people's inability to just fuck-the-fuck off, and not be near him. In his mind, Jack saw this as terribly disrespectful, sometimes even cruel.

"Please just leave. I'm not interested in your chemicals."

"Well, I guess that's your choice, but I don't understand…."

"You don't understand what? How I won't let you fuck me up even more? Is that what you DO NOT FUCKING UNDERSTAND? You did this to me!"

A large red headed man dressed in all white scrubs stepped into the room. It was clear he was meant to be the muscle if Jack got out of hand.

"Now, Jack," Dr. Metz said a little more firmly than before.

"You're not fucking putting anything in me. I refuse your service and advice. Get the fuck away from me." The big white scrubs took another step closer. "No!" Jack said, trying to get up onto his knees to kneel and meet the man eye to eye. *No one backs me into a corner! Fuck this guy!*

"Jack? What's going on here?" Mellie injected.

"Mellie! Please. Don't let them. I'm like this because of people like them." The buffet of blank facial expressions in the room seemed to indicate that no one knew what that meant. Jack was clearly distressed and verging on frantic. He then turned to face Dr. Metz. "You! You fucking did this to me. You and your Goddamn western medicine, and I WILL NOT be a party to it anymore. You don't get to do that to me again." Jack cried.

"Mr. Daw, you are not making sense. I was not part of your last medical team, and I assure you that we have done nothing but administer the best care possible. We're on your side."

"That's what they all say, yet do nothing to understand a person globally. You just see a problem, then attack its symptoms without understanding how it may affect the whole of me. That's why I have this fucked up brain." Jack forcibly slapped the side of his head several times; each whack upside his head gaining more and more force making his hair fly into space. "I was fine…" He sobbed, "and had a real chance at a normal life… but then you Goddamn doctors dish out pharmaceuticals. How much are they paying to destroy people's lives?" When the doctor wouldn't answer, Jack lost it. "HOW MUCH!?"

"Jack…" the doctor tried but was quickly cut short by the enraged patient.

"I used to be normal. I used to be able to be free and walk and be alone or swim, but that has all been taken. BY YOU. I was FINE."

There was a tense silence. Then, finally, nurse Farrow stepped to grab Jack's IV drip line.

"Don't you fucking dare!"

She pulled the needle from behind her to slip strong sedatives into the port.

"No!" Jack yelled, pulling the IV out of his hand. "You don't get to do that. The last time doctors tried to help… well, no one bothered to check if I was genetically predisposed to neurological movement issues. If you had, or even given me the fucking common courtesy to comment on it, because I didn't know what I was being prescribed had potential side effects of triggering what was lying dormant inside me. Again, no one bothered to ask. No one checked, and now I have to live with a crippling fucked up brain. YOU! Your pills and medicine did that, and I will NEVER be the same. Go fuck yourself!" Jack's hand dripped blood onto the bedsheets.

Everyone in the room waited for Dr. Metz's direction. "Understood," the doctor said, indicating that everyone was to leave the room and leave them alone. After they had all left, the doctor turned back to Jack. "What's this all about exactly?"

Before Jack could answer, Mellie sat on the chair next to Jack's bed, tapping the mattress lightly to indicate that Jack should get off his knees and lay down. Next, she turned to the doctor. "Jack has a serious disorder that affects his ability to function. Do you have any of that noted in his chart?"

The doctor had gathered supplies to stop Jack's hand from bleeding. "We have requested records from his primary care physician back in Port Hardy, but we don't have them yet." He turned to face Jack. "It sounds like there might be more here to discuss. Jack, tell me about it. No need to get upset. We're all on the same side here."

Jack relaxed a bit and lowered himself onto the mattress.

The explanation began with a deep exhale. "My disorder is called generalized or global dystonia. It means it's everywhere," an explanation Jack instantly regretted because he was talking to a physician. *Duh, Jack,* he thought to himself. "At least that's what the physical part of it is called, but the neurological issues are often referred to as 'storms' that can be extremely disorienting and sometimes painful if in conjunction with a physical onset as well." He then paused and took in a breath because, in the telling of it, such as this, Jack would often struggle to believe that this was his story; it still made no sense to him. "About five years ago, I began to process much of my past trauma. I had never dealt with it before, and all of a sudden, I was feeling ALL of it at once."

Jack stopped to gather himself for his next truth. "I had a nervous breakdown." The room was silent like an empty cathedral. No one pressed Jack to continue but instead sat in the silence with him. "The doctor's solution was antidepressants and talk therapy. It sounded reasonable enough, so I went along with it. A few months later, my fingers started kinda doing their own thing, independent of me. I figured it was possibly stress or some type of injury. The doctor's solution was to double down on the stress medications because this newfound loss of control was causing me additional stress.

Again, from the outside, that would be a normal course of action. I didn't question it. After a year of my body moving independently of me, I saw every neurologist on the west coast. No one could tell me why my body was losing function and control. The explanations ran from, "It's all just in your head," or "It's just stress," or my favorite from the world's best at Cedars in Los Angeles was, 'It'll just go away.'" Tears made their way to Jack's cheek. "I didn't have any answers until one physician suggested I find a neuro doc who specializes in my disorder." Jack's mind trailed off into a closed heart dead-end.

"What did he say?" Mellie urged softly.

Jack continued looking down. "He said that most antidepressants have the potential for serious movement disorders and that if you're genetically predisposed to it, the meds can bring it to life, a process that once begun cannot be undone. Once you have it, it does not go away. It does not go away for life, and now I'm facing a future that possibly involves me being in a wheelchair. It's just not fair." Jack was emotional.

"I'm sorry…." Dr. Metz tried only to have Jack slap back his hand.

"Get the fuck away from me." Jack's eyes were deadly serious. "You people have done enough, and I will not forgive your entire medical field." There was another long-stagnant pause, then Jack continued, "Why did no one check?" His voice was getting softer. "Why didn't anyone ask me if I was possibly genetically predisposed to such a thing? I knew my father had a mild version of dystonia. So why did no one ask?" Then barely audible, he whispered, "I didn't know. Why was I once again just… never mind." Jack shook his head and turned over to face the wall. He needed distance between him and others. "Please leave. Mellie, you can stay if you like."

Dr. Metz logged into the computer in the room, typed in a list of notes then quietly left the room.

"I'm sorry, Jack," Mellie said, rubbing Jack's back.
"Me too," he replied, willing himself to be elsewhere.

HATCH

A few days later, Jack was released from the hospice care ward, a very rare occurrence for the hospital. They celebrated the victory and sent Jack off with cupcakes.

Standing outside with Jack's things, Mellie put an arm around her friend. "Will you please come home with me? It would be nice to have you there, and you can meet my son. You need to rest, and I'm not comfortable with you being on your own."

Jack smiled, thinking, *Yeah, that's what everyone says. I'm the fucked up one who isn't even adult enough to be alone. Gotta watch the cripple. He might fall and kill himself.* At this point, Jack was fine with these odds.

"Jack…," she complained.

"Come here." He said, extending arms in her direction. They hugged, and Jack said into her hair, "Thank you. You always took such good care of me." The sadness of it hung heavy in the air.

"I can't stop you, Jack, but please call me regularly to let me know how you're doing."

"I will."

"Just like you said to Dennis…? I'm going to need better than that."

It was clear the two had been talking while he was 'unavailable'. The three of them went back a long way.

Mellie pulled something out of her bag. "Here." She said. "It's a note Reason asked me to give you. With everything going on, I had forgotten about it until this morning." Jack took the note and put it in his back pocket.

"…and Jack…," she said, walking off toward her car.

"Yeah, Mel?"

"Don't make me worry about you." She winked.

"You only worry about me because you know the truth."

Mellie looked like she was caught off guard by his response. "Oh Yeah? And what's that?"

Jack thought before speaking but went with his gut. "That sensitive boys on this side of the reservation wall are at best of no value and at worst an abomination. I know my family didn't show up. Not even for this… They're not here are they?"

The air was silent as the mood dropped further. Mellie paused, then managed a tight-lipped expression of sad agreement while she wagged her finger in his direction. That was the best response she could manage. Sometimes there are no words.

"Mellie!" Jack called, turning back to face her as he walked backward in the direction of the Blazer. "Thanks for rescuing Banjo and my car! Oh…" Jack's energy got weird as he processed whether he truly wanted to know what had transpired. "Did you, by chance, ever talk to my mom during this?"

Mellie shook her head 'no' and kept walking.

When Jack reached his vehicle, he had a sweet reunion with Banjo. Dear Banjo. That precious face. They had a long hug and quick playtime then it was time to go.

Jack put Banjo in his co-pilot seat, then walked around the truck, removed the envelope from his back pocket, and then jumped in the driver's seat. He was extremely curious about the note Reason left. He tore the side of the envelope to pour out its contents, but there was no note. Just a single black feather, which Jack thought was a beautiful gift. He immediately grabbed his "thinking cap" disguised as a cowboy hat, slipped it into the side, and popped it on.

"WooHoo!" Jack hollered, putting the stick into first gear. The moment of new beginnings and outdistancing everything else was freedom for Jack. He could soar out here where his tires let fly in a cabin of a truck that was his ride and his temple. Jack gunned it, and off they went.

YIELD

Peace washed over Jack's face as they headed into the first hour of their journey. Like so many things, the flow for Jack was easier to feel in his truck, alone, except for the ever-present love known as Banjo. Here in the cab, going highway speed, the time continuum of the present aligned with Jack's focus because to drive at top speed without crashing, you have to be present in each moment. Here in his edifice of concepts and new experiences, there was much to consider and sort, but only in time. For now, Jack drove. The feeling of being alive was a murmuration of energies that flowed through him as his old broken mind-connections were, replaced by newfound working ones.

The kilometers passed as the two flew on; Kamloops bound, freedom found. Given the past week he'd had, Jack was very aware that he couldn't take his internal vibration for granted. As they drove on, with music for the mind playing in the background, Jack's thoughts briefly stopped on a childhood memory.

A spin of yellow carouseled in front of Jack's eyes while he and Mellie bounded off the Merry-go-round and headed for the soccer field. Jack loved

early summer, with the excitement of possibilities, the warm weather, and the promise of freedom on the other side of the final few days of the school year.

A smile crossed Jack's face as he remembered this feeling and what life was to him back then. He hadn't yet been taught that he was an abnormal and different/wrong sort of human. He wasn't aware that the difference in him wouldn't be tolerated — not by family, friends, classmates, or anyone with authority. They somehow had a collective agreement about who and what he was. Jack would come to learn that their sick perception of him was not rooted in the truth of him but rather in fear of him.

"Hey, Mel! Over here." Jack waved his arms wildly, hoping she'd come to see the treasure he had just discovered.

"Now what, dink?" Mellie's six-year-old self stepped up to Jack, sitting on the grass by a tree and looked at the baby bird he held, maybe just a few days old. "Oh, wow, Jack. Where did you find it?"

"Just here." Jack pointed to the ground next to him. "Maybe he fell out of the tree?" He searched for signs of a nest above them. Mellie knelt down with him for a closer inspection. The chick had most of its fledgling feathers, and it constantly squawked with cries of hunger. They couldn't see where the tiny creature had come from.

"Maybe we can raise it as a pet?!" Jack said in delight, already seeing how wonderful a future would be with a pet bird. "I can ask my dad. Let's find a Kleenex box or something to carry him home in." The three of them headed back to the school buildings only to have their path blocked by Chris K., a kid Jack openly despised and, secretly loved.

"Whatcha got there?" Chris moved toward them with an outstretched hand. Jack did his best to hide the young bird while brushing past him.

"It's nothing, just a dead bird." Jack's joy had melted in the freeze of his fear.

"Oh yeah? Lemme see."

Jack swiveled his body to keep the chick out of sight and move past the bully. "It's nothing. I gotta go."

Chris grabbed Jack's forearm. "Let me see it."

"It's nothing… I just thought I'd put it in a box or something." Jack was very nervous as he waded through this lesson in personal terror. Finally, Chris pried open Jack's hand.

Chris's eyes widened on seeing the bird. "What's this? It's not dead." The taller boy switched his gaze to train on Jack's face. "So basically, you're a liar." Jack was caught and didn't know what to do. "Hey, guys!" Chris yelled over his shoulder. "The faggot brought a pet bird to school. Haha."

Mellie stepped in. "Just leave him alone, Chris. It's none of your busi-ness. Go pick on someone else." It was apparent she wasn't going to let this happen without doing her best to come to her friend's aid.

It took about half a second for Chris to rip the tiny bird from Jack's hand and throw it hard against the brick of the school building. "Haha. Enjoy your pet now. You said it was dead, so I'm just making sure you keep your word. Liar."

"Jerk!" Mellie shot back while Jack chased after the lifeless form of the fallen chick. Jack scooped it up with tears in his eyes. The cruelty of it overwhelmed his young, pre-adolescent, empathic heart.

"Why?" Jack said to no one through tears. Then, finally, Jack wept, drawing the attention of the other schoolboys.

"Haha… Jack's not a boy. He cries. Maybe you didn't hear, fairy, but boys don't cry." The forming crowd began throwing Jack into even more fear and distress. He bolted for the school and safety. "Faggot!" the boys jeered.

It wasn't long after that Jack lost all sense of safety. There was none to be found at home and none in any other place with young men like him. After Jack's father's sudden passing, he had begun his suicide journal by the following year. It was handwritten in the scrawl of an eight-year-old elementary school kid severed from warmth. He didn't know what else to do with all the feelings swirling in him. There was no one he could trust about the journal except maybe Mellie, but he didn't want to be a burden, so it would be a secret kept from everyone. It would be walled off forever. He would be walled off forever.

The distant memory floated away as Jack turned and wound his way through Rogers Pass. "Banjo!" he said, trying to rally some energy. "How about some lunch?" The cockeyed yes from the dog was good enough of an answer as any. "Hold on, buddy… Let me find an exit with food." They arrived at Glacier, a tiny town just beyond the mountain highway that traversed some very steep terrain. Jack noted his energy was slipping, but he hoped lunch would fix that.

Parking in front of the Miner's Cafe, Jack reached for his things, including the Ziplock bag he was discharged with. Rifling through the contents, Jack felt a leather strap wind its way around his finger. He pulled it out to be surprised that it was the "be here" lady's charm. "Ha!" Jack said to Banjo in delight. "Almost forgot about this," Jack questioned whether he was wearing it when they admitted him. He wasn't sure. It laid in the palm of his hand as he more closely searched it for signs of wear or insight. Finding none, his eyes landed on the yin yang of his palm. His eyes then went back to the medallion. Fond memories tugged at him briefly, but then he gathered his hat, black plumage intact, and headed into the restaurant with a new sense of badassery.

"What'll it be?" The waitress asked, looking out the window as he sat. Jack could see that she was 'here' without 'being here'. The aroma of cooked lunches teased Jack's hunger as he quickly conferred with the plastic menu.

"Open-faced turkey sandwich, please… extra veggies." Jack knew the mostly fat and carbs diet could probably use the assistance of a vitamin or two. "Then your fruit cocktail for dessert." The woman on autopilot took Jack's menu from him and walked toward the kitchen.

Kicking back in the booth, Jack let his fingers wander back to the leather strap now encircling his neck. *Totally goes with my vibe... Totally dig it. Oh yeah.* Jack was internally joking with himself. The Autobot restaurant worker returned.

"More coffee?" she droned flatly.

Looking up, Jack became awkward with the question. "I didn't order coffee." She stared across the parking lot some more. "Ma'am?" Jack said slightly louder to snap the waitress out of her "over-there" place. She started to return to the present.

"I'm sorry, what?" she said, lowering the coffee pot she had suspended above the table.

"I didn't order coffee," Jack replied as she snapped back to see Jack for the first time since he entered the place.

"Oh! Oh. Of course. Sorry about that." She wandered off.

"Good lord." Jack laughed.

After twenty minutes, Jack's patience was wearing thin, so he hailed the waitress with a wave of his outstretched hand. "Excuse me." She turned.

"Can I help you with something?" She inquired, walking in his direction with the damned coffee pot. "More coffee?"

"Excuse me..." Jack strained to see her name badge. "Judy, is it?" She nodded to confirm. "Yeah ... it's just that ... well, is my order ready? I have quite a bit more driving to do today, and my dog is waiting in the car, so ...."

"You were the Cobb Salad? Hold on, hon...."

"Excuse me, ma'am. No. Ummm ... Judy. I didn't order the salad. Can you please check on my sandwich?" Despite Jack saying this to her, her facial expression didn't budge. She wandered off again but returned with Jack's order, which he discovered was cold. He sat blinking at his food, plotting his next move. Jack breathed in the stupidity of it all. "Maybe pay attention to your life, lady?" he said under his breath for egoic satisfaction and to dispel some frustration.

Frustration was one of Jack's usual hangouts, especially when it came to others. *Others,* Jack thought with an internal eye roll. *Am I the only one who gets road rage in the face of those who want to chat?* He knew one thing he had to work on was his anger and frustration; Jack's fuse had always been a bit short. He grabbed the strap around his neck and squashed his hat further into his scalp, thinking about the moment he was in.

Why is this perfect? the voice inside him thought, which was quickly followed with, *Because I haven't yet throat punched someone today, and it looks like it's my fucking lucky day.* He laughed at his joke but then let it pass. Thinking about it, he realized he was dealing with what is, rather than, what was.

He inhaled the restaurant fumes again, dispelling frustration. He thought further… *Frustration. Perfect.* Why or how do these two things go together? Because that's what this moment was demanding of him. *Why is frustration perfect? Why is my interaction with this woman perfect? C'mon Jack… What do you have? Thinking, thinking…* Coming up with nothing, Jack sat back in his seat and ate a cold french fry. *Why is this perfect? Why is frustration perfect?*

He closed his eyes and set his mind adrift where it was greeted with his internal voice clarifying, *Because it is here we can have the opportunity to practice being – and practice being a patient human.* Jack's internal response was, *Yeah, no. Who has time to learn patience?* Again, Jack laughed inside over another moment of lightness.

Wow… His insides offered. *Look at you. You're smiling while sitting here after waiting for a half-hour only to be served cold food by a vacant-stared fembot. And your response is smiling. Why?*

Jack's face fell from its humorous position to double down on the discovery of the moment. *Maybe it's not to necessarily "practice" being more patient, but rather to better understand the purpose of frustration. If that part got fixed, wouldn't it then be a good thing? Assigning a useful purpose to it would make it make sense.*

The internal voice retrieved the following and offered it to Jack. *Maybe the purpose of frustration is to be the fulcrum of effort versus letting go. My yang is on one side pushing and doing, the yin on the other allowing and being. The first part, up until you hit frustration, is what can be done to affect change in the world, and the second part, once you're at frustration, is the sign to let go. The second part was often a challenge. To have existence without resistance, to allow flow and manifestation. After all, a watched pot never boils. Part one is putting on the kettle. Part two is then allowing and stepping back. It's the letting nature do its thing part that people with control issues, otherwise known as "the fearful," forget is fully half the equation.*

A calm came over Jack as he watched the absent-minded woman continue on worn paths around the room. He felt tired watching her. He ate his meal and prepared to leave. "Check, please," Jack said across the room.

A minute later, the woman dropped off Jack's bill. He put down cash to pay for his meal but left one more thing. He reached around his neck, took the leather strap off, and placed it on the money. Jack had once heard Dennis say, "What we have, we have to give," and today … in this perfect place where Jack had time to unwind and process, this is what he had to give. He internally thanked the woman for being a disaster so that he could learn (and possibly teach) something new that day. Jack collected himself and his things then set off to hit the road.

LEVELED

About forty-five minutes after leaving the lunch spot, Jack's energy began to plummet. *Damn it,* he thought. He had hoped to make it to Kamloops today, but it wasn't looking like that was in the cards for his still-recovering body. Nevertheless, Jack wasn't interested in making any more problems for himself, so he began to search for a place to rest, maybe even stay the night. Finally, Jack saw a sign that clarified that Craigellachie was ten kilometers ahead. *Perfect,* Jack mused to himself, particularly hilarious given that the word perfect was now his clarifying north star.

"Home of the Last Spike," Jack read, pulling off the highway. Jack entered campgrounds nearby into the GPS of his phone but then had a second thought about the conditions of a campsite. As he looked up from his phone while stopped at a red light, he saw a very unusual building. It read, "The Mash Tun." *The Mash Tun?* Jack let roll through his mind in the search for meaning. *Tun? A Mashed Tun? Maybe a mashed ton of potatoes?* He laughed internally at the thought, then made an agreement with himself to stop into the odd place with the "Pet Friendly" sign in the window. Jack parked the car to check it out. If ever he needed a soft mattress and a warm shower, it was today, and Jack was pleased that he would allow himself this, that he would "treat" himself to something nice. He entered the lobby with Banjo in tow.

"Geez, eh. Close the door, would ya?" was the greeting being offered.

"Sorry?" Jack said, searching for the voice's owner.

"Come on in… Don't stand there like a sod. Fix ya something to drink?" The figure rounded the corner as Jack asked Banjo to sit. "Nice bit of the year here now, but summer has yet to take. Still a bit damp for my old bones." The old dump of a woman rubbed her hands together then dusted off her skirt. Jack wasn't sure what the old coot was doing on the floor behind the desk, but it amused him, nonetheless. Looking up from behind the computer, she inquired, "Who's your friend there?"

"We're just passing through and thought we'd check the place out. It says you're pet friendly and…." Jack was cut off.

"Yep, now. Not an issue with our common area, but we don't allow pets in the room. Welcome to sit a bit in the bar if you care to. Happy hour will be set up in a bit." Booze was the last thing Jack wished to deal with today, and given that their version of pet friendly was not to allow pets, he turned and walked out.

"Where to stay, old boy?" Jack asked Banjo as the old crone from the hotel stepped out onto the curb behind him.

"Yer not be joining us then?"

"Well, with only one of us being able to stay, I need to find other accommodations. Thank you, though."

"Yer needing a place to stay with the pup then?" The pseudo-Scottish or maritime accent making her intention obscure.

"It's okay. We'll just find a campground nearby."

"The bloody balls you will. Come. We have the guest cottages near the river, just this side of the memorial park. Down dat-away." She gestured down the property to a hill and dale of small cottages, each with its own sitting area and garden. "Might now be lovely this time 'o year. Welcome to join us if you like. Given that it's a weekday and all; none too busy. You just let me know." She fished out a key from her apron with the number six on it. "Go then, check it out. Room six down derr. See if she's to your liking then." Jack figured a walk was overdue anyhow. He took the key and thanked the lady, stating he'd be back soon. She turned and headed back inside.

Inside, Cottage #6 was warm, welcoming, and housed a bed that looked more comfortable than anything he'd seen in a very long time. Jack was beat and could feel he had been pushing himself too hard. This level of exhaustion was the siren to dystonic storms. *Not good,* he thought.

They headed back to greet the stout grey-haired innkeeper and checked in. Twenty minutes later, they had everything set for a night of quiet comfort and relaxation, so they headed back to Cottage #6. Jack exhaled long and slow as he lowered himself into the bed's coziness.

It was still mid-afternoon when Jack awoke from an unplanned nap. His first thought was, *Now what?* He didn't necessarily feel like exploring the town or seeing people, so what to do with the rest of his day? He reached for his backpack.

Ah-ha, Jack thought, placing his hand on the journal he bought recently. He had purchased it because the book was so beautiful that he thought it would inspire him to write down his thoughts, but its spell hadn't quite worked yet. Maybe today it would? He cracked open the blank pages and wrote on page one, *Jack's Think Tank,* then on the following line, *DO NOT ENTER.* He laughed, thinking that last part was funny.

Turning to the next blank page, Jack couldn't come up with one thing to jot down. Instead, a voice in his head suggested things he liked… better yet, things that made him happy.

Ok… Let's see… things that make Jack happy…

1. Booze. Preferably dry martinis or an old-fashioned.

2. Mokee pipes and weed.

3. Dark and stormy things such as rainy days, crows, dark amber spirits, leather, molasses, smoke pipes, and dark stained wood paneling in a windowless library with wingback chairs and black Persian rugs.

4. Banjo!

5. My truck.
6. Adventure.
7. Sex… Well… c'mon, it has to be on the list.
8. Making things.

Jack pondered his list, noting that only the superficial made the grade.

"Anything else?" his internal voice appeared again. "Is there anything else that might make you happy?"

Hearing this, Jack paused and thought about it and replied out loud… "Maybe."

"Maybe?"

"Well, yeah. It's just that…."

"That what?" The voice in his head snapped back. "That you can't bring yourself to want? Or won't allow yourself to want, even if it's true for you? Answer the question. What do you want? What makes you happy?"

The thoughts strained through him as he relaxed further into the pillows of downy daydreams. He closed his eyes. *What do I want?* The search through the far corners of Jack's mind offered nothing but static and white noise.

"Jack," his mind's voice whispered again. "I give you permission to want what you want." That thought greatly intrigued his core. He was just permitted to want what he wanted. This was an entirely new thought for him, and yes, it could be anything in the world. So, what was it? What was on that list?

"Sky's the limit, Jack. What do you want?"

Nothing came to him. Searching for inspiration, Jack looked around the room and found nothing other than his reflection in the nearby window. Then, finally, his eyes landed on his messed-up face; the bellwether to the storm called his life.

To not be this broken. To be whole, he said internally while putting his hand on his busted temple. *That's my response. That's what I'm putting on the list. To not be broken.* He further clarified with, *To not be disturbed all the goddamned time. To be free of my past and to find peace. To not physically struggle against my body. To be as I was.*

"Was," the voice chimed in as Jack noted that the word wasn't put forth in the conversation as a question.

"Yes… as I was," Jack replied out loud clearly frustrated.

"Was."

"OMG, bitch, yes. Was. As I was. Past tense."

"Past." The voice paused. "Tense."

Jack understood in a flash. Past. Tense. Was. These three are all not of this moment. *Ugh…,* Jack said to himself. *Be here. Whatever. Yeah, yeah…*

"You know this. You know what this is, and you know what this isn't," the voice insisted.

"I can't do this right now," Jack replied, feeling instantly heavy and exhausted. "Just leave me alone. I just want to go back to sleep. Fuck off. I won't open my heart for this. I just can't. Not now." He went limp and feigned sleep but having just woken up the other side of consciousness, sleep couldn't be reached.

"Up to you… but just know that you must first internalize your sense of safety to protect yourself from the pain. Hold it. Be a slave to it. You've built your entire life around safeguarding against it while it consumes you from the inside. Protect. It's the word you know best, and it's with that mantra you reverberate most. Rest there with that inside you if you like."

Jack was over the conversation and needed it to stop, so he got out of bed, washed up, put on clean clothes, collected his dirty laundry, and set out to find a laundromat, which according to the GPS, was four kilometers away.

Jack spent the balance of the day doing chores, cleaning the Blazer, washing and brushing Banjo, plus lots of downtime to catch his breath and restore his energy. It was a good day.

As Jack was closing his eyes late that night, he felt the familiar pang of the oncoming twinge. Jack was too tired to deal with it and willed himself into sleep before it could overtake him. With rest and unconsciousness resetting his brain from neurological storms, the race was on, and Jack was determined to win this time. He did, and he was asleep in minutes. The cramped T-rex deformed right arm loosened with dreams. The body then rested once the mind did.

INGRESS

It was a beautiful Friday in late May, and Jack woke up feeling refreshed. He stayed in bed for another hour, enjoying the sensation of the bed and the quiet room. The next course of action would be to ask the front desk lady if the room was available for another night. By lunchtime, he had everything arranged, and there was a temporary contentment that came over Jack as he cared for Banjo and himself.

Jack took off for his usual morning run, and even though he had pushed himself the day before, it was still early enough so that his brain would be fresh and not start slipping. Jack didn't have much he could count on, but mornings he knew he could tackle pretty easily without the bedevilment of medical issues. He was always grateful that at least he had that.

Returning to the cottage, Jack decided Banjo needed to go for a walk. So he leashed him up, and they set out to scout the town of "The Last Spike." *Whoopie-shit,* Jack thought. Not exactly grand in historical nature, but he figured this is what the town had to hang its hat on so fine, that's the way it is.

The rest of the day he spent exploring the town, driving around without a destination, and kicking back in the room he had rented for the night.

It was late afternoon when Jack had run out of things to do. He looked out the window and saw the front desk woman walking by holding a tool of some sort. He walked out onto the porch to wave hello.

"Well, don't just stand there waving your flaps about. Come and help me get things set." The directness, and quite frankly, coarseness of the woman was unrestrained by social norms, a trait Jack found endlessly hilarious.

"Aye-Aye!" He shot back as he made his way across the lawn. When he reached where she stood, it was clear she wasn't enjoying the joke as her face read, 'Kids these days'.

"Here, Buckshot. Make yourself useful." She handed Jack a sickle while he was left to mentally whittle on the word "Buckshot."

Was Buckshot somehow directions? Was that a nickname she just made up? Why would she use that word? Was it because of my face? Did she think I've been shot in the head? Jack's thoughts were interrupted by the plump woman physically pushing him down the path toward a field.

Without turning, she continued saying, "Just get us some flowers for the tables. Used to have a floral budget but not since the God damn Province shook us up with them… well, never mind." She walked through the back door and was gone.

"Buckshot." Jack said quietly lost in thought while missing a spray of butterflies that swept the field. When his mind returned to the moment to get the chore done, they were gone.

Jack collected a nice bunch of field flowers and, rather pleased with his efforts, entered the backside of the building where he had seen the innkeeper enter. The room was a staging area for meal prep, odd chores that required more space, and the catch-all for everything else hotel-related that wasn't food or laundry-related. The woman was nowhere to be found. Jack put the flowers on the counter and poked his head into the main reception area. "Hello?" No response. "Ma'am?" Jack forged on to find her.

A dark room at the other side of the area suggested formal dining, receptions, and such. Jack found the woman behind the bar. "Well then, you got it done? Where are they? Come now." She turned and grabbed Jack by the hand and led him back to the staging and prep area.

Jack was now starting to feel a bit forced. "Um…, ma'am. I'm more than happy to help, but I just was thinking I might head out."

She paid his words no mind. "Here." She fetched down some small pitchers from a cupboard. "There you go. Just arrange them, and out they go, onto the tables." Jack didn't move. "Come on then. Don't just be standing like you've grown roots now." Once again, she gave Jack a shove in the correct direction as if his wind-up-toy legs required a jump start in this manner.

"Your name, ma'am? I'm sorry, but…."

"Come along, Buckshot. The day goes on, and we'll be having guests for Happy Hour. Fridays are always best." She eyed him up and down with an air of odd playfulness. "And for all that is money and broken-hearted, would you put on some clothes to impress a person? You're not here to play a bloody match."

"Certainly, ma'am… but how shall I address you? I noticed you don't have a name tag or anything. May I ask your name?"

Without stopping, she offered, "Ana Morrigan… don't be wasting it on yer lips, though. C'mon. Go, go." She shooed Jack into action.

Having delivered the floral arrangements to all the tables in both the bar and the common area, Jack sat in the lobby for a second to catch his breath, noting he still wasn't quite 100%.

Ana approached Jack, and in her funny way, which involved being both warm and cold at the same time, sat also. Jack was expecting the next round of directives, but none were suggested, so he relaxed into it. The silence between them was broken with, "Whiskey?" Jack adored the woman's spirit and nodded yes, accompanied by a you-devil-you grin.

Ana returned with the house best. She served whiskey from their Glenfarclas Family Cask collection. "Where ya from, Buckshot?"

Jack almost choked from the burn of both the drink and the new nickname. "Uh…, the island. Port Hardy. How long have you been here?"

"Gah, none of your business. Let's just say forever and have a nice day." Ana downed the booze and headed off to set things up for the impending Happy Hour. Jack chuckled.

God bless the likes of Ana Morrigan. She is who she is, and it's clear upfront that she doesn't shapeshift for anyone. There's no other version of her. Not a one. That's probably why people can't help but love her. Jack thought of a saying he heard once that felt applicable to Ana. "'When we show up as our true authentic self, we secretly give permission to others to do the same." *And what a beautiful world it would be if we had more of that,* he thought.

Standing, Jack discovered that the booze was now lending him a newfound funk and swagger, which was always his drinking's default fashion. *Fabulous,* he thought to himself. Some in life are happy drunks; others mean drunks… Jack was the "let's get it on" drunk, which often got him into trouble and usually involved him shirtless at some point in the evening. Jack crossed the room to return his glass and almost ran into a woman with long brown hair.

"Oh wow! I am so sorry. I was just…." Jack was frantically making sure he hadn't spilled anything on either of them, only to remember he had finished the whiskey. "Anyhow… I'm so sorry." Jack flushed and excused himself. He headed for the washroom to escape the moment; however, the woman was still there when he returned to the lobby. Jack thought about heading back to his room when she stepped forward with an outstretched hand.

"Sorry about that back there," she offered while shaking Jack's hand. "I'm quite clumsy."

Jack blushed hard over his stupidity and his piercing attraction to her. "It was totally my fault. I'm so sorry." He wanted to smell her hair but thought to himself, *Bet that would be seen as super creepy, so I should probably stick to water for the rest of the evening.*

"Buy you a drink?" she proposed.

"YES!" Jack blurted out far more exuberant than he meant to. Again, Jack was embarrassed. *What is it with me today? Am I that off my game? Dude… pull it together.*

They were headed to the bar when they were interrupted by Ana. "Oh, how ya now, Sharky? Lovely day for it," which meant one thing but then when she eyed Jack the way she did, it completed her latent meaning. "If you gots time for it." The intention was pretty clear. She was clocking them for mischief. "See you met Buckshot."

"Indeed," she said.

"Well, like I said… nice day for it." Ana headed back to the reception desk. She left the two snickering as the young woman properly introduced herself.

"Anyhow… I'm Paula." They shook hands again, hoping to get past the introduction phase finally.

Jack winked. "Nice to meet you, Sharky."

She laughed. "Buckshot was it?" she mused.

"It's Jack. Come." Jack grabbed her by the hand and led her into the bar. A bold move, even by his standards when drinking resulted in anything above not hooking again or not going to prison. That was the bar that drunk Jack could stay above. No other guarantees would be offered.

They sat at the bar. "So why Buckshot?" Paula laughed.

Jack's drunk eyes twinkled. "Ah, Ana." He turned to address the entire rest of the empty room, "Why anything?" Jack turned back to face her. "Best answer I can give, I guess is I don't know… Maybe she thought my face was half shot off." They both laughed hysterically as the drinks arrived. They toasted, and Jack said, "To Sharky and Buckshot!"

It took a while for them to regain their composure, and when the air of normalcy began to return to them, Jack asked her, "Why Sharky?" Paula tried to repress another small laugh.

"Like you, I'm not entirely sure, but if I had to guess, it's because I'm a businesswoman? I don't honestly know." Paula turned on her barstool to face him. "I think she can't remember anyone's name, so she just makes something up." They both laughed some more. Jack was very attracted to her but not just physically; it was her spirit, the spirit of friendship, and "who gives a fuck" that he found very intriguing. He liked being near her.

"Businesswoman, eh? What sort?" Jack inquired.

Paula returned her chin to face forward and took another sip. "I'm a medical rep for a firm that develops drugs for people with autoimmune disorders." Jack's face fell slack.

"You're kidding me."

"I know it sounds posh, but let me tell you, it's just a sales gig."

"No, no, no…." Jack said. "This is super interesting to me."

"Oh yeah?" Paula said, eyeing Jack's "good side." Jack made sure to seat her on his left. "Why's that?"

There was never a comfortable way to out his medical situation. "Ah… it's nothing."

"Doesn't look like it's nothing," she said, making Jack's nerves rattle.

"Oh. It's not because of my…." Jack drew a circle in the air with his finger over his right temple while finding that, once again, he was embarrassed in front of her. He could not figure out how to get out from under this weirdness he kept having.

Paula said the following, which made Jack die just a bit more inside "It's not like your scar is from an autoimmune disease."

Ah! Obviously! Jack thought to himself while laying into the thought. *Things are weird at this moment because I'm weird at this moment.* Jack then tried something he'd never done but had had the experience of it once before, so he figured it was worth a try. He imitated Reason's extension cord disconnect, remembering the healer saying, "This is your problem." Jack adopted that experience internally and, in one second, click, done, gone.

Jack returned to the present free of weirdness and baggage, a moment that had twice now felt like a rebirth, a moment where his senses heightened, the smells of the room flooded in, the feeling of his skin, the closeness, and energy of her, the air filling his lungs, the cough heard from the next room, the wood flooring, the tin-pressed ceiling… in an instant they were known to Jack and all senses were firing one hundred percent. Jack inhaled deeply through his nose, taking in the coffee grounds, the whiskey, the scent of her hair, the growing dusk, and early evening musk. Instantaneously they were there, and Jack took it in deeply with his closed eyes. The wonders of the world from this place were magic. There was no other word for it as he opened his eyes to the dim of the place that newly sparkled. Jack's thoughts were interrupted.

"You ok?" Paula said, putting a hand on Jack's shoulder.

Realizing he had emerged himself in his mind's experience, which excluded his guest for a few moments, Jack steadied himself and replied, "More than okay." Jack put his hand on hers for a second, then spun in a circle on his stool, making fake model poses as he went. He hoped she'd laugh, which she did. Jack noted, *There, did it. Broke through. I'm back. Feels good.* He could relax fully now in her presence without the ever-present tug of past pains and insecurities.

"So, are you going to tell me?" Paula asked, raising her glass.

"Tell you what?" Jack knew he had given himself up. She could tell there was a story there, and she was intrigued.

"Don't play dumb… C'mon… You said what I do for a living is super interesting to you." She stirred her drink. "That's not a usual response when I tell people I'm in medical sales."

There was no escape, and Jack had abandoned the baggage of his past in exchange for the levelheaded cool he needed at this moment, so, *Why the fuck not*, he thought then said, "I have a rare disorder, but you've probably never heard of it. So it's not a big deal."

Paula perked up. "Oh? Try me." This is the part where Jack usually would have angsty guts and weirdness. Still, again, realizing that that part of his brain was no longer accessible to him and that all he had was the present moment, he stated, "I was diagnosed with medically-induced Generalized Dystonia just over five years ago."

"Oh, sure," Paula said with no emotion.

"Sure?"

"Yeah, it's super common in my field."

"Common? But I've never even met anyone with the disorder." Jack's reality had just found a crack.

Paula said again, with no emotion in her words, "Oh, you should hang out with me. We see it all the time." Jack's head, along with the room, was spinning.

There are others out there who are going through this? Well, of course, there are. It's not like it was named after me or I was the first… Of course, there are others. This was a completely new thought for Jack. *There are others.* Jack could not get past how casual the conversation was for her when it was clap-clamoring every nerve and cell in his body. "There are others!" Jack finally said aloud, "I need to meet them. I can't believe you know people like me." Jack was having a hard time putting his finger on everything he was experiencing.

"Oh, sure. If you like." Just then, Paula noticed that Jack was having a moment over this. "It's not like the condition is that rare." This information made Jack's brain stutter. "Seriously, Jack, Dystonia is the third-largest movement disorder after Parkinson's and MS. So it's not uncommon, although it is fairly uncommon in men. Guess you're special." She teased.

"Yeah… short bus special," Jack replied.

"Is it in your brain too or just body stuff?"

Jack couldn't hold the present moment. His walls went up. "Listen…," he said. "I gotta go. I just realized I'm needed back home. I forgot to feed the dog, and it's getting late."

Twinge.

God mother fucking damn it to hell, fuck, fuck, fuck, Jack thought, lowering his chin to his chest. *Why?* But Jack knew. His body was still recovering from his stay in the hospital, and he had just saturated his brain with booze, which could create problems even on his best day. Jack put his drink on the bar and stood saying to Paula, "I think things for me are…." Jack paused and exhaled. "To be direct and to answer your question, yes. Yes, I have the version that comes with storms. I need to go."

Jack made straight for the door, but Ana stepped in to stop him. "I gots the feeling you have something going on. Why ya leaving dat woman there is a fit? Hmmm?"

Twinge.

"Ana, I have to go… I'm not feeling well." Jack ran for the cottage in hopes of getting him and Banjo into a safe space to weather whatever might come next.

DUAL

Back in the room, Jack hurried to get Banjo some dinner, fetch an adult diaper, get himself into some loose, comfortable clothes, and arrange the bed in a manner where he wouldn't hit anything. At that moment, he heard a knock. *I can't do this. Not in the presence of strangers. There's just no fucking way,* he said as he arranged the cushions around the bed.

"Jack…? It's Paula. Is everything okay? Ana said you weren't feeling well." Jack was silent. "Jack, I know you're in there. Are you okay? Are you having an attack?" Jack made no sound. "Please, Jack, if I can help in any way." Jack couldn't speak as he stood unmoving in the room, utterly unsure of what to do next.

Paula wasn't leaving but Jack couldn't do anything about that—and then his wail of discomfort and body hitting the floor gave the woman reason to stay. "I'm coming in." As she entered the room, Jack was on the floor contorted and unmoving. Mouth open, eyes frozen and unfixed. Paula lept to his aid.

"C'mon, Jack… stay with me. I know what this is. Listen to my voice. Focus. Stay with me. We need to get you off the floor. Here." She grabbed towels from the bathroom, looped them under Jack's arms, and pulled him up onto the bed.

Jack was sinking but he was aware. His body was rigid, head pulled back, mouth in a silent unending scream, unmoving, and nonverbal. "Jack?" She lightly slapped his face repeatedly, making his eyes flutter.

"Jack! I know you can hear me. Stay with us." As he watched her lower herself to sit on the edge of the bed, Jack slipped to the other side of consciousness.

The sensation of falling was swirling all around Jack, as he was windswept and thrown through the stinging energy. The blackhole was bottomless as it slapped him like a rag-doll back and forth, falling and tumbling endlessly. Jack struggled to breathe, searching for small pockets of air.

Tumbling and confused, Jack could still hear Paula's voice. "Jack… Listen to me. You're having an episode. There is no need to be scared. This is normal. Listen to me. I'm going to walk you through a series of mental images that I want you to focus on. Stay with me, Jack." But Jack's mind was a swirl of jumble that offered no thoughts, just swirling blackness. He heard her continue quietly, "Can you find a beach? Find the beach, Jack. Sit and breathe. Let's do it together." She slowly breathed in a soothing and exaggerated manner and he could hear it.

"Can you find a beach? Find the beach, Jack," was the last thing he heard before slamming into the first layer of earth. "Sit and breathe." Jack was falling again then hit the first layer of icy water. Jack's next thoughts were pure fear as he could sense the beast rising. Jack fell again, making it impossible to orient himself. In this flailing state, there were no anchors. Moving deeper into himself, Jack managed to eke out one thought. A beach. He plowed through the next layer of earth, fell through space then clobbered the surface of the icy ocean. Jack felt the sting and slap of it. He tried to swim, but the cold made his limbs frozen, hard, and contracted. Jack could sense he wasn't alone in the water. It was coming for him.

As Jack felt the cold stinging air whipping against his face, he could hear a voice in the distance. It was Ana. "Everything okay in there?" which was immediately followed by screams. The kind that escapes a person when they're witnessing something frightening. Jack understood even from this place that the thing that was frightening was him. Jack could then feel his body crash into the first layer of ocean on the back side of his mind while the far off voices trailed off.

Jack swam as fast as he could, trying to outrun the thing that lurked beneath the surface of the icy flow. If he could just make it to shore. *The beach!* came to the surface of his mind. The first thought Jack had managed in this place. Down here, it was mostly a feeling or a knowing, which is very different than thinking, and this felt like a huge breakthrough. *The beach,* Jack thought again as he kicked his working legs into high gear.

Jack saw he was almost there; he was almost to the shore when the fiend grabbed his waist, violently cracking his back as the shocking force pulled him under. Trying to scream Jack's lungs filled with dank water and he could feel his consciousness slip. A very dark place, where the edges begin to blur, and from sheer trial and error, he knew the next best move would be to go limp, to stop fighting it. To play dead. Jack did so and felt its grip loosen and then let go. This was amazing to Jack. He had never outmaneuvered the thing before, and he couldn't help reviewing what was different now. Next, the light through the water changed from dark blue to purple. The addition of red to the place had not been seen by Jack before. He broke the water's surface and paddled with all his might to the beach. Jack touched the bottom, the icy stones beneath him a welcome mooring to his head-spun orientation. He pulled himself onto the shore and sputtered and coughed until he thought he was going to pass out.

Regaining his footing and balance, Jack sat up and looked back to the water. It had indeed begun to have a reddish hue that he had never seen. The water's surface started to calm, as Jack's breathing began to soften. "He'll be fine," he heard in the distance. Jack sat on the sandy beach and took it all in, and it was the first time he saw that this place had the capacity for beauty. It was dumbfounding; it was like watching Satan himself bake you breakfast. The schism of opposing truths queered Jack's mind while the horizon flicked flames of purple heavenward.

Jack breathed it in, the calm within him growing. Looking around to orient himself, Jack noticed a large opening in the rocks behind him. It's voice oddly familiar to him, he stood and carefully made steps in its direction. Jack didn't know what to expect, and he certainly didn't trust anything down here on the backside of his mind. "Hello?" Jack said, which echoed into the grotto of the unknown. Only silence returned, but then Jack noticed movement, making him walk backward, eyes wide. Jack was just outside the cave when the figure showed itself. It was him. It was Jack but without the messed-up face. The moment made no sense. *Perhaps there is a reflection of some sort?*

Jack searched for clues but was interrupted by, "I'm Toby." Jack had no idea what was happening, but the apparition felt real. Jack froze as his twin continued, "Do you know who I am?" Jack still couldn't find words. "There are others. You are correct to have come to this under-standing." Toby stepped into the dim purple light. "Come."

Jack followed himself to sit next to himself by the water's edge. "The beach is always a magical place. The air here is pure. Can you smell that, Jack?" Still wild with emotions, Jack forced himself to inhale through his nose. A whiff of salt was detectable as he became present to meet Toby in the space between them.

"Who are you?" Jack said as he became aware of the drugs infil-trating his system. He knew he was hallucinating.

"I'm you." The figure Toby nodded. "You're me." Jack did his best to take this in.

"There's something not right here. I don't understand. You're not real…." Jack's mind whirled.

Sitting in silence, Toby put his hand on Jack's akimbo-crossed knee. "Can you feel that, Jack? The connection between us?" Jack silently searched for a new sensation. There was a sense of oneness that pulsed between them.

"Yes, but I still don't understand. How are you…?" Jack finished the sentence with a gesture that conveyed 'here and existing'.

"Lay here with me." Toby relaxed back into the sand. Jack followed and, for the first time, noticed the stars that hung in the sky. Their soft purple light was pulsing with life. "When we are born, there is sometimes an accident in the creation of the spirit which splits the being in two." Jack appreciated the silence between them to process this. "You're here." The spirit touched Jack. "And I'm here."

"You're here? You live here in this god-forsaken place?" Jack asked, making Toby laugh.

"Well, not exactly, but also kinda. I'm here. I'm on this side. We are twins of sorts."

"How? What am I a Gemini now?" Jack pressed, more confused than ever.

Toby laughed again. "We shouldn't assume this place is bad, Jack. Nor should we assume this place is good. It is as you perceive it to be." Jack could feel the undercurrent of chemicals flooding his body. He was feeling heavy and drugged. Toby continued. "Stay with me, Jack, as long as you can. Rest but listen. You need to know this." Jack took a deep breath, knowing he'd be unconscious soon, but until then, he wanted to know what he didn't know now.

"When the flame of creation splits, two souls are created instead of one. This is nature's way. All earthly forms have this ability, whether it be man or beast. Our two lifestreams are always corresponding and on the same path. We walk on parallel paths and hold within us the same assignment. Twins are never planned. The split happens out of universal kismet and circumstance." The effortless flow between them expanded Jack's awareness beyond himself, and again he could feel himself outside of his body. It was the same sensation he had with the tree outside his hospital room, only now it extended into the consciousness of another sentient being. It was simply the sensation of knowing and of love, their vital senses swapping in and out of one another. "It's very…."

"…much like the expansion out of self and into oneness." Jack said completing Toby's sentence.

"Yes, however, we are separate but also one. We do not share guides or friends, but we have the same energy. That's why I feel so familiar to you. You are the second half of me. Your density meets my light. We are two sides of the same experience, and I hope we can find peace and balance between us...." Pause. "But that can only happen when you choose to be so. You must decide not to suffer anymore. Right now, you are unaware of the burden you carry because you have carried it your entire life. You know nothing different. What you have experienced of the light is a mere sliver of what is. The eternal hum is unknown to you because you have not been taught it. So we need to begin here. I can tell you have identified the problem, and Jack, that's huge. Give yourself that. I know you own it because you had it to give. That's when you know you encompass it, are ov it... but your understanding of it is limited, and there's still some yet to be identified. The problem isn't found externally; it's the lack of feeling whole. A force that drives all the rest of your decision-making. You will be okay once you're okay with everything."

"Like Banjo," Jack said softly, finally understanding.

Toby laughed with delight and clapped his hands once. "Yes. Banjo doesn't have the bedevilment of his past or perspective of hurt, ego or rage... he just is."

Jack was slipping now. Sleep was upon him. The last part he heard was, "You don't have darkness in you, Jack; you have walls that you raise that block out the light. Don't do that, Jack. Don't do that to us..."

BOXED

The next morning Jack awoke to find Paula sleeping next to him. A mix of emotions caused him to bolt upright. "Oh, I didn't...."

Paula stirred, opened one eye, and said, "Jack, shut up. Lie back down. I'm sleeping here." She clearly wasn't moved by his panic, so he decided things might be okay. Jack lowered himself to be face to face with her. They smiled.

"Good morning, Buckshot." Paula winked. "How'd you sleep?" She rolled over and grabbed one of Jack's arms to forcibly make him spoon her.

"Uh..., fine. I guess..." Long silence then, "Did I...?"

"Jack. You're fine. We handled it. It's all okay."

He tried to relax, but his mind was going a million miles an hour trying to process, what might have been, what did, who was, what happened, what if, why did, if it had been, what did she, why was I?

"Jack...?"

"Yeah?"

"You're fine." And with that, Paula was back asleep.

Jack did his best to be with her in the moment, but his racing mind wouldn't let up. It wasn't just what might have happened in the room during his attack, but it was also what he saw, or at least thought he saw, while he was on the other side. *Toby? My other self?*

Finally, after a long thirty minutes of self-flagellation and angst, Jack decided that was too much work and too much pain. He unplugged from the past, breathed in the room, and eventually fell back to sleep.

"Hey, get up." It was Paula's turn to create a stir. "I have to leave shortly. Let's grab breakfast. They're still serving."

Playing it funny, Jack moaned, "Why?"

"Because I said so, Mister," as she threw his pants at his face.

Arriving at the hotel restaurant, they were greeted by Ana cutting them eyes. "Nice day for it, I suppose?" Her twinkle reeked of scandal, secrets, and untold gossip.

"Indeed," Paula said, moving past her to find a booth.

Ana regained her initial impulse to inquire about Jack's condition. "And you, dear heart, damn near gave us a fright. I had thought you were done for. But here yous is in fine fighting form. Look atcha." She eyed him up and down. "You okay, Love?"

"Better than ever, Ma'am."

Ana, unwilling to completely remove herself from her front-row seat of a still-unfolding rumor, continued with, "Bet yous is, Son. Probably the fine work of a lady to get you on your feet." She winked cheer in his direction then set off to Ana some other place.

Pulling up to the booth where Paula was already seated and reviewing the menu, Jack asked, "Did you hear her? She thinks we're a couple now."

"Well, it's probably more in step with how she was raised."

Jack pushed back into his seat and picked up her hand. "I did want to thank you, and I'm sorry I wasn't a better date."

"Oh, it was a date, was it?" She belly laughed. "Last time I checked, my dates didn't involve making sure someone didn't die. Might have been more of a medical house call than a date." Jack knew she was teasing him. He didn't care. He was enjoying the time they had together.

The morning lazed on. Paula got her things then came to say goodbye.

"Here," she said with a kiss on his cheek. "These are the pill form of what I injected you with last night. Unfortunately, it's not on the market yet, but there's hope for people like you, Jack."

He didn't know what to say. His skepticism of people who dish out narcotics pushed against the idea. But somehow, the rage he'd felt in the hospital was not there. Instead, Jack trusted Paula on a soulful level. After all, she'd facilitated new understanding for him and that was impressive, even if it was merely chemically induced.

"Don't give up on medicine. My number's on the label if you get in trouble." She kissed Jack one more time, then got in her car and drove off, leaving Jack alone, where he realized he hadn't said goodbye. He had just stood there like a lump.

Jack wished he could find someone like that. Like her. Fun, carefree, someone who could tease and be teased. Someone who would care for him without trying to control him or be bossy, but who was willing to take control when the rubber hit the road with his storms. Jack knew he was different in his ways, but he never understood why he couldn't find someone who'd just let Jack be Jack and allow his spirit to be fine exactly the way it was without trying to "fix" him. Someone who would celebrate his uniqueness instead of trying to guardrail him toward a more "normal" expression of what a human does, thinks, and behaves. Unfortunately, he never met anyone who was entirely okay with him his entire life. The world would always find this too big of an ask for someone who lives this far out of the box.

Jack spent the rest of the morning taking care of Banjo, packing, and planning how they might make it to Williams Lake. The almost five-hour drive might be too much for one day, but they would see how it went and how Jack felt after a few hours. He didn't want to push it and take on too much as he was still having issues following his hospital stay.

Turning the small white boxes Paula left for him that contained a heavy sedative that he could use to force himself into unconsciousness, Jack couldn't help but feel small and feeble. Em was right. He couldn't be alone, a thought that bothered him endlessly. Jack didn't want his wings clipped. Not by man, medicine, PTSD, physical issues, or mental ones. Too often, in moments such as this, he thought it would be easier for everyone if he stopped being a burden. He felt exhausted even as the day began. Yet somewhere, in a corner of his mind, Jack also wondered what type of a force he'd be without all the roadblocks life had thrown in his path. Maybe something. Maybe not. He didn't know and was too tired to let his mind wander onto that path of unmet potentials.

Ana stopped by as Jack was loading the truck. "Well, Lad. Glad you had a nice time." Jack found the statement a tad presumptuous as a nice time didn't usually involve those around him hoping he wouldn't choke on his own vomit or anything diaper-related.

"I did indeed. It was a nice few days, and I really appreciate you accommodating us." Jack turned to Banjo for a head scratch. "Right, boy?" Smiles were exchanged all around.

Jack gave Ana a quick hug, put the final few items in the vehicle, and off they drove.

JOLT

The sense of freedom the road provided was where Jack reconnected to himself. It's where he could breathe and think. It's where he could search the thoughts in his head, the emotions of the heart, and his relation to all that is. His cab was his church, and, in this state, with his spirit light blown wide open, Jack connected openly with all that passed before him.

As the hours rolled on, Jack found himself returning to some of the previous day's experiences. His instant connection to Paula, his less terrifying drop into the other side of his mind, meeting Toby and hearing him say that there wasn't darkness in him, only walls that he erected to block out the light felt like something Jack knew he needed to pay attention to.

Walls that block out the light. There was no clear answer. Was he supposed to not protect himself from those things that were a threat? How could he care for himself and safeguard his heart from this crazy world if he was being asked not to shield himself from its slings and arrows? It just didn't make sense. These two concepts were at odds in Jack's mind, and it was still unclear which parts of this required doing versus those that needed undoing.

Jack lost himself in thought. *How am I supposed to feel safe in the world when I'm being asked not to protect or defend myself? This fucking world isn't something one can traverse without some very thick armor. It simply isn't. Not in my experience.*

The voice inside him returned with, "But what are you protecting?"

Jack thought about this for a second and came back with, *My heart, my feelings, and emotions. It's simple. Protecting myself from harm.*

"So, then you spend every day with your pain and fear? Coddling it. Thinking about it. Experiencing it. All while it's locked within you. Rot from the past carried into the now."

Well, not exactly. Sure. It colors my every decision, but it's the only safe way to go through this world. So why am I even having this conversation? Jack thought, getting irritated. He plugged in his earbuds and cranked the music as a wall he could momentarily rest behind, away from the other voice in his head, the one that questioned how he conducted himself in the world. Right now though, Jack just wanted some space. He wasn't interested in the irony that even in his aloneness, he still didn't want to be with himself.

About two hours into their journey, they approached Kamloops, a burgeoning orchard and vacation destination. The Okanagan Valley and surrounding areas had always had special memories because it's where he would vacation with friends as a teen. It was where Jack lost his virginity.

Pulling the truck into Kamloops, Jack searched for somewhere to refuel and check his bank account. They were fed, had cash, and were ready to head back out an hour later. Jack's energy was holding, but he was very mindful to keep an eye on it. It was all too clear he was still in no condition to push himself.

Back on the road, Jack fell back into a discussion with the voice in his head.

So, like I was saying before… How am I supposed to…. Jack paused mid-thought. *Wait. Who exactly am I speaking to here?*

"It's just us."

So… I'm speaking to myself.

"Basically. Yes."

So, if I'm Jack… then you are?

"The one observing Jack."

But how do you identify? I identify as Jack. Are you Toby?

"I don't identify. I just am."

But basically, you're my conscience. Right?

"I don't seek to be anyone's anything. It's not like I'm your conscience as much as I am consciousness. You're down there identifying as the story called 'Jack' and all that is comprised of, and I'm up here not identifying with that story but rather being, being not of form or identification." Jack gulped, processing what was being put forth into his mind. "I hold a relation to the spirit within the one you call Jack but not your clinging and identifying, which is causing you pain. We do not offer that from this perspective, and you have the choice within you to be Jack or to be free of Jack."

Jack shook his head to evaporate some swirls of confusion. *Ughhh…* he complained. *Just make it stop,* as he reached for the radio to punch any button other than the channel that was currently being served in his head.

"It's the Eye of the Tiger; it's the thrill of the fight!" the stereo sang. Jack joined in, thinking it was probably what Banjo was in the mood for. They rocketed down the freeway singing and being stupid because, why not?

Time and towns zipped by while Jack was lost in thought, but its glow started to fade an hour later. They were approaching Cache Creek, and it was becoming clear they needed to stop soon. Jack's energy was evaporating, and he figured this was as good of a place as any to stay for the rest of the day and evening. He spotted a sign for Brookside Campground and pointed the vehicle in its direction.

They drove the perimeter of the grounds before choosing a flat, grassy, and bare spot. Jack had had too much of notable places, people, and things, so a simple option felt like the best solution for Jack's current hopes of less. Less noise, less input, fewer people, and less thought. That's what felt right. They paid for an evening and set about their usual chores of setting up camp, an event that took all of ten minutes, but for Jack, it felt like a Herculean effort. He was spent, his life force a puddle evaporating in the midday sun.

After the initial setup, Jack and Banjo hopped in the back with the tailgate down and laid down to rest. Jack's exhaustion was all-encompassing, and as he drifted into a dreamless state, he did his best not to think, not to associate or identify but just be in the presence of what was, which given the hour, was long rays of sunshine and the occasional bird song. They had been drawn to this simple patch of grass and a nondescript tree in a campsite because this spot was plain and uncomplicated, which was perfect; it was the level of stimuli Jack could handle in the moment. He smiled and let go of the last vestiges of the road.

An hour later, Jack stirred awake and assessed his surroundings. To his surprise, the campground was all but abandoned, so much so he wondered if he should be there. Did they evacuate the grounds? Where was everyone? Or maybe he had finally given humanity the slip? Maybe he could finally fly solo, well, except for his travel buddy, of course. He kissed Banjo and laid back down. *Yes,* Jack thought. *Finally, peace.*

"Your sense of peace can only be found when not in the presence of anything or anyone?" Jack's internal voice said. "Why is peace so conditional for you? Must be difficult to find it then since it relies so much on getting the external being arranged in a certain manner." Jack thought about this for a second and answered.

It is. It's exhausting, and I'm tired. They spent the rest of the day in a quiet hush. As his boredom grew, Jack reached for the whittling stick that had yet to make itself known to him. He pulled out the gnarled twisting branch and held it in his hands.

"What do you want to be?" He turned it around to gain differing perspectives but, more importantly, to listen. Jack wasn't getting a clear directive, so he searched for input from other sources, his senses. He looked at the stick to understand its taste, he smelled the earthen wood to understand its texture, and touched the thing to understand its tenor. This is where Jack began to understand more clearly that he was perceiving objects differently now; that he could use one sense for multiple purposes. His sight wasn't limited to seeing, for he knew from experience he could use his eyes to know more than that.

His sight could inform how a thing would taste, smell, or feel, so it was valid for everything else, turning five senses into twenty-five. The hum of this expansion in perception grew as he turned the wood and let it be known to him not by force but by awareness from within.

After several minutes of interacting with the stick in this manner, Jack started to know its presence. The loving Serpent, the one Great Serpent who arrived with Reason. Jack recalled the incantation … "Wrap your coils of light around us; teach us to shed the past the way you shed your skin." Jack rolled that idea through him again. "Teach us to shed the past the way you shed your skin."

He closed his eyes for further meaning. "You are the skin," his mind replied.

I am the skin, Jack thought. *But how do I shed myself? Or moreover, why would I want to shed myself … and in exchange for what?*

He wouldn't try and figure it out; he would live with the idea in his head until it made its intention known. No push, no work, no doing, just allowing. This felt like the path of existence without resistance. To just let what was not currently understood, to just be. It would reveal itself when the time was right if he set the proper intention. It always had, and Jack knew it always would. He fished out his carving set and began to address the small branch to liberate what was not needed and unearth what was. Jack carved with a spark in him. A purpose, creativity that spoke from the depths of his physical twenty-five senses and from the spirit that connected to them all. Suddenly Jack found he wasn't tired; he was inspired.

There had been several times in Jack's past where such a feeling took hold. He had abandoned the physical drain in exchange for the unrelenting energy source found through inspiration. He often was amazed at the life force within him, and how getting to this place, the intersection of insight and motivation would unleash limitless power, strength, energy, and vitality. There was no stopping Jack when he inhabited this zone. He buzzed with it, and it lit him up, connecting to source and undeniable power. He knew the path; he knew the calling, and he opened it all to let in the light of all that was around him and within him. In this place, he wasn't broken. In this place, he was a force; he was a force of creative spirit.

Jack zapped wood shavings free; he knew what each bump and knot was and what it was to be. He didn't think or choose, but instead, he again listened. His hands turned the thing over and over, paying attention to the directive of what flowed. His strength was on max, and his intuition clear. He toiled for hours, never feeling hungry or tired or anything physical, for, in this space, he was operating from above those places and those needs. He was in the flow. He was in inspiration, which was always a direct channel to the divine.

"This is a gift, Jack." he heard from within.

Yes, it'll make a nice gift. There was a pause in the air, leaving Jack feeling incongruous and like he was missing a mark, but of what? He labored on, unrelenting and unwavering. Jack knew and had never felt so confident that what he was doing was not just his hands, but he was tapping into more than just him, and this inkling he felt needed to be chased down.

He reached for his thinking cap with black feather adornment and put it on his head. However, covering his head somehow felt limiting, and it hushed the surroundings he was trying to tap into, so he took the hat off. Holding it in his hands, he knew the cap was of a lower vibration than he was currently aiming for, so he pulled the feather from it, tossed the hat aside, and simply put the crow feather behind his ear. *Ah.* He thought. *Much better…* The top of him remained open and inspiration continued to flow. Now he was fully charged with internal streaming consciousness and raw energy. Jack had never felt such gratitude. The sense arose that he might have skipped this moment of pure life force, a gift he almost side-stepped in exchange for the easy and the dead. His hands worked faster as he tore open layer after layer of wood shavings and insight.

By the first rays of morning light his work had found completion. He had uncovered the Great Serpent in its truest form, and while one's eyes could see the wriggle of it, its function was only known to Jack, the co-creator of it. Yes, he had carved it with his hands, but its form came from another place beyond that of sticks and curved metal tools. Jack held it in his hand, noting that the wood had give. It was pliable, and Jack knew its possibility from working with its medium. He stretched it gently and slipped his hand through its slither. Gently letting it go, it relaxed into a serpentine wrist bracelet. Its benevolent head was resting on the top of his hand, tongue outstretched towards his middle finger, the body cascading down and around his forearm. It was nothing short of wizardry. A thing created in the beyond and brought to this world through an open channel called Jack.

With his newborn adornment, Jack jumped out of the Blazer, searching for the campground shower where he washed up and brought his energy back to this day. He was shocked that, despite not having slept, he had rarely known such fortitude, and he couldn't wait to hit the pavement for his morning conversation with the world. He leashed up his dog, and they strode lakeside to listen to what the day had to offer. Jack opened his chest to greet the day.

Twenty minutes into their morning walk, Banjo halted in his tracks. "What's wrong, boy?" Jack asked. Banjo didn't move as a man with a gun approached, making Jack clamp off his connections.

"Have you seen anything suspicious?" the man approaching asked hurriedly.

"You mean other than you waving that gun around?" Jack said flatly, not trying to be funny. The man cut him a look and walked quickly past him.

"You need to get out of here. It's not safe. There have been two people killed here just this week. I don't know what's going on, but mother nature seems very pissed off. Either that or some of the bears up here have learned how to hunt and kill tourists. They have no place here!"

Jack thought, *Bears have no place here? Here? Here in the woods? Is that what he's saying?* Jack didn't understand the logic.

"You need to get out of here, Son. Go!"

Jack picked up the pace and headed for the truck, where he scooped up his items and loaded the car. "Banjo! Up, boy." And with that, they were back on the road headed for Williams Lake, the home of Churn Creek Protected Area, where the province's more protected ecosystems remained untouched and wild.

Of everything Jack had studied, forestry, wildlife, ecosystems, and nature held his interest most, so finally getting to see this part of the world was extremely exciting for him. Jack could feel it in his heart, the pull to see, understand, and listen to Mother Earth in her rawest, most pristine form. A place they could drive to in two hours from their current location.

VERSED

As the vehicle approached the wild and untouched span of British Columbia, it was as if they were driving back in time. Herds of wild caribou, buffalo, and bighorn sheep, all wild and endangered, swept the valley floor as migratory birds circled and populated the skies. It was the enchantment of Jack's lifetime, and it all opened before him effortlessly and opened within him even more so. This was the knowing of the universe and its delivery to Jack's senses was immediate and immutable. He could sense its ken, and he tapped into its source as widely as he could, taking it all in, and making it all known to his soul. *All my relations…* He thought quietly as a prayer.

"Banjo!" Jack yelled with excitement. "Wow… We're here! I've wanted to see this my entire life, and it's so much more than what I could have ever imagined." The truck carried them into the park's expanse while everywhere they looked, was a gift from the universe making its way through the world. A brown bear, the swimming salmon, the fox running, dashing and dipping throughout the grassland. The rush of birds was incredible, and the waves of grasslands swayed to the tune of the oceanic winds. Jack had never felt this before and simply had to be in its presence, to be one of this place and one with it without the input of humans. Jack found a dirt road and pushed on, hoping to abandon known roads and trails.

After taking the dirt roads as far as they could go, Jack turned the vehicle back to face toward the direction they had just come. He was in slack-jawed disbelief of its majesty and power, making him feel both puny and powerful all at once. In this space, the smallness of him was as palpable as the vastness of him; it was all one. He was the cell within Gaia in the inner-workings of what is. Nothing more, nothing less. The sensation was profound to be a part of this crown that seated itself perfectly atop the natural world. Jack jumped out of the vehicle to throw himself open and be wrapped in its wild presence.

"C'mon, boy!" Jack yelled back at Banjo as they flew down the hill, running as fast as they could. The freedom, the air, the whisk of it, the smell of it, floating free. Jack had found heaven just as he had hoped and dreamed. It was incredible, and he never wanted it to end. Banjo caught up to Jack, and they ran a circle around the truck, making sure to not stray too far off course, ensuring Jack always was tethered to his line of medical safety. Not a mistake he was willing to make twice.

The run lasted until they could no more. They collapsed into the grass and laid there breathing in joy while beams of sunlight rippled and dashed their way across the world. Jack could never remember feeling such joy and oneness with all. They became still just to take it all in.

Night was beginning to reach into the valley when Jack woke up. He was surprised he had fallen asleep, but given that they had been up all night, he wasn't completely surprised. They wrestled with the truck's contents to make camp for the night despite not being in a designated camp area. A campfire was out of the question because it would draw attention to their location, but a propane camp stove and a battery-powered lantern were all they needed. A great wolf could be heard in the distance as the thunder-beats of cloven hooves drummed the earth's floor. Jack imagined the world in this state instead of how it was, yet no longer is. How humans have strangled the life out of most of what we were offered. An offering from the divine to be met with the scoff of man who wanted more, for humans will be left dying and wanting not because we can't feed the poor, but because we cannot satisfy the rich.

Jack held the Serpent bracelet with his right hand while he wore it on his left, completing its circle of energy. "Teach us to shed the past the way you shed your skin," he said aloud sparking a hum in him. Jack knew this call to change rang true, and probably more for him than others. He did want out of his old skin; it's why he sought out life so often on the other side of him. He was trying to escape it, to not be arrested by it, to not be punished by it. It was his Jack-ness he wanted to be liberated from, for that was what held him stuck at the center of all that that meant.

"*This is your problem, Jack,*" he heard Reason ring in his head. He disconnected the tether to the past and put its cord down. *This no longer serves me,* Jack thought, thanking the Serpent for its gift.

"That is a bold choice, beloved. You see, you no longer need that." The voice said.

Yes. I see that.

"Tell me why. Teach me what you know."

But you already know…

"I do indeed, but one cannot have any mastery without achieving the yin and yang of it. You have been in the yang, the doing, and the learning, but half the equation of mastery is yin, the teaching, the flow outward to others. It's in this where we ultimately teach ourselves. This is when you know the lesson is ov you wholly."

As Dennis said once, Jack thought. *What we have, we have to give… and it's not until you can give it that you know that you have it.*

"Correct, dear heart. Our lessons commence. Begin. Teach me."

Jack inhaled all that is and blanked his mind to still, allowing flow to work through him. *One cannot be in flow while holding onto…*

"Holding onto what?"

Holding onto anything, I guess.

"Correct. So do you want to hold onto your fears and pain, or does that not exist here where we are?"

I choose to be here. Not there. I can be in this world but not of this world. I can be of something else.

"And what is that? What are you ov?"

Jack was silent. *I don't know.*

"I don't know yet."

Yes, I don't know yet, but I can hold a space for it to come.

"You're a good teacher, Jack." Hearing this, he smiled. "How much of this path would you know without your specific journey?"

I don't know.

"I don't know yet."

Yes, I don't know yet… but I'm glad I'm here; that I've reached this point where it gives purpose to life.

"Ah. Do you see that? You see its purpose?"

Yes. Jack thought about it some more. *It's like how I discovered the purpose of frustration, and by giving it a function, it no longer seizes me or inhabits me but rather serves to show me when I need to let go. Frustration tells me when my work is done and when to allow the universe to work its magic.*

"Correct. You have no power over the external despite what you have been taught."

I see that, Jack thought. *We can work and do our best to effect change, but it's in the allowing where change occurs. Not just the doing. That's true manifestation.*

"Bold to think so."

Jack knew what this was. He recognized the test. *Bold to be so.* He smiled and relaxed into the night air.

HAUNT

In the dark, Jack sat upright in a cold sweat. "What was that?" he thought while rummaging through his things in the back of the van for a flashlight or lantern. Then he heard it again. A roar off in the distance which sent a chill down his spine and flooded his body with adrenaline. With eyes wide he quietly climbed out of the truck for a better look. Seeing nothing, he got on top of the Blazer for a better vantage point. The night roar again slapped echos into the basin's walls, sending the guttural moan up, reaching into the dark heavens. His eyes strained against the blackness of night, searching for the source of it. "Maybe we should drive back to the campgrounds?" he asked Banjo. Moments later, Jack froze as his eye caught a white shadow lurking in the brush down valley.

"What the…?" Jack said unconsciously as his mind ran through scenarios and searched for meaning. Then it appeared again… a white shadow. It made no sense. Shadows are black, not white.

"D a n g e r," Jack heard from his gut, but not wanting to head one way or another without more information as to what Jack was dealing with, he stood his ground atop the truck. Down valley rumbled, and the ground started to vibrate. "There it is again!" Jack yelled, pointing in its direction. The white figure flew low and was quickly gaining speed. Jack couldn't tell what it was but could sense its massive form gunning for them. Out of the corner of his eye he saw what looked like a toy moving and dangling from the cooler next to the vehicle.

He scampered down off the car and ran to the kitchen supplies only to jump backward from coming face to face with what he thought was a polar bear cub ransacking his food, but Jack knew they didn't live this far south. Did the province bring in a few for tourists? It didn't make sense, but then he remembered something Mellie's family spoke about, and Jack knew immediately that this was the myth they named. This was the Spirit Bear, and he could remember Mellie's father telling the story…

"When time first began, there was a great white earth that lasted eons. One of its first inhabitants was a Raven. The gatekeeper of worlds – including to the spirit world. Once the Raven had visited earth, he created the green, which lived with the white. Other creatures soon gathered, but the Raven was not yet satisfied with the earth. He wanted a reminder of The Long White Time from Before. So, he chose the bear, the keeper of dreams and memory, to help him out. Raven made a pact with the Black Bear that he could live in peace and harmony forever if he agreed to let every one in ten black bears turn white. This was a reminder of the misery of The Long White Time from Before."

When he heard this story, Jack had rushed home to see if it was true. He looked it up and found that yes, yes, in fact, there was a white-furred black bear sub-species. Jack was now desperate to recall the thing's attributes in his mind.

"Run, Banjo!" The two of them flew down the grade onto the dirt roads that had brought them to this place. Banjo ran full tilt, and Jack did his best to keep up. As they hit the bottom of the slope, the roaring white beast launched itself into their path, making them both veer left down a steep embankment.

Jack's mind swirled, searching for anything he might recall about how to survive this, but his mind couldn't think clearly while steeped in toxic cold adrenaline. They sprinted downhill, and the thunder behind them let loose a torrent of sound that scattered all loose debris ahead of them by bounds. It was a bellow deep, primal, and filled with fury of hell itself. The ground shook from its vibrations, and the gust of its breath sprayed the back of them. They sprinted.

Reaching the base of the ravine, Jack searched for Banjo. They stopped briefly and looked into each other's eyes as the bear's claws tore through Banjo's chest, flinging his lifeless body into a tree. Jack watched as the dog's flank smacked the face of its branches then fell dead to the ground. He could not process what he was seeing or feeling. His mind went blank as the thing came into view, training its fix onto Jack.

In that moment, the world slowed to a stop as Jack became fully present and breathed in the moss, the woods, and the dirt. He could smell the thing and sense its distance without seeing it. He could feel its presence and chose to hold his ground.

"Jack?" The voice of him asked.

Yes. I'm here.

"We need to have a better understanding of why I'm here."

Jack was confused. *Why are you saying this now?*

"Because you're at an important intersection." Jack had no idea what was happening and offered nothing to the conversation. "You have access to information here if you want."

Jack was still confused. *Such as?*

"Such as why is this perfect, Jack?"

Why is it perfect that I'm about to be killed by a bear that I cannot outmaneuver?

"Yes."

Jack, at this point, was pretty sure he had just lost his mind. But, in the millisecond that he had to react, this was how he was spending it. *ARE YOU FUCKING KIDDING ME?!* he internally screamed.

"Why is this perfect that you're facing a fear you cannot outrun?"

The answer was hanging right in front of him, and the simplicity of it pissed him off. *Because one defeats such a thing not by outrunning it but by facing it.*

"Yes. Do you not see the intelligent design of it yet?"

The stillness of the moment, where time was not, gave Jack the answer he needed. *Face it,* Jack thought while also knowing it was going to take everything he had to keep his fear at bay. *I don't know that I can… but I also don't know if I can't.* There were no other options; it was time to put all his faith in the design of him and the design of 'what is'. Jack repeated his answer while seeing it clearly. *Because one defeats such a thing not by outrunning it but by facing it.*

Jack trembled and reached for the black feather behind his ear as the voice within lead, "When you defend yourself, you're defending your walls, so do not defend yourself. Face the nothingness of fear. Do not fight that which does not exist. End your war. Detach from identification with the concept of safety. There's no safety, Jack. There has never been. There just is." The words came swiftly yet seemed to bend and stretch when the bear's shadow descended on him.

Jack felt his knees buckle. "There is no peace in the struggle to defend the idea of solidity and safety. You can do this, Jack! Break the spell of fear. STOP! Arrest yourself. Stand still." Jack thought he would pass out as the loom of the colossal ghost beast leaped for him, the black feather in his hand holding guard against the spirit bear's attack. "It's in the stillness that you can verify that fear lives outside of you. Not in you as you think, and if something is outside of you, then you can choose to bring it in and be ov it, or not. What do you choose?"

Jack was blank with terror.

"WHAT DO YOU CHOOSE?!"

All Jack wanted was to run. It indeed took every ounce of strength to keep his feet planted. His mind worked at hyper speed to access the moment. He gathered himself, the flash of the Loving Serpent coiled and hummed on his left wrist, the crow feather in his right hand which glinted brightly against the white reflection of Mother Moon.

IT IS NOT OF ME. I DO NOT CHOOSE IT. Jack screamed internally beseeching the spirits.

Who in turn rang with, "The moment is owned by the moment, not us. Not you. Do not resist what is."

The fury was now just inches from Jack's frozen form as he registered the hot clenching words. Words that he knew were ringing true.

"Watch, Jack. Stay. Stay and watch."

The air between the phantom spirit and Jack swirled, slamming gusts against the trees.

"Watch the fear. Watch it without attachment."

Jack repeated, *Watch the fear without attachment.*

"Do not grab or cling," his internal dialogue continued. "Don't want. Don't need. STAND, JACK. Take ownership of every millisecond. This is where you meet freedom. DO NOT GRAB. Do not pull fear in. Flow…"

Jack repeated, *Do not grab,* as his hands became alight with his fierce blue blazing personal power.

"This is where you define yourself, Jack. STAND. Stand on what you know. Gird yourself with all you know as true because you will discover that protection is imprisonment here. Abandon the concept of protection. It is not real. Be the one who watches."

Jack immediately responded with, *Be you. The one who watches.*

"Yes, Jack. Be you. The one who watches."

I am the one who watches. The one who observes.

"Yes. You are."

Yes, I am.

With that, Jack's conscious flipped up into the observer deck and took the seat of his soul. He was amazed at the freedom he found there in total detachment of all. The seat of 'I Am' was the seat of his soul and he found the sensation like seeing the observation deck of his mind.

What is this place? Jack asked, then immediately responded with, *This is me. This is my true self. This is existence without resistance. This is I am. This is home.*

With each passing moment, the voice grew more distant. "Use the mind to ponder and create. It is a tool. It is not you. It is secrets, and it is lies. Do not identify with it. Look…"

In that moment, Jack's form became pure energy, and he had ascended to a place were there was no other voice in his head. He was alone, without his thoughts for the first time in his life, and the relief Jack felt was that of a parent reuniting with a lost child.

In this new place within his mind, Jack knew it all at once. He knew the truth of him. He knew his fears were something he could control and dispel because he knew they were not of him unless he chose that it be so. It was all so clear from this place. The fear, the beast it was all outside of him. It was not of him.

Jack thought aloud. "You don't need fixing. The world doesn't need fixing. It's all as it is, not as it 'should be' but rather as it is."

The massive form of the white terror was now but a second from him. Jack stood and blew open his chest to greet the moment the way he would a sunset or a wonderful memory.

Like a loving memory of Banjo… He began to cry.

NO! He stopped himself. *The moment cannot be of this. Use your strength for its purpose, STAND. You may not collapse or weep here.*

You do not have darkness within you. You have walls that block out the light. STAND. Jack doubled down on his opened chest, beaming for all that is. *STAND.* Jack shone and blasted his light to all that is.

Jack with every ounce of his being, stood as the mass of the white ghost blew past him knocking him into a felled tree, rendering him unconscious.

INCORPOREAL

The world had just greeted the gloaming when Jack stirred. He had met the moment, and the lull of distant planes still echoed through him. He opened his eye as a crush of pain scorched throughout his body.

The land had yet offered its face true light, and Jack struggled to make out what he was seeing before him, because what he was seeing didn't make sense. His back was against one downed tree, and what he was fixed on laid against another just two feet in front of him. He searched his mind for clarity as he adjusted his gaze. There, just in front of his face, was an eye looking back at him, its piercing stare rational, unwavering, and unblinking.

"Do you not see the intelligent design of it yet?" rang in his ears. He did. He did see it. The design of him and all that meant even in this moment as his fake iris stared back at him. Jack roused himself to check to see if he was injured. Finding he mainly was intact, he scooped up his eye and held it in his hand the way he did for a tiny fledgling chick when he was a child. He needed a second to regain himself, and he bowed his head silently to replace his eye. In the dim, Jack's next thought was of Banjo.

"BANJO!" he cried, gaining his legs while he flustered to stand. Jack scanned the clearing to find the tree he had been crushed against … and there he was. His lifeless body but twenty feet away was clearly inert and already stiff with rigor mortis. A deafening wail of the pain of a lifetime escaped Jack in a sound he had never heard himself make before. It was a raw cry. A scream. It was the agony of a mind splitting in two delivered from the depths of one's soul that cannot be endured without madness. Jack's mind shook and kiltered. The dimension of the earth changed, sliding, listing to one side, and opening to swallow everything it touched. Jack stumbled and ran and fell and careened until he reached his beloved dead companion. He scooped him up in his arms and collapsed to the ground.

The silent scream that escaped him would last for the rest of his days. The void of Jack's heart met that of Banjo's. One metaphorically, one not. Jack wailed from grief that he had never known. It consumed him until there was no more Jack. Just searing white-hot bays of sobs that would crater his mind and devour his being. As Jack unleashed the torrent of emotion, he wept and cried and screamed until his mind could not take it anymore, and as was custom, he grabbed the escape hatch.

Twinge. Twinge. Twinge. Twinge. Twinge. Twinge.

Black.

Gone.

The process took less than one second…

PRAYER

On the other side of Jack's mind, the moon held its place above the purple water's edge. Jack knew this place because it was where he met Toby, only this time Toby wasn't here. Banjo was. The dog looked up at him with his puppy-dog way and smiled. They sat in silence, looking into each other's eyes in the blueish purple place that buzzed with a purple static and blue hue. Jack heard Banjo's thoughts.

"Goodbye, my friend, my love. I am with you in ways you will know. Watch for me. I always have been with you, and a love like ours can never die. We'll be together again soon."

Jack held his dog as his body heaved with wave after wave of sobs that convulsed through his mind and body. Banjo's form radiated prism light and evaporated into the air. Jack stood on the purple beach, his eyes scanning for the last trace of Banjo, but he was gone. Jack was alone, and the scale of pain he was experiencing made clear that he wanted to die. He couldn't survive this, and he didn't want to.

Jack ran and leaped into the icy water to seek out the beast that had plagued and tormented him all those years. He wanted it to be over, to surrender to the hellion that writhed through him and stole his capacity for life. He swam with all of his might in search of the thing, desperation overtaking him and his death-wish absolute. "KILL ME!" Jack screamed at its vapors. "I cannot do this. MAKE IT END." He dove into the depths with an outcry of the mad. "Where are you?!"

Jack screamed at the invisible thing as he twisted and dove deeper. "END ME."

Water filled Jack's lungs, which had the desired effect of the world around him getting darker. He wasn't sure if it was the depths of the water or the depths of his despair. He welcomed the black fog as it coiled through him. "End me," he begged. Then as often would happen in this place, his brain went "click." It was always the moment when his body, heart, soul, and mind were untethered from one another, and Jack was sent into the abyss of nothing. No thoughts, no forms, nothing. The final place of a storm that was infinite, bright, and white. Jack floated through the obliteration of form suspended, non-verbal, without connection to thought, sound, or light. A place of quiet but not of peace. It was a bright blackhole of agony that sucked all things from what is known into a place where it isn't. Jack's being was empty, his husk floating through the stark vacuum of the universe's womb. His mind was vacant and blank while his body slumped and his bowels emptied.

"Jack?"

He was unable to process, uncoil, or acknowledge it.

"Jack?" silence. "I know you can hear me, Jack."

But Jack had no sense of Jack left. Instead, his mind had fractured into a schism of shards and despair.

"When you're ready, Jack. There is still much to understand – some that will help you in this place, some that won't. The physical when sick is still sick regardless of how it's framed in your mind, but the spirit of the forest does live on even after the fire. We are here when you're ready."

It was two days before Jack became conscious again.

MULLIONED

As Jack began to stir once again, he awoke to the continuing horror of Banjo's death. He had dirt and blood caked throughout his hair and clothing. He was still holding his dog, which had been dead now for days. It was time to let go. Jack tried to stand but was handicapped by grief, nicking his wits and abilities. Jack was as sad as he had ever been. His loss was an agony he wasn't sure he would survive. However, before he did anything else, he wanted to give Banjo a fitting goodbye and bury him in a manner befitting such a great warrior and companion. Jack headed back to the truck to get his short-necked camping shovel. He couldn't stop heaving with sobs, but somehow, he mustered the strength. He would send his friend off to meet those on the other side, and he would find the strength to do what was right.

After Jack buried Banjo, he camped by his plot for several more days, unwilling to leave the dog's side. It was a blurred few days of existence as his mind unshackled while pain blew through him openly like a house missing its windows. His chest was a cavity, vacant and uninhabited. He raved and dreamed wildly as his mind continued to slide, his emotions awash in anguish without light or guidance. He was a free form floating, and he could not regain his footing, not that he cared.

"Jack?"

I'm here.

"Yes. And we're glad you are. You're not okay."

I am not okay. I am broken.

"Yes, your heart is broken, but perhaps you're not broken. Not as before."

Jack thought about this. He didn't respond.

A few days later, Jack's shock began to wear off to where he could at least assess his health and care for his basic needs, but he still couldn't bring himself to leave the site of Banjo's grave. He had set up camp there and knew he would stay put until he had an internal message otherwise. He knew he would know when the time arrived, and until then, he would wait quietly for its message.

Getting back from town and a shower, Jack started dinner in the cradle of the ravine that had become home base. He made his usual dinner of a hamburger patty and the fixings wrapped in foil and cooked on a flame. Jack sat on the earth close to his friend.

"Why is this perfect, Jack? Are you ready for that conversation?"

Jack was silent.

"This part might make it make sense." Silence. "Why is this perfect, Jack?"

Jack didn't want to talk about it. It still ravaged him on the inside to think about it.

"Come. Be still."

Jack was settled on the earth; his legs akimbo, eyes closed, while he thought, *This is perfect because it is showing me the difference between pain that stems from love and that which is self-inflicted. One is of the body and heart; the other is a hallucination.*

"Yes."

And that named the truth of it for Jack. The hole in him was a wound, a scar left by love, and there was no expectation for it to be anything else. Jack saw and accepted the truth of it. He knew it would hurt and that he would suffer for his loss. He recognized that he is human with a human heart which breaks. Jack thought that to have any expectations to the contrary was cruel because it would demand that we not be fully human, when what we're striving for is to be more so, not less.

One more thing…. Jack put forward in his mind.

"Yes."

You said t*he design of us is perfect. Even me?*

"You honestly have no ability to see a thing as it is."

Jack thought that was rude but responded, *Why do you say that?*

"Tell me if I get any of this wrong. You sought additional information from the universe. You sought access to thoughts or perspectives to help us walk each other home. Did you not?"

Jack shrugged yes.

"So, as we always do, we conspire for your success. We gave you not one, but two places to have truly unique insights and experiences. One was given in your physical being and was given in your mind; and they are both portals to another plane—are they not?"

Holy shit, Jack interrupted. Then, in a flash, he got it. He stood involuntarily. *And I respond by thinking I'm going to die.*

"Yes, Jack. Your inability to see a thing for what it is defies understanding. Where did you think the insight and experiences were going to come from? How did you think it was going to show up for you?"

Jack had no answer and felt incredibly stupid for his short-sightedness.

"You lack awareness in ways that are painful and frivolous. Tell me why your design is perfect."

Jack exhaled. *I have been designed perfectly for the information I sought on my path.*

"How so."

Truth is a word for perspective. Your perspective is your truth, as is mine. To better understand all that is, I hoped to see the world from many more perspectives and gain many more data points regarding what remains true for me. To be educated from experience and its understanding. The places my mind and body have taken me are very different from anyone else's.

"This is true."

Yes, Jack said. *For me, this is true.*

"Have you felt your body vibrate with the speed of the humming-bird or be as rigid as a stone?"

I have.

"As your body undulates on its own, to what is it attuned to?"

The sound of the soul and the rhythm of the universe.

"Tell us more about that."

Beyond the 'click', when I detach from all stimuli and I feel the undulating start in my body, it's like the waves of the heavens that I feel like I can ride. I can often hear it, and there's sometimes a peace that comes with it. It has flow. It has a rhythm. It opens my senses because it's a tune that comes from beyond me. Jack exhaled sadly. *It is often comforting when it is not violent.*

"You know this."

Yes, I do, Jack replied.

"And existence beyond the physical? Where have you been taken to that if you had not been designed in this manner, you would have never had the chance to experience? Tell me about those places."

When I am taken under by a neurological storm, I leave my body. Jack paused and slowed. *I know what it feels like to be unrestrained by gravity, senses, and thoughts.*

"That's not nothing, Jack. To have experienced a mind without thoughts for the lengths and duration you have is what people spend a lifetime trying to achieve. We gave you that because it is as you requested. A point of view so ingrained in your experience that you can speak and educate from it."

Jack was embarrassed for his myopic and childish understanding of the gifts bestowed upon him from the beyond. Once again, the words, *If the only prayer you can manage is thank you, it will be enough,* ran through his mind, and coming up with nothing else, Jack acknowledged this, bowed his head, and sent a gentle pulse of gratitude into the world.

It was an early June morning when Jack knew it was time to head out, to continue his walkabout. He packed up with tears in his eyes, blessed the spot where he and Banjo said goodbye, and headed for the highway.

PASSAGE

Jack drove in silence; closed off and unthinking. He wanted to lose himself in the rumble and numb of the countless passing hours and kilometers.

Reaching Prince George, Jack performed his usual tasks of getting gas and money. His heart was no longer in the journey, and his sense of loneliness and loss were inescapable. He got back in the cab and drove more, ignoring his body and physical needs. He just wanted to drive and drive and drive until all of it was behind him.

Burns Lake came into view. It had been an eight-hour journey already, and Jack couldn't ignore his fatigue anymore. He searched for a place to spend the night.

As usual, Jack selected a campsite on the backside of the grounds, made himself dinner, and then went for a walk alone. It would take some getting used to his life flying solo, but Jack could give himself time to heal and time to mourn. Mentally reviewing his affairs, he figured he had about three months left of the Workman's Compensation and the payments from Dennis and Wendy. After that, he could venture out here alone as long as he cared to, but without Banjo, Jack knew his time on the trek would come to an end. His only bucket list item left was the nightless day in the arctic circle during the summer solstice. Those were the directions the universe was writing on his mind, and Jack felt he needed to experience that.

Finishing unpacking and setting up the campsite, Jack's mind sought escape and refuge in the form of distraction. He knew just the thing and tumbled out of the vehicle in search of it.

"You're not tired, Jack."

I know, Jack replied heavy-hearted. *I remember what you said about energy.*

"Listen to your body. What is it telling you right now."

Right now?

"Yes. You just had a twinkle of inspiration. What was that about?

I'm sorry... Twinkle?

"Find your stillness. Tell me what just happened in you."

Bossy, Jack teased but then settled into himself, searching for the meaning of his 'twinkle.' *It was a spark. It was hope. It was creativity.* "It was inspiration," he finally said aloud.

"Inspiration outside of yourself. A connection to source and flow; focus your life source there. Now isn't a time to be inside yourself alone and cut off. Don't do that to us." Jack hung his head while this statement rang true. He had wrapped himself in his protective shell and turned his back on what is to regain himself. It was instinct – the instinct of the hurt.

Jack began walking the site thinking, *I'm not tired... I'm uninspired.* His mind's heaviness pulled and dragged at his soul while he passed a dried up dead tree. Jack stopped walking to focus on 'what is', which popped him back into the present, and from this new place he was aware of where he was, and what was before him. Jack breathed in his surroundings for the first time in days. The relief of shedding his lead blanket of ache felt endlessly light, and he found he could breathe easily again. He looked around him, taking it all in. Jack stepped toward the old dead tree, thinking, *What do you want to be, dear friend?* – and that was all he needed to be zapped with the finger from beyond, waking him from the sleep of grief and finding the connection beyond him to other sources. He searched the tree for inspiration.

Finding the branch that spoke to him, Jack ran back to the truck to grab his camping ax, and within minutes he had welcomed new life into his heart in the form of a dead stick begging for rebirth. Jack could sense it. The pull of it. The whisper of it asking, like the Great Serpent, to shed its old form in search of the new. Jack popped open the tailgate and sat legs crossed to communicate with the spirit of the thing. *Tell me... what do you want to be?* He turned the branch in his hands over and over again until it revealed itself to him. It came to his mind in partnership with source as he recalled Reason's words: "Come and warm your hands by our fires. Be with us. Be here. Whisper to us on the wind. We honor you who have come before us, and you, dear children, who will come after us. We call on our children's children. COME." It was the Spirit of the North. It was his Grandparent's love in hummingbird form.

"The North winds!" Jack said, sitting upright, eyes focused on the newly arriving stars – and that was all it took for source to begin to flow through Jack again... he grabbed for his whittling set, and, with enthusiasm, he started his work.

The joy is in the work. That is the journey. That is connection to source. Begin. The words banged through Jack like he had been clamped into sprinting blocks, and the starting gun just fired. Wood chips started to fly.

As Jack toiled, the plume of his source arose as his five senses moved to their heightened place of twenty-five. The dim around him murmured and hummed. He had found his way back, and he observed how his connections to self and source expanded, moving outward in concentric rings. The pebble of new hope rocking ripples of tides that would meet foreign shores. Jack blasted concentration and vigor. His energy and focus gained measure, which began the sloughing of wounds. Jack knew Banjo's spirit was forever tattooed on his heart and that forever he would be marked at his core. He would carry his companion in him, and he could see the choice of it. He could internalize this pain because it was the pain of love, not fear and Jack would forever be grateful for discovering the difference.

"Why is this different, Jack?"

The pain of love?

"Yes. The pain of love. How is it different than the pain of fear?"

My loss is real. Jack thought. *I will miss Banjo forever. He is a hole in my heart, and I'll be forever grateful for what he brought to my life.* He internally repeated this. *I'll be forever grateful for what he brought to my life... and that's the critical difference – the gratitude for it.*

"Has there been gratitude for the pain incurred by fear?"

Jack blanked, then managed. *Sort of, I guess.* He thought some more on this. *I see how the self-inflicted pain of thought prisons have bedeviled me, plagued me, and I am grateful they brought me to this place of freedom from the habit.*

"There you go. That's it. Focus there. Think of nothing else. FOCUS: You are grateful they brought you to this place of freedom from the habit. You see how they are external, how those fears are not ov you, and internalizing them is a choice."

I see that...

"Pain born from fear does not devour you, Jack. You have been devouring it. Putting it in you. Locking it in you."

And now I choose not to bring the darkness in. It is outside of me. I cannot outrun it, and the only way to defeat it is to stand in the solidity of self.

"Say more Jack... Teach us. Continue..."

When I find fear rising within me, I can pause. I can stop and focus on its source, which I can chase down to discover its habitation and its roots.

"But only if you stand and face it."

Yes. Only if I stand and face it. One cannot assess a threat while running from it.

"Such as your former work Jack. Let's use that as an example. Teach me about those fears; the ones that you allowed to attach and leech life force from you."

I felt like they were trying to peg me as less than.

"Are you less than the other employees?"

No.

"Are you different?"

Yes.

"Yes, Jack, you were trying to do work while having different skills and abilities. Your pain comes from not accepting your differences. You aren't designed for it, yet you insist that you are. Can you see how that flies in the face of how we're trying to help and direct your life? Why do you fight what is with such vengeance? Is what we give you unacceptable?"

There was a long silence as Jack continued to carve, his mind flung into new spaces within him, the discovery thrilling.

Often yes. Often what you have delivered to my life I have found unacceptable.

"Was that decision painful, Jack?"

Yes.

"Was that pain optional?"

Yes.

"Why?"

Because you were conspiring for my success, and I fought it with all I had thinking my life 'should' be different from how it showed up. That I should be different than how I was, Jack halted. *That I should be different than how I am.* He could feel sadness and tears begin to well.

"You rail against existence without resistance. You're doing it even now. Cease your sadness. Cease your illusion. This is how you fail. You resist everything and everyone, even when what you've been asking for is delivered. You have never been taught how to see a thing for what it is. You lack curiosity, Jack. You have exchanged curiosity for judgment when curiosity is the natural first step in assessing something new in life."

I see that now. Jack arrested his tears, clarifying, *We might ultimately get to where a judgment or assessment might be formed, but many steps need to be worked through before that happens.*

"Yes. You have been poorly taught, but the courage to teach yourself, to guide yourself is a valuable asset. Before we move on, let's analyze the sadness that just sprang to your surface. What was that, other than nonsense?"

Again Jack felt the slight sting of it, but also its truth.

His soul continued, "Jack, you were saying 'That I should be different than how I am, and that created sadness. Why?"

Because I'm grasping at 'what was' and have yet to step into the power of 'what is'.

"Thank you, Jack! That is it. You cannot wallow in what was. You do not get to bring that energy into us, especially since it no longer serves a purpose. This self-pity is not ov us, and we no longer welcome it. We are part of the conversation now, and we do not welcome your poison. Teach us more..."

Jack closed his eyes. *When dystonia showed up for me, I cursed it because I did not understand. To watch it snuff out access to my body was wrenching, and I was full of fear because it felt like I was losing something... not gaining.*

"We understand that change can be alarming. However, did you remain curious as to what you were gaining?"

No.

"Why?"

Because fear is what I know.

"Because fear is what you knew."

Yes. Fear is what I knew.

Jack's hands worked at a fever pitch. The shavings and wood chips flew out of the back of the truck as the branch sang its song directly into Jack's mind and resources. It guided him where to place his tools and his focus. His hands became percussive against its toil, and the rhythms of the universe became audible, its pulse swinging at a tempo of all while Jack's mind sparked life, purpose, and creation.

The final crest of the night was falling when Jack took his creation and cupped it in his hands, assessing its completeness. It was done, and it made Jack's heart sing. Joy radiated through him, and the sense of pride he felt over his work filled him.

Slowly time returned to his mind as Jack put down his tools, glanced at the night, then headed for bed. It had been a good day. The kind of day where you are ready to sleep for you have done your work and the satisfaction of that type of tired is its own reward. Jack rolled over and was asleep in minutes.

MOPPET

The next morning, Jack came to life with a better sense of himself. He felt less jagged, he felt calmer. He was refreshed.

After a morning jog and shower, Jack was ready to hit the open road. He planned to get to Dease Lake, if possible. However, there was a lot of road to cover, and Jack was still cautious about pushing himself too hard. Being alone felt like he had no room for error. That said, Jack was feeling better with each passing day, and today was the perfect weather for driving. Cloudy, not rainy. Jack kicked on the radio and hit the open road. He always loved the moment of the first mile, when adventure would motor inside of him, and his sense of freedom would return. Jack gunned it.

Several hours into the drive, Jack became acutely aware of how alone he was during this leg of the drive. There were practically no cars on the roads and certainly no services or towns. He counted the hours between cities. There just weren't any. There was no real civilization to speak of. It was simply a road lined with trees and occasional alternate scenery. Jack also noted how cold it was getting, even for June. He got lost in his thoughts and adjusted the radio.

It was past dinner time when Jack reached Dease Lake. It was somewhat of a relief to be near people again. He noted that, while he fancied himself a loner, the last stretch of his drive was uncomfortable because he felt too alone. Jack was surprised by the feeling but let it sink into his soul.

Jack turned to ask Banjo if he wanted to join him in treating themselves, but forgot he was alone. Then, finally, he took a breath and redirected his question to himself, *How about a treat, Jack?* He thought goofily. *Righteo, mate. I thought you'd never ask.*

This was new for Jack. Being kind to himself and the thought of a warm bed in a heated room felt like heaven to the grate of Jack's wear. He knew he should sleep more at night, but Jack always heeded the call when inspiration struck, and he did so with joy. On this night, Jack found such a hotel room, dinner, then slept for the better part of twelve hours; the time he needed to get his real work done.

The next morning, Jack felt like his old self again, which involved working out, showering, and self-motivating talks in the bathroom mirror.

"Okay, fuckheads!" Jack sexy smiled. "Let's do this! Woohoo!" as he cranked the music coming from his tiny phone on the countertop. He couldn't help but laugh and enjoy his silliness without comment or judgment.

"Feels good to feel good, doesn't it, Jack?"

Jack shot a quick model squint pose into the mirror. "How you doin'?" Eyebrows. Eyebrows. "Lookin' pretty good. Oh Yeah...." Jack thought he looked pretty good for a guy his age. He didn't hate what was reflected, even if much of its perky muscled reflection had been delivered by way of unrelenting cramping; a shitstorm not of his choosing. Jack noted that felt good but also stopped short of reviewing his face in such close quarters. That was generally never an option. Not for some time now.

The morning hit its stride as Jack jumped up into his truck and pointed it toward Upper Liard and Yukon Territory. *Let's see if we can make it to Whitehorse,* Jack thought, pulling onto the highway.

It was a typical day of travel for Jack. Nothing too much to say or feel, and he was happy for a break from thinking or conversing with himself. He often wondered about the one with whom he spoke. "Be me," rolled through him.

I am me, he thought.

"Yes. As am I."

Urrrggghhhhh, Jack thought. *Just shut up. I need a break.*

"From yourself?"

From whatever the hell this is. Jack reached for a joint to make it shut up.

"Ignore me in ways if you like. I still am because you still are."

And you are me. Jack was puzzled without the statement being formed as a question. *You are me,* he repeated. *Then who am I?*

"We don't think you're ready for that conversation yet, Jack."

Arrrggghhhh! Jack thought again while pulling down his cowboy hat with the hopes of cutting the flow from his cranial egress to the beyond. *Just make it stop.* He pushed the truck further and faster, trying to outrun the thing.

Jack had been on the road about seven hours when a sign proclaiming "Swan Habitat Center" came into view.

Swans, eh? he thought. Jack had always felt a connection to birds. Something he found notable given his otherwise very earthy Taurean way. Maybe the feathers and flight offered the yin to his dominant yang ways. Jack parked to check it out.

"What brings you to Yukon Territory?" the man behind the counter asked as Jack closed the door behind him. Jack caught the building's scent of makeshift, which was very common in this part of the world. Building codes and the concept of nice were long ago exchanged for currently standing and working.

"Just passing through." Jack replied. "I was curious what this is all about. Beautiful lake day, though, that's for sure. Some pretty fat honkers you have out there."

"Yep. Thanks. Just the common ones for now, but there are many other avian guests here should ya care for it. Take a self-guided map if you like." Jack was reaching for the pamphlet when he bumped into someone.

"Oh, excuse me. So sorry," he said, turning to see the person.

"Honkers, huh?" The old white guy said. "What's that?"

"Uh, yeah. Hi. Honkers. You know, geese. Canadian Geese."

The old guy eyed the response from under his USA war vet cap. He was dubious of the explanation. "Just yesterday, I learned what a toque was, today honkers. So you people just make up your own language?"

Jack thought, *Nah… We're just not American, so we don't believe everything needs to be adjusted for our comfort.* But outwardly, Jack just smiled and waved.

"Ugh," Jack said under his breath, leaving the building.

Back outside, Jack packed his smaller backpack for a hike around the lake. Opening the brochure was like opening a world of possibility. He couldn't believe the massive amount of wildlife that called this place home. The Common Loon, which was always Jack's favorite, the common Raven or Crow, the yellow warbler, Rough Legged Hawks, the grouse, kestrels, shorebirds such as Lesser Yellowlegs, finches, swallows, owls, ducks, and eagles. He was thrilled at the opportunity to see some of these amazing creatures.

Jack scanned to the next page, where Mushrooms of the Yukon Territory was announced from the top. *Mushrooms?* Jack thought. There was one called the "Slippery Jack." Suillus tomentosus was its genus. "The flesh turns blue when it has been bruised or cut, but not as quickly or noticeably as certain other boletes." Jack read about it feeling weird and tumbly. "Bleh. Next." He turned the page.

"Roadside Flowers," Jack read as his eyes popped from seeing photos of some of his favorites. "Fireweed!" This was always a staple of every painting created in this part of the world. The plant was heavily associated with the Yukon, and Jack loved the sense of it, how its northern beauty calmed his nerves and spoke of long summer nights when the sun was still up well past bedtime.

"Mountain cranberry, Nagoon Berry!" Jack's eyes were bursting with sensations, and his palette swirled at the thought of tasty snacks that might await. He read on, "Rhubarb! Strawberry! Arnica, Sage, Dandelion, Yarrow and Soapberry." Yum… Jack's mouth watered. He could live on this lake forever and never lack for the thrill of life found here. This bleak northern space would always feel like home; Jack loved it here. He loved its simpleness, the uncomplicated nature of the world where people did things for different reasons than was commonplace in other far-flung parts. There was a slowness here that felt right to Jack's way. He grabbed his pack, slung it over his shoulder, and headed out for a day of exploring.

Reaching the water's edge, Jack knelt to observe the swarms of black dots. He leaned in closer to see they were tadpoles. Hundreds of them. Little black squishes that newly wriggled toward food and sunshine. They had just punched out of their clutch as Jack noted that it'd be a few weeks before they become froglets.

The memory of frog stories that he had heard as a child came rushing back…

"Why would someone choose a frog as a spirit animal?" he recalled himself scoffing when he was about thirteen years old.

"No, dip shit," his older cousin Joe said while they were hunting earthworms for the next day's fishing trip. "You don't choose a spirit animal… it chooses you." Jack felt secure in trusting the information from his indigenous cousin, and while Jack didn't always understand the ways and beliefs of his First Nation's relatives, it did always give him the hope he needed while in his darkest moments with his family's

Christian faith. If his Native Canadian family members could value Jack, other groups might honor and cherish him for what he was. The fact that concept existed in his mind, allowed Jack to find space for himself within himself, in a world where he was told he was evil, vile and "an abomination".

"Do you have a spirit animal?" Jack asked Joe.

The older cousin put down his things, took Jack by the hand, and led him to the water's edge. "Look."

Jack froze, feeling like an unbelievable dope because he had no idea what he was being directed to look at. "Cool," was finally his response doing his best not to give away that he wasn't sure what was going on.

Joe looked at Jack's face and sighed; it was clear Cousin Joe needed to start at the beginning. "Like anything with a spirit, it can be a soul friend or guide, a teacher and an advisor. Frogs can be guardian spirits, too, like the helper that appeared to Skookum Jim after he rescued a frog trapped in a deep hole. The explorer later dreamed of a frog showing him a gold-tipped walking stick and told him where he would find his fortune. In the late 1800s, after traveling down the Yukon River to Dawson, Skookum Jim was one of the first people to discover gold in the Klondike." Jack's eyes widened at the possibility of being in union with such a thing. A spirit guide!? Jack wanted to discover that truth in him as well.

"What's your spirit animal, Joe?"

"I said look." Joe pulled back the brush further, but Jack still didn't see anything. Finally, Joe put a finger to Jack's forehead, forcing him to lift his gaze into the trees. He saw it.

"Holy…" Jack said in a loud whisper while backing away. Joe pulled Jack back down toward the earth, keeping him in place.

"Don't move," Joe whispered back. Jack looked up to see a raptor the size of himself. It was enormous. They both froze and witnessed the majesty of the thing. "It's why I carry this." Joe tugged at his necklace made of beads, bone, and feathers. It was beautiful, and Jack's eyes continued to tell his absolute amazement.

Coming back to the present, Jack breathed in the cool air and pressed on from the tadpoles. He readjusted his pack and headed toward a thicket of short trees to see what he might discover next.

Jack spent the better part of the day in the wildlife habitat connecting with his spirit. Hares, Voles, Pikas, and Woodchucks, ran about and showcased their ways, and it was rounding noon when Jack put his back against a boulder to rest and eat his packed lunch.

What am I of? Jack thought mid-munch. The answer had yet to come. He turned back to his meal, where he was interrupted by a visitor.

"Oh, hello there," Jack said, surprised to see he wasn't alone. The tiniest black fledgling was eyeing him from a branch directly in Jack's eye line. The bird switched its head back and forth as if assessing him quizzically from behind blue eyes. Jack tore a few bits of bread from his sandwich and tossed it in the bird's direction.

The exchange between the two lasted the duration of Jack's picnic, but then it was done, and it was time to return to the exploration of the place. So he tossed one last scrap at the bird, adjusted his hat, and headed back into the woods.

"Meep. Craaaa…." the sound behind Jack was unmistakable. He kept walking. "Scraaaa….," it continued.

Now what? Jack thought, turning to see the chick keeping after him. *No more. Sorry, buddy.* Jack picked up the pace and was into the heavily wooded area within minutes.

He was adjusting his vision to the dim of the woods when he heard "Meep" behind him again.

"Oh, c'mon now." Jack pleaded, just wanting to be left alone.

"Scraaaa…," it asked like a question.

"What's wrong, buddy," he said, turning to eye the bird.

"Meep." Jack sat, resigning himself to seeing this thing through while scrounging for the spilled trail mix in the bottom of his bag. Finding some fruit and nuts, he spilled them on the ground in front of him. The bird hopped over and munched some of the treats, eyeing him from side to side.

"So, what's your story, little one?" Jack outstretched a finger to see how the bird would react. It gave his finger a peck then went on with its snacking opportunity. "Where's your mama?" Then, just for fun, Jack put the last pieces of trail mix on his chest and leaned back against a stump. The bird hopped up on him and continued its meal unfettered by Jack's presence. "What are you?" he said, flipping through the Rolodex of his mind that held information on black birds. Finding nothing, he turned to his phone and searched the internet for "Black Bird Blue Eyes," but grackles kept populating the page, and Jack knew it wasn't that because all of its feathers were black, not half black and half blue. Next, he searched for a solution by subtracting the options he knew weren't. Cowbird, no. Starling, no. Grackle, no. That left common crow and raven. "Okay…," Jack said to his phone while typing, "Can crows or ravens have blue eyes?" Remaining in curiosity felt like the next best option. The top-line search result read: "Why does that crow have blue eyes? Despite being roughly the same size as their parents, baby American crows have bright blue eyes. The eye color changes to brown as the crow matures over the summer. Another feature to look for is a bit of pink at the corner of the crow's mouth, called the gape."

"Huh," Jack said, mulling over the new information. He then turned back to the chick. "So, you're a crow of some kind? I didn't know you could have blue eyes. Learn something new every day, I guess." Jack then carefully picked up the bird and put it on the ground, dusting himself free from peanuts and raisins while standing. The thing popped its head up and down then gave clicking sounds in the form of a command. Jack laughed. "Oh really?" he said in a chuckle as he strode onward with his journey.

A shriek arose behind him. "Jesus…" Jack scrambled, looking around only to find the fledgling annoyed and piercing his soul with its very direct gaze. He wouldn't lose this argument, so he put his head down and hurried out into the next part of the trail. Finding Jack had finally shaken the thing, he continued his journey in hopes of seeing other woodland creatures. Maybe a marmot or porcupine? He journeyed on.

By late afternoon Jack was starting to tire from the day of hiking, and he made his way back to the truck where he was greeted with a "Meep." Jack spun around, unsure of what to feel. The damn bird was hopping around the base of his vehicle.

"No, little guy… you gotta go home," Jack said, shooing the small bird from him and his car. "Go on now…."

As Jack was finalizing this performance, the place's owner came out. "See ya met Yolo."

Jack's face showed its puzzle as he threw his backpack in the back seat. "Come again, now?"

"I see you met Yolo."

"This baby bird? His name is Yolo? You know him?"

"Well, technically, she's her, but yeah… she's been trying to sneak meals from our guests for a few days now. It seems she is out of the nest too early." The man shook his head. "Don't know what happened to her parents."

"So, she's an orphan?"

"Yeah, I guess, of sorts." The man went back inside as Jack squatted to see the thing close up.

"Yolo. Odd name for a bird. Native for something?" Jack didn't know. He opened the truck and hopped in, rolled down his window, and started to drive off.

"Meep," it called after him. Jack immediately put his foot on the brake.

"Dude…. you're killing me here. Can you find someone else to haunt?" It eyed him more with a guttural throat rattle. Jack knew that the bird would most likely be dead in a few days without a proper nest and parents, but how could he…?

Hold on, he thought, backing up to the thing then cutting the engine. "Hold on." He said aloud while adjusting his seat back to a resting reclined position. "Be right back."

Hey! Jack thought.

"Yes, Jack. We're here."

So, before they commit me for talking to myself, I just thought I'd give this a try in case there might be some information here. I kinda need some advice.

"You feel that you're at an important intersection."

Jack rebuffed this statement. *Well, let's slow our roll here… don't go putting words in my mouth. Just a little advice. It's not like I'm at, as you put it, an important intersection.*

"As you wish. Your companion here. That's the source of your inquiry?"

Yes… Do I just leave the thing to die, or what should I do here?

"What does your gut tell you?"

This was not welcome advice from his conscience. *My gut?*

"Yes. What is your gut telling you?"

Jack was already tired of the conversation, which was careening its way toward discussions with himself. He was confused. *And I do what now?*

"What are you not understanding, Jack? What is your gut telling you?"

Next, Jack sat silently, focusing his question in the direction of his stomach. *Leave the bird?*

"N o," his gut replied.

No? Jack replied. *No? Ugh….* Jack jumped out of the truck and headed toward Yolo. "Okay, buddy, guess it's your lucky day." Jack stuck his hand out and was pecked. A blood droplet surfaced on Jack's hand. "Gah! Fine." He opened the back of the Blazer, fished out a towel which he used to swaddle the thing and make its place on Banjo's chair.

"Meep," it continued.

I really hope I don't regret this, Jack thought, regaining control of the car and heading out onto the highway.

GLIDE

It was only a short drive into Whitehorse, a special place for Jack where he had spent many summers working odd jobs when things were slow back home on the Island. It's where he first learned of Plexus Foods and how to pack frozen fish and where he got his first driver's license. The Yukon always had the hangover of the gold rush and miners, the zeal for panhandling and the whisper of fortunes yet discovered. This vibe worked for Jack's spirit. The wild and unknown of it were promises that Jack could hear.

"So, what are we going to do with you?" Jack asked the baby crow. Do you just hang here in the cab as Banjo did, or is there another way to do this?" Jack thought it best to let nature do its thing. He cracked the windows so Yolo could escape if she wanted to but otherwise didn't think much of it as he exited the truck.

Jack poked into shops for the next few hours, connected with a few old friends, then got back in the Blazer to head to a campground nearby. He knew the one on the north side of town had the best community facilities.

Once they were checked in and getting set for the night, he turned his attention back to his new traveling companion. "Yolo. As in You Only Live Once? Or what?" Jack's mind failed to deliver additional meaning as he searched his phone for how to interact with the thing.

The remainder of the evening was fairly quiet, and it greatly amused Jack how Yolo would search for things to mess with. The bird was endlessly curious, so Jack thought to have some fun with it. "What if I could train it?"

Suddenly Jack was back in elementary school as dreams of a pet bird washed over him. He noted the energy this brought to his senses as his mind pushed forward thousands of possibilities that might be realized through this. Maybe he had always wanted a pet bird? The notion throughout his life kept resurfacing.

The next morning Jack woke to the sensation of pecking at his hair. *Leave me alone,* he thought, pulling the covers over his head. But his new daughter had other ideas. PECK, PECK, PECK. Yolo continued in her quizzical accosting way. "Damn bird." Jack popped his head out from the covers. "Fine." He got out of bed and searched for some trail mix to throw at the thing.

Figuring he was up now, Jack made some coffee and laced up his shoes for his morning run. "See ya," Jack offered to Yolo while inserting his earbuds. Then, he took off in the direction of the roadside trail. Reaching the paved bike path, Jack sprinted, taking in the world and rejoining its conversation.

"Morning, world!" Jack offered, but something flew right at him with a prehistoric squawk. "Jesus! What in the hell?" he ducked. It was Yolo. "Damn bird……!" as the thing settled a few feet ahead. Jack was honestly surprised to see the thing fly. "You're a bit young to be winging it alone out here, aren't ya?" There was a habit of a new expression that was finding its way regularly to Jack's face. A one-eyed inquisition of "what in the actual fuck, bird?", a clench of facial muscles that encapsulated the feeling of query toward things that needed closer inspection. He remained curious of the bird as it stood there, tiny yet blocking his path. "You ain't short on attitude, are you?" Jack ran on while Yolo trained for another chase.

"Crawwww!" Yolo screamed into Jack's ear.

"Oh… This is a game for you?" Jack smiled and ran on.

Their competition continued the length of Jack's jog, and upon their return to the campsite, they discovered both their souls were smiling. Jack instantly became grateful for his new companion's pip, for it lent his joy back to him, a sense that had been clouded within him for too many of the days since Banjo's passing.

The duo finished their morning routine, or, rather, Jack completed his usual routine. At the same time, Yolo inquired about everything he did while she dusted the spaces around Jack while he worked, an exercise that made Jack laugh every few minutes. Unfortunately, the bird was not short on pesky, prying, eyeing, or personality. "Scraaaa!" Yolo repeated. It wasn't a beautiful sound but a song nonetheless that asked Jack's heart to join in reverence of, what is.

"WooHoo!" Jack yelled, adjusting his cowboy hat and heading north. "Dawson City… here we come." Jack noted that the word "we" returned to his vocabulary, which felt nice.

It was a quiet day's drive other than the meeps, pecks, caws, and scraws emanating from the fledgling while it found its voice. "Sing out, Louise!" Jack encouraged, which was immediately followed by his best radio announcer voice saying, "You Sound Terrific!" Jack's laugh was back.

The two flew down the freeway, voices ricocheting around the cab. Two very different songs that, if you strained to hear something sweet, met somewhere between a dying cat and an elementary school violin recital.

"Faithfully…." Jack's voice quieted for the drama of a Journey song that had to be appropriately and fully realized. He clicked off the radio.

"Are you ready for what's next, Jack?" The voice within asked.

Mother of Saint Francis in a Tonka Truck, Jack thought to himself. *Can I have a minute? I just finished a very important performance where I left it all on the floor.* Jack laughed. *Uhhhh… fine. What?*

"You should clean up some of your mental garbage." It replied.

It was always in these moments, while in conversation with him-self, where Jack was kind of shocked at the rudeness he was met with. *Mental garbage. Mental garbage?! What in the what? Mental garbage.* He recognized the words but was at a loss as to their meaning. *I'm sorry… I don't follow.*

"You feel lighter than before, sure, but you have yet to bring yourself up to zero."

Again! Jack thought. *How is that not fucking rude? Bring me up to zero. Wow. Just wow.* Jack left the conversation and put a match in his mokee pipe.

"How ya doing, sister?" Jack asked the crow, then refocused on the road and sped on.

STUB

"Dawson City!" The sign ahead seemed to congratulate travelers on their arrival. Jack bounced with excitement, encouraging Yolo to do the same. She screeched with sounds of happiness and curiosity. As to what exactly they were doing, she didn't seem sure, but her gleeful cries indicated that she was enjoying the game nonetheless.

"Wow!" Jack crowed. "Look!" Yolo hopped up on the dash and pecked at the glass, leaving Jack to wonder if she actually understood him. *Stay in curiosity,* his thoughts said.

Jack pulled onto Main Street, where the old steam paddle boats and promise of Can-Can girls gave the place a sense of celebration. Jack parked and exited the truck while Yolo hopped on the roof and pecked at the unseen. "Be right back, girl." Jack shot Yolo a kiss while jumping his coat on. "WooHoo!" Jack laughed for no other reason than it felt good.

Diamond Tooth Girtie's Gambling Hall was just ahead, and Jack was not going to miss out on one of his favorite things in the world. A show. Jack walked up to the ticket booth.

"One for tonight?" Jack asked the lady excitedly.

"Ah. Well… it looks like the only one we have as a single for tonight is here." She pointed at a black circle near the front of the stage. "But fair warning, they call that seat 'the hot seat.'"

Jack's smile fell from his face. "I'm sorry? The hot seat?"

"Yeah… we like to warn folks to make sure whoever sits there is game for the girls to interact with. Some people don't like that sort of thing."

People are going to see me? flew into Jack's mind. *Look at me? And people, I'm sure… will be laughing. And what if I don't know what they're laughing about.* Then the words "Mental Garbage" cut into Jack's thoughts as his walls fought to rise. *Mother fucker…* Jack thought. *I hate it when you're right… Fine. Ya. I get it. Mental garbage.* He exhaled the ancient echoes and came back to the moment.

"Fine," Jack said. He paid the $30 and pocketed the ticket. *I should probably shower,* he told himself, heading back up to meet Yolo. His girl. Jack beamed with the thought.

"Yo, Yolo, my solo…." Jack sang, jumping into the truck and getting Yolo seated next to him. "C'mon now!" the joyful battle cry lifted from him as he sped off in search of a nice hotel.

"Just staying the one night then?" the receptionist asked.

"Yes, ma'am. Got a hot date and wanna smell fresh." Jack then realized himself and snapped from his lizard lounge dream. He was way out of line. He corrected, "Yes. Ma'am. Just me. Just one night is fine. Thank you."

The receptionist shook her head with eyes bulging and handed Jack the key and receipt.

"Ooh…" Lip smack. "What's your pet policy?" Jack smiled with a crinkled-up face that conveyed he understood social norms but wasn't really in the mood to care.

"One dog or cat."

"And what about a bird?" Jack inquired.

She erected herself musing on the question. "Bird… ?" She grabbed for the binder near her computer. "Bird…?" she repeated. "Ah… here it is, pets, pets…. pets. Yes. Here it is. Each guest may have one pet per room." She looked up at him. "Doesn't say anything about a bird."

"But it does say one pet."

"Yes, I guess it does. Just pay the pet deposit here…." They exchanged more plastic and paper.

Once in their room, Jack unpacked his toiletries and stretched out on the bed. Yolo ruffled while taking in her new surroundings. She was still adjusting to the concept of "inside." They were both content to just idle here for a while as they reentered themselves and rested. Jack set his alarm in case a surprise nap overtook him.

As Jack stirred alive, he noted that the clock read 6:15. His eyes shot open as he realized the moment and what adventure was yet to come. He jumped in the shower, sang a few bars of "Send in the Clowns," did his hair nice, shaved his face, and added a touch of cologne, which added to his sense of spiciness.

"See ya in a bit." Jack kissed Yolo and set out into the evening.

Strolling downtown, Jack took in the fragmented carnival atmosphere, which was near impossible to reproduce when the sun hardly ever set. What the place lacked in posh, it made up for in roaring kitsch. It was honky-tonk fun, saloon doors, and liquor. Jack had a sense of possibility for the night, and it reveled his stoke to be in it.

Walking the sidewalk, the sunlit night was split overhead by flashing lights as Jack walked under a sign saying, "The Tavern," then scrawled below that was the subtitle "Perhaps the finest dive bar you will ever drink beer in." Jack liked this approach. There wasn't a promise of more here. They just called it as they saw it. *Perfect,* thought Jack as he entered.

"Welcome to the Snake Pit. What can I get ya?"

"Um… your French Dip and a beer… What do you have on the dark side?" Jacked seated himself at the far end of the bar.

Minutes later, his food arrived. Jack never minded eating alone. He felt free of social anxiety when he didn't have to interact with others while he ate. Finally, it was rounding 7:30 PM, and Jack needed to head to the theater. Just then, his thought stream was interrupted by, "Excuse me, mate. This seat taken?" Jack looked up.

"Holy shit…!" escaped Jack's lips as he jumped up to meet the person face to face. "Thad!" Jack yelled with exuberance. "Oh wow! What are you doing here? Yes, come sit, although I only have a few minutes."

"Is that right? You clocking in at the Follies?" Thad winked, making Jack laugh.

"Actually, kinda."

"Ah… makes sense now," Thad said, putting up his crutches, leaving Jack to puzzle on the statement.

"And what's that?" Jack returned, waving over the bartender while miming for another round. Thad joined with a nod that said, "Yes, me too."

"Your star quality," Thad said, making Jack burst into laughter. When Jack regained himself, he came face to face with Thad, and they just stopped for a second to take each other in. The room slowed.

"You know," Jack began while holding his draft mug for the final swig, "I wanted to thank you for something. Something I've thought about a lot." Thad took his coat off, listening for more.

"And what's that?"

Jack wanted to choose his following words carefully. "You made something a possibility in my mind. Something I had never considered." Feeling exposed, Jack clammed, a move Thad sensed, so to encourage an air of safety, he put his arm around Jack's neck and gave him a friendly shake.

"C'mon… out with it because you know…." Thad took his beer from the bartender, "With the amount of sheer brilliance I spout, you're going to have to narrow it down for me." Thad released Jack's neck but didn't abandon the lean-in that the neck wringing introduced to the moment.

"You introduced the concept that, maybe, what was happening to me needed to be assessed from a different place than I had been."

Thad finished a swallow of beer and twinkled. "See, mate," he ribbed. "Stick around. I'm fucking brilliant when you get to know me."

"Actually…" Jack interrupted but then paused, making Thad nudge again.

"Actually, what?"

"Actually, I think I might like that."

"What's that?" Thad sat back, acting surprised. "Do you now?"

Jack was feeling exposed and felt the urge to run. "Yeah… maybe?" Jack stammered while standing and reaching for his coat. Thad grabbed at Jack's shoulder to keep him in place.

"Oh no, you don't…." Thad said, catching Jack off-guard. "You ran out on me last time just when we were starting to have an actual conversation. Remember?"

With that, Jack was returned to their first encounter, how when picking Thad up off the hardware store floor, he noticed that they were roughly the same age, how when Jack asked him if he had support back home, he didn't answer and how once he got Thad to drop his walls that he enjoyed the man's perspective or "truth."

"I guess I kinda did," Jack said, resigning himself back to his bar stool.

"It's the one thing I remember most about meeting you, Jack… well, that and how you insulted me," Thad teased playfully. Jack laughed. "But I also remember how you helped a stranger and how you said from the onset that you felt a connection because of our shared experience." Then to break the seriousness of the moment, "And what the hell was that burger joint anyhow? Rusty's burgers where everything is overly complicated with people's names." Jack's laugh was now being bounced from his belly. "The Sally salad, the Jerry cheeseburger, the Nina pineapple shake." They both laughed. "I think I fucking had the bloody Lee sandwich, WHICH! by the way, I believe was named after Lee Harvey Oswald because that meal assassinated my innards." They were both openly laughing now and making a scene, not that either one of them cared.

A calm returning over the men, Jack turned to face Thad, noting he had grown a beard since their first encounter. It looked handsome on him, Jack thought. "What brings you to Dawson City?"

Thad returned his mug to the bar. "I am on a book tour." This was not what Jack was expecting to be the answer.

"So, you're a writer?"

"That I am. Just finished the tour. Well, actually, tomorrow is the last day."

Jack was taking it all in. So many questions and thoughts arose. "What's your book about exactly?" Jack said, noting the time.

"It's a project I've been…." Thad thought about his answer more closely, "well, to be honest, I've been working on it my whole life. About how we grow through conflict and struggle, so to welcome conflict and adversity, in a way, can encourage growth."

With this, Jack became quiet. "Well, you introduced that concept to me, and I want to thank you for it. It's helped me reframe my life's situation."

"You need to go?" Thad asked, slightly crestfallen.

"I'm not blowing you off, Thad," Jack said as the thought *Well, not yet, but the night is young* ran across his mind, a thought that surprised Jack as it highlighted the fact that he was very attracted to the man. "It's just that I kinda have a commitment. I bought a ticket for the Follie's tonight, and apparently, I'm in 'the hot seat.' Do you know what that is? I sure didn't."

"Yeah… I know what that is. I'm sure you'll do great. Lots of pretty ladies to keep your attention." Thad turned his attention to his phone. "Maybe we'll catch up later."

Putting on his coat, then grabbing an old receipt and a pen from the bar, Jack wrote down his number. "I'd like that. Here," Jack said, handing Thad the folded note. "Text me the info on the book signing thing… or whatever it is… if people can come? But you know… only if it's cool… or whatever." Jack couldn't, yet again, find the end of his sentences while in the presence of someone he found interesting. *Jack, stop being weird,* he thought to himself, then stood, disconnected from the pull of things past, and became fully present to say goodbye.

Before Thad, Jack stood, he breathed in the room and, while fully rapt with his personal strength that sent smiles into them both, asked, "Can I see you tomorrow?"

Thad's face melted into a warm mash of emotions. "I'd like that."

Jack smiled, then turned and walked out the door.

JIG

Jack entered the honky-tonk auditorium and found "the hot seat." He nervously folded his Playbill while pretending to focus on the words when the truth was, on the inside, he was a washing machine set to jumble. This potential stage experience was really out of his comfort zone, but it was something he was willing to wade through to enjoy one of his favorite things of the town. The lights began to fade as the excitement in the auditorium grew – massive clapping and cheers released into the air as the stage lights illuminated a vast red curtain. The music began.

"Ladies and Gentlemen! Welcome to Diamond Tooth Girtie's Can-Can revival!" The crowd cheered wildly, and it was instantly clear that all in attendance were up for the event. An atmosphere of jubilee and gin populated the place while woots, whistles, and cheers continued freely. Next, pretty young women in period dresses began to run around the stage excitedly.

The upbeat music honky-tonked and the girls ruffled in scandal while Jack's knees knocked nervously, not knowing when they might get to him. He focused on the show while his innards tumbled and flopped, but Jack was going to see this through. *Meet the moment. Not as you think it might be, but as it is. Be with what is. Stand.* Jack shored himself against fear's rip current that was asking to take him under.

"And who do we have here!?" The woman yelled into the mic, breaking Jack from his mental sloshing.

Two male dancers rushed down the steps into the audience to grab Jack and lead him back onto the stage. He was being directed to sit in the chair surrounded by dancing girls… but then the world kiltered and slid. Jack froze, facing that chair on stage. Time slowed. The celebration around him grew quiet as the white terror of PTSD attached itself to his cerebral cortex and began to suck. Jack could feel it bite into him, as he was thrown destitute into a suitcase of despair and child-known horrors. Jack couldn't move. The panic of seeing this lone wooden chair centerstage overtook him while the world ground to a halt.

"Jack."

Yes, I'm here.

"What's going on, Jack? You are safe." But the words in his head couldn't outmaneuver the primal cut of him; the cut of the moment, a clamp that knew only one purpose, to wall off, escape, and protect.

Jack began to sob internally. He had never felt so helpless as the wicked within infected his mind, laying waste to his strength. Jack began to panic. *HELP!* Jack's senses flared as his eyes left that one lone wooden chair placed center stage, to searched for an escape route. Again, his mind screamed. *"HELP!"*

"JACK! STAND." The inner voice said.

But he couldn't. Jack turned to face the audience, whose cheers were starting to fade as they observed a man with a deformed skull struggle. Audience members were unsure if this was part of the act.

"Sir," One of the male dancers said to Jack, directly popping him out of his thoughts. "Are you okay?"

There was a hush now falling over the audience as Jack's veins began to accept buckets of adrenaline egging on the fight or flight mode already corrupting and co-opting his nerves. "I'm sorry, I don't feel well," Jack said hoarsely in a rough whisper, his throat and mouth drier than they'd ever been.

The young dancer led Jack off the stage into the wings while another ran into the audience to retrieve another volunteer.

Sitting in a chair the stagehands provided, Jack said "Sorry" to no one in particular and hung his head. *What a fucking failure,* Jack thought of himself. I shouldn't be seen. Not like that. Jack put his face in his hands to regain himself. A few minutes later, Jack excused himself to head out the stage door and into the cool of the bright lit night.

What the fuck was that? Jack asked himself, still astonished at how things had fallen so quickly into a tangle of turmoil and embarrassment. *Ugh…. I'm such a failure as a human,* Jack thought, walking back to his hotel. His phone buzzed.

Hey, mate, the message read, instantly lifting Jack's demeanor. Nice seeing you again. If you like, I'll be at the Bender Street Book Fair tomorrow 11-1.

Jack's spirit radiated as he typed back. Sign me a copy? He pushed send. Dots festooned on the screen, indicating Thad was typing something in return.

Already done ;)

See you tomorrow then. Jack replied.

Jack closed his phone while awash in too many emotions to think clearly. He was just relieved to get back to the room and unwind. He was doing his best to ignore the words "Mental Garbage," the problem never more evident in his mind. That's what sidelined him this evening – mental garbage.

"You're not mental garbage, Jack." The voice pressed into his mind. "That's not what we said. You must stop identifying with things outside of yourself as yourself. It's painful to watch how you shiv such a thing up inside you."

Jack wasn't joining the conversation tonight. Instead, he walled off and headed to bed.

The next morning, Jack found breakfast for himself and Yolo, then they set out for their morning run before showering and getting ready for the day. Once packed and ready to leave, Jack collapsed back into the covers, clean and refreshed. They still had some time to kill, and it felt good to just lay on the bed for a bit while collecting thoughts and unpacking concepts, the pump and pulse of his jog still beating in his ears.

"You're not garbage, Jack." The voice reassured.

I know.

"Why this then? Why this sad tenderness?"

I just can't seem to get so much of life right. I get too thrown by the unseen. Social norms I can't get, things I'm supposed to know that I don't, then everywhere I turn, there are tripwires and triggers from my past. I should just leave.

"Leave?"

Jack was silent.

The voice continued. "You have tools now, Jack. This pain you continue to revisit is optional."

I know, but today I just need to feel it.

"Today, you're choosing sadness."

Yes.

"It is the choice of a wise man," a reply that honestly surprised Jack, but he didn't fight it. He fought nothing but instead just let it all wash over and through him. An hour later, he felt much better from the exercise.

Some days, you just need to be in it, Jack thought.

"The only way out is through…." The voice reassured. Jack smiled hearing this.

Indeed, he thought back while collecting himself. It was, after all, time to go meet Thad.

CRUSHED

When Jack hitched to a parking spot, the bookstore was already abuzz. "BOOK SIGNING TODAY," read the banner with a subtitle of "Meet Thad Pierson, Author," and the following line promised, "Zenith's Peak." Jack thought perhaps this was the title of Thad's book. He internally flogged himself for not asking for at least this bit of information when they met last night. Jack felt embarrassed for himself as he entered the shop.

"JINGLE!" yelled the door's bells a tad too loud for the enclosed small space. A woman in a tool apron approached. "Feel free to sit anywhere," she indicated toward the few remaining chairs. Jack turned himself around a few times before selecting the chair at the back in the far corner. Over the next twenty minutes, the small space was inundated with curiosity and speculation.

"Is this seat taken?" an elderly woman asked. Caught off guard, Jack looked up to respond.

"Oh… no. Here, help yourself," as Jack moved his personal items closer, creating additional room for her.

"Have you ever heard Mr. Pierson speak?"

Jack was unclear how to respond. The question was, had he ever heard Thad speak? Yes. Yes, he had heard him speak because they had spoken before, but Jack sensed she wasn't being that literal. A problem that often occurred in Jack's life. "I have met him but not sure that's what you mean."

"Well, he's an excellent lecturer," the woman said, returning to her affairs. "He's an interesting sort, and my God… what a story. It's incredible that he is still alive."

The words from the woman kept getting stuck in Jack. "Interesting sort." What does that mean? Jack wasn't sure, then the crowd hushed as the lady Jack first encountered in the shop reached into her tool apron to produce a mic.

"Without further delay, we at the Bender Street Book Fair are thrilled to introduce Mr. Thad Pierson." The room clapped, wild with enthusiasm. Jack noted his internal response of being very impressed with his new friend's position in life.

"Hello…" Thad waved into the small gathering. "Nice to be here with you all, and thank you for your interest in my book. Allow me, if you will, to give some of the backdrop and highlights of it then we can have a few questions before the kickoff of the signing. How does that sound?" The crowd cheered their approval.

Thad began with a cool and quiet, "In the past, when I thought about writing this book, I couldn't get past the part where others would read its contents and know my story and my soul. Oh sure, I can gather in a group and tell stories and blather on like someone who knows things…." The group collectively laughed. "But it was the life behind that… The life beyond titles where I *actually* lived. What I do, is not who I am. I am not my job. I am not my title, and that was the question my mind kept asking me to solve. Who is Thad beyond the physical world?" He paused, looking over the crowd, which was now in rapt attention as the quiet way of Thad pulled them in further.

"Who am I?" Thad pondered crowd-ward.

"Who are we?" Another pause for consideration. "I think this is something we all have worked with since the beginning of our consciousness." The crowd murmured in agreement. "My story is, yes, unique, but certainly not special or unheard of." Another pause gave Thad a moment to rearrange himself and move his crutches to a safe resting spot against a chair. "Just another Scousers from Northern U.K. living in Canada, writing books, and pondering life. That's been my lot. That's the bullet-point, cliff notes version… but that says nothing of who I am." Thad then waved exuberantly… saying, "So it's time to cut the crap." Cheering erupted. "That's why I wanted to write this book. To call a thing a thing and clearly spell out my humanity and what I believe lies in all of us. Yes. Some of us have more to overcome than others." Thad raised his crutches in a tone of victory, raising some cheers from the audience, "But even that's not who we are."

The crowd hushed as Thad continued softly. "So yeah…" He eyed the crowd pausing. "Yeah… it's time to cut the crap and understand that we're all far more alike than we are different."

A woman doing her best to contain her excitement raised her hand. Thad chuckled. "Yes, Marcy. Nice to see you again."

Excited noises escaped her, "Oh… yes! So great to be here. Hi, Thad." She didn't so much as say this as flirt it. Thad smiled. "So yeah… wow… I just love the book." She froze, discovering she had caught herself in a pail of awkwardness, but then she tried to swim out of it with, "Not that your other books aren't just as great too." Jack noted the comment "other books."

Oh, so this ain't his first rodeo, Jack thought while being even more impressed. He enjoyed this initial insight into the world of a man he once picked up at a hardware store. Jack was very curious to know more.

The remainder of the hour wore on with fan-girls fan-girling and Thad pontificating about his life and insights, but then the crowd withdrew, and the queue began for the meet-n-greet. Jack stayed put not to draw attention to himself. Another hour passed, and as the last of the Thad Pierson book club left the store, Jack quietly walked up to him.

"I appreciated your talk." Then not knowing what to say next, interjected, "It was nice getting to know you better, getting to know how you think. And your life story… wow. It's amazing what you have survived." At that moment, Jack had all the personal security of a typical fourteen-year-old girl giving her first speech in front of her classmates. He felt all aw-shucks-n-stuff, a sensation that knee-capped his boldness and handicapped his swagger. Jack stood there looking at the ground. Thad grabbed his crutches to stand and look at him.

"I have to pack up and head out of here shortly, but it was so great running into you like this."

Jack didn't know why he felt sad. "Yes. You too," which smacked of fake cheer and disappointment. "Where do you live full-time? Maybe we can visit if I'm in your neck of the woods?"

"Indeed," Thad said. "My full-time residence is the Sunshine Coast. Gambier Island. You know it?" Jack lit up.

"Know it? It's one of my favorite places to visit."

"Well, now you have someone else to see when you do." Thad reached where the stack of books was. He pulled one wrapped in brown paper, and Jack noticed its writing. It was addressed: *"To handsome Jack."* As Jack read this, his eyes welled.

"Thank you. You're very sweet."

"Anytime, my friend. Here." He pushed the wrapped book into Jack and leaned in for a kiss then a hug. Jack then gathered his things to depart. "Okay if I text you sometime?"

Without lifting his gaze, Thad replied, "I'd like that." He then turned, grabbed his crutches, and headed back into the employee area of the store.

Jack stood there wanting more from the moment than it was ready to provide. Finally, he tucked in his brown paper package and left the shop with a sadness in him that he wasn't expecting.

GARBAGE DAY

Jack knew it was going to be another long day of driving if he was going to make it to the Arctic Circle by dinnertime. As morning broke, he stirred himself and got up to start the day.

"C'mon Yolo," he poked at the bird who lifted one perturbed eyelid. "Time to get up." Jack threw on some shorts and a t-shirt to grab a cup of coffee from the lobby.

Back in the room, Jack was still a tad blue. He sipped his coffee and reviewed the events of the past few days, which indeed had only been a few days; however, it felt like months. He stuck his finger into Yolo's neck feathers for a scratch. "Just a quick one today to get the juices flowing," Jack called to Yolo while lacing his runners. They headed out into the morning cold.

An hour later, the truck was repacked, and the two jumped in to hit the road. "Okay, girl. Today is the day. Today is when we cross the Arctic Circle." More than anything, Jack was curious to sense the energy of things, and him, when near the pull of a pole. They drove off with Jack saying a tenderhearted goodbye to his heart's swing and a miss, otherwise known as Thad.

The morning was fading into midday when Jack read a sign saying, "Last service station for 644 kilometers."

"Good lord," Jack thought. "Five hours of driving without so much as a gas station?" He needed to give his sense of exploration a pep talk.

Being removed from civilization on this level called out Jack's lie, the lie he always told himself about wanting to escape and not interact or be important to people. This next part of the journey was as remote and isolated as it gets, and he was about to be served the experience of it. Jack gulped down determination and fixed his gaze. He was ready for it. This is what his soul was asking from him, and he would deliver. Jack stopped at the last gas station for containers of backup fuel, strapped them to the roof, then out-gunned care and left dust in his wake.

An hour later, the false veneer of safety was non-existent. They were alone. Truly on their own, no safety net and no turning back. "Let's do this," Jack said and pressed into the gas pedal.

"So, how does it feel, Jack? This is what you've longed for." The voice said.

I kinda hate you, Jack replied.

"We only wish to bring you your heart's desire, and this is what you have been asking forever since you were young. To be alone and without human interaction. How does it feel?"

Jack knew where this was heading and internally grated against the conversation his mind seemed determined to have. *You know…* he thought as clouds of potential responses breezed through him. *We used to get along better… so why don't we pause from your line of questioning?*

"That's fine, Jack, just answer the question before we move on."

Jack paused but acquiesced. *What's the question?*

"How does it feel to get what you have told yourself that you want?"

Jack's nerves flexed and pony walled. *Well, I didn't know that <u>this</u> would be the reality of it.*

"No, you didn't." was the response, making Jack eye-roll.

No, you didn't, Jack mocked in response. *God…*

"Yes?" Jack froze hearing this because it crossed a line he would not accept. Not now, not ever. He mostly hated these "chats" now. Besides, Jack was still melancholy and didn't want to think or feel this day. Thad's handsome face fuzzed in his memory. He grabbed his Mokee pipe, lit it and dragged hard, as they raced further toward his goal.

"You deflected from the question, Jack."

This fucking guy… Jack thought.

"Please answer it. How does it feel to get what you have told yourself you want? You're alone now. Truly alone. This is the space you hold as the height of your being in order to achieve happiness. According to your desires, total isolation in a cold winterscape. is the zenith of the human experience. Isn't this what you spent all those days and nights hoping for? Because here it is."

Ugh… Jack hated this moment. The moment when he was asked to co-sign his own bullshit, yet found that he couldn't. He was yet again left wanting.

"Tell us the truth of it." They asked.

Okay, fine. Jack collected himself, washing off the layer of "go fuck yourself." He centered and slowed, coming present to the location of where his tires met the road.

"Was your heart's desire a lie? Do you tell yourself lies?"

I don't know.

"I don't know yet."

Fine, Jack thought. He had been caught as the shit-maker he was. *It wasn't an intentional lie. Just made up.*

"Just made up. Is it? You make things up then sell them back to yourself as truth."

Yes. I guess I do that.

He flicked on the radio, but of course, there were no stations here because that would require others, and "others" was a concept Jack had told himself he wanted no part of. The lie had been skinned, and Jack was forced to see it for what it was. An illusion. A fabrication that bordered on a lie. A realization that deflated Jack's mood further.

What am I doing here? Jack asked himself.

"You're realizing your truth."

Jack didn't respond.

The air of the midnight sun grew stronger with each passing hour. It was as if they could sense their flight to the top of the world. The span of sun that endlessly circled the skies and never set was gaining in strength and solar-flared brilliant intensity. It weirded Jack's senses. Something he had never felt before because he had never been this far North before, the sheer vastness and white glare of it inescapable. It really was the land of the True, North, Strong, and Free, but Jack quickly realized that the last part, the Free part, didn't have to mean isolated. Maybe the two words didn't match up as Jack thought. He knew the truth of it, despite not wanting to admit it, even though the stench of the lie permeated every other thought. Jack was lonely.

"How you doin', girl?" Jack asked the nesting crow. Yolo clicked and chortled her response. "We'll be fine," Jack added, doing his best to convince himself while his gut grew concerned. "We'll be fine," Jack repeated over raw nerves.

It was just before dinner when they saw it – the archway that celebrated latitude 66° 33," the road's entrance into the Arctic Circle. Jack's eyes widened, as he threw out his senses, trying to catch any cosmic charges. His feelers buzzed and popped, and he could sense the polar pull. It was electric.

They pulled over near the archway and bounded out of the car. "WooHoo!" Jack announced to the surrounding mountains and wild. "This is amazing." Jack knew he had to be with it, experience it, sense it. He grabbed his running shoes, and they explored their surroundings.

When they hit the crest of the road in front of them, Jack noticed a dirt road heading east. It seemed to head back into the mountain range, which piqued Jack's curiosity. He waved at Yolo, who circled back toward the truck. They ran and got in then headed for the curious off-road path.

Beginning down the lane, the dirt road was winding, and how it arched its way eastward up through the boulders and crags was nothing short of berserk. Jack stopped to assess whether he thought they could make it. He mentally double-checked fuel supplies, food, and cell service. They should be okay, but once the land of the sun engulfed the vehicle, there would be no returning until Jack's inquest was quelled. He would answer his soul's call—and for whatever reason, he *knew* that it was this mountain that he came to best. Jack lowered his gaze to the horizon and threw the metal beast into first which throttled the guts and the zoom of the thing. It took off.

"C'mon, Jack. Steel your innards. Let's go." The words, "The only way out is through," returned to his mind's vision; after all, today was garbage day, and it was time to take out the trash. Jack was of singular goal and purpose. Mental garbage stood in his way, and it was the call of the midnight sun that demanded Jack bring it all into the light so that which held him back, might be turned to ash. He knew his freedom stood just on the other side of that. "I have to see this through," Jack told himself. The truck hit liftoff, and they were halfway up the closest mountain before Jack's mind returned to the moment.

"Holy shit…," Jack trailed off, seeing the land sprawl and stretch beneath them. He felt like he was on a plane. The views were inescapable, leaving Jack agog and empty because it wasn't what he was seeing, but what he was sensing, feeling, connecting to, and becoming one with. He unclenched to allow into his way, its sensory perception—and as it connected to his senses widely, he oddly recognized its touch. It was rocky, challenging, merciless, and without judgment… and it was home. This is what Jack knew, and this is the mountain Jack came to climb. There was no turning back.

"Go, Jack. Go. Trust your design. You have everything within you that is needed for your journey. Go."

Jack didn't know why tears were streaming down his face as he turned in its direction.

It's just been so hard…. Jack thought to himself, overwhelmed with emotions.

"And for that, Jack, you are blessed."

He didn't have the will to fight to deflect, so he was quiet and allowed it to hang in the air.

And for the struggle, I am blessed, Jack repeated with no attachment to the words.

"Why, Jack?"

I don't know why. He said as more tears produced themselves.

"You do know why. There is no 'yet' here. Tell us now."

Jack repeated his words, only this time they formed a question. *And for the struggle, I am blessed?*

"Teach us why, Jack."

I am blessed for the struggle because it's through those fires I have been forged. It's through this process that I know I am strong. I know that about myself. I know I can take care of myself; I know how to take a punch, and I even know how to defend myself.

"Your choice of defend versus protect is correct, Jack. Teach us how you defend yourself. What is perfect of your design that ensures your deliverance from all misery and misfortune?"

My design is perfect for those things because I am not of any of them. My design is perfect because those things do not haunt or inhabit me without my say-so. That's what's perfect about me.

Jack's gut then chimed in with "d a n g e r".

The ring of the words balanced themselves atop Jack's mind as they pushed the vehicle deeper into the stacks of earth and insight. The crown of it was just miles ahead and Jack could feel the mountain in his bones as it wicked at his mind unrelenting, yet somehow, it left Jack vacant. He couldn't gain enough of its presence to determine if it was good or bad.

Hey! Jack internally called. *Is this place good or bad? Am I okay?*

There was silence. Jack repeated louder. *Is this place good or bad?! Am I okay?!* Again, nothing, making Jack's quiet, disquiet. He could sense the creep of the them continuing to move.

"*HEY!*" Jack internally screamed, which was met with not his mind or soul but again from his gut.

"D a n g e r".

Holy shit. Jack's stability was coming undone and there was something he could feel as fear licked at his neck. *I'm alone, and my guides won't help me assess whether this place is good or bad. I'm flying blind here.*

"Was that your question then?" The voice asked.

Jack was shocked that they were back. *I thought you abandoned me. I thought you were gone.*

"That's not possible, Jack. You are, so we are."

Then why wouldn't you answer the fucking question?! I'm feeling extremely uncertain here. A little help, please.

"Answer what question, Jack? You have not posed something for us to answer."

Ugh… Is this place good or bad? Am I okay!?

"Again, that is not a question that can be answered here. That's why there was no response. How is that unclear?"

I don't know, and I don't understand.

"You don't understand yet, but should you care to face it and teach about it, you will."

Gah! Jack let fly. *Always the fucking riddles with you. Fine.* Jack reviewed the issue at hand. *Is this place good or bad? Am I okay?* Jack slowed himself to hear himself more clearly, then continued as the vehicle lurched on its course. *I don't know what I don't know, so let's start with what I do. Am I safe?*

Jack reviewed what he now knew about the concept of safety. He exhaled then opened his eyes to see what was present in the moment while he rolled down his window to breathe in the northern air. *Is there danger present? Well, sure… but when isn't there danger present when driving in a car? So yes, I'm strapped into a vehicle I trust, so I guess I'm safe. I am okay at this moment.*

Jack then focused on the next part of the question. *Is this place good or bad? WELL, IS IT?!* He waited for a response with his good ear turned heavenward. *FUCKING IS IT?*

"Why do you ask questions that cannot be answered?"

How is this difficult!? Is this place good or bad? Very simple. Good or bad? Just give me some direction here.

The beyond then hit a spark of clarity. "Your measurements are not quantifiable."

Dude, da fuck that supposed to mean? Your measurements are not quantifiable.

"Do you have another metric for measuring that which you are trying to assess?"

Jack thought about this. *Why?*

"Because without the lens of judgment, which can only be viewed from behind the human mind, good and bad cannot be quantified."

You don't know what's good? Jack said, astonished.

"Good to whom, Jack?"

That's when he got it. Jack understood it in an instant. *Holy shit… I get that. Good has no tie to a measurable, always true, thing. Good would always be x to some, y to others, and a billion other things to those beyond that. It wasn't a measurable thing when thought about in this light.*

"Yes, Jack. The concept of it holds no ability to measure or assess something universally, only singularly."

He understood. What's good to some is not to others. What's bad to some is not to others. There is no absolute truth there. It's too fluid a concept to be used to answer or quantify anything beyond a singular mind.

"Yes. Good and bad are judgment calls. Not a function we can perform here."

So, if there's no way to appraise the situation using the concepts of good and bad, how do I articulate what I'm trying to discover?

"What other measuring devices do you know that have immutable properties?"

Jack focused on the question as the truck flew past the first crest into the second wave of earthen spires. *Yes, or no? Right or wrong…? No, that's the same as good and bad… Hot and cold? While yes, they're relative, it doesn't get to the point I'm trying to discover. Up and down? Yes, in the concept of measurement, but again, it doesn't get me closer to what I'm trying to determine.* Jack had to stop moving to get to the root of this one.

"Hold on, sister," Jack said to Yolo, side sliding the truck into a roadside pullout. The view expanded when the front window met the side of the steep downward embankment. Jack cut the engine and let his chair recline. He quieted himself and asked the question again. What other measuring devices do you know that have immutable properties? He closed his eyes.

There was a long silence. *Little help here?* Jack asked himself.

"Are you trying to assess safety?"

Before Jack could thoroughly think that through, he yelled *Yes!* But then caught his mistake. *No.*

"Why would you answer that yes, that you sought something that does not exist? Do you often seek out that which doesn't exist? We're unclear as to the point of the exercise."

Jack covered his face with his hands. *Sometimes, I guess I do. But it's more about the second part of it. How can I determine a thing or a situation's essence?*

"How do you assess the essence of others?"

What? Like other people?

"Yes. Exactly. How did you assess Thad?" This put Jack on his heels.

"Stay in curiosity, Jack. How did you assess Thad?"

He closed his eyes tighter. *I dunno exactly… I mean, I thought he was sexy.* Jack smiled at the thought of him. *I thought he was kind and loving. You know, warm and…* he was cut off mid-sentence.

"There it is, Jack. You just said it. You just named an immutable way of assessing and measuring things."

He reviewed his previous thoughts. Sexy? No. Not applicable as to whether this space was "safe." Kind? Doesn't really apply either. A mountain isn't necessarily kind or unkind… it just is. Warm? No. Then, as he thought it, he knew it. *Loving.*

"Do you see it, Jack?"

Yes. The immutable measuring device to assess all things is love versus fear/hate. The simplicity of it is undeniable.

"Ask us a quantifiable question, Jack."

Is this mountain of love or fear and hate? Jack didn't need anyone else's input here. The clarity of asking the right question was inescapable. *Mountains don't hate. There's no vengeance there. They just are.*

"And at the core of all things that are, what are they ov?"

Ov?

"Yes, are they ov love?"

Why do you say it that way?

"Ov?"

Yes. Why do you say something is 'ov' love, instead of 'of' love?

"Because it is the truth of it. Ov. Ovum. Ova. The source; the derivation. The beginning. What is – and what is, is Love. It is used as a function word to indicate origin or derivation on the deepest level. It is the root ov, derived from love that's used as a function word to indicate the cause, motive, or reason." This new information made Jack's brain hurt. He put a hand to his temple to hush the thing.

So ov is derived from love, which is succinctly tied to origin and source.

"Yes. The two are inextricable."

Jack sat back up in his seat and grabbed the steering wheel. The downward-sloping road before them defying worldly comprehension of what a vehicle can do. Jack gripped the wheel with white knuckles clenched in determination. He would see this through. He would test the design of him… and that of the old faithful truck.

Their designs melded as Yolo flew out the window. She sensed the drop of the thing and wasn't about to be captured in that way, not when flight was her design for the moment at hand.

"Scrawwww!!!!" Yolo screamed at the mountain as the truck dropped twelve feet vertically, then caught the gentle slope and nosed toward the flat on the path. Jack exhaled as they leveled out and sped on.

"WooHoo!" Jack said alight as he breathed in the mountain air, the ether of the place now clearly unmissable. He then focused the car toward the next challenge. For hours the old Chevy fell, regained, powered, and dropped. The oneness Jack felt in power and drive set him on fire, causing plumes of life force to lift heavenward. Jack connected broadly to what was and the focus and force he created carved new life into well-worn paths. He would mount this beast, and that would happen today. He dropped the stick into second and floored it, sending stones and mire flying. Some of the debris Jack shucked from the thing flew for miles as they shot outward, rippling into the future.

Jack dropped into himself again. *So, is the mountain ov love or what? Is 'what is' ov something? Does 'what is' beget or begin something, or is it just as it is, no less, no more?*

"What is the mountain ov? What is its source?"

Yes, that's my question, Jack replied.

"Then what's your answer?"

Jack noted this mental running in circles was taxing his strength. *I can't do this right now.*

"You can't do this right now, where you are."

Jack had had enough. He got out of the car and screamed for the better part of three minutes. Then, finally, he collected himself, got back in the truck, and pushed on.

AUGURY

Jack was resigned and exhausted. He couldn't go any further. They parked and got out. He was emotionally and spiritually zapped.

"I guess this is where we camp tonight," Jack said, nudging Yolo as they put the tailgate down, searching the vast expanse before them. Searching for what, Jack wasn't sure. He was too drained to think.

What time is it? Jack wondered.

In this part of the world where the sun was always present, time was a slippery hallucination. A thing that no one could track because it gave no tells as it beamed constant madness into those who held its gaze for too many weeks. It was hallucinatory. It was the song of a siren and the mirage of the north. Everyone in this part of the world knew of its grasp, knew the howl of it, and instinctively knew that it had to be held and bayed with extreme caution. Jack always thought that what frightened people the most about the midnight sun was how it disorients the mind and leads the onlookers into fanaticism and delusion. The tales from these parts were rife with their phantasmic stories and often seen ghosts.

Jack checked the time and despite the glaring sun, he noted it was well past their usual bedtime. Everything felt off. He grabbed some food, hoping a meal would return some sense of convention even if everything else were a fragment of normal in this place where time failed to exist correctly. They ate in silence as Yolo perched on Jack's outstretched thigh, eyeing his demeanor.

"What's that, sister?" Jack asked, stroking her head with his eyes still closed.

The bird pecked and ate, her reply, some chortling sounds that oddly settled Jack. It was the not being alone part that he could rest into while being at this level of exhaustion.

Twinge.

Of course, Jack thought. *I've been expecting you.* He didn't waste any time. He grabbed his meds, quickly placed the banquet of cushions around the cab but then stopped. He just stopped, paused, and did a gut check.

How am I supposed to do this? But Jack's gut was devoid of answers. Jack asked again. *How…* but then was interrupted.

"Jack, it isn't how." He spun a one-eighty to see where the voice came from, but then settled recognizing it's tone.

What's that now? Jack said, again fearing delusion.

"Jack?"

He felt that, yet again, he was losing his mind—and with the impending attack already crawling up his forearm, Jack felt hot and desperate. *Yes! I'm here! What?!* he cried.

"It isn't how, Jack," a statement that had no meaning to him.

It isn't how, Jack reviewed. *It isn't how?! What does that mean?*

"Have you never successfully communicated with the oracle there, Jack?"

Communicated where?! Oracle? Oh my god! What is going on?! Jack was freaking out. This was all new, and it was too much to sort while preparing for a neurological storm that was already finding fire.

"Communicated here, Jack!" The beast of Jack's dystonic form then collapsed him in two with a nefarious CRACK! a contraction of his abs so violent that in one second, it pressed his knee caps into his forehead and knocked out his wind. Jack gasped for air while trying to stay perched on the tailgate. He searched for his breath to recall it back to him.

"It only responds with yes, no, or danger, Jack. It has no other words, but what it lacks in vocabulary it makes up for in clarity and insight." Jack looked at the meds still clutched in his hands.

Got it. Jack thought, filing away the information on how to 'speak' with his gut. *But tonight, we're doing this my way.* Jack forced his lower and upper body apart then stood at the back of the vehicle as he was able. *Tonight, we don't fight.* He reached for a plastic water bottle to clean himself out. *Tonight… We fucking dance.* He was ready to take the lead.

Jack stripped himself of his jeans, took care of business, and then pulled on white linen sweats and a fresh white t-shirt. The monster within made its way around him in its usual form, but Jack didn't complain or fight; he stayed in curiosity. Working quickly—knowing he didn't have much time, he cleared the top of the truck, then threw the mattress atop it and scrambled up, sleeping bag, rope, and pillow in tow. The storm now owned one arm and his neck, but Jack had certainly dealt with worse. He found that this calmer approach slowed it's advance so he could at least work with it; he also hoped it would borrow him some time. Jack breathed, and again with more determination as he echoed, "Tonight we do it my way!" Jack calmed and slowed himself down even more. He grabbed for the ropes and began to web himself in place. This is where he wanted to be while he went toe to toe with the thing. Here. Here atop the truck—nothing between him, the stars, and the gods.

Let's do this, Jack thought, becoming still until the rhythm of the universe was heard as it expressed itself through him. His body began to undulate, his arms curled into nubs while his spine made its pull into his ribs, compressing the air from his lungs. Jack calmed his mind again as a death-wheeze escaped his lips. *Tonight, I'm coming for you,* was the last thing he remembered.

ETHERIC

As always, it began like falling from one plane into another. The rush and movement of energy scattered at Jack frantically and asked for him to participate in terror. *Just stay in curiosity, Jack,* he told himself while tucking himself into the folds of his personal container—the thing he could control. He fell like a bomb, screeching toward earth. The surface of it getting closer and closer. Jack girded himself for impact.

CRASH! He hit the surface then began to slip through its form. Jack dropped out of the bottom of its plane and fell into the next.

CRASH! Jack gasped for air as he violently hit the surface of the ocean. The density of the water gave way to nothing, leaving Jack to slip through it again. He quieted himself further as he let go to fall back into a stream of air. *What is this place?* Jack asked himself curiously.

"Are you asking what this place is, Jack?" The voice inside startled him in this place.

You're here?! Jack's mind was awash in the discovery.

"Your inability to comprehend things as they are on their face defies logic, Jack." Jack knew what this meant as he recalled their previous conversation about not seeing a thing as it is without drama or, fear.

HELP! Jack yelled, desperately grasping at the invisible while continuing to fall deeper into the vast darkness.

"You don't need help, Jack." he heard as he slammed yet again into a crust of the earth, crushing his lungs and rattling his bones.

Jack didn't have it in him anymore. He was too overrun with mental connections yet to take and old ones unmoored and shorting. Jack was defeated and let go of care and effort. He couldn't do this any longer, and he was weary to his soul.

I can't do this anymore…

"And what is it that you can't do anymore?"

Jack hung his head, unclenched, and accepted what awaited him. *This,* he said as his limp body smacked the surface of the ice and water. Jack didn't fight as his body was towed beneath the surface. He could sense the thing coming for him as it always did. The water began to swirl around him, but Jack was resigned. He had no more fight left in him; he simply wanted to be free. He let go, then slid through it to be freed, only to fall, yet again.

"You're okay, Jack." The only response was his hands moving from their normally clubbed and clenched inertness to the tiniest softening. Jack willed it to end, to crash headfirst into a boulder so he could make it back to blue… or the beach… or to Toby or Banjo or anywhere, even the valley of death because at least there the world had form and held the mercy of time and space that Jack understood. Once again, he heard the voice in his head, "You're okay, Jack." But Jack wouldn't respond. His commitment to joining the nothing by being nothing was fixed and unyielding.

But then the words "Yes. This is correct" stopped him cold.

This is correct? he said, remaining resigned.

"Yes."

Yes? That's what I get? Just, yes?

"Yes."

Jesus in Bethlehem lying in a manger… Why do you make this so fucking difficult?

"It's not."

It's not what?

"Difficult."

But that's not my experience!

"That's not my experience yet."

Yes. That's not my experience yet. Why? Maybe teach me instead of the other way around for once!? The lack of understanding I experience is sometimes overwhelming, and I get to the point where I can't fight the fight anymore. Jack's sadness grew in him.

"Good. Focus there."

The design of Jack's deep-purple sadness allowed him to slow all the more, a wounded vibration that was a second skin for him. The wallow of it, the pangs of the misunderstood, and the emotional failures that made up his mind. *I just don't have the fight left in me. I give up.* His final breath of tension escaped his lips as the horizon hummed from purple to white. It was familiar, this bright white, a sensation he first felt when he stepped on a church stage at fourteen years old, and the same ask now presented itself to Jack's mind.

"See… Not as scary when you can't see them. Release yourself into the bright white warmth of it." Rays met his face. He could feel it even with his eyes closed. Jack stopped falling and instead slowed and floated. He took in gulps of air, then coughed and sputtered. The awe of the moment was all-encompassing.

"Welcome, Jack." Hearing this, he started to panic and fall again but corrected the error.

Ummm… what's happening?

"You are, Jack."

Jack laughed. *Oh, I'm happening?*

"Of sorts if you wish to try and bring that into you."

But why am I not falling?

"You can do as you wish in this place, Jack. No one asks anything of you here. Our only job was to deliver that which you asked for. The rest is up to you."

That which I asked for?

"Yes. As discussed previously, you requested access to different information. Information to help us walk each other home. Isn't that true? Was that your ask?"

That is true. I said that. Jack noticed the murk of the place shifting into daybreak.

"Teach me why this is perfect, Jack," he heard as he rolled on-air and drifted between worlds. He pulled himself in closer to formulate the response.

So... I guess... This place is an extension of me. This is happening within me.

"Yes. Say more."

And if it's ov me, of the origin of me, then it is ov my design.

"You have embodied the lesson of 'ov'. Teach us why."

Jack exhaled and dug in deeper, searching for meaning. *What I have been given and how I have been designed is the only way I can have my experience and achieve my soul's assignment.*

"Correct. Say more."

What was, was. It is no more.

"And it now only inhabits in you as a hallucination."

Well... I wouldn't go that far, Jack replied.

"You must go that far."

Wait. What? Jack's confusion was tripping him up.

"You must go that far," consciousness replied.

I don't understand.... He paused then added, *...yet. How far? What are you referring to? How far must I go?*

"You must embody the truth of it."

Aaarrrgggghhhhh.... Jack began to fall again as he yelled in frustration. Realizing he was falling, he righted himself. *Shiny babies, newborn kittens, fields of poppies....* Jack told himself as he opened his eyes to see if he would crash or fall into anything, but he had slowed back to float mode.

"Childish, but a start. Are you ready to be serious, Jack? Going that far will require far more than that which you're doing now, and you barely seem able to hold even this together."

Again, rude, Jack thought. *Gah. This. Why?*

"Because it's where freedom lies for you, but we don't think you are serious. You are slow to learn many lessons, and you are incapable of welcoming anything new without fighting. When presented with new gifts, you fight. When we teach you how to be, you fight. When you ask for help over things we're providing, that you yourself asked for, you fight. This is the truth of you, Jack. No stillness inhabits you. That must change, or you will fail."

Jack understood the message.

"You are a child, Jack. Your mind never developed past that stage. You lack the emotional and spiritual maturity needed to get past this next part. Evolve or fail."

A sadness returned to Jack's mind. *I am a failure.*

"We should end this if you continue to default to the mire of ick. Arrest your sadness. That is drama. There is no time for that now. Why do you allow that to happen?"

I'm fucking entitled to my emotions!

"Yes. You are. You are entitled to your emotions, but that is not what you're doing. There is nothing here to be emotional about, yet you default to sadness and drama. Was that a conscious choice, or are you defaulting to childhood habits?"

There was a long silence.

"We're going to answer that for you, Jack, as it appears, we were misinformed. You are not in the advanced class."

Jack smiled. *Not in the advanced class yet, fuckhead.*

"Ah. Energy. Effort. Sparks of life. A nice change… but are you ready to, as you put it, dance?"

Jack lowered his vibration to that of thunder. *Yeah. Let's fucking dance.* He then folded himself in and began a targeted descent. *LET'S*

GO! WOOHOO! Jack hit the surface of the water and dove and swam with every cell in his being.

CRASH! He blew through the first layer, still focused and diving.

"Teach us what you're doing right now."

I'm staying in curiosity to discover the truth of the thing. And that seems to be e-motion. That's how you steer in this place, isn't it? A question that was met with silence. *Ha!* Jack said, feeling the toehold he had gained in purchase and strength. Jack pushed on, diving into a plane of dirt. Its solidity gave way as Jack discovered it's all like water. All of it. All of the elements were liquid at best.

E-motion is what's driving this thing. Jack triggered himself in differing parts to assess levers and check possibilities. *E-motions are that of your electric soul, mind, and body. The energy you create internally is electric. E-motion/emotion/motion. Energy in Motion.*

"Not up to zero yet, Jack."

He ignored the comment's sting because he wanted to experience it differently, and not be what he was accused of; at the same time, Jack saw the daily lie in his truth. He recalled Sam's words from weeks ago: *People are judged by the lies that we tell ourselves.*

"Yes, Jack. That's something. Focus there."

And I lack emotional maturity—I have distorted lies that I tell myself.

"Yes, Jack. You have not been well taught, and a mind that develops while steeped in internalized terror cannot evolve. Your emotional instability has to be addressed; otherwise, your mind and emotions use you instead of the fully developed mind that uses it. That's the baseline we're seeking. That is what it means to bring yourself up to zero. Are you using your mind, or is it using you?"

A massive pang of sadness swept over Jack, but then he noted the default poison of it, that he hadn't elected to be sad, but rather it was being forced into him whether he chose it or not. He corrected the error and returned to curiosity. *Mental garbage,* he thought.

"Yes, Jack. Mental garbage, and to uncover this deep of truth, you must consult the Oracle. We have done our part for now. Good luck, and know you already have what you need. Trust."

Wait!! Jack said, desperately sensing the guides were leaving him. *I don't know what I'm doing....* He paused again, then said, *...yet.* A smile returned to his lips. *Okay, Jack. It's go time. Let's fuck this shit up.*

REVELATIONS

Jack contorted atop the truck while the beast within whipped his senses and slammed his body into the vehicle's roof and rails. There was no one to ensure he didn't drown in his vomit or wriggle out from under the tied cords. It was raw form here, no promises, no safety—just what was. The midnight sun burned Jack's face and lips as the mountain wind burst gusts of swirling confusion around him.

It had been just over two hours since Jack lost consciousness when the sky began to fill with broad slow circling specters. Yolo was keeping watch, but every minute that passed presented more and more of the things making the sky overhead darken as if it brought a disturbing omen. The shadows of their forms swept over Jack's face, causing it to darken and then lighten, a shift that continued to gain speed. Shadow, light, shadow, light… on and on the raptors flew, gaining in speed and intensity to where it was almost a strobe-like effect that flicked flashes of light at Jack's unconscious state. It was becoming clear that Jack's only protection from the vultures would be Yolo, a bird only weeks old but who was designed as the guardian of the in-betweens and the keeper of hidden truths. There was no fear in Yolo, for she knew the truth of her. Such is the beauty of those who walk the earth without the treachery of the human mind. Clarity comes from such a place, a mind without clouds, available to what is. He was starting to understand the entire reason for such animal spirit guides for they are the access point for man to abandon sight in exchange for 'vision'.

Jack was alone, and the plane where his mind coasted offered little comfort. *"You must consult the oracle,"* still lived in Jack's mind.

Wait! How am I supposed to know where the oracle is?! A question met with silence caused Jack's mood and position on air to slip. *Fuck,* Jack thought, feeling himself begin to fall through space. He righted himself, regained emotional clarity, then paused. *It's not how, Jack. It doesn't know how. It knows danger, yes and no.* He reviewed new questions to pose and landed on, *Can you hear me?* Its response wasn't a voice but a feeling that was vibrationally delivered as the low frequency and rumble of elephants.

"y e s"

Jack practically jumped. He had made the connection. *Uh. Hi. Not exactly sure here. How do I find you?* Silence. *Damn it. That's another how question.* Jack reframed his question. *To find you, do I go up?*

"n o"

Down?

"n o"

Left?

"n o"

Right then?

"n o"

This information picked at Jack's growing frustration. *That's it! I understand the purpose of frustration, which is the sign from the universe to pause and let go.*

"y e s"

Pause and let go it is then. Jack detached the extension cord to his past, bringing him fully into the present, then cleared his mind as if on the white beach after the click. He floated and let go. The universal wind recognizing the call, cupped his frame and began to carry him toward the deep rumbling echoes. Jack fought the fear and walls of protection rising inside him. *Stand,* he told himself as he relaxed into it more, finding the space of allowing.

After a journey through several more planes, Jack could sense his arrival at the place of his destination, which wasn't a fully-realized planet but rather a singular island in space about five acres in size. Jack's feet touched the edge of it, and then he stood. Before him was a 1930's old Soviet abandoned office building. It looked as though it had been through several wars and the apocalypse. It had a creep and a throbbing pulse that unmoored Jack at every level. *What the…?* Jack thought from a place of fear. He instantly was transported back to his physical body, where his eyes opened and saw the clouds. He gasped for air.

Seeing the swarm of vultures overhead, Jack turned to see where Yolo was. "Yolo! Yolo!" he cried, searching the sky, but she was nowhere to be found. *What do I do? What do I do?* Jack thought frantically. *I need to go back and finish what I started.* But Jack knew there was no wishing himself back to the place. He couldn't get there without the portal of a neurological storm to carry him on its gales. He was earthbound for now. He untied himself and hopped into the back of the truck to search for new ways in. *Maybe this,* he said to himself, unpacking a small white box given to him by Paula. *If western medications gave me the thing, then maybe there's a way back in through them as well?* Jack downed twice the recommended dose then slathered sunscreen on his exposed face and hands. *I'm so close. I have to see this through,* Jack told himself. *But what about the winged hyenas circling overhead?* He did a quick gut check. *Am I in danger?*

"y e s"

Fuck. Can Yolo handle it?

"y e s"

Well, there it is then. Jack was clear that he didn't need to protect himself and that between his design and the crow's, they had this handled despite outward appearances. Jack climbed the vehicle to strap himself in again. Twenty minutes later, he was falling through the universal planes found on the backside of his mind.

Again, landing in deep space, Jack searched for where he was as he e-motioned through the gloom, but then he remembered the stream he was supposed to catch, and he detached from it all. The winds picked him up again and carried him to the dank hallows of council and congress. Jack's feet touched the island again. *Stand, Jack.* He told himself as he steadied his imbalance.

The air here didn't recognize the laws of nature, and it swept in ways that made no sense to the human mind. It clustered, chunked, festered and fell, the almost visible form of it, slipping from one thing it shouldn't be into another. Jack wasn't even sure he could walk through it. He took a single step forward only to find the air begin to pebble, each newly formed drone eyeing him from behind eyes of other-world consciousness. It was the creepiest thing Jack could have ever imagined, and as fear and disquiet in him rose, he once again screamed *Help!* It was instantaneous. Jack was immediately flushed out of the space to be thrown back into his body.

Jack opened his eyes with a start while again, gasping for air. *Fuck!* Jack thought, realizing he had failed again. His head spun with the new experience and the toxic chemicals attacking his system. He reentered himself, closed his eyes, and hoped to fall back into the place. *Can I get there voluntarily?* Jack closed his eyes again and relinquished to the realms beyond.

A low articulated grumble met him. "y e s."

A vulture touched down on the truck's hood as Jack closed his eyes and sank. *C'mon, Jack. You got this.* Within minutes his feet again touched the Isle of Congress.

Jack now recognized the place and the game it played. He understood that if he was to make it through that, he had to control himself and not react, cling, or grasp. Any measure to wish something other than it was would repel him back to the physical world. He would see this through. The air eyed him as it shifted shapes and boggled the mind. One step. *I accept what is.* His form held – another step. *I accept what is. I forgive myself, and I forgive others.*

The eyes of the sweeping air circled and inspected him – another step. Jack searched for words to guide and focus his mind. He could not afford to wing off course. Not now. Time on the physical was running out, and little Yolo couldn't be held accountable. She was too young. Jack knew she could at least buy him precious minutes, but he had to hurry.

Off in the distance, Jack heard the shrieks of birds in a death lock, a moment that caused a flicker of distrust that Jack did his best to sidestep. He doubled down on this mind's attention, searching for anything, a Bible verse, a Sanskrit meditation, then he remembered Theta's voice. The Adi Mantra!

I bow to the creative wisdom. Jack flashed from his being. *I bow to the divine teacher within.* The seeing air parted. Jack focused only on those words, and as they left him, they sent flares into the sky, and the words reverberated as *Ong Namo Guru Dev Namo.* Another step. *Ong Namo Guru Dev Namo.* Another. *Ong Namo Guru Dev Namo.* He gained ground and approached the doors. *Ong Namo Guru Dev Namo!* Jack held the ever-watching door handle in his grip and slowly opened it. Stepping inside, Jack was transported to a place of deafening quiet. There was the stillness of death here that Jack recognized.

"Ah, yes. Welcome, Jack," said a woman from behind a receptionist desk. "We've been expecting you." She began to walk down a hall then turned to say, "Right this way." Jack followed her, care in every step he took, trusting himself but not where he was.

At the end of the short hall, the receptionist stopped and opened the door. "He's expecting you. It's the last door at the end of the corridor." Jack thanked her and took the door from her to hold it open for himself. He needed a minute to focus on what lay ahead.

Looking down the dimly lit office corridor, Jack didn't know what to expect, what monsters might pop out to knock him off his trance of chant. He reasserted himself and clarified, *Grasp at nothing. Let it ALL flow through you. You do not need anything to be different than it is. Detach to be in flow. I can do this.*

Jack steadied himself and took his first step while the sensation of cold death rose up his leg. *Ong Namo Guru Dev Namo! C'mon, Jack, hold it.* A pulse of sound and brilliant light cracked the still as Jack's life flashed before his eyes. It was as if someone had taken flashcards of every horrifying event of his life and forced him to relive each scene in rapid succession, the punch of it being that many of the scenes Jack had yet to live. He saw his death. He saw his body rot. He saw all those he loved die and turn to dust. *Ong Namo Guru Dev Namo! ONG NAMO GURU DEV NAMO!* Jack said, gaining in volume and intensity. *They are just pictures,* Jack told himself. They are just hallucinations of the mind. *ONG NAMO GURU DEV NAMO! I BOW TO CREATIVE WISDOM. I BOW TO THE DIVINE TEACHER WITHIN!*

With each passing step, the horrors flashed into Jack's being were monstrous freaks and demons unleashed. He knew them all intimately. He knew them because he had either lived them or could feel the presence of them heading for his future. There would be no escaping them. The only way out is through. Jack put his head down and focused with all of his might. *ONG NAMO GURU DEV NAMO! I BOW TO CREATIVE WISDOM. I BOW TO THE DIVINE TEACHER WITHIN!*

The long dark corridor before him, seemed to have a sense, a being, a consciousness. It was a thing that steamed, shifted, and floated, permeating every cell it came into contact with. He couldn't so much hear it as he could sense and understand it. It had a consciousness that took everything within Jack not to fight but allow it to be as it is. This was the test. *Existence without resistance, Jack. Flow. C'mon.... c'mon, c'mon. Focus!*

A slither of air found its way up into Jack's mind. "Well......., " Jack heard a demon coming from within his mind. "Who isss thisss?" It wafted and pulled itself in for a closer inspection of the intruder. "Why so much focusss to jussst be?" It then laughed wildly; a sound so maniacal that Jack shuddered involuntarily.

Existence without resistance, Jack, he told himself. *Flow. Flow! Don't pull it in. Don't need it to be different than it is.*

"You are but matchesss and sticksss, Jack. Yesss?" Jack didn't take in the thought. Nothing from the serpentine demon entered him as he flexed into the gift of his church-issued impervious hardened shell. If he could survive the laying of hands that almost killed him, he could survive this too. A new lesson of how everything is indeed perfect began to take, and it was in his moment of greatest fear, that he saw how those old wounds of trauma now served him as a superpower. He latched to his all-encompassing shell and on his own say-so, doubled its thickness.

"Isn't that the meaning for faggotsss?" It encompassed Jack, sucking at his mind's armor. "Matchesss and sticksss, Jack, matchesss and sticksss. Kindling, yesss? Isssn't that your form? Matchesss and sticksss?" Jack struggled with all his might, willing himself into total concentration and absolute acceptance of what is. "Oh, you dearsss are fuelsss for firesss. Can you feelsss that, Jack? The lick of flamesss at yousss? You die, Jack. You die today… but if yousss wantsss to play..." Jack sensed a flicker of delight coming from the thing, "…we can playsss. You won't win, Jack. No one ever doesss." With that, the entire corridor became a towering searing inferno. Jack screamed in terror and then woke as a turkey vulture walloped the truck roof next to him. "Yolo!" Jack screamed.

Then for some reason, the words from the guides returned to his memory. *"You can't get there from where you are."* Jack wasn't sure this made sense, but he sure as fuck was about to find out.

RADIATION

For the balance of the bright night, the sun scorched, dried and baked the earth without care or mercy. After hours of its touch, the sun had left Jack's skin bright blood-red. However, for him, there was no turning back. Again, he heard, "*You can't get there from where you are,*" as his angst grew within him.

Bam! Another vulture hit the truck. From Jack's drugged state, he couldn't tell if they were landing or crashing, the sheer size of the things were terrifying. Their long, featherless necks craned eyes that seized him in their near-death gaze. "Yolo!" Jack screamed.

"Jack." He recognized the voice in his head.

Yes, I'm here!

"You're failing, Jack."

With that, Jack dissolved into tears, the weight of the trial too much. Tied atop the truck, with time running out, he willed himself with everything he had. *I DON'T UNDERSTAND!*

"Quiet, Jack. You can do this. Let's slowly review so you can catch up. Still yourself."

Jack did his best, but with so much going on around him, his mind spun in a manner that he couldn't wrap his mind around. The vultures now flew lower to the earth where their menace and glaring gawk was unmissable.

"Listen closely to our words… Still yourself. You can't get there from where you are, so how do you?"

Jack repeated slowly, *Still yourself, you can't get there from where you are, so how do you?* Jack closed his eyes to work with what information he had. *Still yourself… as in quiet or as in I'm still me?* But the answer presented itself to him immediately. *It's both.* He gut checked the answer for accuracy. *Correct?*

"y e s."

Got it. The search was on. *You can't get there from where you are… C'mon, Jack… whatcha got? C'mon!* The vultures were now mainly on the ground hunting. *You can't get there from where you are. Well, where am I, and where could I be? What are my options?* Then he remembered a place he might be able to access it from. *The observation deck of the mind! THAT'S IT!* Jack's face lit up. He knew he was onto it, and armed with this new revelation, he dove headfirst into the unknown. Seconds later, his feet touched the sands of the eerie Isle of Congress.

I can't get there from here. Jack said with his hands in a prayer position held at eye level… *But I can get there from here.* With that, he flipped up onto the seat of his soul where there was no access to fear or attachment; only the observation of these things. It was impossible to grasp or want in this place because everything is as it should be here – nothing more, nothing less. Jack beamed with the expression of it, and he began to run, swimming through it all without attachment; his church-given blessing, by way of an impenetrable shell repelling all that was not him. He ran and observed while staying above it all: the fears, the fires, the pain, and the wallow. Nothing touched him here. In this place, he was untouchable, unreachable because he knew what he was; the maker of stars.

Jack grabbed the front door of the place and flung it open. The receptionist merely glanced up with a chuckle but kept on filing paperwork. He got to the end of the first hall to enter the dark corridor.

"Not too many burnsss, Jack. Not too many yet for matchesss and sticksss. Want to playsss? Playsss more?" There was no reaction from Jack. He took a step in, which was met by another inferno. He didn't flinch, his armor held. Another step as he again relaxed and merely observed what was put in front of him. *Existence without resistance.* He flowed.

Then something new appeared. It was his parents in the flames. They were burning and screaming while the clip of Mellie's conversation with his mother shot through him like an arrow at 90 miles an hour. Her voice was clear.

"It sounds like in his condition, he doesn't need anything. Jack choosing to be the way he is killed his father. You tell him that." But even that didn't touch Jack's heart or mind, because things that live outside of us can only live there, until <u>we</u> bring them in. Jack recognized the test and took another cautious step. *This is illusion.*

"Prostrate yourself before the Lord!" his stepfather screamed from the flames as every sensation of him being mercilessly raped lacerated his will. Jack lifted higher to let it pass under him, avoiding its messy sting.

"You're not good-looking enough to also be an asshole!"

"Turn around, Mr. Daw. Let me see if you understand the basics of scrubbing in for this position."

"It is my job to rip the wheat from the chaff!"

"I CAN'T BREATHE. I CAN'T BREATHE! PLEASE! SOMEONE!"

"Haha. Enjoy your pet now. You said it was dead, so I'm just making sure you keep your word. Liar."

"It's important to be clean. Right, faggot?!"

"Dad! You're hurting me."

One after another, every trial, pain, and trauma flashed at him begging his mind to crater. Jack responded by searching himself in rapid-fire succession.

Gut—My design is perfect for this moment. "y e s ."

How do I find… fuck. He redirected recognizing his error. *It knows yes, no and danger. Umm…* He settled into the upper seat of his mind where a newfound stillness arrived. He centered and exhaled newfound self honor into his way while the bracelet of the loving serpent coiled around his wrist reminding him endlessly of how to shed the old.

With the flames all encompassing and the slither of the hissing demon all around him, he continued his quest to unshackle his mind from false-truths. The visions, the clarity, the things learned from behind the lens of endless power and love. *Find what's real. Abandon illusion.*

From a place rooted deeper than his ancestors Jack gained a clarity; an inkling, a spark that registered within him as the truest true. He named it's energy and in doing so found the switch from the matrix affecting him, to the other way around, and Jack was ready to make the workings of the thing, his play-thing. With clarity and fierce hunger in his eyes, he focused his vision to the horizon.

"Yes Jack. Stand." His guides encouraged. "Name your truth. Name your power."

As Jack's mind slowed and leveled to the still of death, he somehow knew what to do—and for the first time in his life he didn't question what he knew, or how he knew it. He was done forgetting who he is.

He galvanized his truth. "*ONG NAMO GURU DEV NAMO! I BOW TO CREATIVE WISDOM. I BOW TO THE DIVINE TEACHER WITHIN!*" With his mind-connection tied deep into the off-grid, he released the call that ends all illusions, even this one. *I am.*

Jack sank deeper into himself while powering up with all that he had. He focused inward with the guided move that had defeated the ghostly-white spirit bear. A move he first tapped into while simply wanting to greet the day and exchange with its goodness. This time however, the energy exchange was not that of a beginner and he dug deep to gather its lessons. The torrent of energy he found was massive because it was everything he had—and all that he was ov. His origins. His humanness. And his inner God-Being.

He focused it into the form of an all encompassing rocket then unleashed its might—it was an atomic bomb of presence that cleared the room to dust. Its force throwing him back by yards.

Jack blinked as the illusion fell away, leaving in it's place the thing that illusion is made ov—nothing. A clarity, a lesson that Jack knew he would never forget.

Holy shit… Illusion is ov no-thing, he thought seeing clearly that one has to merely challenge illusion to defeat it.

As the dust settled and Jack regained himself he saw a curious thing. Before him the Oracle, not in form but in awareness, a state of all-knowing cognizance and foresight. Their meeting alight as the electric air around them popped, buzzed, and hummed while dust and debris floated and wafted by.

Jack had done it. He had broken through. He searched for his questions, only for simplicity, and for the sake of time, Jack fired them off quickly as statements demanding, *YES, OR NO?! Tell me!*

From my five senses, I can access twenty-five.

"y e s"

In the same manner, I can access information and consciousness in five ways, not one.

"y e s"

My point of view can be from my place here in the observation deck, or it can be viewed from the mind or, as is most often referred to, as Jack.

"y e s"

But I can also see the world from my heart, gut, and sex consciousness.

"y e s"

Jack was rolling with it. The stream of consciousness burning back fears and his eyes found a focus they had never known. *My design includes increased physical strength because of the dystonia contractions. Access to other realms is a sensitivity to perceive beyond what others can, including this information. I am a portal to you, and I have the gift of silence. I can access a blank mind. It is part of me now.*

"y e s"

My design facilitates this, and the gifts you have bestowed on me make this moment possible.

"y e s"

My purpose is to help and guide others.

"y e s"

One finds their purpose by better understanding their design. But, first, one must understand how they were intentionally crafted. For what purpose does your design speak… it's in understanding our design that we better understand our assignment and purpose.

"y e s"

People are unaware of what lack of suffering feels like. They don't know freedom. It is unknown to most and something not currently taught to our children.

"y e s"

Kids are taught fear, because they're taught both good and evil, and one cannot teach both and be considered loving.

"y e s"

It is possible to teach good, without teaching kids evil.

"y e s"

It's my design to help fix this.

"y e s"

But first, we must help others identify the problem, which isn't the external but the lack within of not feeling whole, even though they are.

"y e s"

Personal power can only ever be self-granted.

"y e s"

We must first get clear on the mind's purpose. We have not been taught this. Just now, I am learning how to use my mind, whereas before, it was using me.

"y e s"

The level beyond Earth is the Causal Plane.

"y e s"

It's from there we can begin to tinker with the future. To cause things to be different from the plane we're on. That is possible. That can be accessed from the blank mind. To remember forward, or manifest. To remember things not yet realized. It's the simple notion of a vision board, but it harnesses the power of all that is.

"y e s"

We must stop trying to control what is, and allow. We must get comfortable allowing the beautiful awful, and that can only be done from the seat of the soul, which is accessed from radical detachment.

"y e s"

The past is gone. But, if allowed to, it will bedevil you, many to the point of suicide, over what is nothing more than a hallucination.

"y e s"

Put another way, Jack is a hallucination of his own making. A self-fulfilling prophecy run amuck. Something I must burn to the ground.

"y e s"

I see it now. My story must be scrutinized because, as proven, I lie or sell untruths back to myself. When asked directly of me, I cannot co-sign many of these beliefs as true, or even of my own making. Many of my core beliefs were ones sold to me by others that I bought, and never replaced. I see that now.

"y e s"

This is why we meditate - for the clarity. For insight. For vision.

With that, Jack told himself his entire life's story. Everything he could recall he presented to his mind and then asked himself one simple question. *Is any of this true?*

"n o"

Jack knew the answer even before it was confirmed. *No.* The story he had invented for his life was not true because the truth of something that no longer exists forms, morphs, stretches, and dies with time. It is a labyrinthine game of telephone told over decades of deceit. Something that is not of this moment can be nothing else. Yes, a nice memory if you realize the pitfalls and lies of such a place, but it can never be heart guarded as actual truth, merely perception stored in a feeble mind that skews and melds. *There can be no absolute truth in that which was, only distorted perception—the enemy is illusion.*

A glowing sense of joy came over Jack, and he began to laugh. He laughed like the Buddha, for he had finally untangled himself from the mire and ick of the past. The pull of illusion was gone, and in the present moment, his mind radiated with joy.

In the distance, Jack heard Yolo scream.

BLISS

Jack knew the sound of terror whether it came from man or beast, and he could tell the tone of it in Yolo's voice. He knew he had to act quickly. From where he stood before the Oracle, he dropped down into his festering, swirling mind, punched fear into his guts, and within one second was back on planet earth staring up at the sky.

"Yolo!" Jack yelled, searching for her. "Yolo!" He could feel the fear in him rising as he untied himself from the roof of the vehicle. "Yolo!"

Where is she? Jack wondered, climbing down to survey where they were. There were feathers everywhere and even a few carcasses of dead turkey vultures, but no live birds were in sight. *What the...* Jack said to himself aloud. He spun around a few times and still nothing.

"Yolo!" He screamed again into the mountain air, but she was gone. Jack felt his usual sadness grip; however, he now had a choice whether he would accept its presence or not. *I can do this better without drama,* he thought as he flipped back up to the observation deck of the mind. From here, Jack knew he could think more clearly without the constant chatter and bedevilment of runaway thoughts, emotions, and mental garbage.

With his mind clear and his presence fixed to the present, he once again searched for Yolo but not in how he had. Instead, he quietly closed his eyes and reached one hand heavenward and silently boomed, *Yolo.*

Come. With that, she dropped out of the sky and perched herself on his shoulder.

"Yolo! Hooray! You're okay, girl." They nuzzled each other, and Jack kissed her face generously. "You gave me a bit of a scare… but I have faith in you, sister. You, with your hours-old presence here on earth, I'm certain could teach me more than I could ever teach you. It's good to have you back. I love you." They craned, cooed, and cuddled again, then began to pick up the pieces of the war zone they found themselves in.

After dismantling the makeshift bed atop the truck, they hopped in the back and settled in for a nap. It had been a long blistering night, and Jack's face was sunburned and peeling. He slathered cooling lotion on his wounds and settled down to see if he could rest. He wasn't sure. The excitement was still racing through him; however, it had been a lot to process and he wasn't certain of the condition of his brain. He closed his eyes on the coolness of the sheets and slept for half an hour, but with no dawn, no night, and no sense of time, Jack was feeling lost and off. When he woke, he checked the time on his phone. 9:15. Was that AM or PM? He double-checked. AM. "Oh, good. We haven't lost a day."

The two felt somewhat refreshed and managed breakfast before climbing back in the truck to head for the main highway. "It's time to go home, sister," Jack said to Yolo, whose response was to cock her head sideways. Jack took this to mean, "What home?"

Ooh… Jack thought, realizing there was no home to go back to. Okay then. Jack mentally regrouped and picked up his phone to open his texts. Seeing nothing new, he flipped over to contacts, found Thad's number, and typed:

> Hey. Just finishing up here and was wondering
> if you might like to catch up. I can swing by in a
> few days. You back at Gambier?

A few minutes later, his phone pinged.

Hey, handsome. Nice to hear from you. I'll be back home tomorrow evening. Just have to swing by my office then my ex's place to pick up my dog. The next few weeks are pretty open as I've reserved the time to do some more writing. It would be nice to see you.

Jack immediately pulled over to type back.
Oh, nice! What kind of dog do you have?

Her name is Joy. She's an English Bulldog.

Well, I can't wait to meet her. I have a bird....

Is she a parrot?

She's a fledgling crow.

A crow?

LOL. Yep. She kinda chose me as her dad.

Well, she has good taste then.

Awww… thanks. Same for Joy.

Can I be honest, Jack?

Of course…

I might not be Zenith's Peak, but I'm an open book. lol. ;)

...and a comedian too. lol. Did you read it?

Argh. No. Not yet... but I will. I'm sorry. I've had
a lot on my plate. What was it you wanted to
ask me?

Well, it was more of a statement than a question.

Go on...

I really like you, Jack. Always have. From the
moment we first met.

I feel the same.

Oh? Do you? I couldn't tell and just needed to
put that out there.

Well, I'm glad you did.

You fascinate me, Jack.

That's nice. I just want to fuck your brains out.

LOL!!!!

Jk. ... Kinda.

Well then... I guess it's a date.

I guess it is.

I look forward to it.

I'll text you tomorrow night once you're home.

Jack and Yolo made their way back to the main road and left the Arctic Circle very differently than they had arrived. With the pulse of the place in their rear-view mirror, Jack beamed and radiated bliss to all that was.

"Jack?"

Yes, I'm here.

"Tell us why this is perfect."

Jack internally closed his eyes while still keeping watch on the road. *This is perfect because I know the truth of the thing. I know that we are not bad, simply misled. We have not been taught well — a thing that is easily corrected when new teachers are brought into the conversation every year, teachers who know the truth, and teachers who understand the importance of their work.*

If we are ever to fix humanity and live from a place of love and acceptance for what is, this can be done in one generation. That the awake have one purpose and must not focus on anything else. Teach. Teach everyone but, importantly, the children and the very young ones. We must focus there first. Children who meditate and who grow in power not only physically but wholly and spiritually will lead us into a new earth. A world that will look very different than we are now.

"What does your gut tell you about how long this will take?" His mind asked.

Jack checked in with himself and responded, *Not long. We only have to push the boulder up the hill a few feet. Evolution will take it from there because, here's the thing. Once a person knows the truth of themselves, it is damn near impossible to unknow it. Simply seed the field (Yang) then allow the miracle to happen (Yin).*

Jack flipped on some music and ended the conversation for now. He reached over to give Yolo a scratch then the two headed south toward Thad and Joy. He had a sense of what might come next, and the thought of it excited him. He could see a future there.

A future of Joy, Thad, the crow, and Jack Daw.

The End.

ABOUT THE AUTHOR

Dale Allen-Rowse always knew he was a creator and a storyteller. However, it wasn't until Celine Dion hired him as an original cast member for her show 'A New Day' that he understood his calling. During the almost year-long creation of Celine's Las Vegas show, Dale's vision for storytelling, narrative, and fantasy emerged. He worked for three years under the direction of Dion's director, Franco Dragone, the creative genius behind many of the Cirque de Soleil shows. From that relationship, Dale discovered his voice.

In 2005, Dale left Celine's employment, ending an eighteen-year professional theatre performing career to pursue a new life in real estate. Within three years of becoming a real estate agent, Dale was awarded top honors for individual sales volume for RE/MAX and opened a brokerage firm.

After a twenty-year career as an agent and real estate coach, Dale is adding new passions to his interests, including his spiritual life as a shamanic practitioner and student of core shamanism.

Dale channels his books using 'Automatic Writing,' which he discusses on YouTube.com/DaleAllenRowse channel – as well as many of the topics covered in his books, such as personal evolution, spiritual energy work, core shamanism, manifesting, and evolving. Plus, his talks are set to a disco beat, and that's not nothing.

Dale and his husband John live on a five-acre ranch in Mountain Center, California. They currently have four dogs, four ducks. Other things that keep Dale occupied are his quilts – you can see his work online as the Quilting Cowboy – and his day job as a real estate sales educator and coach.